Praise for *The Vanishing*:

'Think *Wuthering Heights* or *Jane Eyre*, but ten times
darker, and you have *The Vanishing* ... as dark and eerie
and gothic as the Yorkshire Moors it is set on. One to
curl up by the fire with on a windy night'
**Stylist**

'Undeniably page-turning'
**Mail on Sunday**

'Echoes *Wuthering Heights* with its setting and sense of intrigue'
**Red**

'Entertaining'
**Times**

'Vivid, absorbing and wonderfully gothic, with shades of
Sarah Waters and Emily and Charlotte Brontë'
**Kate Riordan**

'Brilliantly Brontë-esque. Perfect reading for a stormy night'
**Anna Mazzola**

'A vivid sense of the period ... which stays with the reader long
after the final page'
**the i**

'The plotting is skilful, with a network of lies being woven so
that no one, characters or readers, can be sure of the truth'
**Daily Express**

'Atmosphere aplenty and some real surprises'
**Daily Mail**

'An atmospheric tale of betrayal and revenge'
**woman&home**

'A thrilling, atmospheric page-turner'
**Metro**

'Playful and menacing, *The Vanishing* is a pitch perfect
evocation of a classic nineteenth century Gothic novel which
confirms Sophia Tobin as a writer of the highest calibre'
**William Ryan, author of *The Constant Soldier***

Sophia Tobin worked for a Bond Street antique dealer for six years, specialising in silver and jewellery. Inspired by research she made into a real life eighteenth-century silversmith, Tobin began to write her first novel, *The Silversmith's Wife*, which was shortlisted for the Lucy Cavendish College Fiction Prize, judged by Sophie Hannah. Her second novel, *The Widow's Confession*, was published in 2015 to great acclaim. *The Vanishing* is her third novel. She lives in London with her husband.

BY THE SAME AUTHOR:

The Silversmith's Wife
The Widow's Confession

# The Vanishing

## SOPHIA TOBIN

**SIMON &
SCHUSTER**

London · New York · Sydney · Toronto · New Delhi

A CBS COMPANY

First published in Great Britain by Simon & Schuster UK Ltd, 2017
This paperback published 2018
A CBS COMPANY

1 3 5 7 9 10 8 6 4 2

Simon & Schuster UK Ltd
1st Floor
222 Gray's Inn Road
London WC1X 8HB

www.simonandschuster.co.uk

Simon & Schuster Australia, Sydney
Simon & Schuster India, New Delhi

A CIP catalogue record for this book is available from the British Library

Paperback ISBN: 978-1-4711-5162-0
eBook ISBN: 978-1-4711-5163-7

Printed and bound by CPI Group (UK) Ltd, Croydon, CR0 4YY

Simon & Schuster UK Ltd are committed to sourcing paper
that is made from wood grown in sustainable forests and support the Forest
Stewardship Council, the leading international forest certification organisation.
Our books displaying the FSC logo are printed on FSC certified paper.

*To Lisa, Samuel and Harrison*

# PROLOGUE

*October, 1815*

The storm was at its height when we left the inn that night. The wind was howling around the outer walls, the draughts whistling through the seams of the windows.

As we opened the door to the moors and the rain, there was not even a glance from those drinking there; not so much as a raised eyebrow. I wondered how much Thomas had paid them to keep silent, or whether they did it for the love of him. With the quiet tenacity I expected of him, he did not complain about the weather. He only pulled his collar high, and pushed the old cocked hat he wore, the fur on it half-eaten away by moths, low over his forehead. He wore it for luck, I knew. By the time he had climbed up onto the box and

SOPHIA TOBIN

gathered the reins, his greatcoat shone like polished jet in the sheeting rain.

It was only then that Emma and I ran from beneath the lintel of the inn doorway through the puddles and the mud to the carriage, the door held open by the stable boy. By the light of the carriage lamps I saw that the child's fair hair was dark with rain, so that he had to blink every moment to keep the water out of his eyes. As Emma climbed up before me, scrambling like a milkmaid rather than a lady, I touched the child's head. It was a kind of blessing; whether for myself, or him, I hardly knew.

The steps were let up, the door was shut, and as the carriage lurched forwards a piece of silver flew past the window, the boy jumping to catch it, and my lady flinched. I reached over, and touched her arm in reassurance. 'It's Thomas,' I said. 'He's throwing the boy a coin for his trouble.'

She turned her face away.

It was not long before we had left the tavern behind and were journeying through open moorland. The road surged downwards, and the horses' hooves caught on the worsening road. I felt the jagged vibration of it through the springs of the carriage. 'Too fast,' murmured Emma. The horses slowed as they began the long climb up to Shawsdrop; as we surmounted the hill, Thomas urged them on. He was a hard driver that night.

'I see it,' I said. Quietly, as though I thought my master might hear me. There were the distant lights – his harbour lights, as he used to call them – shining out across the moor. I wondered if Sorsby was watching our approach from his

2

lodge, the blink and roll of our lamps as we jolted along. It was why we had chosen the height of the storm, the kind of night when every sane person would wish to be at their fireside. Surely no one of sense would travel on such a night.

But I was without sense, and without feeling. I had one goal in view. I was a different Annaleigh from the one who had come here a year before, the bitter tension in me so familiar that it was part of me, and I could seem serene even under the yoke of it.

I was all calmness compared to the woman who sat opposite me in her London walking dress, her cloak fur-lined, her hair a fashionable cascade of curls. How often, in recent days, I had looked for similarities between us. Like me, Emma feigned serenity, but I could see the slight tremble of the muscles at the corner of one beautiful eye, and the sheen of sweat on her face seemed unnatural and marked, like mildew in a grand reception room. I noted the desperate tightness of her clasped hands, still bearing her rings, her wedding ring, even after all that had happened. That alone made me want to roll my eyes in exasperation. *We are such different creatures,* I thought, with surprise, the kind of surprise that made the hairs prickle on the back of my neck with misgiving. She had no reason to care for me; and yet we were here together.

When she spoke, her voice startled me, that sudden gentle voice, amidst the tumult of the storm and the lurch of the carriage.

'If we take his life,' she said, 'we had best do it quickly.'

'Madam,' I said, 'there is no "if".'

3

# PART ONE

PART ONE

# CHAPTER ONE

*One year earlier*

*September, 1814*

'Press your face to the glass.'

The woman's voice was low and soothing. We had been in the stagecoach for an hour, and it was the first time she had spoken. I would have been grateful if our fellow travellers had afforded me the courtesy of silence. In that coach, scented stale by their bodies and breaths, their voices rang strange and disquieting in my aching head. My mind was teeming with memories, so that as we left the streets of London far behind, thoughts of my past streamed on and on like a magic lantern show, as though I was living my life again as an observer.

It hadn't taken long for me to feel sick. The air I breathed felt thick and heavy, and the constant rocking of the coach threatened to bring up the punch I had drunk at the Bull and Mouth Inn with Mr Plaskett. *What had they put in it?* I thought. And then, what had he *asked* them to put in it?

'You're a fine shade of green,' said one of the other passengers warily, a sallow-cheeked gentleman. 'Can you hold off until Barnet?'

'Don't spew on me,' said another. 'You should've travelled on the outside.'

I shook my head. Jared had paid for me to travel on the inside, thinking of my comfort, not wishing me to catch a chill. To criticise this arrangement seemed somehow disloyal to him. So I pressed my face to the glass as the woman had advised, and somehow survived until the next change of horses, my fellow passengers piling out of the carriage with barely disguised eagerness to be away from me.

On the next stretch of the journey, I felt a little better. The sallow-cheeked man hazarded conversation with me.

'I saw the old man that put you on the coach. Saw the look on his face. You're not virtuous, for all that you look so innocent.'

I thought of Plaskett, he who had made my travelling arrangements and ordered the punch. He was one of Jared's customers; the paint was barely dry on his portrait, though we had known him as a visitor in our house for a long time. He had always presented himself as a fatherly figure, but I had begun to notice on my last days in London that he had often licked his lips when he looked at me, watching me with a slight smile. On our way to the inn, he had taken every opportunity to steer me, his hand on my elbow when we crossed the street, rushing to touch me under the shade of solicitude.

He had seemed disappointed when the passengers for the Leeds coach were called. My fellow traveller must have seen him hovering around me, his voice low and urgent in my ear. 'You can always call on me, if I am ever needed. You need not trouble Jared. I may visit to see you are doing well, for I am intimate friends with the Twentyman family. You may write to me at my lodgings in Arlington Street, Piccadilly, or I can always be found at the White Bear – mark it, Annaleigh, mark it.'

The man who had questioned my virtue gave a low laugh at the look on my face. The woman who had soothed me interrupted. 'She's more virtuous than you are, I'll warrant.'

The other man looked harder at me in the jolting carriage, even as I turned my face away, feeling sick.

'Eh? Swear it on a Bible then, eh?'

'I'll not swear anything for you or any other man,' I snapped.

'Injured in love, then,' said the woman softly, who had closed the book she was reading.

'No,' I said, stung into answering. 'A little.' As soon as I said it I regretted it. Presenting myself as alone, a young woman, to this group of strangers. It was my plan to make my own way, to leave my youth behind. Yet here I was, acting like a child. I thought of my home, the house in St Martin's Lane. I had lived there since I was a baby, but as I had looked back at it after leaving, one last turn on that busy street, it was just a house. Another house with a classical façade, the door and windows like the shut eyes of someone long dead.

'It is best you find out that men are faithless now,' said the woman evenly, though the sallow-faced man said a low *pish* under his breath. 'You are young. Best you do not spend your finest years chasing what cannot be.'

She had been meant to travel onwards with us but at the next stop she left the coach, walking out silently into the night, I know not where; her book clasped in one hand, her locking box in the other.

I found some moments of pleasure on the journey. I loved the ancient roads we travelled on, ruts hollowed out of the earth, the branches interlaced above the coach in natural shelter, as though the trees either side had met by mutual agreement.

When we stopped at an inn in Huntingdon, the two children running in and out of the tables in the coffee room reminded me of me and Kit when we were children. A fair boy, and a dark-haired girl, she only slightly smaller than him, their games full of energy but no malice.

In my mind, Jared, Melisende and Kit travelled with me on the first part of that journey, as though they sat next to me. If I closed my eyes, I could catch the scent of them. For Jared, it was the turpentine he would dip his brushes in. For Melisende, the smell of almonds, baked in the tart she taught me to make. For my precious Kit, the scent of his sweat and skin, the musky edge of it, as he reached for me on that last day I saw him, our hands never quite meeting as the crowds on Snow Hill dragged me away from him, Jared calling my name.

They seemed so close to me at first, but on the last day of the journey, I could not summon them. Were there too many county borders between us, I wondered? All I could remember was a stupid, commonplace memory, something I would rather forget and yet could not shake.

It was my last evening in London, and Mr Plaskett was taking me to the coach. Weaving through the London streets, he kept his hand beneath my elbow, always that wretched dry touch of his. 'You must be obedient,' he said. 'I know Melisende trained you in cookery, but you will not be at home, and must think how to please them. Miss Twentyman – Mrs Hume I should say – will take you in hand; you shall be apprenticed to learn housekeeping skills – yes, think of yourself as her apprentice.'

I had nodded, dully. I hardly saw the faces of the people we passed; I was murmuring the apprentice's promise Kit had made. The night before Kit went to be bound as an apprentice, he was fourteen, I eleven, and we sat on the turn of the stairs in our house, a candle beside us, chanting it.

'During which term the said apprentice his said Master faithfully shall serve, his secrets keep, his lawful commandments everywhere gladly do. He shall do no damage to his said Master. He shall not haunt Taverns, or Play-houses, nor absent himself from his said Master's service Day or Night unlawfully . . .'

I fancy I smiled as I thought it, remembering our childish voices together, saying the words as lightly as though they were a nursery rhyme, all our solemnity a play only.

'Annaleigh?' Plaskett's voice, pettish. 'Your lips are moving. What is it you are thinking, child?'

Always the present, dragging me out of the past, where I wanted to live. Always that touch on my arm.

I left the stagecoach at Leeds, and took a further conveyance which had been paid for by my employer. It was a full coach, with four places on the top. As we travelled through the town of Hebden Bridge, the mist clung to the hills, softening the outlines of grey cottages, built from damp grey stone and slate, studding the hillside as the road wound its way upwards, like a thread from Melisende's skein. As we clattered on towards open country the road was bordered by rough stone walls, and high, thick-grown trees. Then the trees fell away to show me the land I had come to.

'They live on the moors,' Mr Plaskett had told me. 'A most respectable family. The Twentymans of White Windows. Discreet, however.'

We were travelling through an openness, an exposed hillside – a green-blue vastness which spread out before me, hills and valleys covered with heather, and the occasional dwelling, miles away, but clear as an outpost on those hills. I stared as the sun appeared from behind the clouds and made the heather on the hills shine as vivid as a bruise. The moors seemed to reflect the constantly changing sky, and were first welcoming under the brief illusion of sunshine, then fiercely barren beneath cloud. In the distance, there was nothing but blue hills. I felt the immensity of it deeply, felt I might be swallowed by it, as one feels standing on the edge of a precipice. It was utterly alien to me. In London, with its crowded streets, dense with voices, colours and smells, I had been raised to think of the people as the threat; but here the vanquisher was the landscape itself. A painter's child, I tried to calm myself by naming the colours: russet, acid yellow, green, brown, purple.

But the carriage was slowing, drawing up. I turned from the moors, and saw that we had arrived at a lone tavern: a rectangular, low, grey building set into the raw hillside. Ahead there was a handful of grey scattered houses, but that was all for miles.

'Becket Bridge, Becket Bridge.'

*No*, I thought. *Not this desolate place.* Obediently, I climbed down, and opened my arms to receive my box as it was thrown to me from the rumble tumble. Then the coach drew off, racing towards some other place.

There was no one to meet me. I was completely alone. I thanked God for the glimpses of September sunshine dealt by the ever-changing sky; it was the only mercy. As the wind snatched at my cloak, I felt it begin to tell on me. I worried the string of coral beads around my neck as though they were a rosary; re-checked the hiring letter, which I had carried in my pocket. I wondered if some mistake had been made and I would be left there, alone at the roadside, in this foreign land.

Then I saw it, at first just a distant shape, moving slowly. As the minutes passed it resolved itself into a man, coming across the moors.

# CHAPTER TWO

It seemed to take an age for the man to reach me. I sat on my locking box, taking in deep breaths of the cold air, trying to suppress my impatience and depressed spirits. The man was dressed in a long brown coat stained with mud, and he wore a hat pulled low over his brow. I was aware even as he approached of a horse, coming quick along the road from the distance with a rider on top, the sharp drumming of hooves on the road in contrast with the slow pace of the man.

'Are you from White Windows?' I called to the man. He looked at me, but my words were either carried away on the wind, or he feigned not to hear. He reached the road where I stood, and came purposefully towards my locking box, but I did not rise from it. I repeated my question.

'Aye,' he said grumpily. His eyes were surprisingly

youthful in his weathered face: clear and dark brown, meeting mine directly.

'What's your name?' I said.

He waited for a moment, looking at me, and I felt him assessing me. 'Sorsby,' he said at last.

'I am pleased to make your acquaintance,' I said. 'My name is Miss Calvert.'

He nodded. 'I'll take your box. We'll have to walk.'

'How far is it?' My horror must have shown on my face. I looked down at my boots; relatively strong, but I had seen the terrain, and wondered whether I would make it without soaking my feet. His gaze followed mine.

'There are pattens at the house to protect your shoes in the future,' he said. 'But I did not think you would come unready. 'Tis not my fault if the cart is not right. Would have been easier for me if you'd come by the Shawsdrop road.' My face clearly showed I had no idea what he was talking about. He sighed. 'You'll be all right. You're a strong enough lass.'

I blinked at him, feeling exhaustion overtake me. He had already turned his attention to the horse and rider approaching us on the road. The large grey horse had plenty of vigour in her; she tossed her head when the rider drew her up, as though annoyed that her trot had been interrupted. The man who rode her was tall and broad-shouldered, dressed in a dusty hat and a greatcoat that seemed to have had several years' wear.

'Good day to ye, Tom,' said Sorsby. 'She's a fine roadster, in't she? Mr Twentyman will want her.'

'That's the idea.' He looked near enough to me in age, but had the bearing of an older man: authoritative, his back straight, his gaze unflinching. His horse danced on the spot, but he was not heavy-handed; relaxed, he took in our tableau, his hands low, his whip tucked neatly in his hand as though carried for ornament rather than use. 'What's happening here, then? Ma'am?' he said, acknowledging me with a touch of his hat, and a nod. He spoke in what Melisende would have called a fine voice: low and strong in tone, softened with the local accent. I had the feeling he observed everything about me, from my locking box to the exhaustion that bowed my shoulders.

'Come to collect master's new housekeeper,' said Sorsby, as though I wasn't there.

I saw a frown crease the man's brow momentarily. 'Why did you not bring the cart? It's not fit weather to make the lady walk across the moors, and they'll be running with water in no time.'

Sorsby looked annoyed. 'Wheel came off the cart yesterday,' he said. 'Needs fixing.'

'I am Miss Calvert,' I said, somewhat awkwardly.

The man bowed, and gave his name as Thomas Digby. 'The rain's coming across the valley,' he said. 'I'll see you to the house, Miss Calvert – if you will permit it. Mr Sorsby will carry your box, and you can ride my mare Quicksilver. She's sure-footed, and won't spill you, I promise. It will save you from walking. Unlike you, she is used to the terrain.'

I looked at the horse: the dark cobweb pattern of grey

on white, her thick black mane, the enormous hooves. The power of her shoulders, kept reined in by him. 'I have never ridden a horse of this size, and certainly not astride,' I said.

Thomas dismounted, and led his horse towards me, with a glance at the horizon. 'She's a steady ride, and I'll lead her,' he said. 'Look.'

I followed his line of sight. The blue hills across the valley were softened by an approaching veil of rain, the outline softening and dissolving as we spoke. I had never seen weather approaching from a distance before, and the sight on any normal day would have entranced me. But it was a sight to be watched from behind a window, with a log on the fire and plenty more in the store.

'Take up the offer or don't, but don't stand there dithering,' Sorsby half-shouted. 'If you do catch your death on the wet ground, master won't thank me for bringing damaged goods to his house.'

'Come now, old Chris.' The young man's voice cut in, firm and reproving.

'Very well,' I said.

Thomas nodded, drawing his mare's reins up in his hand. 'There's no mounting block here,' he said. 'I'll have to hand you up. Do you know how?'

I nodded, miserably. We were both flushed now, with the embarrassment of it. Sorsby made a show of lighting a pipe, a slight smile playing around his features.

I put one foot up in the stirrup; felt Thomas's hands at my back as he counted; then I half-pulled and was half-pushed by him up into the saddle. It was not smooth, and the horse shifted a little.

'Hold the pommel,' he said. 'Are you secure?' I nodded. Just for a moment, he let his hand rest on my wrist. 'Journey's almost over,' he said, his careful eyes reading the exhaustion on my face. His kindness was so unexpected that I could have wept; instead, I nodded.

'*En avant*, then,' Thomas said, half to himself, half to Sorsby, and we set off, Sorsby leading the way, far enough ahead to show he did not want company.

'Forwards,' I murmured in translation, under my breath. Thomas heard, and looked at me with approval.

After a few moments, I learned that the terrain was unsteady, and the most sensible thing was to let the horse have her head, riding out the sudden jerks and pulls, as she went down a stage in the track. Thomas walked beside her.

'She knows the path well,' he said. 'There's no need to worry – she's more sure-footed than you or me. Where've you come from? You're not from anywhere near here.' He said it with a wry smile.

'London,' I said. 'Have you ever been?'

He shook his head. 'No. Nor am I likely to. Father can't bear the place and I have all I need here.' He glanced up at me again, negotiated a dip in the path, then spoke. 'If you'll forgive straight talking, you don't seem like any housekeeper I've ever seen. All the ones I've known are near a hundred years older than you, and far crosser.'

I tried not to smile. 'It's my first place. I was taught how to cook and sew in my guardian's house, but now it's time to make a living.' I said it briskly. I had not meant to reveal so much about myself, but his kindness had unlocked my thoughts. I made a note to check myself.

'I reckon you'll be homesick,' he said. 'I know I would be.'

I looked down at my hands. My fingernails short, the skin already weathered from the work I had done in the kitchen and the studio of my home. I thought of the twenty-one pounds per annum I would receive for my labour here; the first money I had ever earned. 'All is well as long as I can work,' I said. 'Do you know White Windows well?'

'Yes, as much as anyone apart from Sorsby and Jeanne, I expect,' he said. 'I live in Becket Bridge with my parents. Father and I are job-masters, hiring and selling horses. I'm at White Windows every so often, for the master gets through horses. He's a hard rider and – as you can see – he does not care so much for Sorsby's cart, or even the stables, so long as there is a fine horse to put in them. He came here with a town coach but I have not seen it these six months. It will be rotting in one of those leaky barns. I told him last winter that cart would not last for long, and still they all hope it will hold together by some miracle.' He glanced at me. 'Not of any interest to you, I'm sure,' he said without rancour. 'I shouldn't speak of such things, neither.'

'I won't say anything,' I said, 'if you don't tell anyone that I came to be riding your horse astride.'

His eyes crinkled with amusement. 'You can hold me to that promise,' he said. 'Coming from London, we will be a shock to you, I'm afraid. We are all hill farmers and wool combers; we know our own minds and aren't afraid of giving opinions.'

I smiled to show I did not mind it. 'I heard Mr Twentyman is a gentleman,' I said.

'Aye,' said Thomas. 'It was his great uncle who settled here – eccentric old Jack, he was known as. You'll see the carcasses of all the farmhouses he left to ruin, just so he would have moor and clear land, with no folk about him.'

'He came here for the beauty of the open countryside?' I said.

'Beauty?' He smiled at me. 'Do you see any beauty in it today? No, miss. He came here for the bleakness. He came here because he wanted hills and vast horizons and to see a man coming ten miles off.'

I pressed my fingers to my brow, remembering just as I did it that it was a gesture Jared had always teased me for. Something about it caught Thomas's attention too, for he smiled at me, as though he could read the puzzlement and misgivings in my mind.

'As we still have a way to travel,' he said, 'tell me a little of London.'

'There's not so much to say.'

'I can't imagine that.'

I considered the question. 'All of London passed our house in their colour and riot,' I said eventually. 'But I had little converse with them. My world was our house. My

21

guardian, Jared, is a portrait painter, and it was my delight to be with him. London was just a story, told by his quiet voice as I played with my doll in the corner of his studio. And, later, London was formed from the characters who ventured in to have their portraits taken by him, and there were plenty of those.'

'Was your guardian a gentleman?' he said. 'This would be a harsh comedown for you, if so? To go into service?'

'Not a gentleman,' I said. 'A painter of the middling sort, as he described himself. I do not consider this beneath me. Besides, being in the studio was a great leveller. I met all kinds of characters.'

I did not say that I grew up seeing the faces of men who had lost much on the turn of a card, flushed with dissipation; the watery, pale eyes of a merchant who could not, just *could* not, bear to see himself painted as he truly was. Was that, then, a gentleman, I thought? If so I would not be afraid of him. I had already looked into the eyes of a hundred gentlemen sitters, and Jared had shown me their layers as precisely as a surgeon cutting through flesh.

'What a strange look you have on your face,' said Thomas, with a playful glance, then he stumbled. 'Forgive me, I'll keep my eyes on the path. And I'll not ask what you're thinking of. Not until I know you better, anyhow.'

We came over the brow of the hill at that moment, just as his smile was fading, and I caught sight of a house, half a mile away, with moor on one side and fields on the other. I looked at Thomas questioningly, and he nodded.

White Windows. A house built of grey stone, the same

shade as the leaden rainclouds at our back. The only relief its white shutters. It seemed ancient despite its symmetrical, long windows, and the portico which had been added at some point in the last fifty years, its measurements somehow wrong, and jarring. I had not imagined the place until that moment; there was no expectation in my mind, but I felt disappointed. I had come here to escape from sadness, and yet the house in that moment seemed the opposite of a place where one could be happy. It seemed to crouch in the rugged landscape, as though cowering from the rain. The gateway was made of two long upended stones, and I wondered how many horses it had taken to drag them there. A small lodge house sat to the right, and I could just see a scattering of outhouses beyond the main house.

We had all come to a halt, and Sorsby moved to rub the forehead of my horse with surprising tenderness. 'You'd better let her down here, Tom,' he said. 'Master wouldn't like her brought to the door so.'

'Will you ever use my name?' I said, with a little more firmness than before, drawing a low, not unfriendly, laugh from Sorsby. I glanced at Thomas, thinking he might approve, for already a kind of comradeship had grown up between us, but his eyes were on the house, and I could see only misgiving on his face. He managed a brief smile, and a nod at me. 'Just swing your leg over the front,' he said, 'and keep hold of my hand until you're on the ground. Sorsby – that cart should be seen to. My father will see you at the Cross Keys and make arrangements.'

I slid down the side of the horse, my hand knotted in Thomas's, and he kept it there for a moment before letting it go. 'Remember,' he said, 'I live in the last house of Becket Bridge, three miles as the crow flies in that direction. Keep to the path if you are alone, the moors can be treacherous. If you should ever have need of anything – Thomas Digby, at your service.'

I thanked him, smiling, and felt the first sting of a raindrop on my face, raw with cold.

He smiled tightly, raised his hand to Sorsby, then mounted and wheeled his horse around and drove her on briskly up the path without looking back.

'Best not to get caught out on moors in weather,' said Sorsby. 'Come on now, and hurry – or we'll be soaked through.'

# CHAPTER THREE

From the track where we stood, a steep bank descended to the small and roughly paved yard before White Windows. It only took a few steps to get directly from the moors into the yard. Sorsby went first down the slope, my locking box on his shoulder, me slipping and sliding behind him.

I thought we might enter the house through the back, as servants, but he barged through the front door, shoulder first, and as I followed him I noticed that the paint on the door was peeling; once a glossy black, the first layer had come away in patches, revealing the ghost of another. Even beneath the heavy portico, supported by its thick, crude stone columns, the weather had done its worst. Only the brass knocker retained its details, unpolished as it was: a gargoyle, of the type seen on churches, its mouth set in a cackle of menace. I wondered why it jarred in my mind, that painted door; and then I realized it was a town door, a London door, on a Yorkshire house. A more suitable entrance for this place would be made of thick oak, bound with iron. Clearly old Jack really had been eccentric.

'Madam,' went up Sorsby's shout, when he had set my box down heavily on the floor. He made a hissing noise, and a black shape darted past me. 'Emmet, my wife's cat,' he said. 'I'm going to give the horses their feed, then to the lodge for my ale. Wife'll be here directly to show you the kitchen.' And he was gone, closing the door firmly behind him.

I looked around at my new home. Underfoot were uneven slabs of dark grey stone, which clearly had not been swept for some time, and bore the marks of muddy boots, drying to dust. A broad staircase turned out of sight, its bannisters ornately carved with primitive figures, like the figureheads on ships. The walls were panelled with a dark oak, its colour born of centuries of smoking fires; the pale ceiling was decorated with elaborate plasterwork to indicate, I suspected, that this was a house of status, but it was darkened by smoke and too little cleaning. There was an ancient fireplace, its arch pointed, with no fire. In the corner stood a tall clock, its pendulum seemingly long stilled. For all its symmetrical windows, this, it seemed, was a far older house, the shell of which had been refurbished within a generation, but which maintained its dark and smoky core. I guessed that the layout of the house would be irregular and without the logic I was used to, like the inns we had stayed at on the journey: winding sequences of rooms, dark furniture, and plastered walls.

I went to the window, which was letting in precious little light thanks to the heavy clouds. Through the rippled pane I saw Sorsby cross the yard, and pass a woman coming in the opposite direction, seemingly without a word. Large drops of rain came at the window then, suddenly: slanting in angrily as it began to pour. I saw the woman break into a run, her skirts gathered up in her hands.

'Our new housekeeper, I presume.'

I turned around. A woman had descended the first flight of the staircase, and was standing at the turn.

'Indeed, I am Miss Calvert, madam,' I said, and curtseyed low.

'So, you've reached us at last,' she said. 'I am Miss Hester Twentyman.'

'I thought you were a widow, miss,' I said, shocking myself. My exhaustion had betrayed me into saying my first thought out loud. Sorely vexed, I lowered my eyes.

'I am, but I prefer to use my family name,' she said, seemingly without any offence. 'So you use the title "miss"? How strange. As a housekeeper, I expected you to introduce yourself as Mrs Calvert. Still, I suppose you are very young, and not used to the correct way of doing things. It hardly matters here.'

I curtseyed low again, my face burning. At the same moment the front door was thrown open, and the woman

I had seen crossing the yard ran in, brushing off her skirts. She was wearing a brightly patterned dress decorated with printed sprigs of coloured flowers, reminding me of the dresses ballad singers and young pretty women in London would wear, her only concession to the weather the thick woollen shawl she had wrapped around her shoulders. She seemed to be in her mid-forties; her dark hair was cropped close to her head, giving her a stark appearance, and she glanced between me and her mistress with apprehension outweighed by obvious curiosity.

'Jeanne, make us some tea,' said Miss Twentyman. 'I have left the caddy unlocked.'

Miss Twentyman came down the stairs slowly, as though watching her step; everything about her was colourless, like a watercolour executed with too much water. Her hair was a pale mousy brown; her delicate skin dusty in pallor; her slight build clothed in pale, delicate silks which looked faintly unwashed. She brought the scent of perspiration and lavender with her, as though her clothes had been kept long in their presses. 'How was your journey?'

'Well enough,' I said. 'Though it would have been difficult without the help of a Mr Digby, who assisted—'

'I know,' said Miss Twentyman. 'I saw you and Thomas at the top of the hill. An unorthodox way of arriving, riding astride. You should have dismounted sooner, rather than in sight of the house. Come through.'

I had opened my mouth to reply, but she was already walking away.

I followed her into a large room leading directly from the hall where, at last, a fire burned. There was a long oak table with benches either side, together with some ornately carved chairs scattered around. I was comforted to see a little of what I expected: the walls were studded with framed examples of pressed flowers and shellwork, and a large side table held a display of porcelain ornaments, their delicacy out of place against the dark, heavy furniture.

'Where should I sit?' I asked.

'Wherever you like,' she said impatiently. 'I presume you have enough about you to choose a chair. If not, then we have engaged the wrong person.'

Annoyed that my good manners had been rebuked, I sat a little way from the fire, and she took her place opposite me, beside a small table. Jeanne came in, bearing a silver tray with tea things. The tray was edged with tarnish, and I made a mental note to ask for it to be polished as soon as possible.

'Leave it,' said Hester, when the woman fumbled with the cups. 'Go back to the lodge, and tell Sorsby to put his boots back on. My brother is out on the moor and I need him to go and look for him. Tell him to take a lantern; the light is fading.'

The woman's gaze flickered briefly to my face and she gave a small smile before she curtseyed and went out.

'That is Jeanne,' said Hester, handing me a cup of tea. 'She had just arrived from Paris when I took her on to work in my London household a few years ago. When we came here she fell in with Sorsby very well and they were married at Shawsdrop, near here, last winter. He has been here forever; he served my uncle, and knew me as a child. His first wife would take in worsted bundles and spin them into yarn; the house always smelled of wool. We have no truck with that now, you know; you are not to take in extra work.'

'I would not think of it, madam.'

I sat in silence as she poured the tea, noticing that she had not followed the custom of making it at the table, allowing Jeanne access to the tea and to pour the water. Her voice gave the impression of strength, and order, but her movements told of languor. I guessed her to be one- or two-and-thirty, certainly more than a decade older than me, and wondered whether she had always been so lethargic, or whether some kind of malaise had fallen over her. I noticed, close to, that she was untidy. Her hair was poorly dressed, and her gown could have done with some stitches in a sleeve, for all its fine cut and fabric. The high neck of her undershirt was slightly discoloured around the edges. She was a lady; she should have had a lady's maid to tend to her.

My eyes darted away. It would not be the thing to be seen observing my new mistress with critical eyes.

'Now, tell me of London,' she said briskly.

I hesitated. 'It was a fine day when I left it,' I said. I sought for something interesting to tell her. 'There was a balloon ascent last month, for the Jubilee, over St James's Park. It was an incredible sight.'

'I meant a little of society, but I suppose you would not know about that. Of course not,' she said. 'And you are such a young thing. Nineteen, I believe? I do not complain; you are exactly what I requested. But what situation do you come from? I took you on Plaskett's word alone. Not necessarily a wise thing to do.'

I saw the glint of humour in her eye, and warmed to her.

'This is my first situation,' I said.

'Oh, I know that,' she said. 'But what of your family?'

I felt a twist of disappointment in my stomach at the question. 'It is best I am plain with you,' I said. 'I have no real family. I was delivered to the Foundling Hospital on my sixth day of life; taken from it by Mr Jared Calvert, the painter friend Mr Plaskett mentioned to you, and raised in his family. Taught to cook, and clean, and do other things.' I could have said *was raised as one of the family, and thought myself part of it, but was misled.*

'And now?' She waited.

'I wish to make my way in the world,' I said.

She did not smile. 'Nonsense! Plaskett mentioned that there was ... an entanglement. Concerning you and your guardian's stepson.'

I felt the heat gathering in my cheeks; prayed that I had not turned scarlet. I did not know if it was anger or embarrassment. 'I am, perhaps, at a disadvantage. As I do not know what that good gentleman thought it fit to tell you.'

'You are at no disadvantage,' she said, 'if you tell the truth.'

I raised my chin; held her gaze. 'There was nothing disreputable about it. I have been good friends with the young gentleman you mention since we were children. Now that we – are not children – we both thought there might be a chance of something else. A warmer feeling. But he is to marry his master's daughter. It seemed best that I should go.'

'Say his name.'

'I beg your pardon, madam?'

'You heard me. Say his name.'

I looked at her, and gathered from the expression on her face that she was in earnest. Something held me back. I did not want to say his name: to admit something of the past into this new place. My new beginning. But still she looked.

'Kit,' I said. And was rewarded with a smile.

'You are out of danger,' she said. 'I see from your face that your spirit is not quite broken from it. And there is no chance that he will turn up here begging for your hand?'

'None at all,' I said, and was proud to keep any tremor from my voice.

'I can see this is distasteful to you,' she said, reading my gaze with more sensitivity than I had credited her with. 'But you need not be missish about it. At nineteen, we all fancy ourselves half in love with any handsome man we meet. It is good to be chastened a little. I wish I had been, believe me. I would not be living here now, watching over my brother.' Her voice had quietened. Then she rose, and picked up a small silver bell that was on the mantelpiece, and rang it. No one came.

'You will get used to that sound, Miss Calvert,' she said. 'We have no bell pulls, but there are table bells in every room. You will think us old-fashioned.'

'Not at all,' I said. 'I will learn the ways of the house soon enough.'

'Your attitude is a good one,' she said. 'You must learn to keep Sorsby and Jeanne in check. No simpering please; we have not the leisure for it. You will think, of course, that they are rough people, but I trust them. This is the most important thing to me. My brother and I come from one of the best families, and though we choose to live here, it is only because White Windows affords us the remoteness my brother longed for. He is like any gentleman – but the kind who goes to his hunting box for winter, and does not re-emerge.'

'Why does he wish for remoteness?' I asked.

She looked at me then, and I was aware that the benign briskness she had addressed me with had chilled in a moment. I had said something wrong.

'It is not your place to ask such questions of me,' she said. 'Mr Plaskett told me you would be quiet and discreet in your dealings; that you are not a girl who engages in gossip. That is the case, is it not, or I have I been misled?'

I felt the heat rising in my face again. 'It is the case,' I said.

'Good. I do not wish for tea. Bring me that decanter.' I did so, and she produced from beneath the table two glasses which she filled with dark red wine, pushing one over to me. I was not used to drinking wine, but did not wish to seem green, so sipped it. The glasses were old rummers that looked to be fifty years old, and I ran my fingers over the unfiled base of mine.

At length, my mistress began to speak again. 'You, Sorsby and Jeanne are our only servants. It will be hard work; that is why you seemed ideal, as you are not used to a large house where you would be *managing* rather than working. You are not to bother yourself over provisions; Sorsby and Jeanne go into Hebden to buy our food each week, and will present the accounts and bills to you. You may order in girls from Becket Bridge on the washing days, and if you need extra help. But girls are only to be ordered in when you need them; and I must see all the names before any are sent for.' She put the glass heavily down on the table. The harshness in her eyes had not quite softened, but she seemed suddenly vulnerable. 'You are to manage everything, you understand,' she said. 'I am tired.'

'I understand,' I said, taking another mouthful of wine. I wanted to be busy. I knew my thoughts would always return, again and again, to Jared, Melisende and Kit, like a path that leads nowhere but back to the same door again. I would work hard, push all my memories to the back of my mind: that alone appealed to me. There was a kind of strength, I thought, in having nothing, and loving nobody.

'I would like to see London again one day,' said Hester. No smile crossed her face, no intimation that the thought gave her any pleasure. She turned her head as though in response to a silent question. 'Where is he?' she said, in a low voice.

I sensed her disquiet, so sought to distract her. 'What is the routine of the house, madam, so that I may best please you? What time will you breakfast, and dine?' I said.

'I hardly know. And Marcus will not care. You get up early, don't you? Good. Make sure a fire is lit in my brother's library, across the hall. He keeps his collection of glass there – do not break anything. Jeanne has done for us these last few weeks so she may guide you a little, but we are all half dead from the strain of it. That is why he has gone out.' She had slipped into her own world again. 'If we were in London, it would be easier. But here, there is nowhere for him to go to but those wretched moors, running with water and filled with all kinds of traps for the unwary.'

'I am sure he will be home soon,' I said.

She ignored my words and handed me a ring of keys, the metal warm from where she had clasped them, and heavy in my hands. 'This allows you everywhere but the medicine chest,' she said. 'I have care of that, as you will understand.' I bowed my head in assent.

# CHAPTER FOUR

My mistress drank two glasses of wine. I stayed with one, looking around the room where I sat, thinking that I would start the clock in the hall, and put some life into this house. It seemed too grey and dark to me, and if they were as rich as she said, they could afford more candles.

Miss Twentyman watched me looking around the place, sipping my wine as she gulped hers. At length, she drained her glass to its dregs.

'I will show you your room,' she said, rising, and sweeping out. I put my glass down and tripped after her.

We followed the winding staircase up. 'Our rooms, and guest rooms,' Hester said, with a wave of her hand. Then through a door in the panelling, up a back staircase, to a bare-boarded corridor. We passed a landing on the way. 'The back entrance to an old gallery, which we never use,' she said. 'My uncle had it put in so that he could pace up and down it, in the winter, but now it is full of rubbish and we keep the door locked. There is no need to trouble yourself over it.' We continued up a smaller, narrower back staircase, to the highest floor.

'You will sleep up here. The floor itself is yours.' Her expression was indifferent. 'Take one or two rooms, if you wish – though, I see from the size of your locking box, that you do not have many belongings. You look surprised – were you not expecting to sleep on the upper floors?'

I was worried that my face had showed my discomposure. 'I will sleep where you wish me to,' I said. 'I simply thought that the housekeeper would sleep downstairs, near the kitchen and the silver store.'

Her mouth curled in a sardonic smile as she gestured towards the room she had clearly meant for me. 'We are far from London now, Miss Calvert. There is no need to sleep in the kitchen. Sorsby and Jeanne, and my brother's dogs, are good enough security, I assure you. Besides, if we put you on the kitchen floor, what would happen if the brook floods in winter? Submerging you in cold water would hardly be good for your health or your work.'

She directed me to walk past her, into one of the rooms. It was a good size, with a slightly smaller version of one of the large shuttered windows on the lower floor. There was a chest at the end of the bed; when I opened it I saw, with a start, that it already contained a brown woollen dress and a tippet. My eyes darted over it, and the room, and I saw evidence of occupation: a small comb on the table near the bed with a few hairs left in its teeth, and a half-burned candle, the pooled wax left to dry on an uncleaned candlestick.

'Miss Twentyman, whose possessions are these?' I asked.

She was standing at the window, staring out, and turned with a certain impatience, as though I had interrupted some important activity.

'Oh,' she said, and hesitated. 'Those. They belonged to the last servant. She left here in a hurry and in quite a temper. You may have them, if you wish.'

'But they must be of value to her,' I said. 'I'll put them aside. She may come back for them.'

'I don't think there's any danger of that,' said Hester. 'And if she did, my brother would drive her out of here with a horsewhip. But I am worrying you – it is my attempt at humour. You do have courage, don't you?' This she said with a hint of exasperation. She picked up the comb and looked at it, as though it was an exhibit in a cabinet of curiosities.

'She was a strange girl, although when she applied here several people testified as to her good character. But she fled the house, and took one of our best silver candlesticks with her. She is lucky we did not send for the magistrate. But then – we would have to find out where she is.' She sighed, and pressed her hand to her brow, briefly. 'I would not usually speak so informally to a servant, I forget myself sometimes. And I can feel one of my headaches beginning. I suffer dreadfully.'

'I do, too,' I said.

She looked at me with surprise. 'Really? I never think of servants suffering such ailments.'

'It will not affect my work.'

She smiled, softening suddenly. 'Shift for yourself this evening, and rest if you wish. I will not be at ease until my brother is home, so will not bore you with tiresome household lectures. We shall start to have proper dinners tomorrow – you can cook, can't you? Thank goodness, I look forward to eating something other than Jeanne's botched preparations.'

She went, leaving me to dispose of my predecessor's cast-offs. I was surprised that anyone would choose to leave such valuable and personal things, even if she left hurriedly. A girl who had stolen a candlestick would hardly leave a dress, one of her most valuable possessions, behind.

I could not stay in that room; it seemed to belong to another person, and I reasoned that, as I was now the housekeeper, I could move myself into any that I wished. So I went to the next room along the passage, which had a similar bed, and brought the bedding. Then I dragged the table and chair along the passage and put them there. The room was the same size, and perfectly reasonable.

At that moment I heard something; the slightest noise in the country silence, the whisper of a footstep outside my door.

'Hello?' I went out, and looked down the corridor, then down the stairs. There was no one there.

I went to fetch my locking box. As I was bending over to pick it up, the front door opened, and Jeanne came in, bringing some of the cold air and rain with her. I stood up, and caught her eye, and she must have sensed my nervousness, for she grinned at me. Unlike her mistress, there was no hint of fatigue or defeat about her.

'Best not to be tiptoeing around here,' she said, and I heard the slight tinge of a French accent in her voice, 'else, as Sorsby says, they will plough right over you. You look strong enough in the body, but to stay in such a place as this, the will must be strong too.'

'Thank you for the advice,' I said, a little coldly. 'You startled me, that is all.'

'That's what I say,' she persisted, 'best not to startle or jump around.'

I stayed in my room for the rest of the day. The house was silent; the rain beat against the windows. When the light went completely, I closed the shutters.

Alone, the wearing nature of the journey still fresh in my mind, I could not help my thoughts from returning to my family. I remembered how, at nine, I had been rocked to nausea by a hackney cab, as I travelled with Jared to deliver a portrait to one of his grand clients. Sitting in the cab, he had held the painting against him, carefully wrapped in layers of white cloth by Richard, his assistant.

He and Richard had argued that morning. I had witnessed it from my habitual spot in the corner of the studio, forgotten for a brief moment as they embarked on a circular dispute. It was Richard who always provoked these occasional arguments, seeming to stir up the conflict and add fuel to it, so that it was never resolved. One phrase had cut Jared deeply. I had looked up from playing with my doll to see his face.

'Leave be with your plans for my advancement,' said Richard. 'I know you. You collect lost causes. Melisende. Her.' He glanced at me, his eyes hazy with temper. Then he turned back to Jared, defiantly. 'I will not be another.'

In the cab, I observed my guardian's preoccupied expression in the light from the carriage window. 'Why am I a lost cause, Pa?' I said.

He looked at me, a little crease between his brows. 'Did you really hear that?' he said, and sighed. 'You are no lost cause, sweet. He was playing. Remember how we say you were born on St Jude's day? The patron saint of lost causes, for the Catholics? That is all he was referring to. But he said many foolish things which you should not heed. Do not worry. Richard will still be there when we get back.'

I was not worried whether Richard would be there or not, partly because I knew he would. With a child's instinct, I knew he would never have left Jared. There was something else which puzzled me. 'Why did you want me to come with you?' I said.

For a moment I thought he did not hear me. Then he looked at me.

'You know that portrait of Kit that hangs in the parlour?' he said abruptly.

I nodded. I was rather jealous of Kit for having his own portrait. It had been painted by Jared years before, and showed Kit as a toddler, looking out at the viewer with pale, calm eyes.

'Do you remember the piece of coral he's holding?' Jared said. I nodded again. Coral: a talisman, clutched in Kit's chubby hand. To keep the witches away; to keep the child safe; to keep him free of curses; to keep death from the door.

'Well,' said Jared, 'you're my piece of coral.'

No longer, I thought now, sitting in that empty room, one hand clasped tight around the coral beads I wore. I remembered how confidently Jared had dealt with his patron; how he had told me that it was my presence which gave him courage. How distant that seemed now. As an adult, it seemed I was not as vital to his happiness as my younger self had been.

Tired of my solitude, I went down to the kitchen. It appeared that Jeanne and Sorsby – if he had returned – had chosen to spend the evening in their tiny lodge. By the light of my candle I saw that the floor had seemingly not been swept in months; that only the ministrations of Emmet the cat were keeping mice away. Jeanne had not cleaned the pots she had used the day before. There seemed no clear scheme to the organization of the kitchen or its offices; pots and dishes and utensils were piled in different places, even some silver and Sheffield plate mixed in with the china. There was mishap everywhere, and I wondered if it was all Jeanne's doing, or the work of my predecessor. I unlocked the pantry, then the silver safe, picked up the pieces of silver I could immediately identify, and stowed them away. Then I locked the tea caddy, left open by Jeanne and forgotten by Hester. There was, at least, a good supply of flour, a sugar cone, and even a few interesting spices; the Twentymans had brought some of their London tastes with them.

There was a little water in a pail by the door, so I began to wash up. It was not long before I grew tired, but it seemed clear to me that if I did not do it, it would only be the task I began with in the morning. I did not like the strangeness of the house, as I worked: the cold grey stone of the floors and walls of the kitchen, and the shadowy steps leading into the cellar. When Emmet jumped onto a kitchen chair, I caught the movement in the corner of my eye and flinched. As I looked at the cat's glowing eyes, and moved to stroke his head, I realized I had been listening all the time for the sounds of another person.

I left the dishes to drain, seeing only a dirty rag to dry them with, and shooed Emmet out of the kitchen, closing the door behind.

The house was quiet, as if deserted, though as I crossed the hall I saw a dull light from beneath one of the doors, and thought of Hester. I climbed the front stairs then moved up the back stairs.

I did not undress immediately, just untied my hair, and combed its dark unruly mass free of its curls. Something of the shudder and roll of the coach still stayed with me, a faint nausea, made worse by my unease. I hoped, even prayed, that this would not signal one of the headaches which often came to me at moments of tension. Scared of sleeping late – a habit which had always maddened Melisende – I reopened the shutters so that the light would wake me. It was then I saw them – two dots of light, at the brow of the hill, travelling at the speed the horse had when I had ridden it across the moor. I turned away from the window, not wanting to be seen.

A few minutes later, I heard the front door open and shut, heavily, so that the sound echoed through the house. I went out of my open door and walked softly down the back stairs, into the front passageway. There was a sound I would grow accustomed to: the dull thump of boots on the stone floor.

'Hester? Hester?' It was a man's voice: a voice which had its own kind of beauty, but which was pitiful in its grieving tone, and imprecise from drunkenness. I paused, and heard a door open, then Miss Twentyman's footsteps coming to him. Then her voice, low and soft, murmuring, soothing, as though she was speaking to a child. I did not hear what she said to him, only sensed that she was trying to soothe him. I dared not move, or breathe, lest they hear that I was there, listening. There was a long silence, then:

'Is she here?' he said, plaintively. 'Is she here?'

I could not hear her response.

You will think me dramatic to say it, but the truth is I should have gone, that night, as the last woman did. Out onto the moors, leaving all of my possessions behind.

# CHAPTER FIVE

I woke early, with the light on my face. Dressed with urgency, as though someone was waiting for me, and passed the caked boots left at the foot of the stairs. Having splashed my face with the little water left in the kitchen, I remembered Hester had asked for a fire to be lit in the library. Though she had not given me any tour of the house, it was easy enough to find. Coming off the hallway there were four chambers in all: a parlour, a dining room, a second parlour which showed signs of Hester's occupation – needlework, and a Bible – then a room lined with books, which I took to be her brother's library.

The library window faced out onto the yard and moors, dark and forbidding that day, beneath cloud. Near the window was a display cabinet; glittering within it was a collection of glass objects – goblets and the like – some coloured, some clear, but all shimmering in their unusual beauty. I knew only that they were not English; that some great craftsman had made them. My training in art had, at least, given me the knowledge to recognize beauty.

The books on the shelves tempted me; bound in fine, soft leather, with gold tooling on the spines. I allowed myself to touch one or two volumes, and longed to take one out to read it. I wondered if, in time, I could ask to read a book or two from the library; it would be beyond my place, but I had heard some employers were liberal like that. I opened one volume, daringly, then put it back.

It came upon me suddenly: the sense that someone else was there. I tried to shake off the thought, but the air momentarily seemed charged with the energy of a presence: who, I did not know. I had to fight back the panic rising in me, the knowledge that I was not alone. *Be practical*, I thought, and turned to the fire. The travelling, it appeared, had shredded my nerves. But my head was clear, and I focused on the task in hand.

A scuttle of coal had been left with the instruments to clean the fireplace and build a fire. As I knelt and shovelled the ashes out of the hearth, I thought that I had not known my job would be so all-encompassing. It seemed I would really be a maid-of-all-work, rather than a housekeeper. It was not usual for one servant to be entrusted with so much, and yet I did not feel unhappy. Every scrape of the shovel on the hearth was something else to watch, to observe, and take me away from the London that dwelled so intensely in my mind, concentrated in its colours and tastes and landscape. Even that moment of remembrance made me make a mistake, and drop a little of the soot, and I began to cough.

'You shouldn't be doing that!' It was Jeanne, who had come in the open door behind me and was now fussing round, lifting me as I coughed. She waited for me to stop, her hands strong on my shoulders. I felt the heat of embarrassment flare in my face. 'Miss Twentyman said her brother needs a fire in his library,' I croaked, when I had caught my breath.

'And so he does,' she said, 'but I can make that, and I'll do the one in the dining room too. But you have breakfast to be thinking of, and many other things to organize, that I do not have the time nor the inclination for. Miss Hester – Mrs Hume as was – may be good at giving orders, for that is what she was raised to do, but if you do everything she says you will be fagged to death before the month is out. We are here to help you.'

'Thank you,' I said.

'No need to thank me,' she said. 'We are glad to have you here, for I would be dead in a year if I was asked to run the place alone. Now, Sorsby is drawing the water, and he will bring it to you in the kitchen. He has already fed the chickens.'

'What time do the family eat breakfast?' I said.

'Miss Hester is usually up by nine, and I will go and help her dress,' she said, 'but Mr Marcus will not stir before eleven. Just put out any cold meats we have, but he will want hot muffins. If you cook them for when Miss comes down, you may keep them warm in a chafing dish.'

I barely remember that day. Its many hours passed in a blur of cooking, of seeking things, and of trying to get to know the house and its people, in an endless thread of questions. On an ivory tablet, which I had found rubbed clean on the kitchen mantelpiece, I noted the linens, all that needed mending, and made a small list of things that the house was running short of. Miss Hester seemed satisfied with her breakfast, and with her dinner, a boiled fowl with butter sauce and a sweet pudding. I did not meet the master; he kept to his room, and I thought better of enquiring after his health to his sister. After dinner, Jeanne, Sorsby and I ate our own repast in the kitchen, with Emmet, who had taken to me, twining his way around my legs.

'This is the finest food I have eaten for months,' said Jeanne.

'It's good enough,' said Sorsby, with a nod in my direction that I took to be a compliment.

'Is the master well?' I said, a little worried that I had not yet met him.

'Aye.' Sorsby continued to eat. 'He just went to the Cross Keys last night, is all. Madam thinks he spends his time wandering on the moors, when all he really wants is a drink and to be out of this house for an hour or two.'

'I must make arrangements for washing day,' I said, seeing them glance at each other. 'Miss Twentyman said I could ask for some girls from Becket Bridge.'

'Miss Twentyman does not like strangers, nor Mr Twentyman neither, if they can help it,' said Jeanne, concern wearying her normally cheerful face.

I sat back in my chair, imagining wrestling with the laundry. I felt tired to the bone. 'I am not a laundress,' I said. 'I will wait until I am settled here. But if I require help with the linens then I mean to ask for it.'

'Yes, Miss Calvert,' said Jeanne. 'You do look a little worn. But you are new to the Yorkshire fresh air, aren't you?'

'It's not like London here,' said Sorsby, who had pushed his chair back from the table, and was examining his pipe.

'I am well aware of that,' I said.

'You'll grow used to us.' He cast a smile at his wife. 'Like Jeanne did.'

'What about the last housekeeper?' I said. 'Did she come from London too?'

They glanced at each other, and looked ready not to reply until Emmet leapt up onto my lap, breaking the tension.

'No need to trouble yourself about that,' said Sorsby. 'It's best not spoken about. There was a disagreement is all. But I'll say this, Miss Calvert, if you will take some advice – though you seem mighty fiery about my every suggestion – do not get too involved with the family. Do your work, do not mix your life with theirs. Remember always that you are a servant, and that you are free to go when you wish, without bond or tie on either side. Then we shall all be happy.'

The advice seemed a little pointed to me. The uncertainty must have shown on my face. Jeanne rushed to fill the silence.

'You go up to bed,' she said. 'I will make things tidy down here. You said you wanted to write a letter? If you do so, Sorsby will take it to the post at the Cross Keys tomorrow.'

I was too tired to argue; I thanked her, and wished them both a good night, shutting the kitchen door behind me. Despite my exhaustion I was longing to write to Jared. As I walked across the hallway I was already composing the letter in my mind.

'Are you the new servant?'

I nearly cried out in fright, and as I turned suddenly the sweeping motion extinguished my candle flame. I looked in the direction of the voice, my eyes adjusting to the darkness.

'Too vexing,' said the man's voice, 'let me light it for you.' I heard him come towards me, then he tilted his own single candle and lit mine. As it flared into life I saw his eyes, which were fixed intensely on mine for a brief moment before he turned away. As my sight adjusted to the gloom I saw him return to a chair, placed near the empty fireplace of the hall. He walked with a slight limp, and sat down with a sigh.

I looked carefully at him; for a moment I wondered whether a lost traveller had stumbled in from the moors. His clothes were dishevelled, as though he had slept in them, his coat splashed with mud, and his hair dark, loose and unfashionably long. There was something in the way he held himself that reminded me of Hester: a straightness of posture, drilled bone-deep as a child. His face, pale in the candlelight, had a youthful turn to it, its surface clear and white but for a dark patch beneath his cheekbone. I thought I saw – but wondered if I imagined it – the moistness of tears on his face.

I curtseyed. 'Mr Twentyman, sir?' I said, and I realized that my voice sounded small, and worried. He looked at me, and the keenness of his gaze, needle-sharp and perceptive, startled me anew. Even now, I cannot pin down the colour of his eyes, a disconcerting mix of green and copper. I would come to learn that, like the moors, they seemed to change with the seasons. But I remember the quality of that gaze: alive, vivid, and shining with watchfulness.

'Who else would it be?' he said.

I bit back the smart reply which rose to my lips, and stayed a few steps from him.

'Oh, you don't like that, do you?' He reached out, and his outstretched hand brushed at my dress. 'Forgive me.'

I stepped back.

'Oh for goodness' sake, I have no plans to attempt your virtue. I can see it is safely under lock and key.' He reached down to the floor, and lifted a glass to his lips. The bottle sat beside his foot. He must, I thought, have kept it in his room, for I had not unlocked the cellar that day.

'I am sorry to disturb you, sir, and I will wish you goodnight,' I said.

'Wait, wait, wait,' he said, still not rising, but following me with his gaze. 'What is your name? My sister told me, but I forget.'

'Miss Calvert,' I said. One hand still held the candle, the other had moved, without my volition, to my keys.

'I mean your Christian name,' he said, his eyes on me. 'You are a good Christian, are you not, Miss Calvert? Unlike the previous residents of this house?'

I bowed, for I did not wish to speak. I was bridling against his insolent tone. I thought in that moment that he had no reason, or right, to know my first name: surely Miss Calvert was enough. A smile curled up one side of his mouth. 'Haughty, too, for a chit of a girl. Answer me, what is your name?'

I stared at him. The candle flame quivered in the draughts from the front door. I could barely make out his features in the half-darkness, but I could see that his eyes did not leave my face. I glanced in the direction of the parlour.

'Hester can't help you,' he said. 'You have another moment to answer, or I will have Sorsby put you out on the moors this night.'

'I do not think he will do that, sir,' I said, hardly knowing where the words came from. 'Even if he were capable of it, which I doubt. I am rather stronger than I look.'

'You misjudge his strength and his determination,' he said, 'and if he does not do it, I will.' He did not rise.

'Goodnight,' I said. I turned, and walked up the stairs as swiftly as I could.

'Do you disbelieve me?' he called after me, but I kept walking.

It took all of my will not to run up the final few steps; I did not want him to hear my quickened pace, and think that he had unsettled me. But when I reached my room, I shut and locked the door with fumbling hands, waiting for the sound of approaching footsteps. In my last days in London, when I had been difficult and rebellious, Melisende had locked my room door at night. I had thought then there was nothing so terrible as the sound of a key turning in the lock, but now I was grateful for it. I waited, but no one came.

As I turned away from the door, my senses were so disrupted that I could not trust myself to write to Jared, for I knew that I would immediately begin to describe what had just occurred. I had constructed something in my mind for him as I worked that afternoon: something elegant, and delicate, a small miniature of my new situation that would reassure him. But all the words, and even the structure of it, had gone now, knocked out of my head by the unexpected roughness of my encounter with Mr Twentyman. As I sat on the bed, noticing with disgust that my hands were trembling, I wondered whether this would be my experience at White Windows. Would this be my new life? Listening at doors? Wondering what the shadow was at the turn of the stairs, as I had as a child? By coming to Yorkshire I had meant to go forwards, but in that brief moment of fear, I felt as though I was reverting to childhood, at the very moment in my life when

I was hoping to prove I could live without my family's protection.

I took off my gown, and, dressed in my shift, climbed into my new bed. Then I pulled the blankets over my head, so I could only hear my own breathing, trying to block out the dark weather coming over the moors, the wind buffeting the house, and finding its way into every nook and cranny of White Windows. The headache came, a pulse in my skull, rising and deepening until I did not feel the fear any more, only the pain.

# CHAPTER SIX

I wrote to Jared the next morning, before I dressed, wrapped in the warmth of my bedclothes.

> *My dear sir,* I wrote, hedging for formality though I longed to write his name. *The journey was as hard as you warned me, and I fear I was an impatient and sickly traveller, though I am quite well now.*

I looked from the window. There was nothing but white cloud, making the landscape strangely colourless in the dull light.

> *This country is vastly different from London, and though I have met few people yet other than the residents of this house, I hope I will have stories to tell you. I am*

*settled tolerably well here and have not met with any*
*unkindness.*

*I have one thing to ask of you*, I thought. No demands, no
rebukes for all that has happened.

*Will you write and tell me of the pictures you are*
*painting? I should so wish to hear stories of your sitters,*
*of the colours you have chosen, and whether the light is*
*good for you in this current season. I keep your ring in*
*my locking box, and I am fully sensible of the promise*
*you made me, and more grateful than I can express.*
*You may direct correspondence to White Windows*
*care of the Cross Keys inn, Becket Bridge. Believe me,*
*sir, I remain your most humble and obedient servant,*
*Annaleigh.*

I did not know whether it was wise to have mentioned
the promise. It would be a painful memory for both of
us, but I wanted him to understand that I knew, despite
everything, he still cared for me, and that I thanked God
for it.

The morning of the promise, I had been sulking for
days. Parted from Kit, and with no say about what the
next step in my life would be, I stamped around the
house. Kit and I, playfellows in our younger days, were
on the cusp of feeling something more for each other.
But he was coming to the end of his apprenticeship in
a draper's shop, and was meant to marry his master's

daughter so that, in time, he would inherit the business. This, at last, was when I knew that, in Melisende's words, if I intervened in Kit's life, made him reconsider his marriage, then I would be a burden to him, and to Jared and Melisende.

'A poorly chosen word,' Jared had said to her. He never criticized her normally. In the days following, doors were locked, and words were shouted, until Mr Plaskett, having found me on the street one night when I ran out of the house, suggested that I take up the role of housekeeper for a respectable family he knew, in Yorkshire. Jared had not wanted me to go.

'If you must,' he said, when I went to him the morning after I made my decision. He was sitting opposite a half-finished painting, looking at the drapery in the background. He had not touched it that morning but left his brushes in their jar. I held the stubborn tightness of my expression, knew that I could not give up now. He took a ring off: his signet ring, with his initials upon it.

'Take this,' he said, barely looking at me. 'If you need any help, then present it to Mr Arrowsmith, in Leeds. He will assist you.'

'I will be a long way from Leeds,' I said, as I took it.

He rolled his eyes at me. 'I do not know anyone in Becket Bridge, Annaleigh, wherever the hell that is.' A suggestion of a smile began in his face, and I could not help but respond, though I tried to suppress it. I turned away.

'Annaleigh?'

I turned, looked back at him, and he looked me in the eyes at last.

'Don't be my lost cause, little one.'

I dressed, and when the letter had dried, I put it in my pocket. When I opened my door I could hear Jeanne and Sorsby below, lighting the fires, washing out the chamber pots. It was the closest I would get, I thought, to hearing the London street sellers, the milkmaid mewing her wares. In this small portion of time between rising and making breakfast I would simply practise my courage, as Jared had taught me. So I left the back section of the house and went onto the main landing, to the gallery Hester had mentioned.

I unlocked the door of the gallery, and opened it hesitantly. The hinges creaked, as though it had been long left closed. At the sight of it, I exclaimed out loud with delight. It was not a room full of rubbish, but a long, clear gallery, which travelled the length of the back of the house, behind the main apartments. I made my way across the floor, wincing at its creaking, and opened one of the shutters.

The gallery was panelled in the same age-darkened oak as the rest of the house. There were portraits set at equal distances along the walls; many generations of the Twentymans, I guessed, and the first name I saw confirmed it. They were in elaborate frames of gilded and plastered wood; the expense was clear. As I looked at the first one, thick with dust, I was already planning how I would care for it: each day I would attend to one picture, dusting the curls and gaps in the frames with a light brush, so that the grime on them swirled into the air. I wondered if they had once hung in London, gathering soot from the city fires.

I looked at two or three of these Twentyman ancestors, taking comfort from their pale, slick, cracked faces – portraits of fixed serenity, looking down upon me. Their eyes stared out, some without any hint of life, solid and dead with their layers of pigment, but others had something about them, even if it was just a spot of white at the edge of their pupils. The best had a more particular power, as though a fragment of their spirit had found its way onto the canvas through the medium of the painter.

Jared, leaning back, considering the face of one of his sitters. 'Have I got her, Anna?' he would say. 'Is she there?'

And me, leaning on his shoulder, knowing that he would answer his own question, but considering deeply, trying to anticipate his words, so that if my guess matched his own, I would know my judgement was improving.

I was not sure about the first two or three portraits I saw. Their naivety was such that I guessed they were not the work of a London painter. I was trying to tease out their details, to analyse them, when I heard approaching footsteps.

I was walking towards the door when Hester entered. She was dressed in a white frilled morning dress and cap, and she stopped in the doorway, looking unaccountably relieved.

'It's you. Why are you in here?'

'I thought I would look and see how much work is needed on it. It could be cleaned – tidied. Perhaps even used again.'

'Come out, now. We do not use this room. I said it, the first day. It is not as if you do not have other things to do. We do not need this room, not yet.'

'But—'

She sighed, again giving me that impression of exhaustion. 'Miss Calvert, pray do not make me speak sharply to you so soon. Must I cut your tea allowance for this week?'

I came to her, closed the door, and locked it.

'Give me the key,' she said. 'As you seem so determined.' She watched me with a half-smile as I untied the ribbon which had suspended it from the ring, and handed it to her. 'You should be attending to Jeanne and Sorsby,' she said. 'Do not let them run the house, I beg you. We will have coal dust in the muffins and cobwebs in the tea.'

As I descended the stairs to the main hall, I half-expected to find my master there, asleep from the night before. But in the cool morning light his chair sat empty, pulled up beside the clean fireplace. No fire had been lit there, and I wondered how long he had stayed, for he had sat drinking in the coldest room in the house.

When I went to the kitchen I found that Sorsby had already emptied the slops out, washed the pots, and pulled clean water for the day. I murmured my thanks to him, as he sat, bootless, before the fire, smoking his pipe, clearly feeling his work had been done. I began to make

the morning muffins, and found the familiar task comforting: the warming of the milk and yeast, the stirring
in of the flour. But as I waited for the muffins to prove, in
the scouring light of that morning I saw dirt everywhere,
and dust flying in the air. I realized it would take all of
my strength, and theirs, to clean this house. Now and then
I would see where a cloth had been applied to a surface,
in a small sweep, and the dust had built up in the pattern
again. Another hand had tried to change this place, and
failed.

'How long has the last housekeeper been gone?' I said.

Sorsby took his pipe out of his mouth. 'Long enough for
everything to fall to rack and ruin.'

'Was the kitchen arranged well when she left it?' I
asked, imagining her reaching up for the cream ladle,
or carefully stacking the saucepans together. Now that I
looked properly, I could see that Jeanne only used some
things, and left them in disarray. A few vessels had clearly
not been moved for a while, so the last housekeeper's
hands must have put them in their places.

'Do not speak of her,' said Sorsby. 'I told ye before, but
you are mighty slow to learn your lesson. Hush.'

No one came down for breakfast, so we ate a good deal
more than we normally would have done, butter glistening on Sorsby's chin, and Jeanne unusually silent as she
crammed muffin after muffin in her mouth. Eventually
I moved the plate and covered it, in case any would be
needed later. Sorsby declared his intention to ride to
Becket Bridge and collect the post from the Cross Keys. I

thought of the letter I had written Jared, tucked inside my apron pocket. Instead of saying anything, I watched him from the window of the front hall as he led out his horse, mounted and rode away.

I could not hand the letter to him, but I had no idea why. Everything I had written in it seemed to be a concoction. I had not given any hint of my misgivings about my master, no account of what I had seen and experienced. I wondered if the girl who had worked here before had done the same, smoothing over any troubles out of cheerfulness or embarrassment.

'Why, Miss Calvert, you look fit to weep,' said Jeanne, as she came down the stairs. 'Whatever is the matter?'

I felt the cool, smooth fold of parchment in my pocket. 'There is no matter,' I said. 'I simply forgot that I meant to send a letter.'

I was scrubbing the stone hall floor free of muddy bootprints, absorbed in my task, when I heard the sound of horses in the front yard. I set aside my bucket and brush, and opened the front door to see Sorsby and Thomas, and another man, dismounting.

'Miss Calvert,' said Thomas, as he took the reins over his horse's head. He had worn a smile as I had stepped out, but now, he looked at my face as though in deep consideration.

'Mr Digby,' I said, with a slight bow, 'you look very closely at me.'

'It's how he looks at everyone,' called Sorsby. 'Horses,

women, customers – you like to know what you're getting, don't you, Tom?'

'Hardly,' said Thomas, patting his horse's neck. His voice softened. 'I had hoped to see you recovered from your journey, but you look more tired. This place is hard and foreign, if you are used to London.'

'And yet you told me you know little of London,' I said, trying to keep my tone light. 'It's no soft place.'

'She's a saucy lass, Tom,' said Sorsby. 'Don't mind her.'

I cast Sorsby a darkling look before turning back to Thomas. 'Have you come to see about the cart?'

'It is beyond my power, I am afraid – but Mr Deane will see to it,' he said. Sorsby was already leading a man to the stables, chatting away, and carrying a large sack of tools, a cartwheel over his shoulder. 'Sorsby said Mr Twentyman's mare has had her wind broken. I supplied her only two months ago, so I need to see her before I agree to take her back, which is what he will demand.' I watched him tie his horse, and I fancied he did it carefully, looping the rope around, as though showing his expertise. When he had done so, he took a step closer to me. 'How are you faring? I admit to feeling some responsibility, having delivered you to this place.'

'Very well, I thank you,' I said, lifting my chin a little, and giving him a bright smile. 'And I relieve you of any responsibility. I am quite my own mistress, I assure you.'

He looked askance at me. 'Well,' he said. 'I should follow, and advise them. I'll leave you to be mistress of yourself, Miss Calvert.'

I went back into the house, and continued scrubbing the floor with extra ferocity. My encounter with Thomas, although cordial enough, troubled me; in my attempt to demonstrate my strength of character, I wondered if I had been too sharp, rebutting him when he had tried to be kind. I told myself not to dwell on it, and set my mind to the task in hand. Scrub, I went, scrub-scrub. Set up a rhythm which gave me a moment of relief with every pass – my arms and shoulders aching with it already.

I did half of the expanse of grey floor, until my knees were sore and I felt dizzy with the effort. Then I threw my brush in the pail and went back into the kitchen to inspect the sack of vegetables Sorsby had brought back from Becket Bridge. I was planning the dinner when Sorsby came in.

'Tom's off now,' he said, resting his chin on Jeanne's shoulder as he stood behind her. 'Shame. He wanted to get the business with the master settled, and I wanted him here when master opened the post. Extra hands to man the pump, and all.'

I had no time to ask him what he meant by this last remark; I wiped my hands and went out to the front yard, where Thomas was mounting his horse. He smiled at me with the same steady kindness. 'I'm glad you've come out,' he said, when he saw me. 'I wished to make amends if I appeared to pry. I speak a little too plain, sometimes. It is the custom of this country.'

'I will get used to it,' I said. 'And I beg your forgiveness too, Mr Digby, if I seemed to be offended. I am not. I've been busy, is all, and my day's work is not over. When you go I must wash all the china and glass in the house. I am tired, and it was kind of you to notice. May I trouble you for a favour?'

He frowned, and his horse shifted on the spot. 'Of course,' he said, drawing his reins tighter, and patting her neck to soothe her impatience. I reached into my pocket and drew out the letter. Hardly knowing why, I glanced behind at the house before I handed it to him, but the windows, edged by their white shutters, were empty of observers. 'If you could take this to the Cross Keys, for the post, I would be obliged.'

He looked at the letter, and tucked it into his greatcoat.

'It is to a friend of mine in London,' I said, 'my former guardian. There is nothing covert about it. I should have given it to Sorsby, but I had not written it when he went.'

'I have not questioned you, Miss Calvert,' he said, softly. 'There is no need to explain. Of course I will take it for you. I hope to find you in better spirits when I visit again. Good day.'

# CHAPTER SEVEN

In the quiet afternoon, I washed my master's collection of crystal and glass. It was a mixture of lapidary work on rock crystal, and glass; there were tazze, their enamelled stems vivid in greens and reds, hard and bright. Goblets wrought so beautifully they looked as though they were still molten, frozen only for a moment. I felt their cool hardness in my hands, dipping each neglected, dusty piece in the pail, rubbing it dry with a soft cloth, and turning it in the light. For a few minutes, I was so absorbed in my task, I forgot myself.

I owed my care, my missed-heartbeat of love, to Jared. He who appreciated beauty in everything, and had taught me to see it, to know a master craftsman's hand. That was even why I saw it in Thomas Digby, and thus instinctively trusted him, for a deep understanding was embedded in the way he handled his horse: something learned of patience, and love, and perseverance. As I had learned to scrub and cook and brew and bake and be my own self. Perhaps it was possible, I thought, as I placed the last piece on its shelf, to be happy at White Windows.

I went back to prepare the dinner, hearing the heavy footsteps of my master descend the stairs and go into the library. Shortly afterwards the bell jangled; Sorsby went, having changed into a neater suit of clothes in preparation for dinner. 'We'll see how he takes it,' he said to Jeanne. He carried a salver, piled with the letters which he had brought back from the Cross Keys, and a small glass of Madeira.

'What does he mean?' I asked, but Jeanne only shook her head, and asked how she could assist me, all her cheerfulness subdued. 'It's hardly three in the afternoon, and already getting dark,' she grumbled. 'And it's barely autumn.'

After Sorsby returned, complaining about having to light the candles so early in the day, the couple were silent and pensive. Jeanne assisted me with the cooking, whilst Sorsby sat, running his hand over Emmet's head, the cat curled up neatly on his lap. The chicken pie was in the oven and cooking, and I was frying the onions to make a sauce for the potatoes, when I heard a cry and a distant crash, as though a heavy book had fallen from a shelf.

Sorsby moved with such swiftness that I knew he had expected it, rising to his feet so that Emmet flew from his lap with a shriek of protest. But then Sorsby stayed still, in the kitchen doorway, listening.

'Why are you standing there?' I said, a little shaken. 'Will you go and check on the master? He may be unwell.'

'Not unwell,' he said. 'Not as we understand it, anyways. Angry.'

I glanced at Jeanne: her eyes were locked on Sorsby's face. 'What?' I said, looking between the pair of them. There was another crash.

'*Mon dieu*,' muttered Jeanne, under her breath.

'Get the mistress,' said Sorsby to her. 'Drag her out of bed, if needs be.'

Jeanne did not have to be told twice; she sped past us and up the front stairs as though the devil was behind her, before I could stop her. I was so amazed I simply watched her go.

'What is going on?' I cried, moving the pan from the fire to the side, so that the sauce did not burn. 'I insist you tell me.'

Sorsby looked at me. 'Well you're here now,' he said. 'It's hardly as if we can keep secrets from you. There was a letter from his father; I recognized the seal, and the hand. Such letters hardly ever bring good news for him. His father may be a plum but he keeps t'master on a short leash. And it angers him. One time he smashed the front window open, and we were left with a storm howling through until we could get a glazier in from Halifax. We'll just keep our heads down. He'll quieten soon enough, I hope.'

There was another crash from the direction of the library. I thought of the glass, newly cleaned on its shelves; the still lines of books which had seemed so serene in the morning light as I did my best to dust the place. 'It sounds as though he is tearing the room apart,' I said. 'Will you not go in and calm him?'

I thought he might laugh in my face. 'Not I, madam,' he said. 'Miss Hester will speak to him; she will calm him soon enough. It is what she is here for.'

Another crash, and no sound of Hester or Jeanne approaching. I looked regretfully at the onions, their sizzling in the butter quietening. 'I will go,' I said, and had to swallow back the lump that had suddenly risen in my throat.

I crossed the hall quickly, at a pace. As I opened the door to the library, a book flew past my face, and landed with a thump, spread open, on the floor. I did not flinch, or look at Mr Twentyman: I went to it, and picked it up.

'If you do not want it, I will read it,' I said, closing it.

The letters Sorsby had brought back from Becket Bridge were scattered around the salver as though Mr Twentyman had riffled quickly through them; only one had been opened, and it lay on the chair nearby. He had thrown his glass against the fireplace; its fragments lay in the hearth. There were several books on the floor. I turned to him. He was staring at me, and I sensed the shock in him.

'What are you doing in here?' he said after a few moments. He did not shout it, but his voice was hoarse. 'I did not ring the bell.'

'Dinner will be ready soon, sir,' I said. 'As you have smashed your glass of Madeira, would you care for a brandy instead?'

'Damn the dinner and damn the brandy,' he shouted.

I looked around further. He had left his collection of glass, high and untouched on its shelves. I breathed out.

'If something has distressed you then a brandy might assist you,' I said. 'Or are you unwell? Is there a physician at Becket Bridge, who I can send Sorsby for?'

He had covered his face with his hands, but at my words he burst out laughing. His change in mood was so quick, as though a storm had suddenly dissolved into thin air. 'Good Lord,' he said, when he could catch his breath, 'what has Plaskett sent us?'

The door opened at that moment, and Miss Hester appeared, wrapped in another morning gown which I could see had once been white but was now grey, her hair loose beneath her cap. 'Marcus,' she said, looking around, 'what have you done?'

'Where's Sorsby?' he said, ignoring her. 'Cowering in the kitchen? Come out, Christopher, come out, I tell you.'

Sorsby did not appear. 'You have less courage than this poor girl,' he called.

'Marcus, stop this,' said Hester.

He was watching me again, carefully, as though observing every detail of my face. 'You are worn out,' he said. 'I can see it in your eyes. And yet you do not look away from me. I have never seen the flagstones that colour. And my glass – look at it.' He came towards me. 'My Venetian

71

glass, Annaleigh – yes, Hester told me your name, even though you would not. It has not looked so beautiful since I bought it by the lagoon in Venice, long ago.'

'I am glad it pleases you,' I said, dearly wanting to be out of that room. 'I will continue the dinner, now that Miss Twentyman is here. It will not be long; I will ring the bell when it is to be served.'

'Wait,' he said.

'Sir?' I turned back.

'Why are you not frightened of me?' he said.

He looked very young in the firelight. He must have been ten years older than me, yet his face had something vulnerable about it. Despite his temper, he seemed like a child, his eyes a little hooded, as Kit's had been – though his gaze was a different thing, shot through with energy and sadness, whereas Kit's eyes had been blue and gentle with laziness.

'I grew up in a house of men,' I said. 'My best playmate was my guardian's son, and you remind me of him, just a little. That being the case, I could not be frightened of you, sir.'

He let me go then. I went back into the kitchen, passed a silent Sorsby who looked more than a little annoyed that I had survived. As I stood over the onions, frying again, the steam warming my already flushed face, I could not make any sense of what had just happened. Only that I had won some small kind of victory.

'What's gone on?' said Sorsby.

'All is well. Lay the cloth for dinner,' I said.

Sorsby moved silently around me, the table was dressed with an astonishing precision, and I was about to serve when Hester came in. She had neatened her appearance, and Jeanne had helped her to put on a gown more fitted to dinner. In the midst of the cooking, I was only aware of her presence when her shadow came near to me, and I saw her hand, placed on the dresser nearby. She was wearing a ring, with a circular boss of grey carved material set in gold. When I glanced at her face I saw that she had followed my gaze. She was pale, dark shadows beneath her eyes, and her face looked pinched.

'It is carved lavastone, Annaleigh,' she said to me. 'My brother bought it for me in Naples, when we travelled there during the Peace of Amiens. We were different during that brief time in Italy. Happier. What he said reminded me of it.' I continued to serve. 'I do not wish you to be shocked by his behaviour,' she said, 'not that I should care for your opinion, of course, but ... he has always been indulged. It would have ruined better souls. Yet, he has protected me, and kept me safe. His goodness has survived all that the world has thrown at him.'

'You can rely on my discretion, madam,' I said.

'Thank you. And, Miss Calvert?'

'Yes, madam?'

'Did I see Thomas Digby here, again? The horse dealer?'

'Yes, madam.'

'I thought so. I saw you speaking with him from the window. He is rather a libertine, you know – not in the London sense, of course, but locally, hereabouts, he is thought of as rather unsteady ... I know he seems a very honourable type of man, but he is not. I thought I should warn you of that. Pray do not depend too much on what he says. Others have, to their cost.'

I said nothing. I stayed only a few minutes more, then left Jeanne and Sorsby to serve the dinner. When I went to my room I fell asleep, fully dressed, and my candle burned itself out.

# CHAPTER EIGHT

As the days passed, the benefit of my exhaustion was that I slept well heedless of any worries I had about the encounter with my master, of the weather, or the sounds of the old house. I often felt that there were other people there, other presences, and I looked at the last housekeeper's possessions now and then, and checked the rooms to make sure there were no intruders. The rooms were always empty, and I told myself that the feeling was just my sensitivity to White Windows, with its shifting wood, battered by the wind and rain.

I worked hard, and slept so deeply each night that when I woke, I had to remember who I was and where I was. Being young, I adjusted to the work within a few days and learned to be calm in the midst of my master and mistress's demands, Sorsby's mercurial grumpiness and Jeanne's unthinking good humour. I did not enjoy taking orders, but I had decided to form a new Annaleigh, one fit to run White Windows, sailing on through the house's disorder. I knew I could pretend to be capable and strong, until I became so.

On Sunday I had assumed that we would all be going to church, so I rose early and made the fire, cooked the muffins, and then, when no one came to eat, I put on my best dress and green woollen spencer, tied my hair with a broad ribbon, and covered my head with my straw bonnet. Still, the house was silent; I had seen nothing of Jeanne and Sorsby, and I was looking from the front window when I heard my master's foot on the stairs. When I turned, he stopped where he was, and looked at me.

'What a pretty gown,' he said. 'I hardly recognize you. And a beautifully cut coat. You look as though you might be mistress of this house, rather than a servant. Your face has the light on it in that position. No; do not move. You look quite perfect, as though you are ready for your portrait to be painted.'

'My guardian is a portrait painter,' I said, and immediately regretted it. The words rushed from me, and I realized that, though I had cherished my new self-containment, I had longed to speak to someone of the past.

'Really?' he said, descending the rest of the staircase, and coming to sit on that old hall chair by the fireplace. He saw me glance at it, and smiled. 'You shall have to start building a fire here, Annaleigh. Soon it will be winter, and if we are to have all our conversations here, it will need to be more comfortable.'

I smiled. I had discovered that it was easy to forget his temper when he was so contented and receptive.

'Your guardian,' he said. 'Who has he painted?' And he leaned forwards, his hands clasped, that penetrating gaze applied to my face. He was not handsome, but when he was calm there was a sensitivity about his countenance which was deeply appealing. In moments such as this I could imagine that there was no barrier of rank between us. But I was still wary.

'It does not seem quite right to speak of it,' I said. 'That is, I do not wish to. If you will excuse me from speaking it.'

He shrugged. 'I will. Experience tells me that you will not speak of it, even if I demand it.' He drummed his fingers on the arm of the chair, the benign curiosity changing into something darker.

'Why are you dressed so prettily?' he said eventually, without looking at me.

'I was expecting to go to church, sir,' I said. When he first looked back at me, it was as though he did not believe me, but on consideration he seemed to.

'If you are looking for Jeanne and Sorsby you will be waiting a long time, for they are godless creatures, you know, and I do not have the inclination to force them across the moors. They may save their strength for other things, and sleep late on one day a week.'

'Oh,' I said, looking down at my dress.

'I will go to church, of course,' he said. 'My sister and I will follow our usual custom – we will take a walk across the moor to the road near Shawsdrop, where our friends the Robinsons dwell in a house far more handsome than this one. They will wait in their carriage on the road for us. Have you seen Shawsdrop church?'

I shook my head. 'Oh, it is a very handsome building, Norman, I am told,' he said, a smile crinkling his eyes. 'But I am afraid there will not be room in the carriage for you, Annaleigh, even if the Robinsons did allow us to bring an attendant with us. And we are to dine with them – I believe Miss Twentyman did not order dinner from you for today.'

I nodded. 'Can I walk to Shawsdrop?' I said. 'I do wish to go to church very much.'

'It's a little far,' he said, getting up. 'Have you made us breakfast?' And he walked on into the back parlour, where the cloth was laid and the food sat ready. I followed him. 'If you please, sir,' I said, 'Mr Plaskett, in London, when he spoke of the post, did promise me that I would be allowed to go to church, and that I would be given one half day every sennight, for my own use.'

'Where do you get it from? The idea of being good on a Sunday?' He looked at me strangely; I had the feeling he was asking something else.

'It gives me comfort,' I said, watching him uncover the muffins and begin to tear one into strips. He put a piece in his mouth.

'Very well,' he said. 'Go now. If you follow the path across the moor, you may reach Becket Bridge directly and ask someone to help you. There must be a church there, although I can't recall one. Do not spend hours walking around on the Shawsdrop road, it runs for miles. I do not need you to pour my coffee for me.'

'Thank you, sir,' I said, and curtseyed, though I felt it was irregular to leave them without a servant in the house. I hesitated for a moment, and wondered whether I should wait for Miss Hester.

'Go on, I've told you to go.' He clapped his hands. 'Keep to the path, is all the advice I can give you.' He watched me steadily, grimly, and my hesitation seemed to give him pleasure, his previous gentleness all gone. So, with a hint of defiance, I decided to be unhesitating; and I went without glancing back.

I closed the front door quietly behind me and stepped tentatively into the front yard. No one was stirring in the lodge; there was no sign of Emmet, and the only noises I could hear were the horses' hooves as they shifted in their stables, and the occasional cluck of the chickens, the sound carried to me on the wind. Above me the sky was white, banked with clouds, with the occasional glimpse of grey, and I had the sense I was setting out on a thankless journey, in my best bonnet and with no pattens on my feet, for I had forgotten to put them on. If it rained and I was out on the moor, the only thing I could do was put my good wrap over my head; and yet I did not turn back and go into the house.

I went up the bank and out onto the moor. I kept to the path, as my master had said. The moors, in their emptiness, gave me that same feeling I had had on my journey here: that their bleakness was beautiful, yet threatened to swallow me up, or snuff me out. I passed a sheep, escaped from its flock, chewing and gazing at me with unimpressed eyes, and its company cheered me, comical as it seemed. Everything was still; no rain, only the touch of wind as I walked, with the occasional call of birds in the desolation. I looked at the reddish bracken; the tall grasses; the sugary purple of the heather the colour of the fondants Hester loved to eat, the bees buzzing over it, drowsy in the gloom. The grasses were of different colours and forms, from red to a startling green. I wished I could name them; but every sound and plant was foreign to me and fascinating.

I crossed the Shawsdrop road, a thin track, and continued my course for Becket Bridge. My path soon changed from a stony one to the dry dark brown of peat, struck through with grey roots that seemed like fingers. It was springy underfoot and easy to walk upon, and made me feel light, as though I might tap with my feet and find the earth hollow beneath. Used to London walking, I found it hard climbing the hills, using stones as footholds, wondering how the ponies picked their way over these passes. The path took me over the hill, and in the distance I saw Becket Bridge, the grey shapes of its scattered houses. I walked as briskly as I could on the uneven ground, forded a small stream on the stepping stones, and kept my eyes always on the horizon, singing to myself now and then, remembering the hymns of my childhood. In Jared's house, going to church had been a routine, even humdrum, part of our lives. Only now, miles from home, in this strange place, it seemed suddenly important that I keep this trace of my old life, this small piece of the framework that made me who I was.

I do not know how long it took me to reach Becket Bridge; only that it seemed like hours, though it could not have been more than one. I came onto the road at the Cross Keys, the very spot Sorsby had collected me from, and for one wild moment I indulged myself in the thought that I could fly from there and hold tight to the roof of a coach as the galloping horses took me back to London. I could not see a church steeple. When I saw some people emerge from one of the houses, I was relieved – at least I could make enquiries of someone. Then I realized one of the figures was Thomas; he was with an older couple, who I took to be his parents. He left them at one side of the road and crossed to me.

'Miss Calvert? What are you doing here? Are you alone?' he said.

'Good day, Mr Digby,' I said, with a brief bow, remembering Hester's warning about him, yet not seeing any trace of cunning in his direct, open manner. 'Yes, all alone. You would do me a great favour if you would direct me to the nearest church. I had hoped the bells might guide me, but there are none.'

A slow smile warmed his expression. 'Not here, ma'am. The nearest established church is in the next valley. I'll warrant Mr and Miss Twentyman will have gone there. Did they not direct you?'

'No.' I felt foolish. 'How far is it?'

'A good way, if you've already walked from White Windows. But my parents and I are going to worship now, at the Poole farmhouse, if you'd care to join us.'

'Are you—'

'Methodists,' he said, with a slight defiance in his tone. 'Yes we are. Don't let that disturb you, though.'

I looked down the road for the non-existent steeple; brushed some of my hair from my eyes, which had been loosed from its bun by the strong York wind. 'I'd be delighted to join you, if your minister would not object to a stranger. It is kind of you to ask me.'

His smile broadened. 'Strangers are the most welcome of anyone,' he said, and offered me his arm. 'Mother, Father,' he called, and the couple approached us, crossing the empty road, 'this is Miss Calvert, the housekeeper at White Windows.'

I saw them glance at each other: the sweet-faced house-wife, her hair a mix of grey and gold, and her husband, who looked to be a good few years older. His eyes were a piercing blue and, remembering that he was a horse dealer, I felt a little as though he was assessing me; I saw where Thomas got his searching gaze. 'Housekeeper, eh?' he said. 'Tom said you were a slip of a thing. How did you find your way to that hell-hole?'

'Father.' Thomas was jovial, but a little embarrassed, and he led me on.

'Don't be offended, lass,' said Mr Digby, 'and don't be so quick to chide me, my boy. Remember what the Bible says about how to treat your father.'

Thomas laughed, and glanced back, and I felt that I was in the midst of some family joke. The remembrance of such shared laughter came to me with a recognition so sweet it was almost painful.

The Poole farmhouse was a short walk out of town. Squat, perfectly square, and built of the same dark grey stone as the cottages nearby, it seemed to be part medieval hall, part manor house. Forty or so people sat on benches in the main hall, and Thomas explained who people were - this farmer, that farmer. More than once, I felt that I was being watched; I even thought I heard the murmur of 'White Windows' in an unfamiliar voice, but when I turned, I could not locate the source.

'I thought you said I would be welcome,' I said as we took our seats, trying to be playful, but feeling as though everyone's eyes were upon me.

'They're just curious, is all,' said Thomas. 'You'll have a marriage proposal before the day is out. This is my aunt Kat; aunt, this is Miss Calvert.'

A dark-haired woman with the same sweet countenance as Mrs Digby nodded to me. 'She's a bonny lass, Tom,' she said. 'Where did you find her?'

'New to White Windows,' he said.

'Aye?' I noted the incredulity on her face. 'It's a lonely place for such a lovely young thing as you. Well, make sure I have no need to visit you, Miss Calvert.'

I glanced at Thomas; he shook his head. It was only when I nudged him sharply that he whispered in my ear. 'She delivers all the local babies.'

'Well I never,' I said, and thought he might burst out laughing.

'Not used to our bluntness, yet?' he said.

'Why would she say such a thing?' I asked.

His smile lessened in brightness a little. 'Today is not a day for gossip. I will tell you another time.'

Somehow the autumn sunlight found its way from the thick cloud cover onto the whitewashed walls. The thronged voices of the congregation, raised in full song, echoed in the hall with a power that I had not expected. Each person sang as though of their own individual redemption. It was not what I was used to, such passionate singing, at church.

The minister spoke as though not above his congregation, walking backwards and forwards, and gaining their gazes; he presented himself as a working man, like them. He spoke of the day he had been converted to Methodism, and how he had walked from Halifax to the outlying villages to preach, sometimes drenched in rain, sometimes running a fever. 'God loves us – loves us all – rich or poor, high or low. All those who repent may be held in the arms of God, and their souls washed clean of sin. God's love is for you. But you must accept His will. Remember the covenant: "Let me be full, let me be empty. Let me have all things, let me have nothing."'

I drank the words in, felt a chink in my soul be found by them, and let myself be filled with the rapture of the music and the words. When we emerged from the church I felt lighter in spirit than I had in some time.

'Surely you'll not go yet?' Thomas said, when I wished them farewell. 'She may dine with us, mayn't she, Mother?' He looked at her, and she in turn glanced at her husband. Mr Digby stood, watching me steadily.

'It may be that she is expected back,' he said, quietly. 'But if not, you are welcome at our table, Miss Calvert. My wife will wish to feed you, for she has a taste for caring. I'm sure she's been looking at you, and thinking you too pale, and wishing you to eat some of her strengthening Yorkshire cooking.'

'I'm not expected back until much later,' I said, perhaps a little too eagerly, 'but I do not wish to trespass at your table.'

'There's enough for all of us to eat,' he said, 'and they are eager to have you, it seems.'

The food and the company warmed me. As the hours passed, and the tentative sunshine which had cast its light on the moors softened into mid-afternoon, I began to feel unease shadowing my happier thoughts. It was past two when I made my thanks, and stood at the tall front window of their house as Thomas put on his greatcoat. For a brief few hours, White Windows had not existed for me, and now I had to prepare to face its reality again.

I leaned my forehead against the window, realizing how much I missed my family. In the long, lonely days of the past week, I had been forced to wonder whether I had at last been abandoned by them, and when I considered my own soul, it seemed they had done the logical thing. I recognized there was a natural sharpness in me – a propensity to anger, which had long been dulled by the warmth and affection I had found in my family home, in the unruffled hours of light in Jared's studio, and in the tasks I had been taught, and performed to my satisfaction. Only in my last days in London had there been any disturbance to the serenity of my life, and the sudden revealing of my rawness, even to myself, had shocked me, as though I had always borne an early wound, never healed, lying untouched beneath its dressings. Perhaps, I thought, that was why I felt a kind of sympathy with Marcus Twentyman. In my master's flashes of fury and bewilderment, I fancied I saw something of myself. Now – tenderized by worship, made comfortable with food and companionship – I had, for two or three hours, been content again. I did not want to let it go. I did not wish to return to servitude, the punishment I had designed for myself, which my family now seemed content to leave me to.

'You seem to be thinking hard, but I cannot fathom whether your thoughts are good or ill,' said Thomas as he joined me at the window.

'I am tired of being told what to do and being forced into things against my will,' I said, my eyes still fixed on the horizon. I glanced at him, and saw that my vehemence had shocked him.

'No one has hurt you, have they?' he said. 'The Twentymans? If they have been overly harsh, then you need not stay there.'

We heard Mr Digby's footstep behind us at that

moment. 'Now, Tom,' he said. 'Best not to get involved in other folks' business. You should know from experience that no good'll come of it.' There was a serious edge to his gaze for a moment, before he tried to soften his words by patting Thomas on the shoulder. 'Don't fuss over her.' He smiled at me. 'You're a strong girl, aren't you? You can see your way back, if Tom takes you halfway?'

'Of course,' I said. 'Thomas need not take me that far.'

Mr Digby's attention had turned back to his son. 'It's best he doesn't see you with her again, son. You know what Mr Twentyman is: everything is property as far as he is concerned. Remember what happened to the last person who crossed him. And we haven't sorted that business with the mare yet. Sunday's not the day for discussing business.'

'I had planned to take Miss Calvert the whole way,' said Thomas. 'What if the weather changes?'

'Likely it won't,' said Mr Digby. 'Saddle up Quicksilver.'

Thomas went, with a brief glance at me, and I saw his hand brush his mother's shoulder as he passed her. Mr Digby stood beside me, perfectly comfortable, it seemed, his hands clasped behind his back and his eyes, like mine, on the horizon.

'If the weather changes you'll survive, won't you?' he said. 'I've heard they have big fireplaces at White Windows, if you need to dry off on arrival.'

I glanced at him, saw the spark of humour in his eye, and appreciated it. 'I can walk the whole way.'

'I know,' he replied. 'But my son wants to take you, so

we will let him be chivalrous and take you half of it. Make his mother proud.' He smiled. 'I heard what you said – that you are sick of taking orders.'

'Do you find that strange for a servant?'

'Not at all. I never had the stomach for it, though I had to do so plenty of times. And not always in the nicest of language.'

'I could be happy, if I was allowed to be free.'

Something crossed his face: a fleeting expression of pain, as though some nerve had been touched. 'I know that feeling,' he said. 'I used to think that I would be happy too, if only life and trouble would leave me alone.' He laughed, a low, soft laugh. 'I had to travel a long way before I lost that, and realized I needed other folks too. And now, I have my fireside, and I have Rose and Tom. I have built my sanctuary. When you are a little older, I am sure you will do the same.'

'Why should a foundling child ever find comfort anywhere?' I said. 'We are raised to be servants, aren't we?'

He looked at me. 'You are, are you?' he said softly. 'It's not just foundlings. Don't carry that around with you like a scar. I knew you were a London girl. I knew because you're like me – looking around, always ready to face a threat. People always walk too slow, don't they? I saw what an effort it was for you to glide down that path to Poole Farm, when you wanted to dance around the slow folks and run on.'

'You came from London too?'

'Long ago. I was looking for open ground,' he said. 'And

88

now I've found it. What could be more open than this?'
He took in my face. 'Ah, I see you don't find it so. You're
a strong lass, I see it in you. You can face whatever the
Twentymans throw at you, for all your youth. And whenever you step this way again, my wife will be waiting to
feed you. That's not an invitation I give lightly, mind.'

'Thank you,' I said. I felt hope, then, that I had at least
some friends. I had made some slight connection and was
not completely alone in the world.

'And.'

I looked back at him. 'Don't let the anger eat you up,'
he said. 'Pray, Miss Calvert, that's what I advise you to
do, every evening at White Windows, whether those
heathen Twentymans do it or not. Shut out what they say.
Remember that you are one of God's creatures, and say to
Him: "I am no longer mine own, but thine". For the sake
of your strength and your soul.'

Then the door opened, and Thomas came to get me.

# CHAPTER NINE

The sharpness of the breeze caught me off guard as we rode over the brow of the hill. I had wondered how far to let Thomas take me; at each turn of the path I had considered whether I should ask him to turn back, and leave me to make my way alone, but his company was agreeable, and I did not wish him to be gone. Now Becket Bridge was a mere shimmer in the distance, grey houses on a distant green hill, and I thought we must be coming close to White Windows.

'You can let me down now,' I said.

'Just a little further,' he said.

'Must I beg you? I will go now, if you please. I know the way.' This last sentence a half-truth only.

I swung my leg over, the reins gathered in my hands. As I slid clumsily down the side of the horse, my dress catching on the saddle, he caught me, his hands firm on my waist. There was nothing lascivious about it; he kept the length of his body away from my mine, and yet, when our eyes met there was something different in it, and he stepped away quickly, as though to acquit himself from any breach of trust. I remembered Hester's words; tried to see whether I could find any trace of the libertine about my friend's face. But there was nothing there of it; even the look of him, his face brown from his days in the sun, the unwavering slate-grey eyes, went against what she had said. And yet – could it be hidden from me? Was this his Sunday face, washed clean by the preaching?

'Keep to the path,' he said. 'No wandering off.'

'Do I look like a day dreamer?' I said.

'Yes,' he said with a smile, and I could not help but laugh in response as he turned, and mounted his horse.

The peat path was dry and hollow, and I was enjoying the sound of my footsteps too much to look back. Several minutes later I turned around to see him still there, holding Quicksilver, watching me. Only when I waved my arm in a mocking, exasperated gesture of dismissal, did he finally ride slowly away.

I was immediately sorry for it, of course: seeing his retreating back. Thomas's presence had made me feel safe. And the path looked much like any other path; I followed it with the threads of unease twining their way around my enjoyment of the day, infiltrating it like the dark roots of ivy on oak. It was a relief when I came over the brow of the next hill and saw White Windows.

My fears of rain had not been justified, for it had turned into one of those bright autumn afternoons that seem to pierce the soul with their particular beauty, a golden light on the land and the shadows sharp-edged, and the soft light was kind to the house. Nothing could soften those stark outlines, but on a distant green hill the sun shone, and suddenly it did not seem as isolated as it had been. As I passed through the gateway, Jeanne was returning from feeding the chickens, a pail of grain in her hands and a roll to her hips as she walked, and she smiled at me as I approached.

'Did you rest well?' I said, a little more tartly than I had intended, and she laughed and put her arm around me.

'Very well,' she said. 'And now we are ready for more of your good food. Master and mistress have been back this half hour – no, do not worry, they are not looking for you. They let us have Sundays. You see, they are good folk in lots of ways.'

We went around to the back door and into the kitchen, where Sorsby had taken up residence at the kitchen table and was carving a small piece of wood with a knife, Emmet at his feet.

'I must change my dress, and then I will make supper,' I said. I was taking my hat off, and walking softly past the door of the library, when I heard my master's voice.

'Is that you, Annaleigh?' he called. He sounded agreeable.

'Yes, sir,' I said, for I was just a few steps from the doorway.

'Come in to us then, for a moment,' he said.

I found the brother and sister sitting companionably together. Hester's hands were clasped over her stomach; Mr Twentyman was reading. The light was beginning to fade slightly, but the candles were not yet lit. Mr Twentyman seemed relaxed, a slight smile on his face as he put his book down.

'Did you pass your day happily, Annaleigh?' he said, in a mock-stern voice, and when I looked him in the eye – for I had sworn to myself in the Digbys' parlour that day that I would not always be keeping my eyes to the floor – his gaze was curious and friendly.

'I did, sir, yes,' I said.

'What did you do?'

'I went to worship with the Methodists, in a farmhouse near Becket Bridge,' I said. 'I saw Mr Thomas Digby, and his parents.'

He nodded, his smile fading. 'Look at her, Hester,' he said. 'See the animation in her face? Why do you look so alive, Annaleigh? So much brighter than you did this morning?'

'I have been in good company,' I said. 'Mrs Digby was good enough to offer me dinner. And the preaching was interesting, and reviving.'

I thought he might laugh. 'The preaching?' he said. 'You will pity me, then. For I was forced to listen to a long sermon, which I am sure had been taken straight from *Sixty Sermons*, and was without any of the punch which your minister would have had – for the Methodists speak to entertain the common people, and keep their attention.

And then I was forced to dine with tiresome people, and listen to tiresome things – Hester excepted, of course. I wish I had been with you.'

'I must say I am most offended, Marcus, that you would rather spend Sunday with our servants than with me,' said Hester sharply.

'But look how lovely she is, Hester,' he said. 'See how the walk has risen the blood in her cheeks; and she has a bright, clear gaze. Why do you not draw her, now? Call Jeanne, ask her to bring your chalks and paper. Catch that look now, before it flees forever.' He was smiling, and his expression had so much mischief in it that I could not help but return the smile.

'Marcus,' said Hester.

'I do not wish to be drawn, sir,' I said. 'I wish to make the supper. If you will excuse me.'

'Annaleigh?'

'Yes, sir?'

'I forgot. There is a letter for you here. It was mixed in with my letters in the last post.' He held it out to me. When I saw Jared's handwriting I could have wept with happiness. I reached out and took it with what must have been indecent haste, for I saw the surprise in his face.

'Will you read it to us?' Mr Twentyman said. 'There can hardly be anything in it which is not fit for us.'

'Leave her alone,' said Hester. 'Go and make supper, Annaleigh. I am glad you have had a good day. God bless you.'

*

I read the letter that night, when all my work was done.

> *My dear Annaleigh, I have been given a frank to write*
> *to you through the generosity of Mr Beaumont, who*
> *is sitting for his portrait. All places are strange when*
> *they are new and I am sure you will find much to like*
> *in the county of York, for the people are known for their*
> *straightforward nature and I am sure you will make*
> *friends there. Do your best to be happy. Work hard, as*
> *Melisende taught you to. I would have preferred that*
> *you stayed here, but you have chosen to go and I know*
> *you will be a credit to us.*

I read it again, thinking that my first impression was wrong. But even on second reading I could see no trace of his former affection, and disappointment washed over me. It was as though he wrote at one remove from me. There was no mention of his painting, other than the brief reference to Mr Beaumont; no discussion of light, or colour. And no mention of Kit at all, which I could only forgive because he must have thought it was a cruelty to mention him. The letter was dull, stiff and formal, written in a large, heavy hand and vocabulary, when all my conversations with him had always been so full of light and life. If they had been letters those conversations would have been written small, and cross-written, to cram every word, every insight, onto the page.

As I put the letter away, I felt the homesickness in my gut shift, like a fragment of ammunition left in a wound.

How I longed to be nine years old again, standing at the turn of the stairs with Kit at my side, as he lolled against the bannister and called for our maid Alice. The evening after my carriage ride with Jared I had stood so, looking down the turn of the stairs, watching the glow of Alice's candle as she ascended from the basement kitchen.

'Ma said I am to read a verse or two from the Bible,' Kit called, his eyes leaving my face only so he could direct a bright smile in her direction. I had told him that Richard had said I was a lost cause, and he was set on comforting me.

Alice muttered an unbiblical curse under her stormy, heaving breath, but found a smile for him. 'Yes, sir, you go upstairs, ahead,' she said. 'I'll bring it.'

We went to his room. Finally, she appeared in the door-way, a candle in one hand, the large family Bible hooked under the other meaty arm. It was covered in red leather with gold tooling, and Jared had bought it from a book-binder friend when its original purchaser had rejected it due to some small fault in the decoration. 'Which chapter and verse?' Alice said.

'Wait a moment,' Kit said, patting his hand on the bed so that Alice would put the book there. She glanced at me suspiciously but decided not to make anything of it. He opened the cover, and looked at me. I went to him, know-ing what I was about to see, and what it meant. The sight never lost its novelty.

On the front page Jared had begun a family tree: noting his marriage to Melisende; Melisende's first, long-ago marriage to Kit's father, a Mr Jacquard, who had died, and Kit's birth from that marriage.

Below Jared's name, another line, not strong, not broken nor dotted to proclaim illegitimacy, but wavy and hesitant, as though he did not know what to put, his draughtsmanship failing him, just this once.

At the end of the wavy line, my name.

*Annaleigh*
   *Born the twenty-eighth day of October, 1794, Mary-le-bone*
   *Taken from the Foundling Hospital in the epidemic that*
*year, and adopted thereafter.*

I reached out and touched it. Looked at that line between Jared and me; that connection, our names floating together on the page. His decision to keep me, to give me a family, and a name. His decision, every day, to clothe and feed me, to let me watch him paint. Always, Melisende's calm, kind, isolated solicitousness; always, Jared's love. My eyes met Kit's, and his look told me: I was worth recording. I belonged.

I glanced at Alice; she had been watching me with a slight sneer on her face, and I knew the words 'charity child' were on her lips. She saw something in my eyes, a softness, a happiness, and I knew she would move to counter it, the moment she could.

'There's no need to read to me, Alice dear,' I said, rising to my feet, and skipping round her. 'I shall go to bed!'

And I ran, fast as a sprite, bounding up the stairs to my

room, and hearing her roar of 'Faithless child!' with a light heart. Up to my room, in the eaves, away from the family.

I had not thought of it then, my room in the eaves. How many of us were there in England, who had to climb that extra set of stairs, to an unembellished floor? I had never felt separate from Jared, Melisende and Kit until my last days in London. Now I wondered, not for the first time, what the last housekeeper's story had been. Had she always known she would serve? Or had she, like me, ignored the threat of the future, until it had been served up to her in a servant's portion?

As I lay in the dark in my bedroom at White Windows, I thought how my birthday was almost upon me, and how I would not speak of it, or celebrate it. I tried to keep in mind that line between my name and Jared's in the family Bible. I closed my eyes and hoped, and prayed, and willed it: do not forget me, Pa. Do not.

# CHAPTER TEN

After that day I tried even harder to surrender my wish for London. Each morning I looked out of my window at the moors and their changing colours; each morning I hoped to feel something for them, other than awe. But though I longed to feel affection for the alien landscape beyond my window, I found it hard to love.

*Let me name the colours,* I wrote to Jared. *Indigo with blue, grey, brown with tones of ash grey. The sky the colour of a cold fireplace, the ashes not yet raked. From my window I see a sea of purple grasses, and a distant splash of acid green in the midst of it, a drop of poison on the autumn land. Tell me what you paint, Pa. I was thinking last night of that painting you showed me, when we looked through your old sketchbook, the one*

*that had a curve in it, where you had kept it rolled in*
*your pocket for so many years. There was one which*
*I could not take my eyes from, and I wouldn't let you*
*turn the page, keeping my little paw on it. It was a*
*watercolour view of the Thames, painted beneath the full*
*moon, the moonlight pooling on a woman's cloak like*
*quicksilver. You told me that woman, with her back to*
*you, was Melisende, and it seemed so incongruous that*
*you had walked together by moonlight in your courting*
*days.*

I smiled as I closed the letter – Quicksilver, Thomas's
horse, I thought – and I gave it to Sorsby, imagining its
journey from the Cross Keys to St Martin's Lane.

There was a certain brutal intimacy to our days. I could
hear the silver table bells rung in any corner of the house.
There was no luxury for us or them, even, other than that
of a house, its grey stone heated until it was warm and
all-encompassing, and that was shelter enough.

One morning, I was dusting in the library. My master
had chosen to come in and read as I did so, asking me
not to leave. His face was open and agreeable that day; he
was dressed neatly, but with his dark hair loose around
his shoulders. He read silently for some time, absorbed in
his book, then when I turned I saw that his eyes had left
the page, and were fixed on me. The energy of his gaze
seemed to charge the air with a kind of expectancy; it
made my heart quicken.

'Do you read, Annaleigh?' he said.

'Yes, sir,' I said.

'But do you enjoy it?'

'I expect I would if I had leisure to,' I said, and enjoyed the little frown that wrinkled his brow; it was only the truth. 'I'm sorry, sir,' I added, for form's sake.

He closed the book, and put it down. 'There is no need to be sorry to mention your desire for quietness,' he said. 'I know you must wish for leisure. It is akin to the way I felt when I lived in London – surrounded by the whirl and noise, and every luxury and debasement the capital could offer me.' He held my gaze at the word 'debasement'; I blushed, and looked away, and it seemed to please him.

'Forgive me for my frankness. You are a modest girl, I know. But you must understand that whilst there might be barely ten years between us in age, I feel centuries older than you. I lived every moment vividly in those streets. And London stifled me. I told Hester, one day: I only wish for quiet. Will you find me some silence? So to imagine being at White Windows, well, it seemed a kind of heaven to me, that idea. I knew exactly why my uncle had come here. To a small house in a rough country, where he would never have to entertain or . . . account for himself. And now, I am here – as you see – sitting by the fire, with the time to read all of the books that I longed for.'

I looked at him, and he saw beyond the polite neutrality of my gaze to the disquiet behind it.

'Do not judge me harshly, Annaleigh,' he said.

'Why should I?' I said. I remembered what Sorsby had said about him, and told myself: do not get too close, or there will be trouble between us one day.

'You'll judge me,' he said, 'because I find that I am no happier than I was before. The fault is in me, it seems, and not my surroundings. But there are moments, small moments, when I think I have found the eye of the storm. On nights when the rain lashes me, and I walk across the moor, and see the lights of this house – my harbour lights – guiding me home. Moments like this, when my glass, which I left to moulder for so long, glitters in the morning light, because you cleaned it.'

I watched him carefully, and he looked back without smiling. He was not afraid of leaving his face in repose. Puzzle-picker as I was, I could not help but try and unweave the emotions behind his veiled eyes, make him less of a mystery to me. I could not decide if his dominant force was rage, or sensitivity to life. He reacted to everything as though it was magnified to him. How much did Sorsby know him, really? Had Mr Twentyman spoken to him, as he spoke to me now? The mystery of him was beguiling. Unsteady ground, I thought, even as I felt myself intrigued: unsteady ground.

I had looked too long at his face, and I drew my eyes away, turning with a hint of defiance.

'Let me read you a few lines of this,' he said, stopping me again. 'It is a new book I ordered. It came with the post.

*'Thy gentle influence around me spread,*
*And let each soft affection glow;*
*Teach me to feel, the pitying tear to shed,*
*To cheer distress, and light the gloom of woe.'*

He put the book down, and opened his hands.

'It is very delicate,' I said. 'Though I must admit, not the kind of thing we would have read at home.'

'But I see that you understand it,' he said. 'I see you consider it, and weigh it up. Do you know, if I read those lines to a hundred London misses, the kind who wait at the side of ballrooms for men like me, their hair built into towers, their necks and ears glittering with diamonds, not one in fifty would look at me with your understanding.'

'I had best be getting on with the cleaning,' I said, wishing to be gone from the room.

'Annaleigh?'

I turned.

'I have meant to say to you that I am sorry. Sorry that I frightened you, that first time we met, when I pulled at your dress. And sorry also for the temper I showed, the evening you came in here when I received my father's letter. I did not mean to worry you. I thought you would be one of those hardened London servants.'

'Did Mr Plaskett say that was what I was?' I said.

'You are so sharp,' he said. 'Will you ever take a kindness at face value, little warrior?'

'I have stayed too long,' I said. I curtseyed and excused myself; I even managed to smile. But I took myself away, withdrawing into that cold place I was creating. I need nothing, I thought. I need nobody. I went into the kitchen to work, focusing on the feeling of the knife in my hand as I chopped the onions, the sting of my eyes as I did it. I told myself that none of this was real or true, nor would it ever be. White Windows was nothing but a figment of my imagination. London was a dream. Nothing could touch me. If I repeated it enough, I reasoned, I would come to believe it.

I remember the glint of the needle as I plied it, the slight resistance of the cloth as I plunged it in. Red thread on cream cloth, trying to keep my workings and knots on the back as neat as the front. Pierce and pull, pierce and pull, straight, tiny stitches. Struggling to keep my mind on the task, wary of being lulled into bigger stitches, into slanting. Thinking: do not leave the stain of your fingers' sweat upon the cloth.

Miss Hester and I sat and sewed together in the afternoon after dinner. She had particularly requested my company, and I was glad to give it to her, for Jeanne and Sorsby had staggered off to their lodge with lascivious looks on their faces, declaring that they would help themselves to bread and cheese for supper. I was tired from my cleaning work, and I did not care to spend the afternoon alone.

I had already made it my task to neaten Hester's appearance, and was working on one of her shifts.

'Are you quite well?' she said.

'Yes,' I said. 'I have a slight headache.'

She reached out, and touched my forehead, as though checking for fever. 'If you remind me I will bring you some medicine before you sleep,' she said. 'We cannot have you being unwell.'

'Thank you,' I said, touched by her solicitude. Brusque as she was, she often thought of my welfare, her sudden acts of kindness as welcome as they were surprising.

'Your needlework is so fine,' she said, watching me. 'I never cared for sewing. I always wished to be looking at books in my father's library, or turning the globes. My favourite was the celestial globe. I remember saying to him that I wished to travel to the stars, but he said nothing at all in response.' I glanced at her, and she caught my eye. 'Marcus and I are his youngest children. He was indulgent in many ways when we were small. But I believe I tired him sometimes, for my nurse often let me go in to see him, and I always talked to him.' She smiled. 'Constantly.'

'This will soon be finished,' I said, tying a knot. 'And then, if you wish, you can open the press you told me of, and bring out some of your other gowns. If there is a particular one you wish to visit in, I can start with that.'

'God has sent us a gift in you,' she said. In a sudden burst of movement, she came to me and embraced me, tightly. Shocked, I stiffened in her arms. 'The house is so clean, and we eat well at last. But above all, well, you manage my brother so well.'

I was shocked. 'Manage him? I hardly do that.'

'Oh, but he is calmer since you have come here,' she

said. 'I felt quite hopeless before you came. That is why I was so hard on him. But now, I think it quite possible that we might leave here soon.'

It did not seem likely to me, but I did not wish to question her.

'I did wish to ask, madam,' I said, 'whether I could bring in some girls from Becket Bridge, as you mentioned, to help with the big washing day. We can do bits and pieces now and then, but I fear the washing was got behind with before I came, and it would be a great help to me to have some assistance. Sorsby's back was hurting him, and if he was unwell, Jeanne and I would not be able to do all of it. Besides, I wish to wash all of the bedding, and if I am bringing out some of your old dresses, why, I may do them too – I would supervise your clothing myself, of course.'

'Of course you may bring girls in. Speak to Jeanne, and she will help you arrange it.' She rose, flattening down the front of her gown, and smiled at me. I had not seen her so serene before. 'Let me just go and speak to my brother, and see how he goes on.'

I stayed, sewing, hearing her footsteps as she crossed the hall; the now-familiar click of the doorknob as she turned it and went into the study. Though I listened hard, I could not hear his voice.

She was gone for several minutes, and when she returned, the smile was a little more thoughtful. 'My brother wants us both to go for a walk with him, Annaleigh. Will you go and put your cloak and bonnet on?'

I looked at the shift I was sewing. 'I should finish this,' I said to her. 'It is kind of you to ask me, but I need not go with you.'

'Please,' she said, and the note of pleading drew my eyes to her face. She was in earnest, and she was asking, rather than commanding. 'Marcus wishes it, and so do I. Besides, it may help your headache.'

So I went, and found my cloak and bonnet.

We went out of the front door, past the lodge, and up the path onto the moors. The master walked briskly, despite his slight limp, so that now and then Hester called to him to slow his step. 'It is like Sunday,' he called back to her, cheerfully. 'I told you, Hester – you should walk on the moors more, and with a brisker step; it will improve your health. You were so slow last week, when we walked to the road near Shawsdrop.'

She beckoned me to her, and folded her gloved hand in the crook of my arm with a smile. 'Thank you,' she whispered. I felt a surge of protectiveness towards her. I could see it was hard for her, and I understood that although she seemed strong enough, she was still a lady – cultivated like a small, weak plant in a hothouse, to bloom intensely, but have no strength in the real world. Plaskett had told me I would be apprenticed to her, but she had nothing to teach me: she could not cook, or manage. Her only expertise was the quiet, secretive care of the medicine chest, a small corner of the house indeed, and I thought she probably only cared for that because medicine cost money. If she worked with herbs at all she had never shown me.

I realized, keeping my step slow, that she would never have worked physically in her life; never strengthened her arms by kneading bread, or carrying a dense stack of folded linen; never walking other than from her carriage to her door, or taking a promenade in St James's Park, her steps slower than her breath. My strength must have seemed a rough, foreign thing to her.

'Did you ride in London, miss?' I asked, trying to distract her from her heaving breath, but of course it cost her more to answer me.

'I had a grey, Osterley,' she said. 'I would ride in the park, now and then, but he would not fare well on this steep and stony ground.'

Her slow pace meant that I had leisure to look around, for we were walking on a high ridge. In one direction I could see farmland, the irregular parcels of land in their strange shapes: diamonds, rectangles, occasionally a square, a rich vivid green. The view on the other side was all of wild, uncultivated moor, a burnished brown, changing constantly according to the sun and the clouds. The air was clean, but not brisk; I did not feel threatened, as I had on my own when I walked to Becket Bridge.

Mr Twentyman had reached a vantage point, where he had stopped, and was looking at the view. Hester smiled at me feebly. 'I hate to be so weak,' she said. 'And yet it is good to be out of that house.' I said nothing, confident that my support would see her to the top. Those heathen Twentymans, Mr Digby had said to me, and yet, they seemed delicate, as though, like me, they might be swept away by this landscape.

Mr Twentyman turned as we approached. He saw me first; took in what I was doing, then his eyes, freighted with feeling, rested on his sister with a tenderness I had not seen before. 'My dear,' he said, 'am I a brute, dragging you up here?'

'No, Marcus,' she said. 'I wished to come.'

I was too busy watching her, wondering whether she might faint, to regard the landscape properly. He had to catch my eye, and smile, and ask me how I liked it. I had to adjust my gaze, to seek to see how he saw. To pick out, amidst the dark green of the grass, and the grey of the stone walls, what it was that made him happier, that had shifted the look in those eyes from sadness to something approaching contentment.

I could make little out of it, but he saw what had once been there. On that inhospitable slope, there was the ghost, it seemed, of a kind of garden. Small spaces, set with stones, upon which splashes of colour bloomed.

'I will sit, just for a moment,' said Hester, and she found an irregular boulder. I went to her to assist her, and wait with her, but she shook her head. 'Let him show you,' she said, in a low voice. 'It makes him so happy.'

I turned and went back to him, and he offered me his hand. 'The slope is steep,' he said. 'Hold on, so you do not fall.'

His hand was as dry and cool as parchment; somehow, I had not expected that. In a moment we had reached some of the flowers.

'Do you see?' he said.

I saw, or thought I saw, a few irregular patches of colour amidst the stony soil; wondered if my eyes were fading, with all the close work I had done that day. I looked back at Hester; saw her slow, sad smile, which seemed to tell me to play along. 'Is this your work?' I said.

He shook his head. 'My grandfather made this,' he said. 'They are alpine flowers, from his journeys in Switzerland, and he knew they would find a home here, and flourish. I do not see the one I planted, but it is getting colder, so it may not be blooming. It is yellow, the brightest yellow you ever saw, so vivid, it hurts my eyes to look upon it.' He dropped his gaze to the ground.

'And did you bring it from Switzerland?' I said, and saw his face darken.

'Yes,' he said. 'It seems to have been an age since I planted that flower in this inhospitable soil. I have tended it a little. But before long the moor will overtake the flowers completely. See, there.'

We saw its vividness only from a distance, as though it troubled him to go near it. Instead he leaned over a native flower: heather, tiny, delicate, but a resilient purple and pink in the midst of the tough grasses.

'Shall I pick you some?' he said. 'Bring some colour to the house?'

'Oh, don't,' I said. 'Let it stay here, on the moor. See how it moves only a little; see how the bees cluster around it? I will remember it, and that will be enough.'

We smiled at each other. 'You ask for so little,' he said. 'You're just like it, aren't you, the heather? Turning your face to catch whatever light you can; thriving in the rain, and the cold. Hester said you were a foundling from the hospital.'

I felt myself stiffen. 'Yes.'

He drew closer to me. 'The last I heard, it was mainly gentry babies left there. You may even be noble. You have the look of it.' His gaze drew mine to his, and our eyes met with a strange kind of energy. I saw there now some deep sorrow, the bedrock of his gaze. I felt I truly saw him in that moment, and it was then he advanced closer to me, and I did not step away. I heard Hester say his name, and as she did so he moved away from me slightly, almost imperceptibly.

'Most women would wish me to tear up every piece of heather on these moors and lay it at their feet. And you say, "leave it". You will have a home with me, Annaleigh. You will always have a home with me.'

'I am quite strong enough to make my own way, sir,' I said, catching my breath a little. 'Though I thank you for your kindness.'

'Marcus?' Hester's voice again, worried.

He glanced in Hester's direction. 'We should go back, it is getting colder. Wrap your cloak tight around you. You must not be ill, my warrior.'

I stood for a moment, looking out at the view, steadying my breathing, and trying to understand him. As I walked back to Hester, I saw that her cheerfulness had faded into exhaustion. 'Please can you help me up, my dear?' she said, and it took much of my strength to raise her from her cold stone seat.

'There is honey cake tonight,' I told her, by way of a comfort, and she smiled bravely as we began our walk back to White Windows, I on one side of her, and her brother on the other.

After a few minutes he went ahead, as he had before, every step confident and buoyant, despite the slight turn of his limp, and she pulled me a little closer, like a child wishing to huddle against my arm.

'What you must understand, Annaleigh, despite our strangeness, is that I only survive because of my brother's care,' she said. I looked at her face in the fading pale orange light of the sunset as we walked, my eyes dipping to the ground, seeking out hazards on the slope, then back to that smiling face. It was the most serene I had seen her; she smiled like a child about to fall asleep. 'He saved me,' she said. 'He pretends it is the other way around, pretends I am his support and comfort, but without him I would be dead, or wishing that I was dead, trapped in a marriage that I did not want, with a man I hated.'

I longed to ask more, but as suddenly as she had spoken, her softened face closed up again. We walked in silence, until we came to White Windows once more, and she asked for tea to be brought to them both. Mr Twentyman did not go out again that night. For once, he seemed content to be at his fireside.

# CHAPTER ELEVEN

The next morning, I slept late for the first time since I had arrived in Yorkshire. I had gone to bed with a sip of medicine from Hester for my pounding headache, and I woke in darkness, the shutters left closed so there was no light to wake me. Mr Twentyman was in my mind when I opened my eyes. I rose with a galloping heart, and dressed quickly and a little shakily, wondering if I would be reprimanded.

Blinking away my sleep and disorientation, I hurried down the stairs and into the kitchen to find Jeanne and Sorsby sitting at the table. They had been talking, but at my entrance they stopped abruptly and looked up at me.

'At last,' said Sorsby. 'She wakes.'

'Don't fluster so,' said Jeanne, seeing my discomposure. 'The master and mistress have gone to the Robinsons for breakfast, remember?' As I exhaled in relief, she rose and smiled, putting one arm around me and giving me a squeeze.

'And lucky for you,' said Sorsby. To my surprise I saw that he had tallow and sand out on the table. The evening before I had directed him to clean the knives, and it seemed he meant to carry out the task without further nagging.

As I got out the heavy mixing bowl to make breakfast, I asked Sorsby to check all the windows were closed, for there was a chill in the air and I felt unbearably cold. I spilt a little of the flour as I poured it, listening to him as he dragged his feet across the hall.

Jeanne put her hands on my shoulders. 'Mistress said you are looking sickly. Put a little of this on your cheeks, to make you look healthy. A little of the brightness you came here with.' I caught sight of a small jar in one hand, and she dotted something on my cheekbones before I could move away, my hands in the flour.

'What were you speaking of when I came down?' I said, capitulating and letting her smudge it a little, thinking that I would wipe it off the moment I had finished mixing.

I saw Jeanne's lip curl. 'Thomas Digby,' she said.

I tried not to show any surprise on my face. 'What of him?'

She hesitated for a moment, then the words tumbled out as though they were long-saved, and I had turned the key to release them. 'Last market day, I learned there's some girl in Hebden, sick with love for him. He is trying to cut himself loose from it all, but I said to Sorsby, for all his protestations of innocence, he must have night-visited with her.'

'Women,' said Sorsby as he came back in. 'Forever repeating gossip with no care whether it is truth or lies. And look at you lapping it up.' He went to open the door and empty his pipe outside.

I continued mixing the dough, but had little sense of what I was doing, my mind full of what she had said. Jeanne leaned close to me, her voice low. 'You know how men band together. But Thomas, well, I thought I should warn you, for he is due to visit here again today. I know you went to chapel with him, but if you think yourself special you'd best reconsider.'

'You are mistaken if you think I am attached to him,' I said. 'We are friends, is all.'

'That's how it starts,' she said. 'He is always playing at being open, so friendly, like. That's how he gets in. Don't believe me, if you wish. 'Twas the same before.'

I looked at her properly then. 'What do you mean?'

'The last housekeeper.' She saw the sharpness of my look, and gave a little shrug. 'Well, I am through with keeping intrigues quiet. 'Tis best you know, for all that Sorsby says I gossip.'

I heard the tap-tap-tap of Sorsby's pipe against the door frame. 'For goodness' sake, shut the door,' I called. 'I need some warmth in here to prove the dough.'

*

Jeanne's words disturbed me more than I could admit, and I remained preoccupied throughout breakfast. When Sorsby went out to the front hall, and called that Thomas had arrived, Jeanne leaned to me and touched my arm. 'Don't tell on me,' she said. 'Sorsby don't like me gossiping, and if Thomas gets offended he'll make me pay for it.'

'I won't tell on you,' I said, rising as I heard the front door open. I was suddenly desperate to go. I knew that what Jeanne had told me would be painted across my face like the dabs of rouge she had put there. As Thomas entered the room, his face friendly and seeking mine, I turned and was away before he could speak, snatching up an empty pail Sorsby had left by the door. 'Off to fetch some water,' I said, without a glance behind me. 'Good day, Mr Digby.'

I wanted to be far away from the house. So instead of going to the well, I went hurriedly across the field, and down to the brook. It was cold, and I found myself trembling, soon regretting that I had not put my cloak on. I crouched down and held the pail, let the water rush into it, clear and bright, then heaved it out and onto the bank. I had been growing stronger, but I felt weak in that moment, leaning over, my hands on my thighs, the pail resting beside me, as I contemplated the walk back to the house.

I did not hear Thomas approach, so when he spoke I started, and turned clumsily, knocking a little of the water from the pail. As I did so he took a step back; I wondered what he must have seen in my face.

'Easy there,' he said.

'I'm not a horse,' I said. 'There is no need to say easy there, or whoa. Yours is a business call, is it not? Why have you come out here?'

'I just came to see that you didn't fall in the brook,' he said, with a slight frown. 'You were in your own world, it seemed. If you missed your step and fell in there, your clothes and the ice-cold water would have your soul in a moment.'

I said nothing. I turned away and made to scoop the pail into the water again.

'Annaleigh?'

'Miss Calvert,' I said, Jeanne's words all too vivid in my mind. In that moment it was the only way I could think of to put distance between us, and the sharpness hid what I could barely admit – my disappointment. But Thomas was not put off as a lesser man would have been. I saw a faint blush beginning in his face, but he kept his gaze on me, looking into my eyes as though he might see some vital information there.

'What's been said to vex you so?' he said. 'I saw the look on Jeanne's face when I arrived, like a child that's been doing mischief. But I fail to see what that can have to do with me.'

'Jeanne's said nothing to vex me,' I said, rather stoutly, so that he smiled at the effect. 'I've heard there's some girl in Hebden who's sick with love for you.' The words rushed out before I could stop them.

He looked faintly amused. 'I can't stop people from

gossiping. If Jeanne has caught hold of some scrap of information and twisted it, it is hardly my fault. But thank you for your interest.'

'Why, Thomas Digby, you—' I barely stopped myself in time. Seeing the smile beginning on his face, I turned away. The water ran noisily nearby, sheeting down the side of a large boulder, the moors benign under the sunlight.

'As you have decided to question me, I think you may answer a question of mine too,' he said, after a moment, and I heard the hesitation in his voice. 'Who put the rouge on your face?'

My hands went automatically to my cheeks. 'Jeanne. She said I was looking sickly. I meant to take it off before anyone saw me.'

'So you did not put it on yourself,' he said. 'I thought not. Do not let them shape your actions. I say it as a friend.' He tried to gain a smile from me. 'And while I am asking questions, if you will allow me one more. How did you come here? Did the Twentymans advertise in London?'

I remembered Mr Plaskett, the failed poet, sitting for his portrait. His nose pointed up, as he spoke of how his work was not fully recognized, his eyes following me around the room as I lit the candles in the twilight, the session coming to its end.

'A man known to my family, a gentleman, told me of the position,' I said. 'I wished to leave London, and so it seemed ideal.'

Thomas was frowning. He looked over his shoulder,

to check whether Sorsby or Jeanne had come out of the house, but there was no living creature near us.

'You're right that I came here on a business call,' he said. 'But also because I am concerned for you. Unlike others, I am not one to repeat tittle-tattle, and it holds no sway over me normally. But many people hereabouts have spoken about this place in hushed voices for months. Old Jack was an eccentric, but they knew where they were with him, and he bothered no one.'

'So?'

'It is not the same with the Twentymans. The local people suspect that bad things happen here, and no one knows why they came here, so suddenly, from London. I never gave it any truck – it is no business of mine what other folks do in their own houses – but now you are here, I fear for you.'

'What kind of things do they say?' I asked, remembering the looks I had been given by strangers at chapel. His gaze veered away.

'There was talk of the last girl here. Kate. Talk that she had dealings with the master. And no one knows what happened to her. I knew her a little. I don't believe what they said about her – that she took a candlestick.'

*Kate.* The owner of the gown and the comb, the shadowy presence.

'Did you know her well?' I meant it as an honest question, but a defensiveness had crept into my tone.

He sighed. 'I see that Jeanne truly has been here before me. No, not well. Will you speak to me like the rational creature I know you to be? I am trying to say to you that, God forgive me, Annaleigh, there is something about you – a vulnerability beneath all your strong words – which I see. And it is a matter of honour to me that I protect you. I am uneasy about you, and your position here.'

He seemed to expect some answer from me, but I felt overwhelmed, a hundred thoughts circling my mind and blocking my ability to think clearly. 'I am sure there is no need to be concerned,' I said. 'Forgive me, we have said much, I must think.' I started back for the house. 'Do not trouble yourself over me.'

'Does that mean you do not wish me to visit?' he said, following me, taking the pail from my hand, despite my resistance.

'By no means,' I said, struggling to keep my composure. 'You are known to the family, so you are always welcome here. You understand, though, that I must not seem to have too much of a connection to you. If Jeanne can gossip about Hebden, I take too much of a risk to let her gossip about me. I cannot risk my place here. Thank you for carrying that. Would you excuse me?' And I strode on ahead, leaving him to deliver the pail to the kitchen, and went up to my room, without a word to Jeanne.

Standing at my window, my arms folded tightly, I calmed myself. After all that Hester and Jeanne had said, I could not help but doubt my friendship with Thomas; I would be foolish to take his words at face value. And he had said a name: Kate. He had said it just as he said mine, with an almost-tenderness that told of something. In time, perhaps another girl would stand at the brook, and he would speak of the Annaleigh who had been here once. All was impermanent.

I would remember that, in the days that followed. One, two, three, four, I counted: the days that Thomas did not visit. I did not go to church that Sunday, did not seek him out. Five, six, and then I counted no more. I saw the four other people in the house, and only them. I looked after White Windows. I kept it clean, as though by rubbing the silver until it shone I might one day see in it the face of someone who cared for me. One could not feel alone there. There was something in that house, the sense that someone had just left the room. In my moments of leisure, I tried to read the past of that house in its thick air, but I found myself thinking of my own past instead. It was a comfort to me.

# CHAPTER TWELVE

I regretted how I had spoken to Thomas. My behaviour towards him had been coloured by the past. But I did not wish to tell him that.

A week before I had to leave London, Jared had taken me to see a haunted house that was the talk of the town, and drew hundreds of spectators every night. He went against Melisende's advice, scaring me with old stories of the Cock Lane ghost, and took me to Snow Hill, in the City. There, in the crush of people gathered to see any apparitions that might appear, we saw Kit, who waved cheerfully at us. He was with the Whitmore family; his new family. Catherine, the draper's daughter, a year or two older than Kit, was on his arm. I saw in a moment how things were. Saw what Jared and Melisende's careful words had meant. He was intended for the girl.

Jared and I kept our distance from Kit's group. But near to the haunted house the crowds were dense, people packed so tightly that the crowd took on its own life. In the crush I saw Kit look round, and call my name. Our eyes met, and he let go of Catherine's arm with all the restlessness I recognized and loved in him. He was fighting his way towards me through the crowd. I don't remember the panic of those moments, though it must have shown on my face. Jared always said my face told too much of a story; sometimes, it told more of a story than was there. But I remember Kit's expression as he fought his way towards me; remember the pique on Catherine Whitmore's face; remember Jared's hand on my shoulder as he pulled me back, away from Kit, shouting to him to go to the Whitmores. And then Kit stood still, the people flowing around him. The coldness of sudden, unwanted revelation around his heart and mine.

We knew it then, all of us. In the gap between Kit and I, in his growing maturity and my idealistic innocence, something had accumulated which now bound us together and showed itself to the world. After we had extricated ourselves, Jared and I hurried home, silently, my hand hooked in his arm.

'Have you made each other any promises?' Jared said.

'I . . .' My voice trailed away, I could not think what to say.

'You and Kit, Annaleigh,' he said, without looking at me, steering me past a crowd of young ladies. 'Have you made each other promises?'

'No,' I said.

'Good,' he said. 'That is a mercy, at least.'

We walked on in silence. On our front steps, he turned to me. 'Do not speak to Melisende of this,' he said. 'She could not take it. Remember she was alone in the world with him when he was a baby. It means everything to her that he should succeed in life.'

'But—' I said.

'Do not,' said Jared. 'Kit has his path set out for him. Whatever understanding lies between the two of you, you must see it cannot be.' I saw that he thought we had gone behind his back. He did not see that my candid delight glowed because of its novelty. 'We must keep you apart for now,' he said. 'Think of your reputation, if anyone should suspect.'

I could not forget Jared's words, words which were so unlike him. He had never mentioned my reputation before. I thought he saw me clearly and understood me, but he spoke to me as though I had done something wrong. I saw my life in a different, foreign light for the first time.

Kit was persuaded to continue on the path that was intended for him. The potential for us, that brief feeling of hope and possibility – lasted just for a day or so.

I dwelt on the memory one long, lonely evening at White Windows. *Think of your reputation.* The headache I got that night was a terrible one, as though something had been set loose in my head. In my half-conscious haze, I thought the pain in my right temple was a wriggling bookworm which had eaten through one of Marcus's library books, leaving its comet-shaped trace in a hundred pages. I lay there, the worm turning and churning in the right-hand side of my brain. It was a new kind of pain, particular to the headaches I had at White Windows; I got one the last day I looked for Thomas. And Hester, kind and concerned about my pallor, gave me two spoons of medicine in a glass of wine. I slept.

I had been dusting for hours. Rubbing, rubbing, rubbing, with a cloth so black it could have been used to clean silver. Rubbing wax into the dark wood, my knuckles swollen, the nerves in my arms singing with it. I was rubbing dirt onto dirt, and then I was running through the house, knocking on doors that were locked, forcing open the door of the gallery that I had been told to leave undusted. Faces watching me from the walls.

Waking suddenly in the half-light, I saw Hester standing before me in her nightgown, her feet bare.

'I am sorry to wake you,' she said, as I gasped for air. 'Please, you must come and help me, Annaleigh. It is my brother.'

I rose and threw a wrap on, and we went together to the master's room.

Sorsby had tended to this room rather than me; I had only glimpsed it. My master lay on a four-poster bed of carved oak. The shutters were closed, and heavy red drapes hung over them. A whole branch of candles was lit beside him, and a chair pulled up, with a book discarded on the bed. I ascertained Hester had been sitting beside him for some time.

He seemed delirious; agitated, he tossed and turned, his face slick with sweat.

'My dear,' said Hester softly, and he groaned and turned his head again, so sharply and at such an uncomfortable angle that it made me wince.

'Where is she?' he said. 'Hester, where is she? Bring her to me.'

'I am here, my love,' she said.

I stood, hardly knowing what to do.

'Not you,' he said. 'Not you. The one with the golden hair.'

The phrase made Hester flinch and she leaned close to him. 'Hush,' she said. 'Hush, Marcus. That is not who you want, not really. Your medicine is here, drink your medicine.' She turned to me. 'Help me raise him,' she said. I went to the other side of the bed and crawled up onto it. I put my arm under his back; he turned his head and nuzzled into my neck. I moved his face away as gently as I could, whilst Hester raised a glass of shimmering red liquid to his lips. 'Drink it all,' she said. 'Drink it, Marcus.'

He did, in fitful gulps, and we lowered him back onto the pillow. Eventually, he grew quiet, and at last, he fell into a sleep, and seemed to be falling deeper each moment.

'What did you give him?' I said.

'Laudanum, of course,' she said. 'He will sleep now. Thank you for your assistance, my dear. There is no need to wait here.' She sat down in the chair again, and took up her book. When I said goodnight, she did not look up, and I sensed her embarrassment.

I went back to my room with my single candle, leaving them to their part of the house with its chambers, the shut-up guest rooms and the neglected gallery.

I lay very still in my bed, not daring to sleep again, and not able to either, for my brain was alight with the buzz and pull of my thoughts, and my concern for my master. In the passing days I had felt my world narrow percep-tibly. I had liked and trusted Thomas, but he had gone, pushed away by my hard words. As my heart slowed, and I felt myself calming down, I thought of Mr Twentyman, with that strange mournful expression he had, as though he felt everything more deeply than others. Something was happening between us, though I knew not what; a strange mixture of attraction and repulsion, which had me in its thrall. There was none of the easy kindness that had lain between Thomas and I, only a charged tension, a kind of fascination. I did not wish, I thought, to be close to Marcus: when he had put his face against my neck my instinct had been to draw away. And yet my thoughts returned to him repeatedly.

I lay in my bed, thinking of him, twisting some strands of my own brown hair around my fingers. And I won-dered, with a strange animation that could have been jealousy, who was the one with the golden hair?

# CHAPTER THIRTEEN

When I opened my eyes, it was morning, and a different world from that flickering nocturnal realm of silhouettes and candle flames. There was practical work to be done and, having dressed, I took down my chamber pot to empty it, splashed cold water on my face, and went to work on breakfast.

I was relieved when Mr Twentyman did not appear; I had dwelt on my strange feelings for him with such intensity that I could not have spoken to him without blushing, or stumbling over my words. I cautioned myself that being shut up in White Windows had narrowed my world. This, I thought, was why I had imagined some connection between us. Had we passed each other on a London street we would not even have struck a light with our gazes. We would have moved on, to our different destinations, as though we lived in separate worlds. Here, we looked on nothing but each other, and owed our intimacy to nothing more than proximity, and my own tiredness and weakness.

I did not wish him to see a hint that I had dwelt on thoughts of him, for surely some other night he would come home, having tossed back a bottle of claret, and wish to take advantage of it.

Hester came down, ate quickly, then declared she would write her correspondence in the other parlour, and wished to be left alone. As she passed me, she touched my hand.

'He is quite recovered,' she said, in a low voice. 'Thank you for helping me give him the medicine. I could not have done it without you.' She squeezed my hand, then walked on.

I was working in the kitchen when I heard Mr Twentyman's foot on the stairs, and got to the hallway as he was at the door.

'Good morning, sir,' I said. 'Do you care for some breakfast?'

He turned. He was dressed neatly, as though for business, in a black cutaway coat and breeches and carrying his riding crop. 'Good morning, Annaleigh,' he said, and he did not meet my eyes. 'I am going into Becket Bridge today, but I will be back for dinner. Be good, won't you?' There was a certain acidity to the smile he cast in my direction, and he went out of the front door without another word. Puzzled, I walked back into the kitchen, wondering at his manner.

'He's going to see Thomas Digby, Sorsby says,' said Jeanne knowingly. 'Tom didn't want to come back this way, see. Fickle, he is. I told you, miss, you stay here, we'll look after you.'

'You have been imagining things, Jeanne,' I said airily, as Sorsby tramped back in. 'It's naught to me how often Mr Digby visits. I did want to speak to him about engaging some girls from Becket Bridge to help us on washing day, though.'

'Well, Jeanne can see to that,' Sorsby said. 'I'll be going in on Wednesday, we'll pass through on our way to Hebden, for market day.'

'Very well,' I said.

I spent the next hour checking the provisions and listing what I would need from Hebden. Then I set to making a pudding. I must have been so consumed with my work that I did not hear the master come in. So I was surprised when I heard the silver bell in the library. It was their custom to ring it gently once or twice to summon us. Only now the bell rang on and on, an incessant tinkling, until I shouted at Sorsby to put his boots on and go and see what the master wanted.

He went, but returned directly. 'Master wants to speak to you, he'll have nowt to do with me,' he muttered.

'I cannot go. I must finish this and then prepare the dinner,' I said. 'Put your best face on, and see if you cannot please him.'

Sorsby went back to deliver the message, and again

returned. 'He says he cares not what you're doing, and tha'd best go to him, or he'll turn you out, without a character,' he said, not without bewilderment on his face. 'What ha' you done?'

I was staring at him in shock when our master appeared in the kitchen doorway, dishevelled, with his cravat undone. 'Sir,' I said, but he was already crossing the room, and seized my wrist, pulling me past Sorsby, and across the hall so quickly that I almost fell. Trying to keep my balance, I saw that he had left muddy bootmarks across the flagstones. *God damn those boots*, I thought. *God damn that I will be down on my knees scrubbing the floor before this day is done*. That, coupled with the harshness of his actions, lit the rage in me; as he pulled me into the library I managed to twist my wrist free, which I had to do so violently that I thought for a moment we might embark upon a struggle with each other.

'What is it?' I cried.

We stared at each other; I had shocked him into silence and I saw a flash of doubt in his face.

'Will you explain?' I said, rubbing my wrist, my voice still loud with anger, as he began to pace up and down before the fire. 'Why do you seek to humiliate me in front of Sorsby?'

'I would not have done so if you had come to me,' he said, stopping and turning. 'How many times must I ask you to? Is it something in my manner which changes women? You come here as though you are a humble servant, and yet you will have me grovelling to you as though I am some mill hand. I see it. Your expectations are already elsewhere. How long until you steal out of this house and onto the moors?'

Astonished and confused, I shook my head. 'You are mistaken if you think I make a show of anything. I am in earnest. I have no plans to leave this house, though I hazard to say I do not think myself a prisoner, and if I wish to go out I will.'

'I saw it,' he said. 'The way his face changed when he spoke of thee.' The Yorkshire 'thee' had slipped into his speech. 'I saw it!' he shouted; a child suddenly.

My temper overcame my inhibitions. 'You are speaking in puzzles and I do not have the leisure to listen to your ravings. How dare you stamp your feet at me? I do not know of what you speak. I have done nothing but work hard in this house, and do my best. And now, out of nothing and nowhere, you call me in to talk to me of your anger? You, who have pretended to be my friend, who have made a show of understanding me. You tell Sorsby you will send me away with no character. Why, I could smash that mirror!'

'Smash it, or me?' he said, nearing me, and I saw that the light from the fire was rising in his eyes – those eyes swollen with force like the water at the falls – and that his face was flushed. There seemed no way out of this moment, and I had said too much, and knew it, so I turned.

'Where are you going?'

'To pack my bag. Unlike your last servant, I will take all of my possessions with me,' I said.

He snatched at my arm, trying to turn me. 'Stop,' he said. 'Annaleigh, stop. Let us speak sense.'

'It is too late for sense. Let go of me!'

I turned back to him, shrugging his arm off. He put his hands out in a calming motion, and we looked at each other. I wondered whether Sorsby had scampered off to get Jeanne or Hester.

'I was angry,' he said, 'because it seems clear to me that Thomas Digby has a partiality for you. I went to speak to him about a horse, and yet all he could ask of was you. I thought there must be some understanding between you which you had not mentioned to me. Sorsby told me he was here the other day, when both Hester and I were out of the house. Do you see how that seems?'

I shook my head vehemently, and thought that the next time I baked muffins I would jam one down Sorsby's ungrateful throat. In the back of my mind, there was gratitude that Thomas had not forgotten me.

'I was frightened that you would leave here, do you understand?'

Dully, I scrabbled for meaning in what he was saying, or a way to answer him. 'I am virtuous,' I said. A stupid, childish thing to have said, but true.

'I see I have perplexed you,' he said. 'I was foolish, perhaps, to jump to conclusions, but his feelings seemed so definite to me – his face, when he spoke of you – that I thought you must be betrothed.'

'So you threatened to turn me out?' I said. How hellishly familiar. How quickly Melisende had accepted my assertion that I would go. She, who had raised me from a babe. Why I had expected any different from my employer, I had no idea.

'You do not understand,' he said, and his worried face cracked into a smile, an attempt to reconcile, before he failed to see what he wished in my face and turned away. 'I was afraid. I am sorry,' he said, turning back, 'believe me, I am sorry. But you see, Annaleigh, it is important, very important, that we can trust you. You must have no followers, no followers at all, you understand? That last servant that you spoke of – Kate – she robbed us, and under the influence of her lover, who I suspect may even have been Thomas Digby, though I could never prove it. Hester and I have had enough violence done to us, enough to last a dozen lifetimes – and now we must be surrounded by people we trust.'

He was searching my expression with his woeful eyes, like a dog who expects a kick, and I did not want to meet his gaze or be drawn into it. 'I am trustworthy,' I said.

He took my hand, without asking for it, but I did not withdraw it: his cool, dry hand, despite the flush on his face. 'I know,' he said. 'Forgive me.'

'I work hard,' I said.

'I know,' he said. 'But forgive me, Annaleigh. Say you forgive me.'

It happened so quickly, I hardly know how. I had no time to think. He pulled me towards him, gently; and though I instinctively braced myself, he did not kiss me. There was an almost terrible delicacy to it, after the previous moments of violence; I shivered away from it, as one winces at intense sweetness on a dulled palate. He held me for a moment in his arms, and I heard and felt the shivering warmth of his breath as he raised one hand to my face. My mind was racing and yet, despite Thomas's warnings to me, I took comfort in it; I had longed to be touched with affection, and only now did I know it. For one moment, I relaxed, allowing myself to be held in his arms. Then he released me, and I realized anew the danger I was in. I heard Jared's words again: *think of your reputation*.

'I will be gone tomorrow,' I said.

He did not try to stop me from leaving the room.

Sorsby was in the kitchen, and rose to his feet when I returned. He and I looked at the pudding; he had dragged it from the fire, but it was burnt and ruined.

'Sorry, lass,' he said, looking at it. 'I waited for you, but by the time I took it out it was too late.'

'I won't cook dinner tonight,' I said. 'I will bring out cold cuts from yesterday, with bread, cheese and ale. You will serve it.'

He did what I said; there was such vehemence in my looks, it seemed even Sorsby did not wish to question me that afternoon.

# CHAPTER FOURTEEN

At half past eight on the hall clock, which I had got working again, and now wound every day, I decided that I
must leave the kitchen, and ask Hester if she wished for
some tea. I found her in the back parlour, quite alone, and
sewing without me. 'Where have you been?' she said. 'The
dinner was rather unexpected. If you wish to change the
menu you should speak to me.'

'I had many matters to attend to,' I said, stiffly, waiting
for her to reprimand me, and feeling a strange surge of
confidence when she did not. 'Have you spoken to Mr
Twentyman?'

'He has gone to the Cross Keys,' she said. 'There is no
need for tea this evening.' I noticed the glass of wine by
her right hand. 'He left you this quarter's wages. Do you

know why?' I shook my head. I had been there for half that time; his generosity showed his guilt.

'Has he been harsh to you?'

I struggled to keep my composure. I had sworn I would say nothing; I would pretend that what had happened meant nothing. But my face cheated me of hardness. She saw something.

'I have often told you of my brother's nature,' she said.

'And I am afraid the generalities we have spoken of offer little explanation for why he dragged me from the kitchen this evening,' I said, picking up the packet sealed with red wax, impressed with my master's signet.

'How strong you seem, all of a sudden,' she said. 'Sit down, Annaleigh. I must tell you something.'

I did so, turning the packet in my hands.

'Do you remember I spoke to you of being nineteen, and being in love?' she said. I nodded. I could see in her face that what she was about to tell me was difficult for her. For once, she did not meet my eyes, looking instead into her wine glass.

'I told you that was not my experience. It is true. I had a very retired life, was barely in society at all, and it suited me. When I was twenty-five, and everyone had given up hope on me, I fell in love. And it seemed that my beau loved me too. We were married, and it was only then that I learned how brutal he was. He was a drunkard, a gambler, a liar. There is not a single sin I cannot lay at his door. We lived in town, at one of the best addresses, but my life was one of utter misery.' She turned her hand, and regarded the Italian lavastone ring on her finger. 'I used to look at this ring,' she said, 'and try to recall what it was like to be happy.'

'I am sorry to hear it,' I said.

'Ask Jeanne,' she said. 'She was my servant there. The only one who ever tried to protect me from him. And she was knocked around the head by him more than once. She only stayed in our service because he was too drunk to remember who anyone was.

'And now,' she said, sipping her wine, 'I am free. Because Marcus set me free. Because he fought a duel.' She saw the horror dawn on my face. 'I told you we had secrets,' she said. 'I told you, you would not wish to know them.'

'How can he still be living in this country?' I said. 'Surely he would have been prosecuted for such a thing?'

She shook her head. 'My husband did not die immediately. He recovered a little from his wounds, waved off the idea of prosecuting. He agreed to separate from me, and he lingered on, but Marcus had broken him.' A smile moved, seemingly against her will, across her face. She must have seen the revulsion in my expression.

'You cannot judge, Annaleigh,' she said. 'You know nothing of the world, nothing in comparison to what I know.'

'I do not judge you,' I said.

'Marcus had gone into hiding afterwards. In time, he returned to us. When my husband died, at last, it was by his own hand. But still, disgrace followed Marcus, even after all that. So we came here. Because he no longer wanted the crowds, the balls, the beauties who had presented themselves to him once, but who no longer wished to know him. He would be happier, Annaleigh, if it had never happened. He would be different. Do you see – why he has dark moods sometimes?'

I nodded. She tried to offer me wine, but I refused, and after some time in silence, I wished her goodnight. As I passed her, she reached out and took one of my hands, and clasped it. I saw the suffering in her face, and put my other hand over hers.

'You promised that we would paint together, tomorrow, my dear,' she said. 'I found my watercolour box. I did bring it here, after all. I have been looking forward to learning more of painting from you.'

I wished her goodnight again. I walked across the dried mud on the entrance hall floor.

Only when I reached my room, and put my lit candle on the bedside table, did I finally open the letter, feeling sure that it would contain my dismissal. To my surprise, I didn't seem to care too much. When one loses a whole family, never can a loss be as large again. One is always prepared, always braced. I counted out the quarter's money first, and put it carefully in the purse in my locking box, before I sat to read what he had written. His writing, unfamiliar, made me smile; elegant, but unpredictable, with long high and low strokes to it. I could imagine him writing it, bent over his desk, a frown creasing his forehead. Knowing that I would be leaving there somehow made me feel an affection for him, as one always feels for a companion about to be left behind.

*Dear Miss Calvert, I have given you this quarter's*
*wages, for I feel sure that you will wish to leave this*
*house, though it is not my wish that you should do*
*so. I once promised you that you would be safe here,*
*and I know that, in acting upon my passions, I have*
*compromised your position. I will never act so again.*
*I must depend upon you believing me, if you decide to*
*stay. And if you decide to go, well then, for God's sake do*
*it, and without another word, so that you do not add to*
*my self-reproach. But forgive me. Forgive me. Yours, etc,*
*Marcus Twentyman.*

At the time I thought that what he could not have known was that I had nowhere to go to any more. So as I sat, and considered his words, and looked at the ring Jared had given me, and whether I could get to Leeds and claim help from his friend, I decided to stay.

Of course he knew I had nowhere to go. I had told him a thousand times – in my words, in my looks, in my need to belong. I felt I had been strong, but he had read a thousand secret signs of my weakness. And I would be punished for it.

# PART TWO

# CHAPTER FIFTEEN

'Where is he?' I said.

Sorsby rolled his eyes. 'Headed off to Halifax, I should think. You need not worry about that. The master is not a child. I've noticed how you fuss over him now, and I'll warrant he has too.'

I had a vision of Marcus riding his horse off, through this wild landscape. The hard clatter of his horse's oiled hooves on the road. There were times when, with his wild hair, and his dishevelled clothing, he seemed to me to be as defenceless as a child. And then, he would be the man; broad-shouldered, well-dressed, as though some ghostly valet had attended to him. Always that ruffled dark hair though, whether tied back or not. I toyed with the bunch of heather he had left for me on the kitchen table, a small token of apology. That day I had felt a stirring of affection for White Windows; the first sense that I might belong there.

'Last heather of the season,' said Jeanne. ''Twill be winter soon.'

'Yes,' I said, thinking Sorsby was right. I had armfuls of washing to think of and the fact that Marcus had gone was probably a blessing. There were shadows under my eyes. I had spent the day before in the wash house, sorting through the piles of dirty linen, setting aside the finer fabrics and laces belonging to Hester so I alone would wash them, and putting stitches in where they were needed. I was – to echo my constant refrain – so tired. So tired that I could not remember the last time I had not been tired.

'When will the girls arrive?' I said.

'Just as the sun begins to turn on the day,' said Sorsby. 'Around three on the clock in the hall, if I guess right. I have hired Thomas to bring them in his cart from Shawsdrop. He will drop them on the road and they can walk a little way to us. We'll hear them coming with their chattering mouths. You'll have to speak harsh to them else you'll get no work out of them.' He gave me that rare thing: a smile, which still managed to be appealing, despite the gaps in his teeth. 'I'm only playing with you, lass. We engaged Maggie Farley as the laundress and she'll keep them in line.'

I nodded, still worrying about Marcus's whereabouts. Four local girls were coming from Becket Bridge, together with a laundress. They had been promised a good dinner, and to sleep the night in the kitchen, so they could be up at daybreak to begin the washing. Hester, who had taken to her room with a sick headache, had said that none should stay past nightfall on the second day. It struck me that I had not taken the names of the girls or checked them with her, but Jeanne had ordered it all, and it was too late now. I could hardly send any rogue girls off down the road, and it wasn't as if Hester would meet them anyway. I knew the narrative of her sick headaches; knew that she had taken herself away from noise and trouble, and would stay in her room, hiding her eyes from the light. I would send Jeanne up with broth, and she would re-emerge when everything had been done.

Sorsby went to the road to collect the women; I had hoped Thomas would come to the house, but he didn't. As they arrived through the back door, their voices were loud, colourful and full of an energy which startled me. I had not realized how quiet White Windows was; how subdued, framed within its calm routines, which provided a kind of defence against the world. The girls coming through the door, their voices rising in volume as they competed with each other to tell their stories, seemed foreign, and I couldn't help my eyes rising up, wondering if Hester could hear them in her room, and was at that moment turning over in bed, agonized by one of the sudden wracking pains that she told me about so often.

The laundress – an older woman with a lean and lined face – was alone in noticing the gesture. 'Lower your voices, lasses,' she said, and I was glad to hear her voice was harmonious, the kind that could break through their chatter without splintering wood; we shook hands and made our acquaintance.

'Not a chapel, is it?' said one of the girls, who evidently resented having been told to quieten down. Her eyes took everything in: me, the furnishings of the kitchen. She scoured us with her gaze.

'Are you looking for something?' I said.

'No,' she said, though it appeared as though she wished to speak further.

'Then sit your arse down on that chair and stop running your mouth,' said the laundress, Maggie, who was watching as Jeanne poured out small beer for each woman.

I was surprised to see the girl accept this, not without rancour, but giving the impression that she would forget it in a moment. She sat down and accepted her beer, playing with the thick plait of blonde hair that fell to below her waist.

'You'll forgive Becky once she starts working,' said Maggie, with a glance at the girl. 'Look at the shoulders on her. All of my girls are strong but she is near a machine – you get through the washing, don't you?'

Becky gave a sarcastic smile and took another mouthful of beer. ''Tis a pity Tommy Digby did not stop a while,' she said. 'It would be nice to have his company a little longer than the journey from Shawsdrop.'

The other girls giggled.

'Aye,' said Maggie, 'but you'd never get the washing done if he was here. Have you gone setting your cap at him? You'd fair drown him out with that honking voice of yours.'

Thus they continued, happily, spitefully jousting with each other. Tommy, I thought – is Thomas really known as Tommy? It crossed my mind that the girl Becky either knew Thomas extremely well, or not at all, and was feigning familiarity as a way of claiming him. I had felt a stab of irritation at her use of the unfamiliar nickname.

*As if he belonged to you.* It was Melisende, talking of Kit, when I had said he should not be forced into marriage with his master's daughter. Listen to you speaking, she had said. As if he belonged to you.

I pulled myself into the present, and saw Becky watching me, somewhat slyly.

'You'll be sleeping on truckle beds in the kitchen tonight,' I said. 'I trust that is well? It's good and warm in here, with the stone. The kitchen never loses its warmth unless the fire is cold for days on end.'

They all looked at me as though I was mad. 'We know,' said one of the girls. 'We live in stone houses too.'

'Less of your lip,' said Maggie, who had finished her beer, and was holding her mug out to Jeanne for more. 'Never mind, Miss Calvert. I'll say sorry on their behalf. They'd treat any southerner the same.'

The daylight faded, and Marcus and his horse did not return. Both Sorsby and Jeanne were amused by my worry, telling me that it was customary for him to stay away for days at a time, but I slept little.

The girls were quiet enough in the night, and were up even before me the next morning, ready to begin work at an early hour, for their normal process had been compressed to include washing, folding and mangling in a day. I had assured the laundrywoman I would do the ironing myself, with Jeanne.

It was a long day, spent in clouds of steam, accompanied by a gradual numbing of the senses so that the sharp contrast between hot and cold water on the hands turned into a single irritation. We worked hard, alongside each other, Maggie marshalling her girls, correcting technique, and urging them on, so that with every breath I felt I should thank her for driving them when my strength was nearly exhausted. I worked on Hester's clothes, and gratefully did I receive Maggie's advice on removing the stains from lace and linen. She too complimented me on the small, neat stitches with which I had repaired the linens and freshened the embroidery of initials.

'Is this all the linen?' Becky said, when we had worked near seven hours. 'I recall more, last time.' These last two words she said with deliberate clarity, and I had the feeling she would have repeated them if she had not received the response she wanted. I was not quick enough to hide it from her: it must have shown in my face, my unknowing that she had been there before. I bristled with it – for I had begun to think of White Windows as somehow my territory alone – and felt the emptiness of my ignorance, the stirring of something like fear, for this girl with a voice that grated on me like steel on leather obviously wanted me to know something.

'You're not much like her,' said Becky.

'Do you speak to me?' I said, as coldly as I could.

'Aye,' she snapped, 'who else am I looking at?' One of the other girls elbowed her. 'What? I'm not her servant, and she could hardly not pay me for this day's work, washing smoke and blood and shit out of linen. Ah, yes, I know how to do it all.'

'You hold your tongue, Becky,' said Maggie, 'or I'll tell your pa what you've been saying and he'll whip you to kingdom come.'

'As if he could, these days,' said Becky, still defiant. There was something about the discordant notes of her voice, her evident, unthinking arrogance, which provoked a reaction from me. Still I continued with the washing, keeping my eyes on the linen.

'I just remarked that this Miss Calvert is not like Kate,' said Becky, too loudly, 'that is all. And Kate only wished to be known as Kate, not with any high title, as if she were above others. But perhaps I am unjust. Perhaps I only think that because Kate was my particular friend.'

'No she weren't.' Another of the girls, red-faced with steam and resentful, swiped at her. The relaxed physicality of these laundresses was something I had noticed; they were as playful and rough as puppies.

'Where is she?' The question came out of nowhere; Becky stared at me. 'Where is she? Do you know? Is she in the ground, as they say?' The other girls fell silent.

'She would have done anything he said. She would have walked off the edge of a cliff if he'd asked, rolled in a ditch, buried herself in mud. I've never known a man get women to do things for him as Marcus Twentyman does.'

Someone giggled. The others stared. I had nothing to say. I tried to summon a retort in my mind, out of the jumbled impression of words and feelings she had raised in me. Nothing came.

'Get on with your work,' said Maggie to Becky. 'Miss Calvert pays me the money and I'll dock your wages if I judge you've spent more time gossiping than working.'

That hushed them.

I had been working on the same piece of stained linen for some time when Maggie put her hand on my arm. 'Look at it in the light,' she said. 'I'll come with you. See if there's more we can do for it.'

The clouds were moving fast over the hills as we stood on the grass, holding the piece of material to the light, discussing whether it could be got completely clean.

I thought of Marcus, walking amongst the crowded, smoky streets and alleyways of Halifax. I did not understand why he had gone there.

'What Becky said,' I ventured. 'About – Kate – was that her name?'

Maggie had been observing the piece of linen. She lowered it and looked at me suspiciously. 'Aye,' she said.

'Did you know her?' I said, as she folded it and handed it back to me.

'Nowt you can do with that,' she said. Her hands were as pink as broiled ham, raw with the hours of washing and folding. She sighed at my enquiring gaze. 'Aye, I knew her. And she was a flighty thing, one for catching the eye of any man. I wouldn't be surprised if he had his way with her, it's hardly unknown. Has he with you?' She looked at me slyly, and I sensed the layers of her knowing in the relaxed curiosity of her blue-grey eyes.

'No,' I said, more vehemently than I intended to, for she laughed.

'Good for you, if it be true,' she said. 'But as for Kate – well. 'Tis hard to keep any servant in this county, for there is always wool work, which is easier than keeping yourself low, and bowing to the high and mighty. She will be in York, or Halifax, or some other place where she may live her lively wit out, and get hersel' a husband.'

'And Thomas?' I said. She looked sharply at me, and I felt myself blush, but ploughed on. 'Thomas Digby. Was he connected with Kate?'

She raised her eyebrows. 'I don't know. But he's a fine-looking young man, so if she was interested in him I wouldna be surprised. You're mighty curious, aren't you?' She put her arm around me and steered me back towards the others. 'Becky should be still and quit all her mithering. Her voice is enough to set my skin all on a crawl. It grates so that it seems to cut bits off my nerves. Let's get to work and finish off. You want us out of the house this evening, don't you?'

*

At the end of the day we fed the women cakes and ale, and Sorsby went to wait by the Shawsdrop road for Thomas's cart. They were bolting down these refreshments when Jeanne came through and said she'd seen Sorsby waving his handkerchief from the hill. Thus the girls set off, talking and laughing as loudly as if they hadn't done a day's work, Maggie herding them on like a benign shepherd. Wrapping a shawl around me, I decided to walk with them; partly, I told myself, to get some fresh air after the hard day's work. Partly because I was curious to see how Becky would behave around Thomas.

The light was beginning to fade, but we saw them a good way off, Thomas sitting on his cart, talking with Sorsby. I was used to seeing him on a lone horse, and to see him after such a length of time made me somehow nervous. As we came closer, Becky's voice increased in volume, as though she was anxious to advertise her dominance over her fellows, and her good cheer. As I looked to my left I saw another horse and rider, coming along the road at a steady pace.

Thomas looked as comfortable on the cart as he did on his horse, his long greatcoat a little dusty with wear, his cocked hat low on his head. He smiled and nodded in our direction, but did not seek me out particularly. I was disappointed and felt it like curdled milk in my stomach.

'An' here's Mr Twentyman, coming along at a fadge. That horse is good for nothing, Thomas,' said Sorsby with a grin.

'If the horse is tired it's no fault in her fitness,' said Thomas. 'Come now, ladies, up on the cart.'

'Only if you'll help me,' said Becky, but still she stayed by the road, her eyes moving now and then to the approaching horse.

'Now there'll be trouble,' said Maggie, getting behind one of the other girls and pushing her up into the cart. 'Becky, don't you go bothering Mr Twentyman with your fantastical gossip. Get up here.'

Marcus was close upon us now, only a few yards, and he slowed his horse to a walk and then a halt. The mare was panting, her flanks slick with sweat, and I saw something of annoyance about Thomas's jaw, as he looked down at his hands. Suppressing it, he tightened the reins instead, not looking at anyone.

'Good evening to you all,' said Marcus. 'Is our washing day done? I thought you would already be gone.'

'I bet you did,' said Becky. I felt, rather than saw, the other girls' horror; a little ripple moved through their ranks, and all their glee was gone as they moved closer together in that cart on the Yorkshire hillside.

Marcus looked down at Becky, then turned his gaze on the laundress. 'I hope you've been paid and well fed for your trouble,' he said. 'I'll wish you all well now. Best you get back before darkness falls.'

'Where's Kate?' said Becky, her loud voice booming in the evening air. 'Last time I saw her she could speak of nothing but you.'

'God damn it,' muttered Sorsby, under his breath.

'Do I know you?' Marcus said. I saw, for the first time, something cold in him. This was not temper; not child-ishness. Those eyes with all their molten feelings gazed coldly at her. He was so angry. I was afraid.

'Is she dead?' she said.

'Again,' he said. 'Your name?'

I thought she would say it; but her courage failed her, at last. 'I'm nowt to do with you!' she shouted, angrily.

He dismounted, took the horse's reins over its head, and advanced towards her. She was such a big and strong girl, they were almost equal in height. His eyes glittered and his fists were clenched. Such was the fury I sensed in him, I feared he might strike her. 'But apparently you are something to do with me,' he said. 'For you seem to think yourself my interrogator, so now I ask you again: who the hell are you? Some representative of the thieving, wretched whore I turned out of my house?'

It was at that moment Thomas intervened. 'She's a girl with a smart mouth, is all, Mr Twentyman,' he said. He had passed the reins to Maggie; now he jumped down and took Becky's elbow. 'Now sithee,' said Thomas, 'there's no need for you to be saying such things. Climb up here and we'll be on our way.'

'I'll not say sorry to him,' she said, in that loud, wretched voice of hers that made every phrase a shout.

'Shut your mouth,' hissed Maggie, and with one of the other girls pulling and Thomas pushing, they got her to scramble up onto the cart.

'I'll wish you a good evening,' called Thomas, for the

first time a little awkward as he climbed up, and took the reins back. Becky had wriggled past Maggie to sit next to him, and she wrapped her hands around his arm, and rested her chin on his shoulder. He did not respond. She cast a look at me as they moved off.

In the midst of my bewilderment at what had just occurred, I felt concerned and, I admit, proprietorial about Thomas. I felt hurt that he had ignored me, but at the same time I had seen that he did not seem to favour Becky, and his only thought had been to try and prevent a row. Still, as I looked at my master, and his ebbing fury, my main hope was that I could speak to Thomas in the next day or so and discuss what had happened.

'Who brought that wretch into my house?' said Marcus. I glanced at Sorsby, and saw that his eyes were fixed on the middle distance.

'I must take responsibility for it, sir,' I said. He handed the reins to Sorsby, who took them and started to lead the horse back to White Windows, across the rough path and the moors.

'Did Hester approve your choice of girls?' Marcus said, as we began the walk back.

I had to prevent myself from rolling my eyes. 'No,' I said. 'And I'm sorry if they did not meet your idea of moral characters.'

He grabbed my arm and turned me to him. 'Are you toying with me?' he said.

I caught my breath. 'No. No, sir. I am sorry if I sounded smart. I did not mean to.' I waited for him to speak about what had been said, to express anything other than his anger. To speak more of Kate, and say that what Becky had said was rubbish.

Instead, he looked down at my sleeves, rolled up; at my hands and my arms, reddened and sore from the day's work. 'Look at your beautiful skin,' he said. 'What has happened?'

The question was so incongruous, I felt I might laugh out loud; instead, tired and perplexed, I answered him. 'It is the action of the washing, Mr Twentyman. I am responsible for Miss Hester's very best things. It is the water, and the soap, and the other things that we are obliged to use.'

He let his hands run down my arms, and took my hands. A shiver ran through me. It was as though someone had walked over my grave, and yet it was pleasurable to be touched so gently.

'We will talk no more of it,' he said, and we went into the house. 'It is getting colder,' he went on. 'I will not wish to venture out when the snow comes. Make sure there is enough coal, Annaleigh, before you send Sorsby to Hebden. We must be warm, you and I.'

Later, Sorsby found me, tidying the kitchen. I did not hear him come in, and flinched when I turned to see him standing close to me, his expression blank, without any currents of the malice or amusement which usually defined his expression.

'What is it?' I said.

'I told you, Miss Calvert,' he said. 'It is best if you do not get too close to the Twentymans. I saw what he did.' He looked at my arms. He looked tired, disappointed, even a little angry. 'Do not think he is your family – do not be—' He paused, and shook his head. 'You should not grow even a little fond o' them. I am, 'cos I've known them since children. When you've seen someone as a child, well, you can never quite shake that. My life is tied up with theirs now and I've done well out of it. They have all the blood servants they need. Do not be foolish. I say it for the last time. You are a sharp thing, and I had high hopes for you. But do not be foolish.'

# CHAPTER SIXTEEN

Of course I did not believe Becky when she said that the last housekeeper was dead. But the sound of her voice found its way into my thoughts as the nights lengthened.

Thomas did not visit. No letters came from London, and I remembered what I had written; unpicked it in my mind, wondering whether I had caused offence. I thought of other letters I might write. I even considered advertising for another position, so that I might go somewhere different, perhaps in a town, where it was not so bleak and isolated. I was still often woken by the sound of footsteps, or disturbed by the sense of someone else having just passed out of sight. I still saw reminders of Kate: a fingerprint of jam on a label, a discovery of more linen, neatly folded in a press. I had packed her belongings away, in the chest with her dress. Now and then, I checked they were still there, without knowing why I did so.

As the air chilled and told of winter, I busied myself with baking, and keeping those rooms I had access to as clean as possible. And the bitter weather helped, in its own strange way. When one is cold, really cold, the physical feeling of it provides a distraction. Breaking the thin skin of ice on the pail of water in the mornings made me concentrate on the here and now.

Then it was decided that we were to have visitors.

'A gathering,' Jeanne had said, with a little whoop. 'Wine and good food and the master's friends from London. It shall be a moonlight theme, the master says, on account of being held on the full moon.'

Sorsby looked at her glumly; looked at the floor. 'You'd think it was your party, the way you're behaving,' he said. 'But it's not. And not yours either.' He looked at me. 'I can't be doing with all the fuss. Old Jack never bothered with such things. This house was made for solitude. If he wants people around him, master should go back to London.'

Marcus hired a French cook from a Leeds tavern, who arrived two days before, and spent his time haranguing Sorsby for further supplies, though he had brought a good amount of spices and secret ingredients with him. We called him Monsieur. Although he raised one black eyebrow at the sight of my kitchen, and blustered about how ill-equipped and small it was, he nevertheless complimented me on its cleanliness. He promised to teach me how to make certain dishes, though he said his range was restricted by the lack of equipment.

On the evening of the party, before the guests had arrived, I was helping Monsieur to prepare a dish of game, when on turning I saw Mr Twentyman. He had come in silently – I had no idea how long he had been there. I could only think that his soft tread was on purpose, to watch the chef and I at work, and his expression was indulgent.

'May I get something for you, Mr Twentyman?' I said.

'Do you wish to learn how to make sweets and jellies?' he said. 'Do you see yourself in some other house, some grander place?' He smiled as he said it.

'It is good for you, is it not, Monsieur?' said the chef. 'You see I am telling Miss Calvert some of my magic, so that she may sprinkle it on this rough barren country.'

'Most generous of you,' Twentyman said. 'But I have come to tell her to spend the evening away from the kitchen.'

'Sir?' I was puzzled. 'But that is impossible. It is the busiest evening since I've been here. There are the lanterns to hang, and a dozen other tasks to be seen to.'

'Jeanne and Sorsby are doing them,' he said. 'What is the matter? You have already prepared so many things over the last few days. Jeanne will assist Monsieur in the kitchen. Sorsby has brought in those two boys from Hebden – who are probably drinking in the lodge with him now – to serve at table.'

The arrangements seemed so shoddy, so without true organization, that I hesitated, still standing by the fire.

Mr Twentyman watched me for a moment, then smiled. 'Do not worry, you will not miss out on it. Go up to your room, Miss Calvert, and when you come down later it will be to direct Sorsby and that is all. There is a gift for you upstairs.' He walked towards me, touched my shoulder. 'You are so stubborn! Must I tell you again?'

'I hope madame will be able to eat a little of my cooking here in the kitchen,' said the chef. As I walked from the room I saw him glance away from his precious sauce, in the grey light of the kitchen, and catch my eye, with a glance that was suddenly serious. 'Who is this man,' he muttered to me, 'who does not respect the state of master and servant? Will you send that French woman to me? I cannot do this without some assistance.'

The gown lay on my bed. It was a pale, simple dress of white muslin, so sheer as to be almost transparent, with a wrap of shimmering grey satin. Next to it lay a domino mask, also covered in grey satin, edged with some glittering substance which looked to the world like silver, though I later thought it must have been fool's gold. It occurred to me the moment I saw it: the colour of moonlight.

It did not seem like a dress meant for me. It was a dress made for a lady, cut to cling to the body, and in a style I had seen in the fashion plates Hester looked at, when she spoke of longing for London. I searched my mind, wondering how the dressmaker had known my measurements, then I remembered how a month before Jeanne had put a string around my waist, in one of her silly games, and held the place there, for a moment, with her thumb.

There was a knock at the door, and Jeanne entered, a dumb smile on her face, something unsavoury in it, though I pushed it from my mind.

'Monsieur needs you,' I said. 'Hurry down to the kitchen.'

She seemed unbothered. 'Mistress says I'm to help you dress,' she said. Then, at the sight of the outfit, she gasped and came forwards. 'It is more beautiful than I thought,' she said. 'I hardly dare touch it.'

'Who ordered it?' I said.

She looked at me, shook her head, as though the question was irrelevant. 'One of them wrote to York,' she said, 'I don't know which. If I had to guess, I'd say Miss Hester.'

'I don't want to wear it,' I said. 'I don't know what it means that I have been given it.'

I could not fathom it. It seemed wrong. Some debt would have to be paid for this dress, I knew. Had we been in the town, I would have been able to slip out of the house, and I cursed myself for being too lazy to have placed an advertisement. In a bigger house, with other servants, I could have taken myself elsewhere, drunk a dish of tea. I could have gone to church. But there was nothing for me beyond that dark square of window. If I pressed my face to it, I would hear only the winter wind.

I turned and looked at Jeanne, toying with the edges of the dress with her hands.

'Oh madam,' she said. 'You look terrified. I told you a thousand times, you must be braver than that.'

'I do not wish to be part of the gathering,' I said.

She looked a little serious then. 'If you do not go, then Mr Twentyman will send the mistress to fetch you, and it will make her so cross to be sent to get the servant,' she said. 'You are making it worse for yourself by hiding up here, and I would fancy you would enjoy the evening. What I would give to wear a dress such as that.' She glanced behind, as though someone might come in. 'Hurry now, or if you *will* cause such a problem let me begone and tell Miss Hester, so that she may calm her brother before the guests arrive. She has already had to open the medicine chest once this day.' She looked sullenly at me. 'Why would you wish to anger him?'

I did not wish to anger him. I had seen his anger at Becky. 'Very well,' I said. She helped me undress, then supported the gown over my head and laced me into it. It lay lightly over my shoulders, ending in a deep V over my bosom. 'It is the fashion,' said Jeanne. She puffed and played with my hair, draped the cold silvery wrap over me, and finally tied the mask around me, so that at last I was hidden.

'You look a little pale again,' she said. 'Shall I fetch the rouge?'

I shook my head, remembering Thomas's words, and feeling a sting of anger that he had abandoned me.

The noise of hooves in the courtyard and raised male voices heralded the arrival of the first guests, and as

Jeanne moved away to go downstairs, I turned and took her arm, suddenly afraid.

I don't know what prompted me to say it. Perhaps it was that she seemed so calm, so unruffled by the appearance of the housekeeper in a dress made for a lady. That same, strange mirth permeated her expression, as though nothing unusual was occurring at all. 'Has this happened before, Jeanne?' I said.

The grin faded then, completely. Faded to an empty expression. I had never seen her show fear, but now I think that was it.

'No,' she said. 'He simply wants you to dress in accordance with his wishes. Get hold of your wits.'

She ran away. I heard her footsteps fade as she returned to the front hall, heard high, chattering voices.

I left my room. I walked along the corridor, went to the chest, opened it, and looked at the last servant's possessions: the comb, the dress, the candlestick. They were exactly where I had left them.

# CHAPTER SEVENTEEN

When I could postpone it no longer, I went downstairs, having untied the mask and left it on the bed. I felt ridiculous wearing it. I put on the pale slippers that had been left with the dress, wrapped my normal woollen shawl around my cold, bare shoulders, and silently tiptoed down. I hung back in the entrance hall for a moment or two; they had left the door open. I was tempted to run back to the kitchen, and tie my apron on. Despite the paper lanterns, and the smell of the mulled wine thickening the air, the sight was amusingly domestic. There were ten or so men, and two women, apart from my master and mistress, and a crescent of chairs had been made around the fire by the visitors, unused to the biting Yorkshire cold.

As I edged into the room one of the men was making

some jest, and the guests roared at it, their voices made louder, it seemed, by the stone walls.

'My dear Twentyman,' said another, 'you've brought us halfway across the world to this folly of a house – and on horseback. I feel that London belongs in another life. I hope you'll have some fine entertainment for us this evening.'

'I am hardly Beckford,' said Marcus, acidity entering his voice.

'No, quite,' said another. 'You could hardly drive a carriage up your staircase – but then your father doesn't keep you well-supplied enough, does he?'

'Yours neither, from what I've heard,' said Marcus. 'But I promise you there will be fine food, diversions, and good wine.'

'I'll raise my glass to that,' said another.

At that moment, my master turned.

'Ah,' he said, and there was a quality to his voice which made the other men look at me. One or two rose, and bowed; the others stayed in their seats, taking me in with their eyes. One of the men who bowed was Mr Plaskett.

'I see you have invited the goddess of the moon to our soirée this evening,' he said. There was something in the way he said it which both horrified me and made me want to laugh out loud, and it must have shown in my face, for when I looked at my master he was suppressing his mirth, glancing at me as though we were in on a secret joke.

'Exactly what I had in mind, my dear fellow,' he said.

Hester was away from the fire, dressed in a high-collared dress with a yellow bodice that I had altered especially for this occasion, her hair fashionably wrapped in a yellow turban-style cap. As I looked at her I could not see approbation in her face. If anything, she seemed puzzled, her eyes searching her brother's face for signs of something, as though she wished to read his expression, and could not. She gestured to the two local boys to pour the wine, for they were lingering awkwardly at the far side of the room.

It was then I found myself regarded by the two females of the group. They had turned their faces from the warmth of the fire and now I could observe them properly, I saw that they were not virtuous women, although they were dressed elaborately, and expensively. Their faces were painted exquisitely, their lips and cheeks expertly drawn and redder than the roses I had seen hawked at Covent Garden. Their eyes glittered, and they wore numerous patches on their faces. Their dresses were cut even lower than mine, so that their breasts were almost completely uncovered. The dresses were made of floaty, gauze-thin material, cut high to the waist, showing slight, agile figures. Unlike in colouring or facial features, in their expressions they could have been twins: they shared the same hard, appraising glance which showed me they had seen and known everything, and now wore it on their faces and in their hearts. The Yorkshire boys' eyes were wide; I wondered how far Sorsby had gone to recruit them, and thought that he should have gone further than Hebden Bridge. It was no wonder that people spoke ill of the house.

'A glass for me, and with thanks, m'lud!' said one of the women, snatching a glass from the salver offered to her. I wanted to tell her that my master was not a lord, but he seemed amused by her words, and it struck me that she, with all her cleverness and knowledge of the world, had chosen them with care. When the other spoke, I knew it for sure.

'By Gad, m'lud, I had to ride astride across the moors to get here – with all the jolting, my virtue is quite lost!' she said, and one of the men gave a shout of laughter.

I went then. I turned on my heel, slipped past the boy who offered me a glass of wine, and ran through into the kitchen, where Monsieur was cursing at Jeanne for being too slow. At the sight of me he stopped reprimanding her. 'Mademoiselle?' he said, then his gaze focused on something past my shoulder.

My master had followed me; he caught at my hand as I moved to go up the back stairs.

'Annaleigh,' he said. 'Where are you running to?'

'I am running to put on my working dress and my apron, sir,' I said. 'I have no place in there. I do not wish to drink, or eat, I only wish to work – that is,' I saw the anger darkening his face, 'that is, I am sensible of the honour you have done me in inviting me, but it is not my place.'

'And now the truth,' he said. Looked at me mournfully, with intimacy.

'I do not like the way your guests look at me,' I said.

He chuckled, shook his head. 'My, my, what strong principles that painter of yours instilled in you,' he said.

'It's the women, isn't it? You are right, Annaleigh, quite right, that they are not ladies. But I did not know they were coming – Tranter brought them – and I am not the kind of gentleman to turn them out on the moors on a winter's night like this one. Would you have me do that? I own, when you look at me as you do now, I would do anything you asked of me.'

My astonishment must have shown in my face; I saw him as he observed it.

'Do I surprise you so much?' he said quietly. 'Let us talk quickly, before Hester comes and wishes to be in on our confidences. Tell me, what do you want to do this evening?'

'I wish to read in my room, or, if that is not to be, to stay in here, as your housekeeper, and assist Monsieur with the preparation of the dishes,' I said.

He shook his head, it seemed regretfully. 'No,' he said. 'If you must, rest now. But come down later. And wear your mask. Has chapel made you so dull? Have the Digbys removed any hope of sophistication from your mind?'

'I do not understand, is all,' I said, bewildered. 'I do not understand what you wish of me.'

'I wish only what I just asked for,' he said. 'And just for once, I wish you not to be that silly little girl that you were in London. The past has gone, Annaleigh. You have a new life here.'

It struck me hard; I felt his words as I would have felt a physical blow.

He left the room, and I turned to look at Jeanne, who

was holding a bowl for Monsieur as he whisked a sauce. He glanced at her, and at me, then said something in French. 'He says,' said Jeanne, 'he'll be glad to leave this house.'

I did as my employer asked. I went down when the visitors' sharp, boisterous voices had softened to lazy jollity. They had eaten their dinner, and it was clear that they had drunk a good deal of wine too. I made my way quietly in, and found a dark corner. I had tied on the mask, as he had asked me to, but my heart ached at how strange it all seemed. As I came in, Hester passed me. 'Do you wish me to attend to you, Miss Twentyman?' I said, hoping she would give me a reason to leave the room.

'No,' she said. 'Stay here. You will be needed, I am sure.' A few minutes later, I saw Jeanne follow her upstairs to help her prepare for bed.

I had been noticed by Mr Twentyman. He sent a boy over with a glass of maraschino. I had seen the bottle in the cellar, many times, labelled with an unfamiliar hand. Kate's hand. I took it, and sipped. It was fiery and sweet.

The air was thick with their smoking; some of the lanterns had gone out, and I extinguished one which threatened to ignite its paper shade.

'I am sure one of these ladies has a fine singing voice,' said Mr Plaskett, drunkenly. 'Or Annaleigh? I believe I heard you sing once in London. What a lovely, slight, delicate voice you have.'

'I am not sure singing is the entertainment these

gentlemen had in mind,' said Mr Twentyman, his words drawing a laugh from one of the other men, who was caressing one of the prostitutes, gently stroking her on the neck, as she sipped her wine. I could not draw my gaze from her face; her eyes, glassy, glistening in the light, were fixed in a strong unblinking gaze. She neither swooned in ecstasy nor drew away with disgust. I had no idea what she felt, in that moment. She had gone into some darker land, known things I never had. I felt curiosity stir within me.

'I forget, Plaskett,' my master continued, 'you have never been to one of my gatherings before. I fear you may be expecting poetry and intellectual discussion, but there's little of that. We are mercilessly shallow creatures, my guests and I; we deal in pleasure, a little in dark-ness, a little in the poisons God gives us to sweeten our existences.'

Mr Plaskett gave an uneasy laugh; he was clearly out of his depth. Many times he had said he was a man of the world, and yet I had always known, even as a child, that he was not who he pretended to be. I had always been uneasy about him, in those days of unclouded judgement. And yet, I thought, I trusted him to find me this situation. I took another mouthful of liqueur.

'I am honoured to be here,' Plaskett said, with a little flourish, and a half-bow, that no one acknowledged. 'Is it my reward for sending you the sweet package over there? Is she the subject of the hunt this evening?'

Another of the women had crept over to my master.

He did not acknowledge Plaskett's words. I saw only the woman dip her head, and begin to kiss Marcus's neck, before I looked down to the floor, sickened with some emotion I could not name. It was as if, in that moment, my mind made an end of any hope I had of staying in the house. Rooted to the spot, not wishing to attract attention, I realized I would have to go as soon as possible. Thomas was right; the house was not respectable, and I would be compromised if I stayed. I tried to distract myself by imagining my guardian's studio, a world away from these dark stone and wood-panelled rooms. I had never longed for the safety of his house so much until that moment, my careful mind ticking with plans to leave as I tried to ignore the sensuality which was unfolding before me.

'Enough.' I heard my master's voice, soft but firm, and glanced back to see the woman walking away from him, flouncing a little as she did so, stepping with a certain elasticity. He had spurned her. 'We are not quite at that point in the evening, gentlemen,' he said, signalling to the man who was attending to the other woman. 'These boys who serve you drinks – this housekeeper of mine, so painfully shy in her white gown – they are virtuous people.'

Too late, I thought. Too late. Glancing at the round eyes of one of the Hebden boys, who was handing out drinks still, before he hurried out into the kitchen again, I wondered if Monsieur had finished for the evening, and was sitting drinking amidst the pots and pans. Despite myself, my mouth twitched in amusement.

'Is she a puritan miss?' said Plaskett, who was clearly

trying to break into the manly swing of things. Oh God, I thought, he is speaking of me again; why does he keep glancing at me; why does he constantly seek my eyes; why does he lick the edge of his glass in such a way as he looks for me?

'She needn't be so precious,' he continued. 'The man who raised her paints mere portraits – a practitioner of the face business. He is not a history painter and his art is carried out for business only ... yet the way in which she always worshipped him, as a child, you would have thought he was one of the gods of the Academy, touched daily by the muse. Oh, I do not complain, my dear. The capacity for worship is such a useful thing.' Again, his tongue flicked over the edge of his claret glass, and I simultaneously wanted to gag and throw it at his face.

But still he was not finished. 'As for him – and your so-called family in St Martin's Lane, *missy*.' His eyes darted over the other gentlemen as he emphasized the word, seeing whether his companions were impressed by him. One gave a slight smile, which seemed encouragement enough. 'They do well enough without you, from what I see. I saw you to a good enough situation. Where is my payment for it, that's what I want to know? And Mr Twentyman does not even have to pay tax on you, unlike his other luxuries.' These words brought a suggestion of laughter from the other men; they approved the mention of economics, it seemed.

'The knowledge of your good deed should be payment enough,' I said. 'And I am a housekeeper, not a luxury. I am the reason why your cutlery is bright and the glasses are clean. My labour has been bought and paid for by my master. As far as I can see, he owes you nothing, and neither do I.'

Mr Twentyman gave a shout of laughter. 'She says well, Plaskett,' he said. He leaned a little closer to his guest. 'And there is plenty of entertainment for you here tonight. Do not continue to trouble Miss Calvert with your looks, or with the thoughts that are contained within those looks. In short, if you touch her, Plaskett, you shall have me to answer to.'

That, at least, was a relief. Plaskett was a coward to his core, and my master's words made him bristle, but also made him afraid. He turned away from me, shadowing his eyes. 'I was just playing with the little chit. Of course she does not hold a candle to the beauties here.' He looked hopefully in their direction, but neither of the women would go near him, and not merely on the basis of his ugliness; they sensed he had no money, no charm, and that there was something unsavoury beneath it all. Instead they concentrated their attentions on Twentyman's other friends.

The group was not done with me yet. 'She is a spicy little piece underneath, I'd say,' half-shouted one of the drunken gentlemen, as though the conversation was being conducted in some foreign language which was only slowly being translated to him, thus accounting for his delay in understanding. 'But what happened to that sweet one we met before? She was uncommon ripe, that one, sweet as a berry. Kate, was that her name? Was it Kate?'

Twentyman turned angrily; I saw something ripple in his jaw. 'Do not speak of her. She was turned away for stealing.'

'She was a spinner, was she not?' said the man. 'Dextrous. What a fine arm she had; what a fine hand.'

'Take something in exchange for your ecstasy, did she?' said another. 'I'd forgive a poor girl that.'

Twentyman jumped to his feet; the other man took several steps away. 'No offence meant, Marcus. I was in jest.'

I did not wait any longer. I left as quietly as I could. I heard my master's voice as I walked away.

'Give me a few grains of what you promised me,' he said. 'Help me to think clearly again.'

# CHAPTER EIGHTEEN

I stayed in the hall for a few minutes, sitting in the cold oak chair near the fireplace, hearing the guests talk and laugh. The servants were dismissed, Sorsby and Jeanne trooping past me, out the front door to their lodge, Jeanne touching my shoulder as she passed. They both looked exhausted. I wound the clock, and wondered what my master had meant, and what he had taken, but I heard his voice no more. Eventually, thinking that I would not be needed, I went out into the kitchen, longing for the clean Yorkshire air rather than the warm fug of dinner and wine, where I found Monsieur, curled up and asleep in the warmth, on the rolled mattress he had laid out, one of his hands still tight around an empty bottle of red wine. The Hebden boys were wide awake, chattering softly to each other, shocked into silence by my appearance. Their truckle beds had been pushed into the corner of the short passageway leading to the back door.

'Hush now,' I said. 'You must be tired. Go to sleep.' Rather grudgingly, they settled down, and I gave each of them a cup of spiced milk.

They had drunk it, and were falling asleep, when one of the women came marching in, still carrying a half-drunk glass of wine in her hand and a candle in the other. 'I need a pot to piss in,' she said shortly, slamming the glass down on the table. 'The ones in there are stinking and full. Well? Where is one, you bloody wench?'

I went to the cupboard and handed her a clean pot. She squatted over it, before me, and relieved herself. The Hebden boys were wide awake now, staring at her from their vantage point by the doorway. When she had finished she rose, with a curse, and looked me in the eye.

'I should throw this over you,' she said.

I said nothing, holding her gaze, trying to control my anger.

'You stand there so proud,' she said. 'For a man such as Mr Twentyman, to show partiality to you. You should be crawling on your knees to him. You should spend your nights curled up on these cold flagstones, and not think yourself worthy of him. That dress must cost four times your annual salary – oh yes, madam! I know what things cost! And yet you walk as though it is an encumbrance to you, with some strange pretence that you do not wish to be seen.'

'I do not have to answer to you,' I said, 'and I did not choose this dress.'

'No, you were given it,' she said. 'Do you not see what a gift that is? What it means?'

My face must not have given her the answer that she craved, for she took a step closer to me, holding her candle level with our faces, as if to seek something from my expression, to measure my ingratitude.

'Play the virgin if you wish,' she said. 'If you do still have it – and that I doubt, for it's always the prudish ones you have to watch – then you won't have it for long. Will you struggle, do you think? Will your virtuous front have you pretend not to enjoy it?'

I did not think about what I did. I slapped her.

Only when my hand connected with her face, hard and smart, did I realize what I was doing; the instinct to strike out had come to me, pure and without reflection.

I thought she would hit me back, drag me by the hair, or at least throw the pot over me. Instead she stood, one hand pressed to her face, the candle in her other; she was angry, but she had control. She was no brawling whore on the streets of London, I realized. She had been selected for gentlemen, and had learned how to please them, with perfectly distilled self-control, and she exercised it now, though rage filled her eyes. She breathed through her nostrils, hard as a racehorse, as she fought it.

'If we were alone,' she said, 'I would beat your head against that hearthstone until your skull had lost its shape. But you know, don't you, that you have him as your protector? That if anything happened to you at my hands, I would suffer for it. You need not worry, though. I will remember you, bitch.'

She went back out, leaving the glass on the table, the candlelight trembling slightly as she went.

I turned and leaned on the table. It was then I caught the eyes of the Hebden boys, and Monsieur, who had woken and seen it all.

'You clouted her good and proper,' said one of the boys. 'You've got a strong right hand like me ma.'

I looked at them all, my gaze sweeping them coldly, feeling alert and alive. 'Thank you for coming to my aid,' I said sarcastically. 'The best thing for all of you to do is to keep quiet and go to sleep now. It won't be long until morning.'

If only what I said had been true. The night stretched on before me. I wanted to escape and yet beyond this house I was hemmed in by the moors and their treacherous paths. I tell you now, I was afraid. More afraid than I had been of the dark corners in the passageway of my child-hood home, or the shadows at the turn of the stairs. The darkness beyond the windows seemed so immense that I could not go past it. Even with my lantern, and Thomas's words – 'keep to the path' – I did not feel able to break out of the house.

I was, unaccountably, sad too. We had been here alone: me, Sorsby, Jeanne and the Twentymans. Every word or look Marcus had given me had been my own property. Apart from Kate, whose shade had hovered at the corners of my mind, he had never mentioned other women, other people, as if White Windows was its own discrete world, fully contained, like the sphere of rock crystal Jared would look at by candlelight. I had come to depend, just a little, on that world. That was why I had not yet advertised.

I stayed in the kitchen, feeling strangely safe near Monsieur and the Hebden boys, though I was not sure what use they would be, if pressed. There was no sign of Jeanne or Sorsby. I stayed long in the kitchen, until I felt I could not bear it any more – my mind circling over everything. I went quietly from it, opened the first door, then the next, so slowly that I would not be heard by the men and women, drinking, smoking, easing their minds with substances.

I paused as I passed the doorway of the dining room. Saw that two men were asleep. One of them, mercifully, was Plaskett; the others played cards, some kind of strange game, which they were lost in. In one corner of the room another man was lying on top of one of the women, grinding his body into her, her face lost in that same glassy look. My master observed it all – the cards, the coupling – and then me.

He rose to his feet and ran after me swiftly, knocking a glass to the floor as he did so, and it was only from the look on his face that I realized he knew I was afraid. I was walking backwards across the hall, to the front door, and let my hand rest on it as he came towards me.

'You should not have come in,' he said. 'I thought you were abed, dear Annaleigh – I would not have had you see that, he is a brute.' He stood still, no longer pursuing me. 'Men are brutes.'

I said nothing. Already I felt the cold at my back, seeping through the gap between the door and the door frame, already the coldness sticking its claws into me, and I wondered how I would get to my cloak and my clothes, how I would drag my box across the moors at this time of night without freezing to death. I looked out of the window. It had started snowing, a silent warning in the darkest hours of the night.

'I have frightened you, haven't I?' he said. 'You look as if you might flee, this moment. I cannot bear it.'

'I will not say anything, sir,' I said, thinking that he was worried about the reputation of the house. 'I am not a gossip. I will stay in Becket Bridge for as long as it takes me to get a coach. No one will hear anything of what I have seen.'

He smiled. I knew he must have taken some drugs, but his senses seemed sharper than I had ever seen them, for he looked at me with the same expression of focus, that sharpened intensity, as though I was the only person in the house, his familiarity soothing in that dim candlelight. 'It is not that I meant. Damn the world – damn what the wretched people round here say of me. I care not about that. Oh, God, you really do not understand, do you, Annaleigh? I cannot be without you. There is only one woman I want, and it is you. You are strong, and capable. You make me good again. You make me believe I might be all that I once thought I was.'

I stared at him, trying to fit his words into my experience of the world. 'Sir – I do not understand ...' I could not believe he was genuine, and yet he looked at me so.

'It is the truth. I knew it from the first moment. They spoke of Kate, who was here before you. It is true, I dallied with her, but it was nothing – nothing compared to this. To the regard I have for you. Never mind, you do not have to believe me now. But I will help you to see it, if you let me. I cannot think – my head thickens with the wine and the opium – I cannot find the words I need, not now. It is meant to help me think clearly and I did. But then I saw you, so afraid. Do not go, not yet. Stay until the daylight. Things look clearer then. I promise I will make you forget all you have seen, all you have suffered, for it is written on your face, my dearest. You are so good, so strong. I need you, you understand? I cannot survive without you.'

I could not believe what he was saying; my master looked as though he might fall onto his knees at that moment. Stay until the morning, he had said to me, just as Jared had. Things look better in the daylight. I should have stayed in London, and instead I had come here.

I walked away, into the kitchen, closed the door, and turned the key. I sat down on the kitchen chair, the snores of Monsieur comforting in the darkness, and when Emmet leapt into my lap I had never been happier to see the cat. I stroked his head, felt the delicate outline of his skull beneath my hands, felt him purr. The warmth of a living creature was what I needed in that moment of fear and indecision. It was thanks to his presence that I slept at all that night – for minutes only, here and there, until the sky was a milky grey.

Marcus never tried the door.

# CHAPTER NINETEEN

The morning light came like a punishment, its scouring white blasting my eyes open and irritating my sensibilities. The snow had not settled, and I sent up a silent prayer of thanks for it.

Most of the visitors had not made it to their beds. They rose when discomfort stirred them, yawning, dressed in their clothes from the night before. I cooked with the kitchen door locked, Monsieur watching me, the bags heavy and layered under his eyes. I kept the Hebden boys in the kitchen and let them eat first, solicitous as a mother, then, when Sorsby appeared, having tended to the horses, I made him take out coffee and muffins to the guests who were still draped over the dining room, with the instruction to pull the drapes and shutters open, to let the light in, and not mind their curses. 'You can do that, can't you?' I said.

'What's got into you, hard all of a sudden?' he said. 'Been watching and learning from those other ladies, have you?' I lifted the kettle and poured the water.

The Hebden boys left, each with a generous slice of pie and their wages. Only Monsieur stayed, drinking coffee and complaining about his head with a certain bitterness.

It was mid-morning when I decided to take a tray up to Hester, and see if I could read her face after all that had happened. I went quietly, not wanting to attract the attention of the guests that remained. As I approached her room, I heard raised voices. Hester's and Marcus's. I stood there, and listened.

'I thought this was all over,' I heard Hester say. 'What was your purpose, giving her that dress? You wanted virtue, and you have it, and you seem to wish to ruin it. If you mean to do this thing, why do you dally so? Playing with her as a cat plays with a mouse, just as you did before.'

'Is that how you see me? As cruel, by nature?' His voice was hoarse, and he sounded excitable. 'I am not toying with her – if I am hesitating, that is to my credit, surely?'

'I do not know.'

I knocked on the door. When I opened it, their faces were a picture. For Hester was wearing her nightgown, and her brother stood in his clothes from the night before, his hair loosed, his fine garments crumpled and half-ruined. The next washing day, I thought, had best be someone else's problem, and they can speak of the woman who was once here in hushed tones. Becky can carol out about that cold Miss Calvert, who has gone back to London, swinging her locking box merrily.

'Madam, sir,' I said, and put the tray down on the table near Hester's bed. Hester said my name, but Marcus put his hand up to silence her. 'Annaleigh,' he said. 'We were just speaking of last night.'

'I would prefer it if you call me Miss Calvert, sir,' I said. 'I have left the gown upstairs in the attics. It should be put away in one of the presses, properly wrapped, so it does not spoil or the moths get to it.'

He paused. 'Yes, very good.' He smiled at me, a smile of youth and openness. 'You are the best of servants. I really would not know how to replace you.'

I looked at Hester. She looked as though she might weep and I wondered at her fragility. 'Why have you put the keys on the tray?' she said. 'Do you have the headache, dear Annaleigh? Let me bring you some medicine. You should rest today.'

I ignored her. 'Thank you,' I said. 'But it is all by the bye. I will be leaving today. I give you notice of it now, so you do not think I have gone without saying goodbye, or in some covert way. I will take nothing with me that does not belong to me.'

They stared at me as though I had announced the death of the King. As though what I said was so extraordinary, they did not understand it at all.

'But – listen,' said Marcus. 'My visitors are, even now, saddling up out there. Do you hear the sound of their horses' hooves, of their voices, complaining about their sore heads?' He tried a smile, but I did not respond. 'Sorsby is seeing them onto their horses and directing them to the Shawsdrop road. By the end of today you will not know that they have been here. We will be quiet again, Annaleigh, quiet as you would wish us to be.'

'The noise does not matter to me either way,' I said. 'I wonder that you speak to me as though I am some kind of invalid, as though you are caring for me. But it has been quite the other way around, has it not?' I turned away, then felt sorry for my harshness. When I looked back I tried to put some kindness in my gaze. 'I have been a good servant to you both, I hope, and as I said last night, you can depend on my silence. But I will be gone this evening.'

I turned away from them. I did not wish to look into his eyes any more, for his gaze was having its effect on me, that current of mourning softening my resolve. 'How will you leave here?' he said. It burst from him, aggressively. 'I will not let Sorsby help you.'

'That is none of your concern,' I said. 'I will make my own way. I can fend for myself. Goodbye. I will remember you both in my prayers.'

'We will need them, without you,' he said, and I heard Hester go to him. And he said my name once, and then again, as I hurried away.

I remembered the prayer I had learned. *Let me be full*, I thought, *let me be empty*.

I packed one thing that was not mine: the comb that the girl Kate had left behind. I had tried to ignore her, but she had been there all the time. That person who had stood in my place, slept near me on the servants' floor, carried the keys from her waist as I did. I wondered that I had not seen her touch everywhere rather than just the occasional fingerprint, cleaning away the traces of her presence with my brisk, over-anxious energy. Wanting to do too much; seeing nothing, only acting. I don't know why I took the comb. I knew, somehow, that she would never come back to get it now. Perhaps I thought I could keep it with me, for her; that whatever fragment of herself she had left behind, it was safer with me than with the Twentymans. As I picked it up, I noticed that the hairs left on it were red. She, at least, had not been the girl with the golden hair Marcus had talked of in his delirium. How many other servants had there been? The thought made me shiver.

There was not much to do or to pack. I wondered how I would get to the stagecoach with my box. I had saved the quarter's wages given to me in advance by Marcus after his argument with me. Once I had reached Becket Bridge, I would write to Jared, finally with the intensity the situation deserved, and hope for a response.

At length I went down to the hall, where Sorsby looked at me. 'I've heard you're going,' he said. 'I am just walking Monsieur to the road; I've made arrangements with Thomas to pick him up and take him on.'

'I will come with you,' I said.

'Hoping to throw yourself on his mercy?' he said. 'I'm sure he will listen. He's a soft one. Come on, then.'

*

Sorsby was right. My friend did not fail me.

'I'm glad to see you,' he said, as Sorsby heaved Monsieur onto the tough little pony Thomas had brought for him. I explained that I wished to be gone; he listened, nodded. His eyes roamed my face as I spoke, reading my thoughts and feelings, and I sensed relief and concern in him. He promised to return in the late afternoon and take me to Becket Bridge. He said his mother would give me a bed for the night before I could make arrangements to travel on. 'And if you will listen, there are things I wish to say to you first,' he said. The formality in his voice was new to me; in my nervous mood, I only nodded, and put the thought aside. I dared not dwell on it, but I gave thanks for him. I could have kissed his hand with gratitude. Then he rode off with Monsieur.

On my return to White Windows I did not wish to speak to Jeanne or Sorsby, or to hazard coming across my master and mistress. Instead I stayed in my room, waiting as the time passed, occasionally going down to the entrance hall to check the time on the clock. I was sitting in my room when I heard doors slamming and the sound of raised voices. Still I stayed where I was.

When a knock came at my door I rose, thinking it must be Jeanne or Sorsby come to say goodbye. When the door opened, it was Jeanne, but her expression was fearful and urgent. 'We need you,' she said. 'Mistress is insensible. Please help me. I know you must go soon, but we need you one last time.'

I went reluctantly. Hester was in the dining room. It

had not been cleaned properly since the night before; a goblet was left on its side near the fireplace, the dregs of wine staining the stone. She was sitting on the floor, still and silent, and not responding to Jeanne's admonishments. There was no sign of Marcus; my every sense was heightened, listening for him. We tried to rouse her, Sorsby watching appraisingly as we did so.

'She speaks no sense,' said Jeanne, taking Hester's shoulders, but Hester wrenched herself violently away. I got on one side of her, Jeanne on the other, and we each took an arm firmly and raised her to her feet.

'Needs a good shaking,' murmured Sorsby to me, but I glared at him. Hester pulled away from us and walked up and down, and when she looked at me I saw a deep distress break through her self-control, the tears filling her eyes. 'I thought you might save him,' she said. 'But you have not.' It was terrible to see her so broken. When she raised a hand to wipe her tears, I saw that she was shaking.

'Be still, madam,' I said. Jeanne was pouring a glass of wine. She handed it to Hester but Hester dashed it out of her hands in a movement so quick I hardly saw it. It smashed against the wall. 'Holy hell,' said Sorsby. 'Waste of a good wine is that, Miss Hester. Waste of a good wine.' He raised his voice to her, spoke slowly, as though to a child, and I was reminded that he had known her her whole life. I wondered if he had spoken to her so when she had had a tantrum in the nursery. Or had he just known her from when she came to visit her Uncle Jack?

'What shall I do?' she said, turning this way and that,

and I could see that she was in the grip of her emotions, working her mind into ever tighter circles.

'Sit down,' I said. 'We cannot help you, madam, if you will not tell us what ails you.'

She would not sit down, but her breathing steadied a little, and she found some words. 'My brother has gone out onto the moors,' she said. Sorsby tutted; we all looked at each other: to the Cross Keys.

'He'll be back when he's had a few bottles of claret,' said Sorsby, 'whether it's tonight or in the morning. No need to make such a fuss.'

'You don't understand,' Hester said. 'He told me he was quite lost, now that Annaleigh is going. He said he would destroy himself.'

A silence. 'He has never said such a thing before,' said Jeanne.

'He's a little wild sometimes, is all,' said Sorsby.

'He was completely in earnest,' said Hester, taking Jeanne's hands. 'You know what he is like when he speaks so? As he did that night on Park Street. He meant it. He meant he would kill himself, if he has not already done so.'

I looked at Sorsby, feeling ill with apprehension; looked for signs of disbelief, or cynicism. His lips were pursed, as though he might whistle, but he was pale too, his skin faintly yellowish. Jeanne wore that empty look. I saw that they were both afraid. I saw that they believed her. Sorsby turned to me. 'Thomas will be waiting for you. Best go now, we'll see to this, it's nowt to do with you any more. I mean it. She shouldn't have come and got you.'

'Thomas will wait a little longer. What does she mean by Park Street?' I murmured to Jeanne.

'The night of the duel,' she said.

'If he is dead then I will die too,' said Hester. She was not crying now; her voice was low, taut and credible.

We heard the shift of the front door then. I went out into the hall, and as the door opened, I thought it was Marcus. Thought I saw the shape of him, his hair loose down his back, his boots dark with mud.

'Miss Calvert?' It was Thomas. He took his hat off. 'I waited a little while at the road, but it is raining now.' He lowered his voice. 'I tried at the back door, but it was locked. Are you ready to go now?'

'Who is that?' Hester's voice, wretched, like a child who does not wish to come out and be seen.

'It is Mr Digby,' I called, then came towards Thomas. 'I must ask your help on her behalf,' I said. 'One last time, if you will. Mr Twentyman has gone out onto the moors and he must be found.'

'It is his custom,' said Thomas, tightly, and I saw his eyes dip to his hands on his hat. I had seen him do it before, when he was suppressing annoyance.

'It is different, this time,' I said. 'He said despairing, violent things, and talked of harming himself. You know there are places he can destroy himself. What if, when distracted, he stumbles into a bog?'

There was impatience in Thomas's eyes. 'He is a child seeking attention. He will find his way home soon enough.'

'Thomas speaks the truth,' said Sorsby, who had joined us. 'Whatever is to happen, 'tis best you go now, Miss Calvert. I'll bring your locking box down.'

I thought of Hester, and all that she had told me of her marriage. I remembered the suffering I had seen in her eyes, and how she had clung to my hands when she had told me of Marcus, and what he had done for her. 'I cannot leave now,' I said. 'Not with her in such a state, and blaming me. I will see this fixed before I go.'

There was the noise of Hester weeping. Half-wail, half-cry. Thomas's eyes flicked up, and I saw the pain there. A soft one, Sorsby had said. Cannot bear suffering. A libertine, Hester had said.

'It will kill her if he dies,' I said. 'Please, will you just look for him. Then I will leave, I promise you.'

He sighed. I saw his reluctance, saw how I was pushing my fellowship with him to the edge of his patience. 'Very well, as you ask me to go. But I do so only for your sake,' he said. I nodded, and, by way of thanks, stood on my tiptoes and kissed him on the cheek. It had such an effect on him; it changed him, as the sunlight changed the moors. He brushed my face with his hand. 'If you only knew what you do with such a gesture,' he said. Thus I sent my only friend out into the wilderness.

The rain poured for hours. Night had fallen when we heard the wrenching sound of the front door being forcibly opened.

When we came out the master was sitting on the

flagstones before the low fire. I could see his fine clothes were soaked through with the rain, his dark hair wet. Hester ran to him, telling Sorsby to heat some water. Thomas stood just inside the door, his gloves in one hand, a lantern in the other; he too was dishevelled and soaked through. He smiled at me, and I just managed to return his smile. I saw how it gladdened him.

The master was weeping. He groaned and sobbed into his hands, and each time he fell silent he seemed to be taken with it again.

'Annaleigh,' said Hester, her voice quiet. There was still the shock in her voice, but it was tempered by something.

'What is it?' I said. 'All is well, now. I will go.'

'No.'

Marcus looked up then. He held his hands out to me, from his seat on the floor, and when I looked into his eyes I felt sorrow fill me, sorrow as intoxicating as the dark liqueur we had drunk at the party, black with the berries of past seasons.

'I live only for you,' he said. 'Please.' The tears were running down his face.

I sat down on one of the chairs near him, and touched his head. He came to me, on his knees, put his head on my lap, and wept more. I felt the weight of his sobs, and let my hand rest on his head. I had felt worried for him. I felt a little sick, a little shaky, like the day when he had gone to Halifax, and I had been worried he had fallen from his horse. I was so tired. I did not wish him to be harmed; I wished him well. And in that tired, heartsick moment, it passed, perhaps, for affection.

He clung to me. 'My beloved,' he said, his voice soft and low.

I had not thought tenderness was a dangerous thing. When I looked up, at Thomas's face, softly lit by the flickering flame of the lantern he still held, I saw then that something had changed. There was something there – a terrible thing, no normal disappointment, an assumption of so many things. It had stuck him, that thing, like the feeling of a knife. I wanted to say: my dear friend. I wanted to explain to him. His gaze was cold on me, and it froze me; I stayed where I was, my hand still on Marcus's head, as it lay in my lap. I did not move. There were so many things I wanted to say, but I did not speak.

Eventually Thomas pulled his gaze from my face. He bowed to Hester. 'I will wish you all a good night.' He turned abruptly, opened the door onto the night, and slammed it behind him.

'Jeanne,' called Hester, 'do not let him go. We should give him some ale – or he can stay the night if he wishes. Do not let him ride out into that storm.'

Jeanne ran out of the front door. My master had stopped crying, though he still lay in my lap. 'Will you rise, sir?' I said, looking past him, hoping that at any moment the door would reopen and Thomas return. 'Sorsby is heating the water. You must change your clothes. You will be ill if you do not.'

'Yes.' He looked up at me, wiping the tears from his

face. 'Yes, I will do anything if you ask it.' He got up off the floor, and Hester went to him. 'Do not fuss, dear. I will be well, now that I am home, and I have my dear little warrior with me. Tell Sorsby to bring up the basin when it is ready. Goodnight.' He turned and touched my face, and I, kept still by the same dazed disbelieving, did not move. 'Goodnight, dear Annaleigh. I am glad you have decided to stay. By staying, you have saved my life.' Hester followed him.

I went into the kitchen. Sorsby shook his head as I entered. 'I told you to go,' he said. 'Once you'd spoken to her, I told you to go. And now – this. You may as well have opened your legs for him.'

'How dare you speak to me in such a way?' I said, my voice low, so frail that it hardly counted as a reprimand.

'How dare I? Because you're a damned fool. I knew it would end badly, bringing a chit of a girl into this house again – and no need to raise your voice to me, madam. You're nowt but a child in understanding. These are not people to be meddled with. Ask in the dark corners of your precious London if you don't believe me. God damn you, you foolish wench.' As he leaned against the table his frame was tense with potential violence.

The back door opened and shut, and I hoped to hear two sets of footsteps, for I was longing to speak to Thomas, and to explain to him that I did not love Marcus. But it was only Jeanne, wet through from the rain, and cursing as she brushed back her sodden hair, the remains of the powder in it running down her face in grey streaks.

'Where is Thomas?' I said.

'Gone out onto the moor,' she said. 'He said he would not stay. Not if you paid him a hundred pounds.'

'Where is Thomas? Where is Thomas?' mocked Sorsby. 'If he ends up in a ditch riding hard because he can't feel his heart beating in his chest any more, then we'll have his father here too, wanting to beat my brains out, no doubt.'

'But . . .' I said, 'why?'

'Because you've broken his heart, you wretched little slut. Can you not see what is plain before your face?'

'Not true,' said Jeanne, her low, soothing voice breaking through his rage. 'Not true, not true. Do not listen to him, Miss Calvert. Sorsby is just sore again, as he always is. Thomas might have a little pique at the moment but he'll be over it tomorrow. We must all sleep, and all will be well. And in the morning I'll have Sorsby apologize to you – won't you, Christopher? You'll apologize to her for all the terrible unchristian things you have said this night.' She heard a chime, and groaned. 'It's near one on the clock. For God's sake, let us go to bed, and say our prayers.'

'Yes,' I said, my mind still echoing with all the things Sorsby had said. 'Yes, let us all go to bed, please.'

I went out into the hallway, but something made me stop and listen.

'He'll fuck her halfway to kingdom come, and when he wants rid of her I'm the one that'll have to dispose of her. I thought she had more to her than that.'

Jeanne's voice, urgent, low. 'She does. She's cleverer

than the last one. It won't be like last time. Have faith, Christopher.'

'You stupid bloody bitch, you've encouraged it, haven't you? Will we ever have some peace here? They should have sent us some old hag with a face like a cracked windowpane, and then at least I would have some rest.'

I walked up the staircase slowly. I had come down it only hours before, thinking I was walking into a new life. A door opened down the passage, and Marcus came out. We met at the top of the stairs. The very look on his face showed his confidence in my affection. It was too much, suddenly, to see that openness. I shrank away from it; for it seemed that his turning from despair to comfort had been too sudden. So sudden, that I doubted his despair had been real. It was true, I had been fascinated by him, but our drawing together had been too violent and quick, too contrary to all the rules I had grown up by.

He came towards me; I stepped away. 'What would you think,' I said, 'if I said to you, sir, that this last night has carried us too far. That, in the daylight, we should look at it clearly, without fancy, and take it no further.'

He did not stop moving as I spoke. He stopped a few steps away from me, his face serious again.

'I would say that it would be unfair to have led me thus far,' he said. 'I would say that you have already declared yourself, and that my sister, and everyone in the room this night, knows it.' He lowered his face and brushed his lips against the side of my neck. A shiver ran through me, whether of fear or desire, I could hardly tell. Even now, I do not know, truly, what I felt, other than a tempest, other than a great swirling conflict.

'I am unwell,' I said, and I went past him, up to my room.

Once inside, I locked the door.

# CHAPTER TWENTY

I didn't light the fires the next morning. Shivering, I rose in the cool light, and saw my new dress and silver wrap, laid carefully across the chair in the corner of the room, a reproachful reminder of the past few days. Then I climbed back into bed and went back to sleep.

I was shocked awake by a sharp knock on the door. It was Hester's voice that called for me, brisk and no-nonsense. I got up, and unlocked the door, then stumbled back to my bed lethargically.

'Marcus said you might be unwell,' she said. 'He has sent me to tend to you.' She said it as though it was not unusual at all.

'I do have the headache,' I said. It felt as though I had only just fallen asleep.

She carried a dish of weak tea, and some bread, which

I recognized that I had baked, for it was half-stale. She had dolloped blackberry jam onto it. I thought of the jar, labelled in an unfamiliar hand.

'Did Kate make that?' I asked. She frowned, stood up, put the tray down on my bedside table. From her pocket, she took a small silver box, and opened it. 'Have two of these,' she said, handing me two small grey pills. 'The ordinary dose will not help you, by the look of you. They help me to feel better, when I have one of my sick headaches. You do not have to work today. Jeanne will do everything.'

I took them. She left me, and after her footsteps had faded I locked the door again. I sipped the tea, and ate the bread, then took the tray down to the kitchen, seeing no one.

I dressed in my working clothes, went out of the house, and onto the moors, not knowing why, or what I hoped for. Then I realized I wanted to see Thomas. I wanted to speak to my friend, watch him galloping towards me, his hands floating, light as air, his coat its many patches of dark and dust, his face as kind and wise as ever.

He was not there.

There was no sunshine, either. Only an anaemic grey light, the shades of brown and dull green and purple deadening my gaze. I thought I would walk to Becket Bridge, then I did not seem to know the path at all. One moment, all was familiar; the next it was strange, the alien land I had first come to so many weeks ago. But something seemed to come off the land; the air had a strange shimmer to it, a sickly look of expectancy. The headache had indeed gone, and I felt as though somehow my gaze was readjusting itself, my sight refocusing. Everything seemed sharper and more vivid. I marshalled arguments in my mind; I developed a great confidence that I would be able to handle the days to come. I did not return to White Windows until night had fallen.

That evening, I slumped. The sudden, vivid focus I had achieved died in me, snuffed out. I lay, curled like Emmet the cat, in my bed. Hester came for me, her soft knock-knock-knock rousing me from sleep, continuing until I opened the door, and I noticed that the knuckle of her index finger was red. 'How long have you been knocking?' I said. She did not answer.

'I would like to leave,' I said, 'that is my intention.'

She tilted her head, looked down at me. Then she put her candle on the bedside table, and sat on the end of my bed. She reached over, and pushed the hair out of my eyes, pushed it higher up my forehead, with a natural, motherly sweep.

'Really?' she said. 'You could have left today. Why did you not?'

I buried my head in the pillow. I could not leave without Thomas, I thought. I was to have met him at the road. I needed his help. And yet – I could have walked across the moors, to Becket Bridge. Even if I did not take my box, even if I only had my wages in my pocket, the ring that Jared gave me, and my coral beads. The thought of Jared drew a sob from me. I felt Hester's hand on my head, her touch light and soothing. Then her hand moved a little, and her fingers raked through my hair, until her hand lay close to my scalp, as my hand would move over Emmet's head and feel, beneath, that small skull, so seemingly fragile.

Why did I not leave? I thought.

Something had taken hold of me on the moors, in the shimmering light, each hour passing as though it was a minute. I had been there, and yet not; in my body, and yet free of it, dancing like a spirit over the landscape. I had walked on the hollow peat path, and I had seen the white roots that were men's fingers. I lay on my back in the heather and looked at the sky. I saw the clouds pass. I could differentiate every shade of colour. I could love, at last, God's creation, without fear. I was not afraid, I saw clearly at last. In this ecstasy I had spent my hours on the moors. Fascinated by the changing sky, and the sigh of the breeze through the grasses, unheeding of the damp ground. How did I tell her that?

'I will leave tomorrow,' I mumbled.

There was a silence, but she did not stir.

'Suppose,' she said, 'you do not go. Suppose, I take you downstairs now, and you curl up on the couch in the library, just as you are now, but in the warm? There is a good fire.'

I looked up at her. 'Oh Annaleigh,' she said. 'But you do look tired, my dear. Those beautiful eyes are edged with heather-purple – do you remember, just like you told me? Heather-purple; fox-russet? All those pretty colours in your mind.'

'I do not wish to be your servant any more,' I said.

'That is good, because we do not wish that either,' she said. 'You are released from it. Only stay here a little while, and see if it does not suit you.'

'What?' I said. My voice was as fractious as a tired child's; I did not fully recognize myself. That, I thought, is what exhaustion does. I found a little of my old spirit. 'I will not be your brother's mistress,' I said.

I thought she would be shocked, or at least pretend to be, but she did not. 'No one has asked you to,' she said. 'But come down to the fire, and be warm. How will I face your guardian – Jared, you said his name was? – how will I face him, if you return to him so pale and ill?'

She gave me more medicine that night, this time a red-tinged liquid in a glass, and I slept. 'Tomorrow, I will leave,' I thought, as I closed my eyes.

Overnight, the snow fell, and it kept on falling. Silently it coated the roof and sills of White Windows. Cloaked the hills and the moors, painting out all colour, so that you could hardly tell the land from the sky. It was the sky's turn to be granite: harsh, the snow clouds moving like a cloud of city smoke. I watched from a chair in the hallway, that never-ending snowfall. White on white, and cold on cold.

'He'll never come back,' said Jeanne, stirring the fire as she tended to it. 'Thomas Digby, if that's what you're thinking. We're your family, Miss Calvert. Don't know why you want to leave us. Won't you come into the library, and let Mr Twentyman read to you? You're not well.'

As the days passed, more snow fell, and I stayed still in that house, bound by something I could not name. The dress stayed on its chair. I thought of putting it away, delicately, like the good housekeeper I had been, but instead I only looked at it, watching it crease as it had fallen, wondering how long it would take for a layer of dust to gather over it.

Hester tended to my illness with her medicines. Some days I felt better, and refused them, and she accepted it with equanimity. But there were other days when I was shaken with spasms, and she would watch, dispassionately, until my distress drove her to care for me, whether naturally or through force of will, I could not tell.

As the days passed, it was as though something vital had been separated out of my character, as cooks separate an egg yolk from the white in their careful hands. All division between me and my mistress had melted; all firmness and resolution in my character lay at rest. When a brief thaw came, and the moorland paths were clear again, I did not go. I tolerated Marcus in the room, and spent my evenings in the library, dozing, near him. The medicine made me feel well and calm; but also outside myself, and unaffected by the trials of normal emotion. In the moments I woke from that feeling, and became me again, I was cursed by pain in my head and tremors so harsh that I all but begged Hester to give me more medicine.

But one thing did not change: I would not have him. Waking one evening as I lay sleeping by the fire, I felt his hand slide up my leg and rest on my inner thigh, and I thrashed violently like an animal, smashing a glass on the floor in the process. I had to be soothed by Hester, who had been in the next room, and who came in with the expression of one expecting to see something terrible.

'Forgive me,' he said. 'Dearest Annaleigh, dearest one.'

'That is for my husband,' I said. 'That is not for you.'

'Very well, my sweet,' he said. 'If that is what you want.'

He came to me the next morning, into my room, which I now left unlocked, knowing that any attempt to keep the Twentymans away was ineffectual. He gave me a glass of wine to drink, telling me it would help me wake up and restore my wits. Hester stood behind him, worrying at her dress with her hands. Groggily, I looked at her. 'I can put a stitch in your dress,' I said.

'Never mind, Annaleigh,' said Marcus soothingly. 'We do not need you to serve us, my dear. You are not our servant any more. We are getting married today, my love. Do you remember?' He took my face in his hands. His smile was wide, and broad.

'You are not smiling,' I said, trying to rub the mist out of my eyes. I could still see the sadness there. See it even when he smiled.

'Hester will bring you some medicine,' he said. 'Now you must dress.' He opened my locking box, and rifled through my belongings. I heard myself whimpering, murmuring reproaches. At length he pulled out my Sunday gown. Not the one he had ordered from York, which lay on the chair. The one he had seen me wear so many Sundays ago.

'Let me be full,' I said, quoting the minister. 'Let me be empty.'

'Stop talking nonsense,' Marcus said. 'Put this on.' He had recovered the note of command in his voice. Hester dressed my hair with the help of the grinning Jeanne. Sorsby had been banished to the kitchen, muttering curses; his temper had worsened over the weeks. They tied my straw bonnet on my head. Then we went outside. The dress, once my favourite, seemed tawdry to me now, fluttering in the cold Yorkshire air, the slippers ruined on our walk up the hill. I had no shawl or pattens, and complained. Marcus took off his coat, and draped it around my shoulders.

'Where are we going?' I said to him. Hester followed us at a distance, struggling to keep up.

'To Shawsdrop, my love,' he said, the grin on his face and the tone of his voice at odds with the loving words he spoke to me. 'We are to be married, as I promised you.'

'Will the Robinsons be there?'

'Who?' He yanked my arm as I tripped on the uneven path.

'Your friends the Robinsons?'

'Oh no, my love.'

I looked back. Hester had stopped walking, and was

watching us. After a few moments, she turned back, and began to stumble off in the direction of White Windows.

'It is too far,' I said.

The walk to Shawsdrop took a long time, and I fell more than once on the journey, lifted up by Marcus, brushed off, and shaken like a doll who was not right for his game. Eventually we came to a tiny hamlet, and I saw a church. It was the one I had looked for long ago, with a tall Norman tower, its crammed churchyard tiled with so many gravestones that there was barely a blade of grass between them.

Marcus led me up a cobbled alleyway and opened the door. It did not feel like a sacred space, with damp creeping up its walls, and the air foul and noxious with the smell of damp and sewage. A bird had somehow got into the church, and I heard the flap and flutter of its wings high above us, the sound of desperation. The breezes moved eerily through the organ pipes.

My brain was foggy as I made the promises. There was no ring. The clergyman, his stock tied crookedly, watched, and had to be prompted to speak. I smelled the liquor on him and I wondered who he was. When he declared us man and wife, Marcus held my face in his hands again, and looked into my eyes. I thought he might kiss me, but instead he said: 'Remember, I have done what you asked.'

'We must sign something,' I said. 'We must.' So they found a page, and they dipped the pen and put it in my hand, and I was content.

*

Marcus did not wait to eat the wedding breakfast. I could think only of my tiredness, after the walk over the moors. Hester had been watching from an upper window, so when we opened the door, Jeanne and Sorsby stood waiting in the hall, in a parody of a servants' line at a grand house. The Annaleigh I had once been would have stood with them, and all of a sudden I envied her: so neat, so controlled, the keys at her waist. How had I come from that, to this?

'Where are my keys, Mr Twentyman?' I said. Marcus did not reply. He had hold of my hand, and pulled me past them, and up the stairs. He yanked me into his room, shut the door, and locked it. I stood, dazed, as he pulled his shirt out of his breeches, and undid it. I could not even muster the energy to pull my gloves off. I wanted Hester to make me one of the special warming drinks as she normally did at this time of day. Fear was far off, like a distant person calling out across the moor: the suggestion of a noise, nothing more.

The shutters of his room were open, and I could see the moors beyond.

'Not in the light,' I said, as he undid my bonnet and then began to work at my clothes, but the clothes were beyond him, so he tore my Sunday dress, and I watched him as he did it.

He lifted me on to the bed with a little jump, and laughed. I laughed too, but it was as though I was only echoing him, and it grew into hysteria. I could not make a decision for myself. I had enough resolution, still, within me, to feel apprehension at the sight of his naked body.

He pulled me to him, urgently and roughly, but I had the feeling he did not see me. 'Be convenient,' he murmured, and his breath was stale, the acidic smell of hunger, for no one baked for him now, and he had not eaten a thing.

He found the place with fumbling hands, and thrust into me, and the cry of pain I gave seemed to please him. He did not stay his movements, but held me in my place as I scrabbled to move away.

I had wondered, in the past, if I would ever know a man in this way. After the first moment of pain, I felt nothing – nothing delicious, nothing painful, only his frantic movements, with the sound of his breathing as it caught on the arc of each thrust. I watched, outside myself, looking down upon my own empty face. I saw the rhythmic rise and fall of his body over mine. I felt nothing.

And then I saw, over his shoulder, in the corner, a figure.

It was me. Me as I had been. Neat, and young, and untarnished, in my best dress, and my clean apron, and in my hands the keys. She watched mournfully, an observer. Plain as day in the white light from the window. But I saw also that she had much in her: passion, and delight, and courage. I saw, all at once, that Annaleigh was different to the dead thing on the bed. That Annaleigh might have longed for a man's touch, though she was scarcely able to admit it to herself. The clasp of Thomas's hand over hers might have sent a thousand delicate sensations through her; made clear, suddenly, the insubstantial veil of gauze that lay between earth and heaven. But now. Whatever fire was in me had been quenched. I closed my eyes for a moment, and when I opened them, she was gone.

My husband finished, with a cry: of rage, or ecstasy, or pretence, I could not tell.

He put his hand down and raised it; showed me the blood on his fingertips. 'God bless you,' he said. And he smiled a wide, carefree smile that I had never seen before.

'All sadness gone,' I said. I wondered if Kate had seen that smile.

'Will you eat the wedding breakfast?' he said. 'Jeanne will have made something, even if it is foul. If I help you dress?'

'No,' I said. 'Let me sleep.'

He shrugged, standing, a little unsteadily, and putting on his clothes. 'Sleep, then.' As I heard his footsteps fade, I uncurled myself a little. Looked over my shoulder at the empty room.

After a little while Jeanne brought me a drink mixed by Hester. I knocked it back. 'What was it like?' she said to me.

'Go away,' I said. Then I turned on my side, and heard her creep out.

I slept fitfully in that strange bed, drenched in the musky scent of him. I heard voices, and it seemed Sorsby, Jeanne, Marcus and Hester talked as they ate and drank, as though nothing had happened. In the early hours, the hours of densest darkness, he came into the room, and lay down beside me. I could smell the drink on him. When his hand rested on my hip I recoiled.

'I will not force you,' he said. I was glad not to feel his touch again.

When I woke in the morning, he lay alongside me, fully dressed, not even his boots cast off, his mouth gaping in a snore that made me want to put the pillow over his head, and keep it there. I looked at him dispassionately. My husband.

The thaw was only a brief respite from deep winter, for we had descended into the longest month of January. Even before the wedding, Sorsby and Jeanne had left their little lodge and come into the main house for warmth, in case fuel should run short. 'You never know how long it might last,' said Sorsby. He no longer looked at me, but always directed his words to whoever else was in the room. I had the sense I had failed him somehow, and that his disappointment had curdled into malice. But this, like everything else, did not concern me.

The sickness came only a few days after that first night. It coincided with another heavy fall of snow, so that when I ran from the chamber I now shared with Marcus, and out into the white landscape, I fell deep into a drift, and vomited there.

He and Sorsby lifted me from it, and carried my trembling body into the kitchen.

'You must not go out into the cold,' said Marcus,

stroking my face as they put me in a chair before the fire. He smiled, and shook his head with disbelief as he looked at Sorsby. 'I had not thought,' he said. 'So soon.'

He questioned me each day as to whether my monthly had come, and when I said no, and buried my head in the pillow to sleep, he would smile with delight, and send Jeanne up with a bowlful of one of her dreadful soups, grey, with yellow globules of fat floating in it. I was desperately hungry, despite the nausea, so I made myself eat it, but when I asked her to bake muffins for me, she shook her head. 'Can't do them as well as you,' she said, 'you'll have to come down.'

So after that I spent each afternoon in the muggy warmth of the kitchen, sitting in my chair, supervising Jeanne. I saw little of Hester; though I knew she was active in the house, for Jeanne was given a list of things to make for dinner, and our supplies were being marshalled and rationed. Also, she clearly unlocked the medicine box, for Marcus brought me my special drinks, and maybe a pill or two, when I felt very unwell. I welcomed them; they helped me sleep, and sleep was what I wanted. A beautiful, unknowing sleep.

Once, I went to the window of the library, at the sound of a horse's hooves, and I saw Thomas, searching the house with his eyes as he turned Quicksilver on the spot. I raised my fist to bang on the glass, but before I could do it I was pulled away from the window by Jeanne. It was the first time she had ever been rough with me. Marcus went out, and spoke to him, and I heard him go. I cried then, for the first time in a long time. Cried until Jeanne tired of me, and left me alone.

'We are to celebrate,' Marcus said. He had shaken me awake, and I could have struck at him for it. He got me out of bed, and helped me to dress, then led me down the stairs to the library.

Hester stood before me. She had changed into her yellow dress, at her brother's command, it seemed. But how she looked at me. I was the creature she had created, and yet she looked frightened of me.

'Greet her, then,' my husband said.

I went to her obediently. I kissed her pale, dry cheek.

'Call her sister,' said Marcus.

'Sister,' I said, but it sounded strange to my ears. Hester's expression broke a little. It was beyond her control, as though she had come too close to soured milk. A gut-deep, instinctive tremor of disgust made her move away from me.

'Sit together,' said Marcus. 'I will go and speak with Sorsby, and ask him to pour us all a good drink, and bring in some little sweets.'

Hester and I looked at each other. Even in my sleepy state, I saw that her appearance had reverted to untidiness, even dirtiness. She looked even worse than she had on the first day I had come here. Now, I did not care.

'We won't run out, will we?' I said. 'If more bad weather comes. We won't run out of medicine?'

An expression I had never seen on her face before. Pity.

'No, Annaleigh,' she said. 'We won't. Marcus has said I am not to use any of the medicine even if I have one of my worst headaches. It is all for you now.'

I felt sorry that she would have to deal with her pain without the relief of medicine. My scrambled mind could not produce the words. Instead, I reached out, and put my cool hand on her forehead. She looked so sad, when I had meant to comfort her. I looked down at the gown I had put on. It was creased and stained. I could not remember being dressed in it. I put my hand to my neck, where my coral beads had always hung, but they were not there.

'I cannot remember,' I said. 'Why am I like this?' It was a rare moment of clarity. These moments were becoming less frequent, and when they came it was frightening, like standing on the top of some precipice, about to jump off, staring into the landscape of Yorkshire, the green divided pastures. All those shapes made by grey walls: diamonds, squares, rectangles, rolling before my eyes, far below.

'You have not been well,' she said. She moved closer to me, looking around fearfully. 'I am sorry,' she said, and her voice was almost a whisper. 'I am sorry if we have kept you here against your will.'

I stared at her; somewhere in me the old Annaleigh was fighting to get out. The anger of her, the innocence. Tears gathered in my eyes.

She spoke again. 'We have come too far to renege now. You have been very strong, Annaleigh. Please,' her voice shivered, trembled like the wind through the reeds, 'please stop fighting him now. Do not waste your energy.

Once the child is born, you can be free. I promise you.' She touched my face. 'Do not hate me, Annaleigh.'

I blinked, let the tears fall.

Then she regarded me long, taking in, I am sure, my own untidiness, my unhealthy pallor, the tightly drawn back wiry greasiness of my hair. 'I did not think it would go this far,' she said.

Marcus returned, carrying a tray of glasses filled with a pale wine. 'Let us drink,' he said, raising his own, without handing either of us one. 'A son, for Gracegrave.'

I looked at them both; him drinking his back, her swallowing each mouthful painfully, as though there was an obstruction in her throat.

'What is Gracegrave?' I said.

They glanced at each other. 'Have your drink, my love,' he said. 'Then I will take you back to bed.'

# CHAPTER TWENTY-ONE

As the snow melted, and winter moved on into spring, looking at the clear bright moors intensified my sense of isolation. I was not allowed out, but the snow was not the reason, and the pretence of it was no longer made. It was simply that I was not trusted to leave the house. It was thought that I might miss my step on the moorland paths, and lose the baby. Marcus explained this, couching it in many soothing words, but I heard underneath the level, unwavering tone of command, no matter how softly he spoke. He would never be convinced of anything, other than what he had thought of. The energy with which he spoke, once so attractive to me, became something I hated. It was inexhaustible, whilst mine was finite. So I learned that silence was my friend. If I argued with him he would only repeat himself again, and again, and was sometimes still speaking in that low, irritating murmur, when I finished my drink and went to sleep.

I missed Thomas, and that missing did not cease, but remained the still, molten core of my memory, even though I had given up hope of ever seeing him again. Only now he had gone did I realize how much I wanted him with me. I thought over our past encounters, and they seemed more vivid than they had been when I had lived them. Re-seeing them in my mind, at a distance, I examined what I had felt for him. I had loved the scent of him. Had loved not just his kindness, but the physicality of his presence: the touch of his hand, the strength he had shown. I had not known it: poor, innocent Annaleigh, I thought. Running from the past, but not yet looking to the future. Pretending she needed nobody. For a while I let myself hope. Whenever I heard hooves in the courtyard I would pretend that he had come for me. When I reached the window I would see Sorsby, or Marcus.

Marcus and Hester went to church each Sunday; Sorsby and Jeanne went to town to fetch supplies. They maintained the semblance of normality. Only I lay, still and weak, in Marcus's bed. I had been lost to the world. I wrote to Jared again, and sent it off with Sorsby, but no reply came. As the moors came fleetingly to life in the spring sunshine and showers, I sickened.

It may have been grief, I do not know. My hunger died, and I stopped eating, my hands soothing the bump in my belly, apologizing, murmuring, hoping with every fibre of my being that the new life forgave me. On the rare occasions I forced myself to swallow food, I could not keep anything down. My skin grew grey. I heard Marcus and Hester arguing in her room, heard her weeping in the nights, until I rose and banged on the walls, and told her to be quiet.

No one could care for me. No one knew of children, not even Jeanne, who would shrug at me and say that as she had never had one, she had never missed one.

So one day, Marcus came from Becket Bridge, and a woman rode alongside him, a woman he said would help me, for she had children of her own, and was known for birthing babies. I saw Sorsby's face change at the sight of her, and for the first time I felt hope, real hope.

It was Kat, Thomas's aunt, who I had met so long ago at worship. She sat in the kitchen drinking tea with Jeanne and Sorsby for a while, then at last she came to me. A comforting, solid presence, in her clean clothes and her woollen cloak.

'That's them on my side, then,' she said when the door had been closed. 'Now, you poor lass. I did say to you I hoped I'd never have to visit this house.'

When I witnessed Marcus's humility towards Kat, I realized how much he wanted me to carry our child to full term. But this, even combined with the fact that he had fathered my baby, did not make me love him, or even tolerate him. The smell of him sickened me. Kat saw it all, and banished him from his own chamber to one of the guest rooms. He went, and it was she who lay beside me, raising a glass of water to my lips when I woke feverishly in the night, cooking the things I wished for, and bringing them to me.

I tried to ask her of Thomas, but she would not speak to me of him. She said little, but everything she said was soothing.

'Will I live?' I said.

'Aye, lass,' she said. 'If I have anything to do with it.'

She accepted each tray Jeanne brought up with a smile, and a 'thank 'ee', but on the second day she sat down beside me and did not pass me my drink.

'Annaleigh,' she said. 'They are drugging you. You know that, do you not? And it will likely kill the child, and perhaps you, if you keep on with it. These rich folk who think themselves so clever know nothing at all.'

'Let me have my drink,' I said. 'I need it, to sleep.'

She let me have it, that night, but as she soothed me, her words knitted into my thoughts.

It was she who helped me unlace myself from the drugs. She secreted them in chamber pots, threw drinks from the window. She told them I was unwell, and needed only her, as I lay awake and saw so vividly and violently the scenes of my childhood. I imagined the characters in stories Jared had told me, as though they were there, in miniature, marching up the length of my leg; sometimes, larger than life, their faces so close that they seemed to be sucking the air from my lungs. From a half a glass, to a sip, to nothing, Kat stayed with me those weeks, feeding me, steering me through hell, through craving, sleeping alongside me in bed like a parent with a child who is tortured by nightmares.

Still, the baby clung on to me. I wept for it. 'You are doing the baby a service,' she told me. 'You are doing this so that the baby might live.'

I was well, at last.

I know not how they found out what she did. Only that, in the midst of one black night, Marcus came into the room and woke us, and dragged her away, so that I screamed for her, and heard only her cry of 'God bless you' as they took her out into the night.

'Will you kill her?' I said to him.

'Kill her?' he said. 'Is your mind addled, Annaleigh? Of course not. I hardly want the whole of Becket Bridge at my door. Sorsby is taking her back, is all. We do not need her any more. You used to be so clever. How can you say such a thing of your lawful husband?'

It was in the way he said lawful: the slightest hesitation in his words. I saw clearly, for the first time in months. Shook my head, and turned away from him. He left me alone.

I felt the distress, the fury at losing Kat, awaken the sluggish blood in my veins. I opened the shutters, and decided I would begin to fight. I had energy. I even had strength. Alone in my room, I leaned against the wall, pushing myself up and down, willing my muscles to remember their previous strength, the months of housework, the scrubbing, the polishing, the mixing.

As the days passed I did not show Marcus how much my strength had returned. But I refused to drink the special drinks they brought me, or to take any pills.

'You must,' he said to me.

'I will not,' I said. 'I will drink only from the full pail of water drawn from the brook. If you think to drug the whole pail, you will use a month's quantity of laudanum in a day. And if you try and force me, I swear I will starve myself and this child to death. I will destroy us both.'

He stared, and I felt him turning inwards, the summoning of a deep hatred that he could barely control. I saw it in the tic in his jaw, in the way he froze, his hands firm on his hips, his anger giving him strength. 'You are a wild bitch,' he said, turning away from me.

'Would you rather I was weak and obedient, like one of those débutante beauties in town that you said you were so tired of, standing at the edge of the ballroom, waiting for the scrape of a violin bow on strings?' I said.

'What do you know of that?' he said, and the sudden anger in his voice lit my suspicion.

'You defend those ladies now, do you?' I said. 'Is that where you wish to be? Do you no longer wish for quiet, for peace? How you bleated about London, how you hated it. But it is just one more lie in your tapestry of lies, *husband*!'

I picked up the nearest thing and threw it. It flew past his head and landed on the floor. He picked the book up, straightened one crumpled leaf, and closed it. 'Like old times,' he said.

Then he went from the room, slamming the door

behind him. A few minutes later I heard it: the creak of his footsteps in the long gallery, which ran parallel to the sleeping chambers. Step, step, step. What did he see in those faces?

A portrait, Jared would say to me, is not just a portrait. It is a presence.

# CHAPTER TWENTY-TWO

The following day Marcus had gone out, and I was on my knees, dipping my cup into the pail of water, when I heard the rattle of keys. It was a familiar sound, from my old life as housekeeper, but when I looked up, it was not Hester holding them, but Jeanne. She put them down on the table, and went to stir the roux. It was already burnt; I knew from the sound and the smell, but she would never know that, she who had no sensitivity to anything, blundering on, with that faint smile on her face.

'Jeanne?' I said, my mouth cold and fresh from the water.

She looked at me.

'Will you let me walk in the gallery?' I said. 'Let me take the key? It is only tied with a ribbon. Where is your mistress? I will ask her.'

'Miss Hester has a sick headache,' she said. 'Luckily we have got some more medicine now, enough for her to have some, rather than just you. But she would not want you to have the keys.'

I struggled to keep my temper; it was so close to the surface then. 'Just the one key,' I said. 'That is all. I have no access to silver or food or the special medicines.'

She pouted, but kept stirring the roux. Sorsby came stamping in, looked at me as I dipped the cup again and took a gulp.

'Let me into the gallery,' I said. 'Let me walk; I need to, for my strength, for the baby. Unless you will let me out?'

Sorsby snorted. Jeanne frowned at me. 'You're definitely not to go out,' she said. 'And that is that.'

'But the gallery,' I said. 'There would be no harm in that.' I did what Marcus did; talked low, and all on one note, and said again and again and again that the gallery would do no harm, until Sorsby's temper snapped.

'Just give her the key, woman,' he said. 'What's the worst that can happen? She's not leaving here anyway.'

Jeanne, rather moodily, left the clumpy sauce and untied the key.

'Go on then, my pet,' said Sorsby to me, sarcastically. 'Go and have your little play in the gallery.' He put his arm under my elbow, and pulled me up. 'Give the family my best,' he said, mockingly.

I unlocked the door to the gallery. As I walked down the short narrow corridor into the main body of the room, I wondered whether Hester would hear my footsteps from her room. I decided not to worry because she was probably opiated out of her mind, and what was the worst she could do to me? Turn me out? Strike me and risk the baby?

I unhooked the catches and opened each shutter, one at a time, unleashing light into the room, seeing with a kind of delight the shimmer of the gauzy cobwebs which hung from the brass chandeliers, and one or two of the paintings. Despite the creak and give of the dark floorboards beneath my feet, I walked softly enough, up and down, up and down beneath the gaze of those portraits which, in another life, I had intended to care for and clean free of their veil of dust. These portraits which Marcus himself had come to look upon, brought here long ago by his uncle Jack.

Those first two or three were familiar from my last visit, but I lingered by each of the others. Eighty, seventy, fifty years old, they were: and then.

The portrait of a woman, her hair veiled, wearing fashions only ten or so years old. Not that she looked familiar. But the hand of the painter did.

I felt dizzy before I realized I was holding my breath. Sick to my stomach in a sudden, urgent way I had not felt since the early days of my breeding time. 'Why?' I said, to the empty room. 'Why you?'

For the painting had been done by Jared. I knew it at once, in the stroke of his brush and the shape of the sitter's hands. In that particular way he had painted the light in her eyes, the glisten of white on her skin to show the shape of her nose, and the sheen of her cheekbones. I knew it before I saw his signature, in the right-hand corner. Jared Calvert. A signature neat and precise, as though he was an illuminator rather than a portrait painter.

You would have thought it would have been a comfort to me, to see that familiarity in this strange and foreign room. But it did not comfort me. It seemed suddenly cruel, to have this reminder of someone I loved so close. And yet he had not replied to my letters. He was lost to me, as I was lost and my childhood was lost. I could reach out and touch where he had touched, but the painting was of no use to me.

I had no more tears in me. I walked to the window, and looked out at the moors, veiled in the blue mist of late summer, autumn beginning already. Unmoving and unconquerable. I had been here so long.

My mind, active since Kat had gone, would not let me walk away. I returned to the painting. If it had been painted when I suspected it had, I would have been living in the house. I might even have met the sitter, observed her from the corner of the studio, where I often watched, drawing smiles from the visitors, softening the atmosphere in the room. The sitter was not named on the frame or the canvas. I struggled, dredging my memory for her. Found nothing there except my own imaginings.

There was one more picture, at the end of the line. Not hung, but leaning against the wall.

The beginnings of one, at least, although not by Jared. A girl with red hair. There was the outline of her: the features of her face sketched in a cool brown on an ochre ground. No layers had yet built up the enamelled depths of Jared's painting. There were a few strokes of her hair, the red of a sunset, as though the painter was trying a shade out or, perhaps, catching it in his memory so he knew what to recreate when the sitter was gone. Strangely, he had painted her eyes, so that they looked out at me intensely, the human eyes of a spectral presence, that strange green of foliage on the forest floor, something alive, now decaying.

I turned the picture, looked at the label on the back. A painter in York, a vaguely familiar name. Why would he deliver a half-finished portrait? I was so lost in trying to decipher it that I did not hear the creak of the boards until it was too late.

'A flower picked and already fading.'

I flinched with surprise, and turned to look at Marcus. 'When did you get back?'

'Just now,' he said. 'Sorsby looked at me like a Papist who has missed communion, so I knew you must have done something wrong. Do you like the picture?'

'Who is she?' I said.

'Her name was Kate,' he said.

I bit back a sour hiccough of release. 'The housekeeper before me,' I said.

He pulled a face. 'Hardly. You were much more efficient. A better servant certainly. But when it came to me – she was not unwilling, like you.' He seemed to take no pleasure in the words; he looked at the floor. I sensed regret in him. He turned away, walked a few steps, and looked out of the window. 'I wonder why I even went through the charade of a service. It did not melt your resolve. It still felt as though I forced you, which was not what I wanted. One should never have to force a woman. But not Kate. She actually did want me. Imagine.'

'And where is she now?' I said.

He laughed. 'I do not know. Far away from here, I'll warrant.'

'You tired of her.'

His face darkened. 'No. It was much worse than that. She was the worst kind of woman. Not merely disobedient or wilful, like you.'

'What was her sin?'

He took the painting and put it down gently, the face turned to the panelling. 'She was not pure,' he said. 'Some other man had had her.'

'Surely you were used to that?'

He rubbed his eyes, and when he spoke the tone of his voice, pained and angry, showed that his self-control was wearing thin. 'I am tired of talking. You tire me, Annaleigh. And yet, when I met you, I was both – inflamed by you, but my soul soothed. All the pains I get – in my joints – all those times I wonder whether Hester might poison me, one day. When we first came here, she shut me up in the house, you know? No fresh air, and mercury pills, four times a day. I thought you would fix all of these things. So strong, so firm. Then I touched you. And you shattered into a thousand pieces.'

'I did not ask you to,' I said, walking to Jared's painting. Looking at that familiar hand. 'Do not ask me to feel pity for you.'

He sighed. 'No.'

'This painting was done by my guardian,' I said. 'Who is it of?'

I looked at him. His face was still, ungiving.

'Not that I should care,' I said. 'It is he who has left me friendless in the world, and in the power of a man like you.'

Marcus began to laugh, partly out of exasperation I could tell: but it was a great rolling laugh which, once it had seized him, did not let go. How handsome his voice was; there was a time when that laugh would have drawn the brightest smile from me, perhaps even a laugh of my own.

'Oh, do not judge him too harshly,' he said, once he had caught his breath. 'If he could see you now, so heavy with child, with the fire alight in your eyes, he would be proud of you. I will not let you think harshly of him any more, my poor little warrior. You have had too much unhappiness for that. I am sure he still loves you. Who could not? Look in Hester's cabinet. You will see your last few letters there.'

'What do you mean?' I said, something terrible, unthinkable, turning in my mind. 'Did he write for me?'

'For a sharp girl you are so very dull in many ways,' he said. 'Your letters left this house in Sorsby's pocket, and their life out in the world lasted only for the circuit he rode, until he brought them back here, and gave them to Hester, by her command. I believe your painter may have written once or twice after that first time – you got one letter to him, didn't you? But she burned most of the others. *She* did.' He leaned forwards, gazing at my stupefied face, not with even a glimmer of triumph, only sadness. 'Your Jared never received them,' he said. 'So let him have your forgiveness. But you are right in one regard. No one is coming for you, Annaleigh. I can promise you that.'

# CHAPTER TWENTY-THREE

I lay on my bed in the sickly morning light, where Marcus had supported me after I had fainted in the gallery. A whole night had passed, and Marcus was not beside me. The baby beat its fists within my belly, a drumming, an alarum that urged me to my feet.

Drowsily I walked through the moonstone-coloured air. Unhooked one of the white shutters, opened it, and looked out.

'Press your face to the glass.'

I remembered the woman on the coach, her steady gaze, filled with confidence – in what? The world seemed to me to be something I should not have confidence in. Somewhere in that woman, there had been steel, something forged in pain or trial or prayer, I knew not.

'It is best you know now,' she had said. 'When you are young.'

Drum, drum, drum went the baby's fists. Sending its warning, this life that had clung to me – was clinging to me – so resolutely.

Quietly, I tried the door. Marcus had left it unlocked. I dressed, quickly, knowing that he would still be abed in another room. Sipped the cup of water beside my bed. Layered over my thin dress with a cloak I had not worn for some time, other than when Kat had covered my sleeping form with it. Put on my bonnet, and tied it.

I ran down the stairs, and saw Sorsby and Jeanne, coming out of the kitchen into the main hall at the sound of my step on the stair. The smell of baking bread filled my nostrils.

'I will be gone,' I said, running towards the door, one hand cradling my belly, thinking that swiftness was the key.

I felt no pain when Sorsby brought me down with his foot. No pain as my head hit the floor, face first. Only surprise as I looked up, and saw something terrible had happened from the horror on Jeanne's face. I put my hand to my face, and felt the blood, a warm sticky flatness where my upper lip had been.

'Christ, you've gone too far this time,' said Jeanne, falling to her knees beside me and trying to dab at my mouth with her apron. I batted her hands away, not wanting her to touch me, not wanting anyone to touch me. The baby was still, and my hand stole to my stomach, in sudden fear. Like a wounded animal, I wished to crawl away into some dark corner, but Sorsby stood before me, blocking my way. 'It's what you've needed from the first, someone to take you down,' he said. 'You'll listen to me this time, high and mighty miss that you are.'

He considered the booted foot that had brought me down. I could tell he was assessing whether he could kick me in the face or, even better, the stomach. I could feel him wanting to do it, his malice so tangible it was almost a presence in the room, alive and vital. As Jeanne dabbed at my face, my body came alive again, and I felt not just the heat but the pain.

This was it: the pain. It had hovered out of sight, my whole life, and now I knew what it was, just as I knew what the metallic taste was in my mouth. I was nothing; I had nothing; there was no law that would protect me, nothing to keep me safe. I had always been falling and only now did I truly know it. With it came a clarity, a sudden knowledge of my own stupidity. Why had I not seen clearly until this moment? Why did I imagine that I might have some fellowship with Sorsby, that he might even have a grudging affection for me, after the hours I had spent here, improving this house, cooking his food? The pain brought emptiness, and then something new within me. Real hatred. So rare and searing. The baby stirred.

'You poor thing,' said Jeanne. I put my hand up, pushed hers away.

'God damn you,' I said, and Sorsby dragged me to my

feet. I snatched my arm away. 'Get off me,' I shouted. 'Or will you strike me again, and kill me and the baby this time?'

He brought his face close to me: unshaven, now, his breath sour, he had grown unkempt as the others in this house had, disturbed as they waited, waited, waited, for me to be delivered.

'You brought this on yourself,' he hissed at me. 'You thought yourself so clever. I told you, keep your distance, and yet you had to meddle. I have no pity for you.'

'You took my letters,' I said.

'I was ordered to!' he said. 'What, do I serve you now? If you'd had even half your wits you would have saved yourself.'

I stepped away from him. 'Do not come near me. Do not touch me. I swear before God I will have vengeance upon you if it is the last thing I do,' I said.

'Will I ever be free of women mithering?' he said. 'Get out of my sight, and do not try the door again, or I'll mess up more of your pretty face.'

I crawled up one step, then another, shaking off Jeanne's attempts to assist me. As I tried to rise to my feet I felt the rush of warm liquid between my legs, the shifting of something, and then a sudden, sharp pain slice through me. I did not hear what they said as they came towards me, Jeanne's lips moving, soundlessly. I heard my own scream, and then felt hands either side of me, lifting me up, raising me to my feet.

*

The labour went on into the night, with the shutters open to the black and star-pocked sky. Marcus stayed away, as he was meant to, and so it was Jeanne who stayed beside me. I felt the force and cruelty of nature as it picked me up and shook me like a mouse in the jaws of a cat. As the hours passed the certainty of death grew in me.

In a rare moment of peace I pulled Jeanne to me. 'Please, get Kat,' I said.

'We've brought the best sheets out for you,' she said, unfolding one, the fold mark in it deeply ingrained. 'Miss Hester kept them in her room.'

I stared at her with horror. 'Never mind the sheets,' I said, every word an effort in the mire of my exhaustion. 'Get Kat. Send Sorsby to her. I will die without her, and the baby too.'

She covered me with the musty sheet, then came back and took a tight hold of my hands. Her face was two inches from mine, but she did not waver, or pull away, or show that she meant to do anything at all to help.

'He won't go, even if they asked him to,' she said eventually.

'My baby will die. I am going to die,' I pleaded.

'Oh, *chérie*,' she said, the slightest trace of pity in her eyes, as her voice dipped to a whisper. 'It would be best for you if you did.'

The child was torn from me in the early morning. Before it happened, I heard Marcus say he would cut me open himself, if it did not end soon. A stinging pain, a moment of silence, and then the cry: that brief bleat of infancy, that shriek of anger into a room that, a moment before, had three people in it, and now had four.

I saw the bundle, in Marcus's arms. The pink, wrinkled face; a head of dark hair.

I held my arms out, but nothing was put there. Heard the cry again, and then it retreating, as it was carried away, away, that cry a thin thread holding me to it as my body's tissues once had.

'A boy,' said Jeanne to me, a warm whisper in my ear. 'A fine boy.'

And then she went, and she closed the door, and I was alone. I opened my mouth, but no sound came.

I saw myself from above, as I had on the night the child had been conceived. No ghost of the former Annaleigh, for I had come back to myself. Conscious. Lying in the midst of a spreading bloom of dark blood. The linen sewed with someone else's initials. I turned my head to the stale sheet, and saw it, close to my eyes. EJE. Tiny, in a corner, badly sewed. EJE. I closed my eyes, and knew that my life was leaking out of me.

And yet, I did not die.

# CHAPTER TWENTY-FOUR

Jeanne had the kindness to feed me, when I woke, after what could have been hours and could have been days, in the stale air of that chamber. She would not answer my questions, my continual asking: where is the baby? But she fed me, and brought me untainted water and, at last, dragged the blood-encrusted sheets from the bed and changed them. I had known I was trapped before but now my world contracted further; the door to my room was always kept locked.

I had convalesced for two days when I decided to make as much noise as possible. I bound my aching breasts, heavy and leaking with milk, dressed, and began to stamp around the room, screaming and shouting. Deep in me was a hope that my noise would wake the baby, that I would hear again that tiny cry. If he could hear me, I thought, and I could hear him, he would know that his mother had not abandoned him. Every other connection had slipped from my mind: I longed only for my baby.

At length the door was unlocked and opened, and Marcus came in, unprepared when I flew at him with the last of my strength. He caught one wrist as I swung to hit him, then another, and wrestled me onto the bed.

'Give me my baby,' I said to him. 'Give him to me, and let me leave.'

'Oh for God's sake, go quietly,' he said. 'I thought after everything we could put you meekly into the coach for Edinburgh.'

I spat in his face, and his grip on my wrists tightened. Then, releasing one hand, he slapped me hard around the face. 'Be still,' he said. 'You know there is no fighting me. Christopher!'

Sorsby came in; I realized he had been standing just outside the door. Together, they bound my hands, and I could tell the pleasure Sorsby took in tying the knot. 'Why do you hate me so much?' I said, in a whisper.

'Because you, like all women, have caused trouble, when all I wished for was peace,' he muttered. Then Marcus sent him out, and locked the door again. As he turned to me, he was short of breath.

'I am sorry to do this to you. But you will now learn, I hope, for your own sake, that you must quieten yourself and you must accept how things will be. The baby is mine. The baby is what I wanted, from all of this. And a little something else, which need not trouble you.' He was still Marcus. He still looked sad, as he smiled at me, hoping in some way that I would smile back, it seemed. 'We are finished with each other now. You may begin again, as you did when you came here. My little foundling. Find another life, another man, be free.'

'We are far from finished. Give me my child, and we will be finished.'

'Where has all this fire come from, Annaleigh?' he said. 'Yes, you were always strong, but you were sensible, too: practical. Say if I gave you to Plaskett, you would have a comfortable life. Why are you shaking your head?' I sensed he was about to lose his temper. 'You are not on stage in Drury Lane, and all this makes me very tired. I have seen enough of death in my life. You are too alive to die, and yet you struggle, knowing that I could snuff you out, like that.' He made the pinching gesture he had made against the candle on so many of our nights together. 'And watch your soul float off like candle smoke.'

I stopped struggling. It seemed to soothe him a little.

'Do not think I have no affection for you. You were here for me in my darkest hour – there was no one who would have me, after the last girl. I was sure of it.'

'And now?'

'Now, I am not so sure. I feel well again, you see. And you were a virgin, weren't you? I'm not saying I didn't doubt it; after all, Plaskett brought you from the streets of London. But there was always something so innocent in your look. Mind you, there still is,' he brought his face level with mine, searched my eyes, 'even after everything you have seen. So such looks can be deceptive. But I know you were a virgin.' He came close, whispered it to me. 'I felt it.'

I felt the acid rise in my throat, choked it back.

'I just want my child,' I said. 'And for this marriage to not have existed.'

'Oh do not worry, the marriage does not exist, but then you knew that, didn't you? You were drugged half out of your mind, so a little trip to the church was enough to dissolve your fiercer struggle, though you were hardly a willing partner. As for the child, he is mine in law, you know that. You must give up hope, completely. He is gone.'

I thought he meant dead, for a moment. But as I looked at him despairingly, I saw that he was happy. That his aim had been accomplished, for whatever reason.

'Where is he?' I said.

'Far away from here,' he said. 'Being cared for by his aunt Hester. Now I will not answer any more of your questions. I am advising you, in a friendly way, to tame whatever wretchedness is within you. Give up hope. Then let us see if you do not think my plan is a good idea.' I could hardly believe it, but there were tears in his eyes, as there had been the first night I had met him, drinking by the fireplace in the hall, filling and refilling his glass. When he spoke, it almost sounded as though he was pleading.

'Please, Annaleigh. Do not make me do what I did with the last one.'

*

As the days passed, I nursed the fury within me. I grew it as I had grown my child, from the seeds of something that felt like sickness, until it was strong and kicking inside my gut, with a life all its own. The fury gave me a cool detachment: it focused my vision. When members of the household visited me, no gesture went unnoticed; no glance or movement unstudied. And my mind worked and gathered detail, and plotted until I was as cunning as a watchmaker. The house was my mechanism, and I could read every sound in it, every vibration in its frame. That was their first mistake: to let me sit and wait. To let me live so long.

I knew Marcus had gone that day, because I knew the sound of his step on the yard. The particular way he would drive his horse from standstill to canter, with a scrabble of hooves, without the poor animal adjusting to the fact it had a creature on its back. He had always been a terrible rider, I thought, remembering Thomas's annoyance with him. Before, that memory would have brought tears to my eyes. Now it made me smile; it warmed me.

A few minutes afterwards, there was a knock at the door, and Jeanne came in. She was struggling with a large tray that bore a decanter of red wine, and a plate piled high with rolls. 'Thought you might like some victuals,' she said, that faint smile on her face. 'Sorsby's drunk himself to sleep. He won't wake for a while.'

'Where is the master?' I said.

'In his library,' she said. How easily she could lie.

She unbound my hands, wincing at the chafe marks on

my wrists. I poured a full glass of the wine and drank it, then hungrily tore into the doughy flesh of the roll. Jeanne joined me, and I sensed she was relaxing slightly.

I waited until I had eaten a roll, and drunk back a whole glass of the wine, before I spoke. 'They are going to kill me. You know that, don't you? Why do you bother to be kind to a dying animal?'

'Oh madam, don't say such a horrible thing.'

'Where is the baby?'

She gave the briefest moment of consideration before she said it. 'He's been taken to London.'

'To London? Why?'

She shook her head, refilled my glass and hers. 'I've said too much already. Sorsby'd knock me into the middle of next week if he knew I was up here, spilling so. Drink up. I'd best go back down.' She took her drink with admirable speed.

'Wait,' I said. I drank the wine and gave her back the glass. 'Let me go. Let me leave the house now.' She shook her head. 'You can say I pushed you, hit you, overpowered you. Consider it carefully, Jeanne. Do you want to see me dead?'

Still, she shook her head at me, and her silence maddened me. Beneath the covers, I had gradually worked my legs around to the side, so I was ready to jump out of the bed. As she gave that final shake of the head, I knew I would have to move quickly, more quickly than I ever had. My botched attempt to get past Sorsby haunted me. I pushed Jeanne's kindness to one side. Her kindness, after all, did not extend to saving my life. So I would have to save it.

She turned away from me to pick up the tray. In the same instant I snatched up the jug beside my bed, and smashed it over her head. She fell to the floor without so much as a cry.

For an instant I stared at her in disbelief. Then I put on a greatcoat of Marcus's that he had left on a chair. I had noticed that it was the same pale brown as some of the moorland plants, and hoped it would camouflage me a little on the moors. I went out, through the unlocked door, and down the stairs, carrying the length of rope with me that had been used to tie my hands.

I had already made the calculation in my mind, and yet I went against it. Tried the front door, and realized that it was locked. Turned back, as I should have done in the first instance, and went into the kitchen.

The sound of his wife falling to the floor had not woken Sorsby. He was asleep in the chair by the kitchen table, the poker left in the fire where he had been stirring it, his head tipped back, his mouth open as he snored drunk-enly. I thanked God for Thomas, that he had always been showing me his equestrian skills. I knew how to make a knot for a horse. Thus it was that I gently slipped the rope around Sorsby's neck, and only woke him when I pulled it tight. He scrabbled at his neck with his hands, rolled his head back and saw me.

'Bitch,' he said. I pulled the rope and brought him to his knees.

'More docile,' I said. 'Give me the keys, and I will not harm you.'

I was standing a few feet from him, the length of the rope. He would not be told. I saw the calculation in his face. I did what I had to do: kept hold of him with my right hand, and with my left seized the poker, candent from the heat, and then hit him hard on the arm. I heard the hiss of it against his skin and his arm collapsed beneath him, the rope pulling tighter. I dropped the poker, loosened the knot a little. He had rolled onto his back, his eyes wide open, nostrils flared with distress, and with the shock at what I had done.

'Sorsby,' I said, calmly. Still his eyes roamed in their sockets. I slapped his face. 'Sorsby! Yes – making all that pastry means strong muscles, doesn't it? I haven't quite wasted away. Now listen to me. Let me out of the house or I will kill you.'

He stared, as though I was a ghost.

'Sorsby? Look at me.' He did. 'Give me the keys, or I will kill you.'

He began to scrabble in his pockets with his uninjured hand. His other arm lay still, and prone.

'Throw them to me,' I said, and he did as he was told.

'That was easy, wasn't it? Now you stay here, or I swear to God I will batter your brains out.' I put the poker in the fire again, waved it in front of his face. He nodded. I dropped down, picked up the keys, turned the bunch in my hands until I had found the one used on the front door. Wondered if I should kill him anyway. Decided I could not. So I let go of the rope, ran out the kitchen door, and locked it.

I heard the scrabble of his feet, a croak – not a roar – of rage. A thousand thoughts crossed my mind: Jeanne would be waking, she might have heard his shriek, Marcus might be returning. I unlocked the front door, and opened it. I ran out across the yard, batting away one of the dogs who ran beside me, feeling blood warm between my thighs. I looked out, across the moors, and I plotted the course to Becket Bridge, the course I had taken so many Sundays ago. There was no horseman in sight, and in my hand I carried the poker, still.

I did the only thing I knew how to do.

I ran.

# CHAPTER TWENTY-FIVE

A blast of the cold Yorkshire wind hit my face as I ran up the bank and onto the moor. The air was harsh and intoxicating all at once, after so many days locked up in White Windows, watching the dust motes fly in the air. I found the strength to continue running, spurred on with the terror that someone was behind me. The coat was rough against my skin, with the smell of Marcus imprinted on it.

Do not look back, said the voice in my head. Do not look back. Then, Thomas's voice, from a better, safer time: keep to the path.

I could not keep to the path. They would be after me. They would find me. Run, run, run, said my harried brain – but if I ran through the thick bracken and grasses, knee-deep, they would bring me down. Keep to the path.

I pulled the collar of the greatcoat high, kept my head

down as I ran. I could see the Shawsdrop road and any-thing on the Shawsdrop road could see me, but it was empty. I thanked God for old uncle Jack and the derelict farmland, uninhabited, without anyone to see or betray me. I kept alongside the high, roughly built stone walls. Followed the seam of ownership, built out of grey stone.

I heard hooves, or thought I did, on the wind. I dived low behind the wall; looked through its many holes, and the wind whistled through the jagged gaps. I looked at the road, and saw nothing. Waited there for many a minute. I felt the blood, warm and rich as the earth, beneath my legs. I began to pray. Dear God, under my breath, and there my memory ended. Dear God, Dear God, Dear God, was all I could say. I was shaking so much I thought I could not stand again.

Then, the briefest moment of peace. The whitewashed walls of the Poole farmhouse. The words of the minister. *Let me be full, let me be empty. Let me have all things, let me have nothing.*

My ragged breath slowed the slightest bit. I regained some fragment of clarity. I could not shelter behind the wall forever. I knew I must go on, keep the coat all around me, to camouflage me just a little as I moved across the moors. It was not exactly the same colour but it was close enough. I set off again.

I was so weak. I stumbled and fell, more than once. I no longer looked around. I knew if I saw anyone – Sorsby, Marcus – then my life would be over. I would end it myself rather than be dragged back to the godforsaken White

Windows. How I hated that house. I mistook the cry of an animal for Sorsby, and I ran even faster. Looked back once, and saw nothing.

Again, I fell and lay close to the earth. Felt the grasses waving around me, heard the tick of insects close to my ear, heard the wild calls of birds. And it crossed my mind that I could surrender. Let the life slip out of me, gently, in this clean air. The moments passed. Then I got up again. Getting back on my feet felt as hard as climbing a sheer rock face. I continued to run.

I don't know how long it took me to reach Becket Bridge, but it felt like hours. The light was fading as I ran across the road, and hammered on the Digbys' front door. It was opened by Thomas, and he took a step back as though he had been struck.

'Dear God,' he said.

The sight of his face was too much for me. I stepped forwards, and wrapped my arms around him, a terrible, shivering bundle for him to hold.

It was Rose who urged us out of the doorway. She took my hands and pulled me into their hallway. She stroked my face, and called me her dear child, and all of a sudden I was weeping at her kindness.

'Where is the baby?' she said to me, gathering me into her arms.

'They have taken him,' I said.

'Look at your poor, dear face,' she said. I saw Thomas turn away.

'I am bleeding,' I whispered to her. She brought me a

folded wad of linen, and pushed Thomas out of the parlour so I could see to it. I was shivering so hard my teeth
were chattering. When he came back in, Thomas put his
coat around me, a coat smelling of horses and hay, and of
him. I clung to it gladly. Rose brought me egg hot, a mix of
beer, eggs, sugar and nutmeg. I sipped it, but felt nothing,
only vaguely aware of Thomas wrapping another shawl
around me, as though blanketing a baby.

'Are you warmer?' he said. I nodded, but I was not. I
only wanted to temper the sharp, raking anxiety of his
gaze, wondering if it might be dangerous, if he would
head back over the moors. Still I felt Marcus was behind
me, that he would come and fetch me as his property, and
when a gust of wind palmed the window and set the pane
rattling in its frame, I turned, half-expecting to see his face
at the window.

'You are safe.' It was Thomas again, trying to comfort
me. 'I'll put the bar across the door.' I nodded, disbelieving.

Before he could get there I heard the front door open,
boots grinding on the stone floor. Rose was in the hallway
in a moment. 'Edward?'

'Aye.'

'It's just Edward, lass. Edward,' she said, soothingly,
but I could see fiercely and sharply how the blood had
drained from her face at the sound. Every colour and
sound was magnified by my fear, as it had been when I
gazed through the gaps in the stone wall.

'Well.' Thomas's father stood in the doorway, bootless.
He looked at me, at Rose, at Thomas, and it seemed to me

he assessed every current in the room, every possibility, dismissing some in a moment, allowing room for others.

'Forgive me for greeting you in my stockinged feet,' he said, walking past Rose to the fireside, brushing her back with his hand as he passed. 'But I've brought half the moors in on my boots, and my wife would not thank me for dragging the mud to her neat hearth.'

I said nothing; he warmed his hands. I saw him look at Thomas's face before he turned back to the fire.

'Well, lass,' he said. 'They're out looking for you on the moors. I saw the lights as I came round the Shawsdrop road. Be a while before they get here.'

'Father.' Thomas leapt to his feet.

'She'd rather know,' said Mr Digby. 'Wouldn't you?'

I nodded. Having opened my lips, no noise come out. Nodding, it seemed, was the limit of my communication.

'You'll be safe here,' said Rose.

'I can brazen out anything,' said Digby, 'and they'll come here first, there's no doubt about it. Though I'd rather trouble didn't come to my door.'

'She's no trouble,' Thomas said.

A smile crossed Mr Digby's face. 'Not to you, at least,' he said. Then he looked me in the eyes. 'What will you do?' he said.

I swallowed; my throat felt tired, my breath staled by the egg hot. 'Go to London,' I half-croaked, half-said.

'That's it, girl,' said Mr Digby. 'Get your voice back. But what do you have to do in London, pray?' His eyes flickered to the floor and back to my face.

'My child,' I said, and I knew my face showed everything; felt it change as I said it. My feelings were just below the surface, and he had scratched something and brought them to light, like dark, infected blood welling up from a sudden wound.

He nodded. 'Now, look there, my boy,' he said to Thomas, 'look direct and hard at it. That's trouble.' He turned to the fire, his back to me.

'What do you expect her to do?' said Thomas. 'What kind of woman would she be if she did not care what happened to her child?'

'My kind of woman,' said Digby, and Rose tutted at him. 'It's not the caring that I mind. It's what she'll do under the influence of that burden. I can see it in her eyes.'

'I must find him,' I said.

Digby shook his head. 'If I were you I'd concentrate on running from your master, not finding the child. The child is lost to you, and belongs to the father by law. You know that.'

A noise issued from my lips. Thomas made to say something, but Digby raised his hand to quieten him. He sat down opposite me, in the heavy carved oak chair stationed near to the fire, and leaned forwards towards me, his elbows on his knees, his hands clasped.

'These folks have their ways,' he said. 'They win, we lose, and there is nothing you can do about it. I know not what Twentyman wants with the child – he has been little but a stranger to us since he came here – but all I do know is, if you are fighting him, woman, then he will win.'

I looked at him as though he had said nothing. He searched for a response in my eyes with his own.

'There will be other children,' he said.

I shook my head.

'Heed me,' he said. 'I've left behind things, more places and people than you can imagine. I know when an ending should be made, and this is one such moment. Because wherever you go, whether to Newgate or Bridewell, I see from my son's face that he will go with you. He may pretend otherwise, but he's thought of nothing but you over these past months.'

'Do you truly expect her to think of me in such a moment?' said Thomas softly.

I held Mr Digby's gaze, cleared my throat again. 'I know you wish to protect Thomas,' I said. 'But I don't ask for him to come with me, nor do I expect him to. I cannot leave my child unlooked for in the world. Even now, he must feel my loss as I feel his.' I spoke with absolute certainty, feeling the pull of the thread in my guts, as though the sound outside was not the wind, but my son's cries. Though he had been torn from my body, my knowledge of him had not.

Mr Digby looked at me. 'I hurt like you, a while ago. My Rose effected a cure of some sort, she was something I had never expected or looked for in life, after I left London. And I did leave, left as if the devil was on my heels. So I know what I speak of. You are young. And I am asking you, with my hand on my heart – do not begin your life with a crime. The way back from that is only so much harder.'

I said nothing. I knew, even then, not to make a promise I could not keep. For with that blow to Sorsby, singeing his flesh, I had already seen myself capable of violence.

'Very well,' said Mr Digby. 'If you won't listen to reason, we must help you as best we can. They won't find you on the moors, so I'll hazard Twentyman will send a man door-to-door. He's probably in the Cross Keys now, recruiting. Tom, you'll hide her in the cellar. Behind the barrels, and put some of that cloth over them too. Or the old priest's hole perhaps. This house was made to be hidden in.'

The knock at the door came a few minutes later. Alone in the darkness of the priest's hole, I heard the thump of footsteps and the shape of voices. I pressed myself back against the cold rough stone, as though I might be able to make myself disappear.

'Search the house from top to toe, if you wish,' shouted Mr Digby.

It was the longest half hour of my life, listening to the rhythm of their search: their boots, their voices, their laughter, a blunt cacophony of looking, of doors opening and closing.

Then there was a long, unyielding silence, before Thomas yanked open the door and I gasped for breath.

'What did they say?' I said, as Thomas helped me out. I had never seen him look so shaken; he, who rode over moors and harnessed wild horses, was pale with worry, his eyes bright with the shock. 'All is well,' he said.

'First of all, don't fret, for they suspected nothing,' said Mr Digby. 'And the good thing is, they don't care either – it's not as if they have any loyalty to Twentyman, and he hasn't thought to offer a reward. They said, would you believe: "We are after Miss Calvert. She has taken off with a silver candlestick." Yes, madam, a capital offence, and so soon.'

'I cannot believe he would say such a thing,' I said.

'Can you not? Then you are a fool,' retorted Mr Digby. 'No, Tom, don't be saying nothing. I don't know what madam did to get out of White Windows, and whatever it was, I salute her. But it is only the start, the very beginning, and a silver candlestick won't be the worst of it – don't flare at me, I'm not saying you took one. I haven't seen one secreted around your person, and from what I can see you're not guilty. No, you're burning with that holy righteous anger which,' he sighed, 'is such a waste of time. And now we have to get you out of here. And we'd better be quick sharp to move you without being noticed.' He groaned. 'I have ease now. Why would I ruin it, to get involved with something that has naught to do with me? Risk my fair set-up here, my family, my livelihood – Twentyman's a nasty piece of work, something you're only now acquainted with, and he would finish me like that.' He snapped his fingers.

'Why are you helping me?' I said.

'Above all, because of my boy,' he said. 'But also because something in my gut tells me it's the right thing for me to do. It's to your advantage, so don't press me, wench. And if you're going to have egg hot, I want some too.'

Rose went to the kitchen, and returned with it for all of us. As we sipped it, Mr Digby and Thomas discussed the routes out. In the end Mr Digby decided it. 'Best if we go a little roundabout. I'll take you to Hebden Bridge. From there you can ride the Enterprize to the Devonshire Arms at Keighley, where you can pick up the Leeds coach. When you get to Leeds, go to the White Horse, Boar Lane, where the London coaches start from. If you can catch the Royal Mail, take it: it leaves at nine in the evening. If not then take the True Briton at three in the morning. It will see you into London by dinner time the next day.'

'What if we are seen leaving here?' I said. 'Will they tell him – Marcus?'

The men glanced at each other, and it was Rose who spoke.

'They'll be careful who they tell. There are men in this place who watched my son take his first steps on that windblown main street. I don't believe those men will betray him for anything, and if they do they'll have me to answer to. It's time for you to cover that beautiful face of yours, and be gone.'

# PART THREE

# CHAPTER TWENTY-SIX

Thomas and I travelled as brother and sister, under the name of Bay, his mother's maiden name.

'I never thought you such an efficient liar,' I said to him, after I'd watched him say it without the slightest hesitation, as he paid for our room at the inn.

'I'm not,' he said shortly. 'If I dissemble, it is for your sake. Don't believe me to be like Twentyman.'

His words silenced me, and though we sat alongside each other in the coach, and slept in the same room, he kept his distance from me. I grew accustomed to the shape of his back, clothed, across from me, in the night. That memory of him, and the long rise and fall of his breath in deep sleep, will stay with me until my last moment.

I had escaped only in my shift and Marcus's coat, and it was not safe to travel in the coat. So I wore a dress of

Rose's, and kept my dark hair tied over with a black scarf, whenever it was not covered by the hooded cloak she had retrieved from a chest in her room. She had given me my new clothes silently, and without any sense of grudging, though they were valuable. She had helped me dress, binding my aching breasts, and seeing to my hair when I, exhausted, would have gone out into the night with it loose around my shoulders. When I had thanked her she had only smiled, and said: 'I'm not losing them forever. You will come back to us, won't you? And with your bairn in your arms.'

We came into the heart of London, assaulted by the crush of carts and carriages, sedan chairs and traders, moving slowly, and then stopping completely.

'Not another damned stoppage,' said one of our fellow passengers.

'Are you coming to view the Waterloo museum?' said another, who had taken to Thomas. Cheerfully, he waved his copy of *The Times* at us. 'It is the most capital thing.'

'London, London, how I've missed you, you filthy, rotten city,' I murmured, under my breath. Then I saw Thomas looking at me. Not with that same happy, calm expression he had always worn in the days I had first known him, but with a grave watchfulness. The coach lurched forwards.

'What is it?' I whispered to him.

'He has changed you,' he said.

'I have changed myself,' I said, knowing that I must

have looked hard to him. 'Besides, nothing ever stays the same.' I turned to watch from the window again. How I loved those people walking the London streets, lost in their anonymity, uncaring of me, even if they caught my eye. There was no emptiness, no vastness here; only these tight, crowded streets, thronged with people who had no connections to each other, and wanted none either, with horses that threaded their way with bloody-minded toughness. The noise, the energy, the freedom that was possible in all of this. A place I had been kept from was suddenly home. I turned to Thomas.

'We will be safe here,' I said.

Thomas secured us a room in a lodging on one of the dark streets off Piccadilly, saying his father had recommended the house. His grim countenance seemed to both impress and chasten the landlady, who asked no questions and took the money cheerfully enough, showing us to a small, gloomy room, with a mean fireplace and a tiny window. When Thomas sat down on one of the truckle beds, he gave a deep sigh, and I could tell it was not out of show. I sat down beside him.

'I am sorry to have drawn you into this trouble,' I said. 'I can hardly remember our journey – strange as that may sound – but I feel sure that I have been harsh to you. You are the last person who deserves harshness, so I am sorry for it. If it makes you happier to hear it, I feel safer here. I could almost be myself again, if I had not been so very changed.'

He rested his hand over mine, the first touch he had given me since we had left Becket Bridge, and looked at my face with a brave smile. 'Your mouth is healing,' he said. 'Soon you will look just like the old Annaleigh.'

'That is not what I meant,' I said.

'I know.'

We went to find a tavern at my insistence. As we came out onto the street a passer-by hit Thomas's shoulder without apology, and I saw him flinch. 'It is London,' I whispered to him. 'I'm afraid it happens all the time.' And, at last, his troubled expression broke into a grin.

'You will soon grow used to it all,' I said. 'And, I know you to be of good temper, but – try not to anger too swiftly. Londoners are always only waiting to fight or to riot.'

He looked vaguely troubled, despite the mischievous look I cast him. 'What do they riot over?'

'The price of bread, the price of theatre tickets,' I said. 'And you think Yorkshiremen are opinionated.'

In the Nag's Head, Thomas asked for a meek tankard of porter. When he turned to me, I decided to choose something new. I remembered a sitter of Jared's long ago, in the shadows of one evening, when Jared was busy and so spent many evenings painting by candlelight. The man was an actor, and when Jared offered him wine, he had wondered aloud if something else was available.

'I'll have a flash of lightning, if you please,' I said, and watched as the innkeeper poured me a gin with a smile. I took a sip, nearly gagged, then another, until I was used to it.

'Is that wise?' said Thomas.

'Probably not, but it will give me courage to face the night again, when you have fallen asleep,' I said.

'What do you mean?'

'I sleep for one or two hours if I am lucky. I long for rest, and yet, when I lie still – God, what torturous images come to my mind. I have come to dread it now. Perhaps this will knock me out.'

He considered his drink. 'What will you do?' he said. 'When you find the child?'

It was the first time he had asked it, and the first time I had thought about it. I had been living from moment to moment, thinking only of the time of reunion, and whether it would ever come. To hear this question woke doubt in me, an unwelcome visitor in my frantic thoughts. 'I do not know,' I said.

I had spoken to him a little of my imprisonment, and I sensed that there were many questions he longed to ask of me, and yet could not. He who had seemed so strong in Yorkshire now seemed to be someone I should protect. There had been moments, on our journey, when I had longed to lay my head on his shoulder. I thought his touch would offer me relief, as one longs to put cool water on one's face in the densest summer heat. But I had held back from seeking comfort from him, because I sensed the great swell of his feeling for me. It puzzled me.

'Sorsby said you cared for me, the night you left,' I said. 'I only half-believed him. Yet when I came into your house, from the moor, the look on your face told me the truth of it. You seemed to have cared more for me, since I was gone, than you did when you could talk to me.'

He half-choked on his drink. 'Really? You can say that? If I kept it hidden it was because I was not sure of you or whether I could offer you ...' He let his voice trail off. 'Enough,' he said. 'It is wrong to speak so. There is nothing to be done about the past.'

'There are plenty of things to be done,' I said, and I took a bitter mouthful of the gin; felt it carve a path down my gullet.

I saw in his hesitation that one of his questions was coming; one he had kept dammed in. 'What kept you there? I thought, that night I brought Twentyman in off the moor, that you would leave with me. And yet you stayed, not just that night. Why? Did he threaten to ruin you? Did he show violence towards you?'

'He did not threaten me. Not then.' It made me sick to say the words, and see him take them with a quietly suppressed bitterness, and another mouthful of porter.

I shifted on my seat, let my hands play over the dense, hardy cloth of my gown. 'You are right, I could have left and I should have done so. But I felt bound to that place. I know it must seem hard to understand. Sitting in Becket Bridge, surrounded by those who love you, the situation must have seemed very clear. It was not so clear for me; I am alone in the world.'

'Not now,' he said.

'Perhaps,' I replied. 'As to what made me care for him enough to stay, that first night. You said once I had a vulnerability which – God save you – gave me a kind of appeal. I denied it then, but it is true. I may be quick to anger, but I am quick to show tenderness too. For my whole life, I have longed to be able to love. And when such a desire is held in – well, it can be forced in the wrong direction. He saw that in me, and he used it. He knew I would not condemn him to death. The strongest card in the pack, and he played it. And you did not come back. I wanted to speak to you that night, but when Jeanne came to get you, you did not come back.'

'Came to get me?' he said. 'She did no such thing. She stood in the rain, and watched me ride away, without so much as raising her hand.'

I had had so many shocks, that it should not have affected me, but it did. 'Was anything the truth, there?' I said.

Thomas sat, his chin resting in his hand, stooped over the table a little. He did not look at me as I took another mouthful of gin.

'And did you like him?' he said, quietly. 'Before then? He was a gentleman. Good with women, so the gossip went. I wondered if you liked him.'

'If you must know,' I said.

He nodded.

'He had a kind of fascination. He showed interest in me. And there were moments when I believed him, when he said that he cared for me.'

'I suppose he had his fortune, which is always an attractive quality,' he said: glumly, tightly.

'Now I see your pa in you, thinking only the worst,' I said. 'I am not a fortune-hunter. I felt a sympathy with him. His interest flattered me. Now you say it, because you see things so clearly, unlike me, perhaps my desire to be free in some way – free from drudgery. Perhaps that lay beneath it too. Who does not long to be free? But, I did not love him. I can tell you that truly. I did not love him.'

He brightened at that, and I wondered at it: that he could see me as a mercenary, and not be distressed by it. We sat together in the shadowy corner, watching a couple argue nearby, over the man's wandering eye. *Stop looking at her arse*, the woman yelled, her tongue loosened by drink, so that Thomas and I could not help ourselves from laughing.

'Very well,' Thomas said at length, sitting back in his chair. 'How do we begin?'

'I do not know,' I said, overwhelmed, and put my head in my hands. How would I find my child in this city? I felt the tension flood my head, the warning first stab of a headache. I grasped at my one certainty. 'I must go home first. They will help me. We must walk to St Martin's Lane.'

'Tomorrow,' he said. 'Rest first. Have you stopped bleeding?' How suddenly intimacy had been forced upon us, and yet he did not baulk at it. I nodded.

He seemed content with that. 'It has been a long journey for us both. I will go to one of the coffee houses, read the newspapers and make enquiries, see if there is any mention of Miss Hester.'

'She won't be in society,' I said.

'I would not assume that,' he said. 'You always said she spoke of how she missed London. And for all that you liked her, I fancy her soul is as cold as ice.'

# CHAPTER TWENTY-SEVEN

The next morning, we made our way to St Martin's Lane. The walk was piercingly familiar, and I felt the nausea of anticipation mounting in my stomach as we came closer, wondering if I would be welcome. As I knocked on the door, I noticed that the knocker was no longer polished. The front steps were a little muddy, the scraper had a thick pat of mud on it, and a mush of wet autumn leaves layered the steps. I had prepared myself to see Alice's sour, doughy face, to register and respond to her surprise. So when the door was opened by a maid who was probably my age or younger, it was I who started, and drew back slightly, holding my hood partially closed.

She looked afraid, the timid little thing. 'Yes, 'm?'

'I am here to see Mrs Calvert,' I said, and I felt Thomas's shift at the words, for he had come to associate that surname solely with me. At her hesitation, I continued in a firmer tone: 'Will you tell her Annaleigh has come to see her? She will know who I am.'

'Madam is not at home,' she said.

I looked past her, at the stillness of the grey passageway. There was something dead about the house and yet, with my animal senses, so strongly developed from being chased, I was sure that Melisende was there. She had retreated, as she so often did, to sew by the fireside; to be quiet, and pretend that the world and its attendant noise and shocks were no longer there.

'She will see me,' I said. 'Just go and say my name.'

The girl hesitated. She did not want to be shown to be a liar, and I understood that. But she eventually turned, closing the door quietly on me.

'Something is wrong,' I said to Thomas. 'The house was always full when I lived here. I have been away too long.'

'Do you wish me to come with you?' said Thomas. 'I can easily amuse myself for half an hour.'

'Why?' I said. 'Have you seen a girl you like? Is it the orange seller? I can see you with her. Look at her beautiful, fresh face. Take her to Yorkshire and she will bear you a dozen fine children with the same delicate colouring.'

He half-smiled, half-grimaced. 'God damn you, Annaleigh, I will come in with you,' he said.

The door opened again; the girl's eyes were cast down in shame. 'Madam says to come in,' she said.

'Scrape your boots,' I told Thomas pertly, and got a dark look in response.

It had been only a year since I had seen her, but Melisende was visibly smaller. Not just in waist or shoulder, but in her entirety, as though her very soul had shrunk. She was dressed in grey with black trimmings; grey to match the grey light in the corridor, and the room. There was no fire. She did not rise and come to me, so I went and sank down to kiss her cheek. She took the kiss; bore it as though it was a burden. Her hand fitted over mine for a brief moment, before she gestured towards the chairs near her.

'Janet did not say there were two of you,' she said. Then, turning to the maid, who was already trembling with some kind of fear or exasperation at her error, asked her to bring the flavoured brandy drink, Noyeau, and whatever cake there was in the larder.

'Unless you prefer tea?' she said.

'I think we would, if you do not mind,' said Thomas, looking a little queasy at the thought of us all drinking strong liquor. I too was alarmed; her suggestion, made in a tone of deep exhaustion, was not what I expected of her.

'Please, madam, there is no tea,' said the maid.

Melisende sighed. 'Just bring what I said, then; you will have to make do, sir, I am afraid,' she said.

All of this time the realization had crept over me that Jared was not here. There was nothing of him in this room, or in her manner – for her life had been shaped around his, and not around a glass of spirits in the morning. And more, the house was silent: no sitters making their way up and down the stairs, no assistant tramping out to fetch colours or complaining about canvases. The place was eerily still, just us, Melisende, and the maid pattering around like a spider.

'You look poorly,' she said to me.

'Where is he?' I said.

It was as though I had stuck a fleam in her, to let out the blood. She stared at me with such force that I knew the old Melisende was there somewhere, living beneath the layers of her lethargy. 'How can you say such a thing?' she said. 'He is in the churchyard, as I wrote you, waiting only for the day of resurrection. Where is the Noyeau? It is the only thing that keeps me warm, and calms me.'

I choked on my own breath. I covered my face with my hands, but could not weep, made cold and still by all that had happened in the past few days. I felt Thomas's hands on my shoulders. 'She did not know,' he said.

'But I sent word to the address in your letter,' she said. 'First when he fell ill, and again when—' She broke off.

Thomas squeezed my shoulders. 'It is monstrous cruel, lass,' he murmured, into my hair. He looked up, at Melisende. 'She never received your letters, ma'am, apart from the first. She has been locked into a bad situation which she alone must acquaint you with.'

'Well,' she said. 'Well.' Then the door opened, and after the maid had set the table and gone, she took a glass of the Noyeau and drank it down. I smelled the fumes of it: that strange mixture of brandy with the scent of citrus, sugar and bitter almonds. 'You too,' she said, as I looked up at her, and she pushed a glass towards me. Thomas took a slice of cake, and ate it carefully.

'He did ask for you,' said Melisende. 'He did say, "where is my little girl?"'

I could not bear it. I put the glass down without taking a sip, and began to cry, trying to do so silently, until my ragged breath caught, waving Thomas away when he came to me. He drew up a chair, and I heard his voice, low and steady with its Yorkshire softness, telling Melisende a brief summary of what had happened. I had wiped my eyes and blown my nose before I could look at her again.

'I am sorry for you, child,' she said. 'I will pray for you. But our business together is done. You left this house in a fit of pique, and though it is not long on the calendar it seems like a lifetime ago to me, after all I have suffered. He did grieve for you, you know – oh no, do not turn away, you were not the cause of his death, little one. I see how sensitive you still are to all suggestions of blame. He fell ill at the tavern one night, with Richard. He did not die of grief, but of some illness sent suddenly upon him. But I cannot help you now, Annaleigh, I do not see how. This house is to be shut up, and I am to go to my sister. Your companion seems to hint that you require secrecy. That, I cannot give you after today. I will live around people again. I will go to church. I do not want solitude.'

I drank the Noyeau now. I wondered if she was right; I could not help but think my absence might have injured Jared's health. His coral, as he always called me, his talisman. I thought of my coral beads, still in my room in

Yorkshire. As I drank, I looked at Melisende. I saw that she had deadened herself to me, perhaps to everything except her prayers. My thoughts moved to the other constant presence in my childhood: Jared's assistant.

'Where is Richard?' I said.

'That, I can help you with,' she said. She went to her desk and drew out a card with an address on. 'You may find him there.'

'Will you receive me, after this?' I said. 'Once you have gone to your sister's house?'

'If you wish, you may visit.' She paused, and looked at me carefully, sorrowfully. 'You were always more Jared's child than mine. I will always think fondly of you. But I am tired. If you wish for answers – for I see in your look that I have not given you everything you wanted – then you must ask for them now. Let us be done with this.'

I glanced at Thomas, saw the pained expression on his face. But I would not leave without asking more. Jared had been taken from me in a moment – he was gone, though I could not yet accept it. I had to know more of him, like someone gathering scraps of memories, as the London pigeons gathered crumbs, pecking at the seemingly empty ground for something, anything.

I asked the one question I had always wondered about. 'Why did he choose to keep me?'

Melisende took a morsel of cake and ate it. I sensed the question was something she would never have answered before. Now her tongue was loosened by desolation and the strong liquor she had drunk.

'He knew your mother. No, he was not your father – I see that wanton hope written all over your face.' Her lip curled, a sourness I had never seen so openly expressed, though I thought now it had been there all the time, in her sudden anger, her wish to be alone, in every perfect stitch, set with a controlled ferocity which only came now and then. 'Jared's real inclination was not for women. He cared for me, but not in the way most men care for their wives. He was a warm and kind stepfather to Kit, but I came to accept that we would never have any children of our own.'

Thomas cleared his throat. She continued without a glance or change of expression.

'You were the child of a servant, a girl he befriended before he was married to me. She was in the employ of a friend of his, and would help in Jared's studio sometimes, and when she fell, they dismissed her, although they gave her enough of a character to ensure that you were accepted by the Foundling Hospital when she petitioned them, and some money to pay for it, I believe. It sat badly with Jared, when he learned that she was destitute. He insisted on supporting her, and finding her lodgings, but she died. Her name was Anna Leigh. When he went to the Foundling Hospital, and persuaded his connections to let him adopt you, which was most irregular, he removed the name they had given you – some patron's name – and called you after her. He said it sounded pretty. And how much tenderness he lavished on you. He said that the Anna he had known had been bright, and strong, and talented; that she would have had a different life, if she had been born in a different house.'

Melisende had said this all in the same unhurried tone, as though it was a story that bored her, and that she did not wish to tell other than without emotion.

'That is why I found it so strange, that you should so fight against your duty,' she said, pouring another glass of the Noyeau. 'You came from a family of servants. Generations of them, stretching back, as far as I could tell. And yet you always had such fight in you – resisted any attempts to make you humble – and then, when what happened with Kit happened, I saw how futile my attempts had been, how your manner was just the semblance of humility. I blamed myself for it, for I thought it must have been the way we raised you. I did try to make you like the kitchen, to make you think of it as a place of sanctuary.' She sipped the Noyeau. 'But you were always in the studio.'

It was Jared, I thought. Jared who had always shown me, in a thousand ways, the secret of my potential, as clearly as if he had whispered it in my ear. I wondered if he had seen it in my mother too. My mother: a presence, with a name, suddenly. And I saw the line drawn in the family Bible, between Jared's name and my own. Melisende had always envied that. Jared had loved her, but never in the way she had wanted. How tired she looked, from asking a question of him, again and again, and still asking it now he was gone.

'It is time for us to go,' I said. 'Forgive me, for taking

up your morning.' I rose, noting the slight surprise in her face, leaned over her and kissed her cheek. The scent of her brought the past rushing back to me. She took my shoulder.

'I did not fail you completely, did I?' she said in my ear. 'Annaleigh? I loved you in my own way. I will always think of you as that little scrap of a thing. Do you remember our cooking lessons? Do you remember the day I taught you how to sprinkle rosewater on the crust of an apple pie to make it fragrant? Your face was so bright that day, bright and sweet.'

'Yes,' I said. 'I remember.' I tried to draw away, the tears blurring my sight, but still she kept me. 'Do not go to Kit,' she said. 'Leave him in peace.'

I kissed her cheek again, and it seemed to be enough of a promise for her to let me go, and for Thomas to make his bow and say farewell.

We went out into the hallway, and I fought the urge to go up the stairs, those stairs that Kit and I had lingered on so many times with our stories and our games. To see if every trace of Jared had gone.

'Annaleigh?' Thomas tried to bring me out of my thoughts, as the maid came scampering up from the basement, so much lighter in step than Alice had been. 'What are you thinking?'

I looked at his kind, honest face. 'There is nothing to hold me back now,' I said. 'Nothing to keep me from doing whatever I choose to do. I thought I would make my confession to Jared, for he was the only soul who ever loved me truly. He would give me penance, keep me gentle, steer me on the right way. But now he is gone.'

'You are not thinking right,' said Thomas. 'Let us go back to our lodgings, have some coffee, and make our plans.'

I gave a coin to the maid and told her to buy some ribbons, then asked her to leave us for a moment, saying that we would show ourselves out. As she walked down the hall, I remembered how I had gone, that day I left for the county of York. Following Mr Plaskett, without looking back.

And there, I imagined what I should have done, and it was as vivid to me as if I *had* done it. I never closed the front door, or walked towards Plaskett, his face caught in that half-smile I would come to hate. Instead I turned back and ran up the stairs and through the studio door into Jared's arms. My father: the thing I never called him, but which he was, in reality if not in blood. I buried my face in his paint-spattered coat that smelled of turpentine and the tang of his hours agonizing over portraits, and I felt his arms around me, those arms that had carried me from the Foundling Hospital and brought me to a place where I had learned to love colour, and light. Where I learned that life is not just the same old day-to-day things we see before us; that it is not just ordinary, but that in every moment is the seed of something sublime. And in my mind, I told him the one thing I should have said to him. For I owed him it, the truth of it as pure and heavy as gold.

When I spoke, it was to the empty hallway, Thomas watching me with a curious look on his face, trying to see what I looked at so intensely before me. 'Thank you for giving me my beginning,' I said. 'If I have ever loved, since then, it is because of you.'

# CHAPTER TWENTY-EIGHT

'Now it is my turn to have the headache,' said Thomas, when we had returned to our lodgings.

'It is the Noyeau,' I said, with a laugh, then felt sorry when I saw him wince. 'Shall I get you a capuchin? It will set you right. A nice milky coffee is what you need.'

'It is not the Noyeau, it is London,' he said. 'I am a country boy. All this noise. All these people. Not a single half hour passed without carriage wheels, or shouting, or some scream in the distance whether of animal or human. I think I may never sleep here. Last night I lay awake and listened to you breathing.'

'As I did you,' I said. 'You should have spoken. But it is quieter here now than at night. At least our downstairs neighbour is not brawling with some bawd. Why do you not lie down, and sleep? I have another friend I wish to see. Someone who may tell me where my child is, who may even know why I was trapped in such a way.'

He had sat down on the bed when I started talking, but at my words he swung his legs round to right himself. 'I will come with you,' he said. 'I cannot let you venture out without some protection, after the shocks you have had today.'

I put my hand to his forehead, and saw how startled he was by this small act of tenderness. 'Protection?' I said. 'Do not worry. I have the knife your father gave me, and I will take your stick too, if you'll allow it – do not worry, I will be quite safe. I know this city, and I am not troubled by it. I have someone I must see.'

He protested a little more, but eventually let me go. I could see he was exhausted; he was pale, and there were shadows beneath his eyes. I stayed long enough to see him fall asleep.

I went to the White Bear, where Plaskett had told me he would be all those months ago, if I should need his aid. The landlord was suspicious at first, but his curiosity outweighed that. 'You're the first woman I've ever known enquire after Plaskett,' he said. 'He gives all the talk, but as for actuality – it's only debtors ever ask for him here.' I heard him laughing and saying the words 'some poet' as I walked out.

He had directed me to Mrs Keeple; I found her house on Arlington Street. Each floor had been let out to lodgers, and on the ground floor the woman herself was at home, drinking tea. Her maid opened the door, and when I told her I too was a servant, confirmed that Plaskett lived there on the second floor, but said she could not show me up, for 'mistress keeps the keys and likes to keep note of callers.'

'Where is she?'

She jerked her head towards a nearby door. 'In there, sitting on her fat arse and drinking tea.'

I slipped her a coin. 'Make yourself scarce, and don't come up again for a good half hour,' I said. She went without a word.

'Mary? Who is it?' The mistress herself opened the door. I stood there, looked at her, and lowered my hood. I smiled, as kindly as I could. She glared at me.

'Who are you?' She was a fleshy woman, powdered and painted beyond the bounds of respectability, I noticed. The house seemed quiet enough, but I had pushed my way through a small group of finely dressed whores to get to it.

'I've come to see Mr Plaskett. I'm told he lodges here,' I said. 'Is he at home?'

'Why should I know?'

I looked pointedly at the brassy tangle hanging from her waist.

'He may be out, although sometimes he writes in the afternoon,' she said, with a sniff. 'He does not like to be disturbed. Locks the door. Not that he has many young women like you calling upon him. He tells me if there are visitors due; tells me what they want; sometimes invites me to meet them.' She sounded proprietorial, and

I mentally applauded Plaskett for having any woman interested in him. Still, her pretensions were no use to me, and I could sense that she was actively hostile towards me.

'I need to speak to him, and can wait if he is out,' I said. 'The second floor, I believe? Will you show me up? Or, if you do not wish to climb the stairs, give me the key?'

She put out an arm, and barred my way. 'What do you need to speak to him about?'

'I have urgent business with him.'

Her face changed. 'You're that little strumpet chasing after him, aren't you? He described you to me.'

There was something about the way she was looking at me which sickened me. My mouth felt dry, and my skin hummed with tension. 'You know nothing about me,' I said.

'I do. You are younger than I thought.' I could see her making the equation in her mind, and the sum failing to add up. Plaskett had spun her some tale about a woman pursuing him; he thought himself a catch and, in some ingenious way, probably through repetition, he had per-suaded her of it too.

'I know all about you, offering yourself to him – as if a man of his talent and respectability would be taken in by a loose woman.'

I felt my grasp on my temper beginning to slip. 'Madam, I have asked kindly. If you wish to see what I have to say, you may show me up.'

'Not now. Knowing what I know.'

I took a step closer to her. 'You know everything, don't you? Let me make it plain. You either let me upstairs or I will beat you into unknowing.'

A moment was enough; she opened her mouth into a shape that had enough of outrage and pride in it that I knew she would not help me. Praying that the maid would keep her word, I hit her broad across the stomach with the stick. I was fast and she was slow, so she did not see it coming, only felt the blow, which first bent her double then brought her to her knees, coughing and gagging. I raised the stick over my head, and hers. Her mouth opened in a soundless scream, but pain had quickened her.

'No!' It was a croak, barely a sound.

I held off, the stick above her head. 'Get into your parlour, and let me have your keys,' I said. 'Your maid will not come. If you stay silent, as God is my witness, I will not harm you. My business is not with you. But if I hear another scream from you – another murmur – then you will feel the full weight of this stick.'

She did as she was told, and told me which room was his. Each key was carefully labelled. When she had crawled into her parlour I locked her in.

I ran up the stairs, past the first floor, up to the second. The door was locked. I knocked. Silence.

As I fumbled in the half-light, trying to find the key, my temper overcame me again. I kicked the door, hard, then ran at it with my shoulder. I heard a voice in the room beyond, imploring in note.

'I have the keys,' I said. 'It is Annaleigh. Spare me the

trouble, for if I am in a temper when I come in it will be worse for you.'

He opened the door quickly then, stood there, looking at me. His eyes were a cloudy grey like tea with too much milk. 'Little Annaleigh,' he said, and he began to laugh with relief, quietly at first, as relaxed as though he was watching a play at the theatre. He was not afraid at all. This tall, hunched man, with the drop ever at the end of his nose, the man who had sent me to Yorkshire, as though it was a safe place, who had guided me through the streets of London with his hand upon my elbow, who had delivered me into the arms of Marcus Twentyman, all the time hoping he might have his own time upon my body. He was laughing at me, and not just at what I had been – little Annaleigh – but at what I had become.

In that moment, something broke within me, and let out the violence and the anger which had been brewing in me since the day I had woken from labour.

I did not think. My body worked of its own accord.

I stabbed him.

# CHAPTER TWENTY-NINE

'Why would you do such a thing to me?' said Plaskett.

'If you laugh at me again, I will finish the job I have begun,' I said.

He was rocking himself as I tied a cravat hard around his thigh to stem the bleeding, and bound the wound under his direction. I had tied his hands behind his back, his wrists as frail and thin as a boy's, his skin faintly grey. I could have felt pity for him in that moment.

When I had done the job I rose and went swiftly to the window. I longed to open it, to breathe even the street air of London, but I did not want to weaken myself in his eyes. I looked around his room. To hear him talk in those long portrait sittings with Jared, you would have thought him a great man. I had expected to see prints on his walls, to see shelves of books, perhaps touristic fragments of the travels he said he had taken. Instead there was a bed, unmade; a handful of books piled all upon each other, and his linen, hung all around the room and before the small fire. A certain grubby domesticity pervaded the room: a teapot, a cracked cup, two dirty glasses and a frying pan littered it alongside a few other utensils. There was some trace of his trade: a small writing desk sat near the window, and pages of paper, written and cross-written in poor erratic handwriting, peppered with blots, telling, it seemed, of joyless hours spent waiting for the words, or of writing when intoxicated.

There were no prints, no fragments of great civilization. Mr Plaskett had lived a grand life in words, and a miniature life in action. I recognized the decanter of ruby-coloured liquid, my mouth watering so that I had to turn away.

'What are you looking for?' he said, rather sadly. He does not write in the afternoons, I thought. He drinks, and drugs himself, and – well, I did not want to think what else he did. But he was alone, quite alone.

'Where is the portrait of you that Jared painted?' I asked.

'I could not pay him for it.'

Mindful of the landlady below, I turned back to the matter in question. 'Why would you leave me open to such violence, and not expect violence in me?' I said.

'I do not know what you mean,' he said, but fell silent when I switched the air with my hand. His leg wound, small as it was, had cowed him a little.

'You sent me to Yorkshire, to the Twentymans. For what purpose?'

'The purpose I described to you.'

'With no other incentive? Why not send someone else, better fitted for the role of housekeeper? Why involve yourself at all?'

'My dear girl, if there is an answer you want then you will have to ask for it.' He was only silenced when I brought the knife close to his face again.

'I'll be blunt then,' I said. 'Did you send me as a present to Marcus Twentyman?'

His lips parted as though he was suddenly short of breath. 'No – nothing as gross as that. Of course, I knew that Marcus had certain – tastes. It is true I knew he would find you attractive – but what man would not? – that was at the back of my mind – I thought of your good too – you said you wished to leave London.'

'I have borne him a child, and the child has been taken from me,' I said.

'Oh.' He looked a little older then. Drew his mouth tight, and I wondered if he might lecture me, like a clergyman. The rage swelled in me; I trembled with the effort of containing it. I was itching to slap him around the face, but reasoned that I had probably hurt him enough.

'That is hardly my concern. I am not responsible for your virtue,' he said.

'He took me to bed as his wife,' I said.

He was incredulous. 'Did you think yourself married

to Marcus?' He laughed again, despite his fear. 'You? An illegitimate servant? You really think too much of yourself, Annaleigh. There was no intention of that. Besides, didn't you know—'

'Did you tell him I was a foundling? Was that part of it all? Knowing I had no one to protect me?'

He shook his head, watching my hands, knowing that the knife was there.

'Where is my child?' I said. 'Where is Hester?' My voice rose to a scream. He was leaning away from me, still shaking his head.

'I do not know, Annaleigh, I do not know. I would tell you, I would tell you.'

I walked a circle, breathing hard, trying to gather my thoughts. I thought of Thomas waking in our lodgings, wondering where I was. I thought of my child, and how he would not wish his mother to be a murderer. Plaskett interrupted my thoughts, his voice breathy and slight in that room and its sickly sweet fumes. 'Please,' he said.

I looked at him. 'I cannot decide whether to let you live, or slit your throat now and spare the world more of your poetry,' I said. 'Tell me something. Persuade me to let you live.'

He drew his breath in. 'I am sorry,' he said, finally. 'Truly, Annaleigh. I do not know where Hester Twentyman is. You saw how they were with me. They despise me. They only invited me that night, I think, as a reward for sending you to them, and to make you feel a little safer – not that I even did that.'

'I do not believe your apologies.'

'Do not, then. But they are true. And I am sorry that you went through the charade of a wedding.' His face looked old in the light; he looked tired, and sad. 'I thought you knew he was already married.'

# CHAPTER THIRTY

I weaved my way through the crowds at speed, eager to be away from Plaskett's house. Thomas had told me London was full of men home from the wars; but I had no trouble. I was nimble and light-footed, and I did not stop for anyone. It was only when I reached my lodgings that I felt it: exhaustion, heavy on me, almost taking my legs out from under me as I sat down on the bed. Thomas had been pacing our dark little room by the sickly light of a taper; when I entered he rushed to me, but I said nothing.

'Where have you been?' he said.

I smiled, weakly. 'You are playing the brother role rather to the extreme,' I said. He turned away in exasperation, and swore under his breath. Then he was silent.

I closed my eyes, my head swimming.

'Why is there blood on your gown?' he said. 'Are you bleeding again? Are you unwell?'

I shook my head and swallowed hard. 'Do not worry,' I said.

He stared at me. 'We cannot continue this together if you do not tell me what you are doing, or what you plan to do. You have hurt someone, haven't you? Unless you are injured yourself, and you would tell me if that was true.'

I told him what had happened. 'He will not die,' I said. 'Men like Plaskett never die.' I thought of Sorsby, grinding his teeth with rage in the kitchen. And then of Jared, who had always been so gentle and full of goodness. And yet he was gone, and the wretched Sorsby lived.

'Annaleigh,' said Thomas. 'Listen to me. I understand all that has gone before, all that has brought you to this. But you are endangering your life, as well as your immortal soul – no, do not laugh, do not shrug, the girl I knew would never have taken things so lightly.'

'Lightly?' I cried.

'Will you stab me now, because I am not agreeing with you?' he said. 'Do not let your rage drive you. Plaskett is good for nothing, but you had no right to hurt him in such a way. No, you will not speak back to me on this. I know what is right. You must promise me, Annaleigh, that no matter what anger is in you, you will not hurt another person. You could have killed him. If you do this again, then I will go back to Yorkshire, and I will leave you to become a murderer and a thief and a whore, because that is what you will need to become to survive.'

I turned away from him, but he followed me around the room. His voice was softer when he spoke again.

'You are not those things, Annaleigh, but you could become them in a moment. When I look at you, I still see the girl who climbed down from that coach at Becket Bridge. That is who you are. Live as she would have lived and choose as she would have chosen. If you choose to follow your anger, then you will never get your child back, and Marcus Twentyman will have won.'

I gave him the knife, sat down, and put my head on his shoulder. We sat there for some time, in our shadowy room, as the light of the autumn afternoon faded outside. I told him Marcus had been married. At length he put one arm around me, and I tucked my tilted head beneath his chin. It reminded me of a time, long ago, when I had held a friend's baby on my lap, its little head looking out at the world, yet fitted comfortably beneath my chin: warm and safe.

'Does the man need a surgeon?' he said. 'Should I call upon him?'

I shook my head. 'The wound was slight, I promise you.'

'If you are lying to me—'

'I am not.'

'Very well,' he said.

'He told me nothing of use, Thomas. I am no closer to the child, or to even understanding why this happened. I do not know what to do.' Jared rose in my mind again, the shadow of hopelessness darkening my thoughts. 'Perhaps I must come to terms with it. The vanishing of everyone I ever loved.'

He squeezed me, and let me go. 'Do not give up. I have made enquiries. There is a house we can try, on Park Street. Hester lived there, when she was married, and I am told it is still held in her name, though it is shut up. We can go there this evening, if you wish.'

'To stand outside an empty house?' I said, disconsolately.

'It may not be empty,' he said. 'There are always servants.'

Hester had spoken of her grand life in London. Park Street was a short walk from Bond Street. Though it was elegant, it was not quite as I had imagined; from Hester's description, I had thought it paved in gold. We walked along the streets, passing houses lit by flaming torches, the stately rhythm of horses' hooves as grand carriages passed us, and the occasional flaring rage of a sedan-chair bearer being nudged out of the way by a hackney cab. The street was full of life, but when we reached the house that Hester owned, the windows were dark and shuttered.

Thomas tried the gate to the basement steps, but it was locked.

'It is closed up, as you were told,' I said, and realized, from the prickling of my eyes, that I had allowed myself to hope, for a moment, that my child might be there.

Thomas went up the front steps with a shrug, and knocked briskly. He stayed there a good length of time, knocking and knocking.

'I have to admire your patience,' I said, putting my hood up, and he raised his hand to quieten me.

'There is someone coming,' he said.

The woman who opened the door was an elderly servant with grey hair and reddened eyes. She looked tired and rather frightened. My presence agitated her; she constantly sought to make out my face beneath my hood, but Thomas soothed her with his presence as he asked for Hester, using her married name of Mrs Hume. As with horses, so with women, I thought, as he spoke to her gently and with a kind of tact that I could not have managed. At length she opened the door a little wider, and told us that Mrs Hume had not been there for over a year, nor was she expected. I could see that Thomas believed her, but he put a little doubt into his words, and so it was that she ushered us into the hall, and, having closed the front door carefully, opened the doors to the drawing room. 'Look, if you do not believe me,' she said, with a note of defiance, and walked ahead of us, holding her branch of candles.

I had been listening the whole time for a baby's cry. But there was no sound other than the click of the servant's boots on the floor, no matter how hard my raw senses sought for one. The drawing room was still and dead, the furniture covered in dust sheets, the clock stopped on the mantelpiece. One table had been left uncovered, a pretty little table which I could picture Hester taking tea at, and when I ran a finger along it the dust was thick.

"'Tis impossible to keep anything clean in the London air,' said the woman. 'I spend most hours in my parlour downstairs. There's been a spate of housebreakings recently. I have a pistol.' I could see her fear, and instinctively knew it was unlikely that she knew how to use the gun.

Desolate, I looked around the room. 'Is there anywhere else your mistress could have gone?' I said. It was the first time I had spoken, and I saw from the look on her face that I had startled her. She shook her head.

Thomas looked at me warningly. 'Forgive my sister, she is over-tired from the journey,' he said. 'But we are anxious to see Mrs Hume and we heard most definitely that she was returning to London from Yorkshire.'

'No.' The woman looked a little rattled; perhaps she thought she would have to clean the house, her nervous disposition fluttering over the idea that a letter had been sent which she had not received. 'I would have been sent word,' she said, 'and funds to re-engage servants. And Yorkshire? I have never heard mention of that.'

I could not help myself. 'If she would not come here, perhaps she would have gone to her brother's wife? She would have a child with her, a small baby.'

I saw her lips part slightly, the slightest movement, but one that betrayed her sudden agitation. It may have been my over-excited imagination, but in the uneven candle-light she seemed to have grown a little paler. 'I cannot help you,' she said. 'It is best if you go.'

'But you know something, do you not?' said Thomas

softly. He held out something to her; I saw the pale circle of the coin as he gave it to her.

The woman took it, and regarded it long before she spoke. 'Another visitor came looking for her. It was at least a year ago, perhaps more, I cannot tell. Time goes so slowly being in the house alone. She asked for a baby, too. Not for Mrs Hume. Just for a child.'

It was lucky that my shock rendered me speechless. I felt Thomas's hand on my arm. 'Did she give her name?' he said.

'Kate.'

I felt a swell of emotion rise in me, threatening to engulf me. I stayed still, knowing that I should not speak, Thomas's hand tight on my arm as he thanked the servant. When he asked for the address of Hester's sister-in-law, she shook her head.

'I have already said too much,' she said fearfully. 'I will not send you from this door to hers. Do not make mention of what I have said to anyone.'

Thomas's grip on my arm stayed me. 'We will keep your confidence, of course,' he said, and he gave her some more coins. 'But if, by any chance, your mistress does return, will you – quietly – send for me? My name is Bay. I am a friend of the family, and may be found most days at the Gloucester Coffee House, on Piccadilly.'

She nodded, but almost pushed us out of the house, back onto the steps. I saw her look up and down the street fearfully. As we walked away, she spoke again.

'She won't come back here, sir,' she said. 'Not if she can

help it. The day she left, she said she would only come back if she were driven to it.'

He nodded, tipped his hat, and took my arm. 'Don't say a word,' he murmured to me. So we hurried off into the night, and heard the slam of the door behind us.

# CHAPTER THIRTY-ONE

I dreamt of my son, that night. Dreamt that I held him close to me, felt his warmth and his life. His eyes were unseeing, and yet he knew that I was there, his skin against mine.

When Thomas woke on his truckle bed in the corner of the room, he heard me weeping, and came to me, putting his arms around me. 'Why are you crying?' he said.

'I cannot remember what he looks like,' I said. 'My son. I decided I would call him Jared, when I find him again, but how will I know it is him?'

I repeated the question, my face pressed against his chest. 'You will know,' he said, and he held me tight and rocked me like a child.

'And you were right,' I said. 'I do not know what I will do when I find him again. The law will not help me. I must run with him. How will I keep him? And yet I must go forwards. You understand, don't you?'

'Yes,' he said, in the darkness. 'I understand.'

I decided that I would disobey Melisende, and seek out Kit, though it took another flash of lightning for me to tell Thomas of my relationship with him, and the hopes I had once had. Grudgingly, he agreed that Kit might be able to help us in practical matters. I remembered well the name of the family he had married into. We took a hackney cab to Cheapside. He was not in the shop, but we were directed to a house a short distance away.

'So he doesn't live above the business?' said Thomas to me.

'He must have moved up in the world,' I said. It was a neat enough house, but the door was opened by an aged servant with an ancient and crooked wig, and when I looked at Thomas's raised eyebrows at the servant's airs and graces, it was all I could do not to laugh out loud.

We were shown into a panelled parlour, and within a few minutes I heard quick approaching footsteps. When the door opened, what I saw surprised me.

It had been little more than a year, but I sensed instantly that the young man who stood before me was a different Kit from the one I had known. His face was ruddier, and squarer somehow. Every feature had thickened. I wondered if I appeared so too, to him. What distressed me most were his eyes – those lazy blue eyes which had looked out from Jared's portrait of him as a toddler, and out of his face as an apprentice, were now reddened with tiredness, a certain fleshiness beginning below. I wondered at the sudden change in him over such a short time. A year had added ten in looks.

He still knew me: read the expression on my face, unguarded.

'Am I so different to you?' he said. And in answer I ran to him, and flung myself into those now sturdier arms.

He squeezed me, then released me, and nodded to the far corner of the room, where Thomas had turned away, seemingly to examine an ornament on the mantelpiece. There were lots of ornaments, and none of them in Kit's taste.

'Your name, sir?' he said, not unkindly.

Thomas presented himself: hat off, hand outstretched, he met Kit's eyes. 'Thomas Digby, at your service.'

'He means Thomas Bay,' I said, glancing at Thomas and realizing he was nervous, and had been shaken in some way to forget our cover.

Kit nodded as though nothing unusual had been said. The years of working in a shop had perfected his manners, I saw – like me he was made to serve, though in a nobler kind of way that didn't involve being on his knees and scrubbing floors. He had learned never to appear ill at ease, or short of words.

'I am pleased to meet you, Mr Bay. Miss Calvert is a kind of sister to me.'

'I know what she is to you,' said Thomas shortly.

'You will find us blunt,' I said. 'It is not ill-mannered,

where we have come from – things are spoken of differently in the north.'

Kit nodded again, and I could see him studying Thomas. I felt like telling him not to bother – that he would never win Thomas's approval after all I had said under the influence of gin. Thomas considered him weak in resolve, the very worst of sins.

'Please, both of you, sit down,' said Kit. 'I will ring for some refreshment. Though it will be basic – some beer, perhaps?' He went out, and came back some minutes later with a tray bearing beer, and some biscuits. 'I am afraid the apparatus of hot drinks is my wife's domain. I would need her here, to make it for me.' I sensed he was still trying to win Thomas's approval, debasing himself at his feet as though Thomas were some pagan god, emerged pure from the Yorkshire hills. He glanced at me too, but I was prepared, for we had both known the moment would come when I would have to acknowledge his wife.

'Where is Mrs Jacquard?' I said.

'She is resting. Our first child was born but a fortnight ago, and she is a little slow recovering her strength.'

I looked down to hide the tears that welled at the edge of my eyes. Heard Thomas mention horses, awkwardly and abruptly, so Kit could gratefully take up the conversation, and they could discuss things that had nothing to do with children, or tears.

When I had recovered myself I saw that Kit had not drunk a drop. He looked, stricken, into my face.

'It is not what you think,' I said. 'I am happy for you both.' Thomas downed his beer in one go and put the tankard haphazardly back on the table. He stood up, went to the window, and looked out, on watch again.

'Dearest Kit,' I said. 'I have come to you because I need your help.'

I told him my story, as briefly and quickly as I could, garbling some elements, rushing on as I saw horror and incomprehension cross his face. I had wondered how much to tell him, for it was possible it would change his feelings for me. I, after all, had been the innocent playmate of his youth, an unsullied love who had now fallen from his respectable world. When I had finished he put down his beer, still untouched, and stared at the floor.

Thomas still stood at the window, his gaze directed at the street.

'You are the only friend I have in London,' I said to Kit. 'Will you help me? I am glad you have a child. I weep for the loss of mine.'

'Did you go to Mother?' he said dully.

'Yes,' I said. 'But she never loved me as well as Jared did, and I cannot trust her.'

'Yet you trust me, when I failed you so grievously?' he said. 'You must know that I have often longed to see you, to weep in your lap and beg your forgiveness.' At this, Thomas cast him a look that was half-contempt, half-incredulity.

'There's no need for weeping,' I said, more stoutly than

I had intended, for it made Thomas smile. 'But I do need your help, and your loyalty.'

'You will have one, and you already have the other,' he said, and I saw then a flash of the old, dear Kit.

'Thanks,' said Thomas.

'We need a place to stay,' I said. 'We have already stayed too long where we are, and there may be people looking for us. We need somewhere decent, but where no questions will be asked. And I need money, Kit. Mr Bay has a little – and he has been a true friend to me, a brother indeed – but I do not wish to exhaust his resources.'

'My resources are yours,' said Thomas, low, but loud enough for Kit to hear.

'Anything I can do, I will,' said Kit.

The door to the drawing room opened then, with a little scrabble and fuss, as though the person behind it wished to announce themselves in some way. I rose to my feet and went to Thomas.

'Mr Jacquard?' Her voice was slight, a little dis-cordant. She stood in the doorway, uncertain in her own house, as Kit went towards her, saying her name soothingly. This then, was the woman I had envied. The woman I had glimpsed long ago in the crush at Snow Hill. Of course, she looked completely different, for memory and emotion are difficult bedfellows, and my mind had become a poor recorder of things. My memory had made her taller, more beautiful, elegant and in command. In truth she was small, slighter than me, and with rather bad teeth. Her skin was a particular shade of white – whiter almost than white – and it had a shine to it. Her hair was black, and her face had a kind of sweetness, dormant at this moment, but still visible. She, I gathered, was the owner of the ornaments, for she walked over to the mantelpiece and adjusted one that Thomas had touched.

'I thought we might walk out for half an hour,' she said, and I read the astonishment in Kit's face. I wondered if she had called the maid to report on the visitors, and had dressed accordingly. Fittingly for a draper's daughter, she was beautifully attired in a pale grey walking dress and a purple coat with blue piping, a purple bonnet tied on her head, bobbing with a plume.

'If you wish, my love,' Kit said. 'But first, may I present you to Mrs Bay, the daughter of a former servant of my parents, who requires some help of me.' Such a smooth, uncomplicated lie, spoken without faltering. His wife showed no flicker of recognition of me in her face. 'We grew up in parallel, and were friends when we were very young.'

'But you look so much older than my husband,' she said.

*You know me then,* I thought. I curtseyed, and answered her with a thick Yorkshire accent. 'I wish you a good day, madam.' I saw Thomas's back shaking slightly, for he had turned away, obviously amused at my poor attempt at the accent. I was worried that he would end up in a hysterical laughing fit, which had threatened me plenty of times over the past few days, and so we wished the couple farewell.

We were in the hallway when Kit came out, and sent the servant away.

'I know a lodging place for you,' he said. 'I will come to you – where are you staying?'

We named the street. 'God, Annaleigh,' he said. 'That you should have fallen so far.'

'I am not altogether lost yet,' I said, a little sharply. 'And I can order a good dinner. We shall expect you for it, this evening, at the Nag's Head, if Mrs Jacquard can spare you?'

'I cannot come this evening, but I will the next night. God bless you, and keep you safe.' He glanced at Thomas. 'Both of you.'

'My mother always warned me of the wiles of women,' said Thomas, when we were out on the street once more. 'She said some were half-serpent, and now I know what she meant. I was proud of you, Annaleigh. You kept your temper, for once.'

'Do not speak to me of my temper,' I said. 'What do you expect me to do? Besides, I owe her a courtesy. She is Kit's wife.'

'And a poor inconsequential thing she is too, to talk to you so,' he said. 'I am not surprised he wanted you instead of her. Fine clothes don't make a woman.'

'You have the vastly pleasing, but inaccurate, habit of comparing me favourably with every woman we come across,' I said. 'I thought it was the horses that wore blinkers, not you. I know what I am, dear friend. I see it in that little fragment of mirror in our room, every day. There is a scar on that fine mouth of mine, and my hair is turning its colour. I fear my spring and summer have come to an end. From now on I am autumn and winter.'

Thomas came to a halt, and turned me to look at him. 'Do not say such things of yourself. And will you at least let me, as a man, decide what I want to look upon? You are troubled, Annaleigh, but I swear I would rather look upon your face each day than any other woman's.'

The sweetness of his words, and the evident feeling with which he spoke them, shocked me. I pulled away, trying to lighten the tone when I spoke. 'If you continue to say such things to me, I will lose sight of all else and we shall be caught. No, Thomas Digby, do not try and kiss me. You are my brother, remember? We should not stop here. We should keep moving. If we must talk in such an earnest way, let it be in shadows.'

He had taken my hand, and in that moment, I was once again on the moors, on a distant Sunday, when he had taken me halfway to White Windows, and helped me down, my hand in his. That person seemed so distant now – and I but the shell of her, held together by my love for my child and my spleen. Was a part of her still on the moors, I thought? It comforted me, the idea that a trace of my spirit might be left behind, bedded down in the heather and the deep grass, beneath the hazards of the changing weather.

I drew my hand away from him. 'We will talk of this another time, and in another place,' I said. 'We must discover what Jared's connection with the Twentymans was, and if he knew more of them. Some small piece of information may help us find my boy. And I know who to ask.'

# CHAPTER THIRTY-TWO

We stood outside the colourman's shop in Long Acre for some time, watching people go in and out.

'It is not like you to hesitate,' said Thomas.

'Richard did not care for me overmuch as a child,' I said. 'I fancy I always took a little too much of Jared's attention.'

As I stood there, I remembered the way they had worked together, anticipating each other's thoughts. Their mutual understanding was so well-developed that they could spend hours working in silence alongside one another. In the studio, Richard, normally so clamorous, so full of energy, became quietly receptive to Jared's mood. Often I would watch them, Richard standing behind Jared's shoulder, the two of them silently regarding a painting, until they were ready to discuss what should be changed, what was right, and what was wrong. When I was older, I would stand there too and be part of that discussion, sensing without naming Richard's disquiet at my interruption of their perfect union. Jared was the sun around which we moved.

'Come on, then,' I said to Thomas. 'It's best we go in before I lose my courage.'

The door was sturdy, sticking at my first attempt to open it, so that Thomas had to pull hard, the bell clanging as he did so. I took a few steps into the shop, and the sight made me catch my breath: red, blue, yellow, violet – the light scintillating across the pigments in their bottles. The colours wild in their intensity, for all the perfect order and neatness of the shelves. Everything a painter wanted could be found in the shop: brushes, pencils, chalks.

I need not have worried about asking for Richard. He was the first person who came out at the sound of the bell, dressed in black with a neat white apron, his hair tied back, as always, his eyes that same mixture of keenness and cynicism. I only got a hint of his shock when he saw me. He stopped, and his lips parted slightly, but there was no other sign of emotion.

'Annaleigh,' he said. Then, looking down at the counter, and shifting something on it: 'You are a little late. Several months, if you wished to see him.' Something told me that he could not, yet, say Jared's name; that the sound of it would force emotion from him.

'I did not know what happened,' I said. 'Until now.'

His eyes roamed the colours on the shelves, and I had

the impression he was avoiding my gaze. 'Have you come to buy something?' he said. 'Can I interest you in vermilion? Orpiment? Prussian blue?'

'No, thank you,' I said, trying to ignore his scathing tone. 'I did not picture you in a shop. How do you find it?'

He shrugged. 'Mr Roberson is amiable enough. I mainly serve on the counter. Sometimes I stretch canvases. Sometimes I grind colours. I cannot handle the donkey that pulls the grinding wheels so well. It has taken against me.'

I heard Thomas give a splutter of suppressed amusement.

'Were you not able to find another studio?'

'Yes. But my affections were not in it. For a while I painted drapery for . . .' he paused, '. . . another fellow, but we oftentimes did not agree. A studio can be a close place, and a closed place.'

I smiled, remembering Jared and Richard's bickering on the rare days they did not agree, the occasional argument, the quiet silence Jared would adopt when Richard flung around his insults, the wire of his temper tripped by some stumbling remark of Jared's. Richard had lived too long with someone whose affection gave him freedom. I could not see him ringing up painters' accounts, or dealing with abrupt enquiries, with good humour.

'I may try another studio soon,' he said. 'Strange, that I should end up working somewhere like this. It was the colours that killed him, I think. I always told him he used too much lead white. How did you and your companion find me?' He had taken up a small item which had been put under the counter, and was working with his same neat thoroughness, wrapping a cake of colour in paper with a precision that was so redolent of the past, it was painful to look upon.

'Melisende told me your lodging address. I went there and they directed me here. I must speak with you on an urgent matter. But not here. I must – remain unknown, Richard. Please do not mention my name to anyone.'

'I wondered why you were cowering so mysteriously beneath the hood of your cloak. Stop it at once – you are drawing attention to yourself and every person in here can see your fear from a mile away. Come to my lodgings again tonight. I will hold off on my normal entertainments.' He said it with a certain bleak sneer. He waved away my attempt to come to him, for I wished to kiss him on the cheek. He went into the back of the shop without another word.

As we went out into the mid-afternoon light, the streets full of shoppers and traders, Thomas nudged me. 'He's right,' he said. 'You've been growing more stooped by the day, and people are looking at you. Stop trying to be covert, Annaleigh.'

I clipped him around the ear and tucked my hand in the crook of his arm.

'Have you thought more of what you will do?' he said. 'When you regain the child?'

'Why do you ask me that again?' I said. I felt cold. The future lay ahead, grey and blank, as the sky had so often been over White Windows. I had not dared to delineate any kind of future, without knowing whether my child would be with me. Whether he would live.

'I just think it is best to plan,' he said hesitantly.

'I will shift myself somehow,' I said to him. Then, changing the subject, 'It was good to see Richard. But ... he seems so hardened.'

'Why? Because he does not weep?' said Thomas. 'Grief takes different forms in different people. A man may seek to lose himself in a thousand different ways which show no sign of his deep wound to the watcher.'

'And what do you know of this?' I said, meaning to tease him. But he only looked annoyed.

'Do not jest with me,' he said.

'Thomas. Tom! You are my very dear friend. I did not mean to anger you.'

'Is that all I am?' he said. 'Is that all I'll ever be?'

There was something so set in his countenance, a toughness to his face, that it frightened me, then angered me, the two emotions coming upon me all at once, in one disagreeable combination. 'Now is hardly the time for making choices,' I said.

'What about my choice? I could be at home, but I have chosen this. And when you tease me about it, I can only wonder why.'

We were passing people: shoppers, sellers. I glanced worriedly around us.

'Only you can answer that.'

'I see. You have answers for everyone else, but not for me.'

'I have no answers!' I cried.

I carried on, striding forwards, then I realized he had stopped. Turning, I saw him standing there, his face ashen, staring at me. Then he came towards me, driven it seemed by some sudden impulse, and gathered my hands into his as he would a handful of reins, the sweet roughness almost making me laugh if it had not been for the serious look on his dear face.

'Will you marry me?' he said, and the words came out with such a burst of emotion that I knew he must have meditated on them for some time. Earning a cluck and a stare from a passing lady, who craned her head round even as she carried on down the road, to see if we were somebodies. But we were nobodies.

I touched his face, looked all around us, still in fear. 'Now is not the time,' I said. 'I cannot think.' I had wanted him once. Now, I had been emptied out by all that had happened. When I excavated for an emotion, nothing came.

'I am a man,' he said. 'I sleep in the same room as you each night. Have I ever complained? Ever been anything less than honourable?'

'You have been beyond honourable,' I said. 'But please, do not push me on this. I cannot help but see love – the love between a man and a woman – as a kind of plot, a way strewn with traps and hazards. What I feel for you is clear and plain – I beg you not to make it something different. It is about comfort, and kindness – do not look away – do not think I demean you with these words.'

He let go of me.

'Thomas, do not turn away like that, as though you were some stupid conventional lover spurned. I do not sigh over thoughts of Marcus. I am exhausted. For now, I only have the energy to hate. If the time comes when I am able to feel as a person should, I would wish to love unencumbered by all the shadows and darkness that crowd round me now.'

'It is all the same to me,' he said. 'The same answer, no matter how you talk around it. We will not talk of it more. I wish I could leave you, at this moment, dishonourable as it is, but I cannot.'

'I am sorry for it, to be a pain, and a trouble to you.'

He saw off my words with a shake of his head. 'I will accompany you back to the lodging,' he said. 'Then I must go to the coffee house, and see if there are any messages for me. There is work to be done. That is how I will view it, from now on.'

It was his turn to walk ahead now, and mine to watch him. He was so tall, his greatcoat almost down to his ankles, and he walked straight and strong, alongside the palisade of black iron railings, on this London square.

When he returned that afternoon he told me of what he had read in the London papers, and it was not the Waterloo subscription or the situation in France which had caught his attention. It was the bad money uttered, the skirts and shifts stolen, and the mad bull being kept for baiting in Westminster. 'This is a dark city,' he said to me. I could not help but think that he now thought of me as part of the darkness.

*

Richard lived in a house on Great Queen Street. When we arrived, a little after seven, he was not there, and his landlady made us wait rather awkwardly in the front hallway, going back to the warmth of her fireside and shouting warning to the maid. Thomas was still cross with me, and he paced up and down, slowly, without speaking.

A few minutes later I heard a scrabble at the door, and Richard came in, calling to his landlady as he did so. He was neat and perfectly groomed in his black coat and hat, holding a paper package in one gloved hand, a silver-topped cane in the other.

'I have bought some hot chestnuts for us, little one,' he said. 'I remember how you loved them. I have rooms on the first floor. I will lead, and mind your step – the stairs are steep. Good evening, Mrs Wilcox, may I light my candle?' The last was shouted in a jovial, I thought rather theatrical, tone.

The room we entered was all in darkness, the shutters already shut. 'I never open them,' he said, lighting tallow lights, and stirring up the fire in the grate which his landlady had set for him. His sitting room was neat but crowded, with pictures and sketches pasted or hung in every conceivable space on the wall. Many of them were by Jared, and shock pierced me at the sight of them. It was like seeing the handwriting of one loved and long-dead on a letter, tricking the mind into believing, just for a moment, that they live again. With his usual flair Richard had increased the cosiness of the room by layering rugs on the floor. These too were from the studio, and although they were threadbare there was still something of their scarlet plushness about them.

That he had remembered the chestnuts silenced me with emotion; I sat down, looking at them as he tore the packet open.

'I thought I was a burden to you, as a child, always under your feet,' I said. 'I never expected you to remember such a thing.'

'So you are,' he said, hanging a kettle above the fire, 'but Jared loved you, and now that he has gone, I love you for his sake. I meant to ask earlier – what happened to your face?'

'An accident,' I said.

'And who are you?' Richard said to Thomas, leaning on the edge of the mantel. 'Did you do this to her?'

'I did not,' said Thomas heatedly, abruptly.

'That's good,' said Richard. 'A fine, strong answer that leaves no room for doubt. Take a seat by my fire, then, and eat some of the chestnuts. You were together earlier – is he your shadow, Annaleigh?'

'And my protection,' I said, not daring to look at the wounded expression on Thomas's face, for I could see what today had cost him, though others would only see his sternness.

I did not realize how hungry I was until I began to eat the chestnuts, the skin charred black, the succulent earthy flesh awakening my taste with an intensity so keen that it almost sent a shiver of hurt across my tongue. Thomas ate too, more politely and slowly than I, and after a moment or two a grin spread across his face at the sight of me wolfing them down. 'Don't stand on ceremony,' he said.

'Cram 'em in, little one,' said Richard. 'I don't care for them myself.'

We drank weak tea together, as I told Richard my story, another retelling which seemed to bring it nearer to me yet make it more tenuous, somehow eluding my grip. As I told each person, I found I watched the ways in which the listener reacted, any flicker of incredulity a hurtful doubting of my own private sorrow.

'There was a portrait in the house,' I said. 'It was painted by Jared, and signed by him. It was one of the only modern portraits there, so Marcus must have taken it to Yorkshire with him.'

Richard frowned. 'Had Jared known anything of the family which echoed what you have told me, he would never have sent you there. You surely do not suspect some connection?'

I was silent, the chestnuts all gone, always straining to hear over the sound of our conversation and the crackle of the flames, thinking that there might be a knock on the door. I doubted everything.

'She must have sat for a portrait,' I said.

'The name is not familiar,' he said. 'But I have Jared's visitors' books, and we can look through them.'

'You kept them?'

'Of course. I kept as much as I could. It was a way of keeping him with me. And Melisende was no use. He was only just cold before she cleared the place out. Said she could not bear to see anything of his. And of course, I was the first to go – I took what I could carry.'

He brought the books out in his arms, well-thumbed, slim little books, covered in scuffed red morocco. We sat down and looked through them, all three of us, companionable in the warm silence.

Name after name passed my eyes, in Jared's neat, beloved hand. He had been meticulous in the way he recorded his sitters, and as I read the entries I could hear his voice, for he had often told me of the characters of those he painted.

'Thursday last, Mrs McIntosh. Has seen the portrait of Mrs P, and wishes something similar. Claret-coloured silk and wishes much made of her hands. Agreeable. Children: James, Edward, Jemima, Rebecca (now dead, not forgotten). Likes music, be sure to raise it. Gives an animation to her face that speaking of her husband does not.'

It was hard not to be caught up in his words, in those careful notes which had made him such an excellent host and a perceptive painter. Still my eyes moved on, up and down each page two or three times, to be careful I did not miss something.

'Annaleigh.' Richard reached out, and touched my arm. I leaned, looked forwards over his shoulder. I could see no Twentyman in the first column, where the sitter's name was recorded.

'Where?'

'Look.' He had to point at it, the tiny note beneath the name.

'The twenty-second day of September, 1803. Miss Emma Faulkner. To be married to Marcus Twentyman Elton, Esq, this winter. A portrait for her father.'

'Do you not remember her?' he said. 'I do, now I see it written there.'

I shook my head, trying hard to be calm, for at the sight of Marcus's name, even with the unfamiliar addition of the surname Elton, the vision of him had come to me powerfully. I could see him, smell him, look into those mournful eyes. I felt Thomas's hand on mine, unfurling my fists. 'Take a deep breath,' he told me.

'She lives in Mayfair,' Richard said. 'On Bruton Street, Berkeley Square, I believe. I thought her husband was abroad in the wars, though I do not know what gave me that impression. But you should remember her, Annaleigh. The day of her first sitting, you watched from the studio window as she came down from her carriage, two hours late. Jared was near-frantic.' He glanced at Thomas. 'Children never remember the same things as the adults do.'

I tried to remember, and though something shifted in my mind, the stirrings of a ghost of a memory, I wondered if it was my imagination.

'She was very beautiful,' he said. 'She goes by the name Elton, the family name of those who own the estate, Gracegrave. That is why I did not think of her immediately.'

'I know the name of the house,' I said, 'it was told to me once. But Marcus never said he was from the Elton family. He only went by Twentyman.'

'That was old uncle Jack's name,' said Thomas. 'And convenient enough for him to use, if he did not wish to be known, which he evidently didn't.'

'What else do you know of her?' I said.

'Golden hair, and blue eyes,' Richard said.

The words tapped a deep recognition in me which the painting had not. The girl with the golden hair. Marcus turning, in his bed, asking for *the one with the golden hair.*

'I always wondered who she was,' I said, half to myself, and saw that Richard was no longer looking at me, but at my companion. I glanced at Thomas. He was frowning, and I saw the signs of strain on his dear face.

'Thank you, Richard,' I said. 'You have helped us so very much.'

'Let me write her last address for you, as I remember it,' he said. 'And if you need anything else, little one, then I am here many evenings. You and this very handsome young man may consider me your friend.'

Later, as I lay in bed back at the lodging, my head resting on one arm, searching my memory, it came to me. 'My God,' I said.

Thomas turned and looked at me enquiringly.

'I remember it. The day she came to the studio. I cannot – can I? It seems so clear, and yet, I do not know if I can trust my recollection of it.'

The evening of the day Jared and Richard had argued, I had heard it: but just the wisp of it, like candle smoke. Their voices, Jared's and Melisende's, distant, raised – perhaps anger, perhaps despair, but something uncommon. Something I did not want to hear, in that house, with its beautiful midnight stillness.

The special chicken dish Melisende made the next day for dinner did not heal Pa, or make him less restive as he prepared for the lady who was coming to have her portrait taken. He and Richard moved the canvas scores of times, as Kit and I sat quietly in the corner of the studio, playing with Kit's model soldiers. Jared asked for one canvas; then another, primed, a different size.

'Where is she?' he said eventually, looking at his pocket watch.

'There is plenty of time yet,' said Richard softly.

'The light is changing,' said Jared. He knew every tone of light and shade in that room, knew how a face would be softened or brightened by it. A person, he had told me, could have a dozen different characters, depending on the light you saw them by.

That is why I left Kit playing, and came to be at the window when the carriage arrived outside, so I could be first to tell Jared to stop fretting, that she had come. I was used to watching sitters arrive from the window of the studio. I liked to watch the patterns of expectancy on their faces, their doubts, their pride, their hundred different emotions as they walked up our front steps. I did not watch openly – what fine lady or gentleman would want a little girl's eyes boring into them from an upper storey as they negotiated the steps of their carriage? – but covertly, from the side of the window, half-obscured by the heavy green drapes which Richard drew every evening after Jared had finished his work and closed the shutters.

'She is here!' I shouted, joyful.

'Kit, clear those toys away, I have told you a hundred times,' said Richard, clapping his hands, watching, as he always did, my father's face. There was so much love in that house: layers of it.

The lady stepping delicately down from her carriage seemed wary of the street, of the very air, as though it was contaminated. She was wearing a hooded cloak, which gave her a clandestine air. Her maid, rather than a male servant, waited patiently for her, holding out her hand in case she wished to take it.

The lady looked up at the window and, unusually, caught sight of me. Her face was unremarkable, apart from her eyes, which, even at that distance, had a haunting quality, piercing in the demi-gloom of the autumn afternoon. In a strange way, just like Marcus's eyes. I see them as blue in my memory, but I can hardly have seen their colour from such a distance; I had filled in my memory, shaping it from Richard's remarks, as Jared did when he touched his paint onto the canvas. Her gaze moved away, and she went forwards, out of sight.

'Who is she?' I said. I felt the reverberation of the front door as it shut behind our visitor. Our house was so elegant, with its à la mode classical proportions, but the walls were like paper.

'If you mean my afternoon sitter,' said Jared, gazing at

his watch, 'she is a young lady who is about to be married, and you'd best go.'

If he hadn't been in such a subdued mood, he would have allowed me to stay, shyly watching from the corner of the room. Would things have been different, if I had stayed? I know now that a single word can alter the course of a whole existence, and on insignificant moments are whole lives built and lost. I wonder if that lady might have sent me on some better way. But Jared was sad, from his arguments with Richard and Melisende, and so he made me an outsider. Sent from the room, I saw her only from a distance.

The first Mrs Twentyman.

# CHAPTER THIRTY-THREE

I lay awake all night, thinking of Marcus's first wife, wondering if she had ever been to White Windows. Hester had told me that he had gone into hiding, after the duel. If it was true, his wife must have stayed in London. Yet, in his delirium, he had asked for her. Her initials had been sewn on the sheet I had been wrapped in after the baby was born. I had looked for signs of Kate, the former housekeeper, everywhere in that cursed house. And yet, there was another: her portrait in the gallery, her initials on the sheets. I needed to see her face.

It was not hard for us to find the house where Emma Elton lived. The address Richard had given us was an old one, but when I made enquiries at Gunter's Tea Shop on Berkeley Square, I pretended to be a servant, and mentioned the past address as the one I had served at. I was directed there.

'I have never seen such a place,' said Thomas, looking at the tall, elegant houses, and the maturing gardens of the square. 'It is grand indeed.'

I had been trying to shake off my unease. I could see nothing beautiful in the houses, or the serene square. I longed to be back in the clamour of a busier place.

'Let us go there, then,' I said.

'It is the visiting time,' said Thomas. 'You cannot expect her to see you if she is already called upon. Even if she is alone, they may not let us in.'

I saw the quality of his glance in my direction. We were not dressed to call upon such a house. I shook off Thomas's suggestion to go to the tradesman's entrance. 'Then, she will not see us at all,' I said. 'It is true we do not have the town polish, but I will make sure we get entry, believe me.'

The maid who opened the door had a pointed incredulity to her expression when we asked to see Mrs Elton. 'Do you have a card?' she said, when Thomas handed her a coin.

'I have no card,' I said, interrupting Thomas before he could say anything. 'But you may tell your mistress that I come from White Windows.'

Her face told me everything; a moment of shock, then she slammed the door.

I reached for the knocker, but Thomas stayed my hand. 'Easy, lass,' he said.

We stayed on the front step, and at length the sound of footsteps approached the door. The maid opened it, her façade once more in place, but her pertness gone. 'Mistress is not at home,' she said.

'I'll wish you a good day then,' said Thomas, tipping his hat, and pulling, half-dragging me down the front steps. 'Keep walking,' he said. 'It was dangerous enough to come here. When we see your stepbrother tonight we must press him to find us another place to stay. If this Mrs Elton is as Richard says, she will have no scruples, just like her fine husband.'

We walked briskly, side by side, and I was lost in the agony of my thoughts, so we did not hear the pounding of running footsteps mixed in with the sounds of London, but when a voice came crying 'sir, sir', Thomas turned.

It was a footman, dressed in a fine livery of green coat and black plush breeches, but with his wig off, as though he had been sent quick from the house.

'Begging your pardon, sir, ma'am,' he said, with a look that indicated this was the very last thing he was doing. 'Mistress says will you come back?'

We glanced at each other. 'Gladly,' said Thomas.

The boy took us into the house through the tradesman's entrance, through a corridor with service rooms coming off to the left and the right, the staff in them still and watching, one moving forwards to throw the footman his wig, which he positioned as he walked. As we came up into the entrance hall I gripped Thomas's arm. It was so beautiful, the walls painted in imitation of Italian marble, the gilded details in the ceiling picked out in a backdrop of searing white.

The footman showed us into the drawing room. I saw her back at first, dressed in a gauzy white dress decorated with thin green stripes, her hair piled high and fixed with a plain green ribbon, a straw bonnet on the chair nearby. She had been about to go out.

I crossed the room quickly, a little too quickly, so that we could see each other at last. I wanted to look her in the eyes.

When she turned, I caught my breath in the shock of recognition, even though I had expected it. Here was the woman in Jared's painting. He had caught her just right, although not the air of gentleness with which she moved, something in direct opposition to what I had thought about her.

She was less than ten years older than me, and yet, from a different world. I had learned to work, to make things. The only time I had to think of my hair was on a Sunday; when I was working my only concern was whether it was tied back neatly enough, and the cost of clothing had made it a secondary concern. This lady was different: I observed her pinned curls, the large pearl drops which must have cost Marcus a king's ransom; the fine fabrics which wrapped her slim body, showing the white skin of her shoulder, every curve visible, yet covered. She was everything she was meant to be.

*The girl with the golden hair*, I thought. How bitterly

Marcus must have regretted parting from her. Was it her presence, then, and not Kate's, that I had felt so often in White Windows? Just out of reach, as though in the next room, or moving ahead, just past the turn of the stairs.

She looked at me, and then spoke to the servant. 'Devon, make sure to close the shutters in the drawing room by the middle of the day. Imagine if the paintings and furniture were ruined by the sun. It is strong, even at this season.' She turned back to us. 'My father-in-law would be so angry. And tea, please. At once.'

The footman left the room. She smiled at us, her eyes lingering on Thomas. 'I call them after the counties, you know. Devon, Dorset, Kent. It saves me having to learn their names, which would be so very tiring. He is my third Devon, and I do not think he will stay here long. He seems so very cross when I ask him to do things.'

She came towards me without any hesitation, with a focused energy, so that I had to suppress the desire to step back, as she extended one beautiful white hand. 'I am Emma Elton.'

'Do you have a servant called York?' I said. I saw the perfect sense in her eyes.

'Annaleigh,' said Thomas, in a low voice.

'Please, do sit down,' she said. 'And no, Annaleigh, I do not have a York. I am a woman of sensibility, and to say that name would be very hurtful for me, do you understand?' She sank down onto the ottoman, upholstered in green silk. I couldn't help but notice that the stripes on her dress matched the furnishings, and felt a twisted glimmer of humour. It was best that I did not laugh; I knew that if I began, I would not stop.

'How do you know my name?' I said.

'I was told to expect you,' she said, a little discomposed for the first time.

'By your husband.'

'Yes,' she said, rising again and going over to a small table, where she opened a drawer and withdrew something. 'By my husband.' And, as if to offer proof, she handed me a portrait miniature.

It was of Marcus, and it was a picture of perfect sensitivity. He was alive in it: the same dark, unruly hair, the same nervous quality to his gaze, as though a fire might be lit in his eyes at any moment. He had always been on that edge, I realized now: ready at a moment's notice to cover one with kisses, or else hurl a chair across the room.

'It is very like, is it not?' she said.

I was still staring at it when the footman brought in the tea. She made it herself, telling him to leave, then handed each of us a cup.

'I must be frank with you,' I said.

'Must you?'

'You seem to know of me, but I know nothing of you. Marcus married me.'

'Please.' She held up a hand. 'If you must speak of him, call him Mr Elton. If he has led you to think such a thing, then, I am sorry. He goes to such lengths, but I did not realize he would pretend such a thing. And I really know little of you, other than that you had a little baby boy, and he is beautiful. He is not here!'

I had risen to my feet, and Thomas also, putting his cup down with a clatter. 'Do not trifle with us, madam,' he said. 'Where is the child?'

'I do not know,' she said. 'I have not been told that. They would hardly bring him here. And the truth is I know little of you. I met the other girl.'

'Kate?' Her reaction was enough to confirm it.

'Yes. She came here once.'

'And she had a child too.' Thomas's voice was low, and grief-stricken.

'Yes, a girl. Marcus did not want a girl. And besides, she did not fulfil her other purpose.'

'What other purpose?'

She looked at the miniature, now in her hands. 'I am not to speak of such things.'

'Speak it!' I could have struck her, and it must have been clear in the way I stood, for Thomas came to me and put his hands on my shoulders, partly to comfort me, partly, I believed, to hold me back if necessary.

There was resoluteness as she said what was obviously far beneath her.

'She was not – *virgo intacta*? – not pure. You see, he wanted two things: a son, and to be cured.'

I remembered suddenly Hester, Hester with her intricate medicine cabinet, filled with packages and pills.

'He said his body ached all the time,' I said. 'I thought he was melancholy.'

'A friend of his swore he was cured by being with a virgin,' she said, her eyes down. 'He was not ill when we married. There was such a quality of sweetness to him – to his melancholy. He has a great soul. If he was a little wild, then that was only from the company he kept. He became ill the year after we married.' She swallowed, hard, and I wondered if she would manage to speak the words.

'What is it?' I said. She could not meet my eyes. Just for that moment.

'The French pox.'

I stared at her. 'Say the word,' I said. 'You may read it on the front of the newspapers every day. Or shall I say it? Syphilis.'

She looked down at her right hand, her thumb flicking at her little finger. 'He did not tell me until it was too late and even if he had – I would have stayed with him. The doctor was very harsh to him. He said it was a death sentence, but I do not believe that. You see how well I am? And Marcus too has been well, for a long time. Not like his older brother, Robert. He is mad, now. I was meant to marry him; we were intended as children. He will never breed now, and there must be an heir.'

I looked at Thomas. Saw that his hands were shaking, and that he stayed standing where he was only through force of will.

'Why did you not bear him a child?' I said, and it came out as an accusation.

She looked up at last, and I saw that I had remembered that piercing blue glance correctly. 'I did. The baby was unwell, although I saw the perfection in him. When the sores came, I could not look at him any more. I could not bear to hear him cry, knowing that I, we, had done that. He died. There is a memorial to him at Gracegrave, ten times the size of his tiny body. It shows how we wept for him.'

'Dear God.' Thomas rose from his seat, and turned away; paced the length of that grand drawing room.

Emma Elton needed no further encouragement to speak. 'That girl – Kate. She would not go away. She would not be quiet. In the end, they were forced to quieten her.'

'Is she dead?'

'Of course not! At least, I think not. She was transported for stealing. When she came to London, Hester said she had taken a candlestick, and she was put on trial for it and found guilty. So you see, Annaleigh. You must be quiet. You are better than her. Marcus wrote to me once, "she is so innocent", and I see that you are, even after everything. And if it means anything to you, I am so very sorry.'

I rose. I watched Thomas, continuing his pacing, as though he was alone in the room. She took up the miniature again.

'I met him at Almack's. Do you know they have waltzes there, now? Imagine it. Those bare rooms, and the worst refreshments you can imagine.'

I brushed at Thomas's arm. 'We must go.'

'I will help you,' she said, as we made our way across the room. 'If you will only be quiet. You may have money. And you seem a very sweet kind of girl. Let me help you find another place. You may begin again.'

I said nothing, but heard the patter of her feet behind me.

When I turned, she stood close to me. Held my gaze, looking at my eyes as though they had resolved out of the dirty London mud.

'He has hurt me,' she said. 'I have wished, many times, that I was not bound to him. I am not meant to say it, but I say it to you, because you have known him. That is the third miniature I have owned. Every time I break it, he replaces it. You may be free. I cannot.'

I thought of all that she had told me. 'I do not think either of us can be free now,' I said.

# CHAPTER THIRTY-FOUR

I remember every step I took to get back to our lodgings.
I remember the colour of the paving stones, rough-hewn
and pale, so different from the grey stone of Yorkshire.
I remember the mulch of the autumn leaves which the
crossing sweeper had not cleared away. I remember
the slip I took, the almost-fall, putting my hand out to
Thomas, scrambling to stay upright, and how I suddenly
became aware of my heart, beating so hard in my chest, as
though it might rise up and burst out of my throat.

*I am still alive*, I thought. And then: *I want to live.*

I scrambled up the staircase of our lodging house
before Thomas, knowing that I would be overcome. It
was as though I stayed the shock of the blow until I could
finally release it, and when I sank down onto the bed
in the corner of the room, it came from me in juddering

gasps. It was not just the discovery of the illness Marcus had; the putting together of a thousand pieces into one, terrible whole. It was the knowledge that my child might be ill too, and that Thomas and I could never be together now.

'You may not have it,' Thomas said to me, his voice hopeful but broken.

'And yet I may, and my poor boy too,' I said, and turned away from him. 'Do you still want to marry me now?'

Behind me, he put his arms around me. I felt his face against mine. I could not see his face, but I could feel the reverberation of my grief in him.

'I do,' he said. He rocked me gently, as I had rocked my doll when I was young, and we wept together, without looking at each other's faces. When, at length, I had ceased to cry, and spoke again, it was with a resolution which rose spontaneously from the ashes of what I had been – suddenly, and whole.

'You should leave me to finish this alone,' I said.

'I cannot go,' he said. 'I will not go. It would be easier for me if I could, but God knows it is as if my feet are fixed to the floor in any room that you are in. And nothing, nothing that that uncommonly dull woman can say, will send me from you.'

I wriggled free of his arms. Saw that his face glistened with sweat or with tears, I could not tell. 'I am so sorry,' I said. 'It is likely that I am infected. I am unclean. How can I ever be your wife?'

'I love you,' he said. And he kissed my mouth, and my

cheeks, and my forehead. We lay alongside each other, closer than we ever had before. Looking at each other with care. I remember every detail of his face. Just as I remembered the shape of his back on the journeys we had taken. By the evening, he had grown a shadow of hair on his face, and even now, I feel the bristle of it on my fingertips.

That night, we had agreed to meet Kit for dinner. He came promptly, moving with a briskness that surprised me. He seemed a little puzzled and disturbed by my reddened eyes and our subdued demeanours. The dinner was poor, despite my vouching for it. He talked of his business, of his child and his wife, and I saw that he was contented with his lot. Melisende, I thought, had been right after all.

I toyed with my greasy chop, but the men ate heartily. I wondered at my nausea; wondered if I, like Emma, had been given the disease by Marcus. I remembered a sitter of Jared's, a minor nobleman, and Melisende talking of his fate. She had viewed the disease as a punishment from God, and had spoken of its symptoms until Jared hushed her. She had meant me to hear. Protected as I was, she wanted me to know of the dangers that she had observed inflicted on others: faithful wives, she hinted, could end their days in the Lock Hospital, thanks to unfaithful husbands. Perhaps I too would become ill, as that nobleman had done, the inner tissues of my body bubbling with corruption, destroyed from the inside out. In my seemingly healthy body, the silent traitor would work on dissolving me, until at last I became mad.

I watched Kit talk, and remembered how, as an apprentice, he would go out with the other apprentices into the London night. He had told me a little of it, the strange new knowing in his eyes, and I wondered if he had been with women of the night, the beautiful ladies of Covent Garden with their feathers and their powder, like the women who had come to masquerade at White Windows. I did not doubt it. And I wondered too if he had briefly borne a black chancre, the signal of the beginning of a process, the blighting of a life.

'But enough of all this merriment,' said Kit, rather falsely I thought, so that I had to suppress a bleak choke of laughter. I had not listened to a word he had said for the past quarter of an hour. He drank back the contents of his glass. 'We must act, it seems. I said I could give you lodgings – well, I can, of course, if that is what you wish – but some people came to the shop today. They were asking for you.'

'What was their appearance?' said Thomas.

'I can say that plainly. They were members of the watch. They were seeking you, Annaleigh, saying that you had taken a precious silver candlestick. They know of your connection with me. I do not believe a word of it, of course I do not. What I am saying is, that I will find you a lodging, of course, if you wish, but—'

'But you cannot harbour me,' I said.

He looked a little ashamed. 'It would be death to my father-in-law's business, and to my livelihood, if I was found to be helping you. And it seems to be not good sense to do so. You are hardly safe, as they know of our connection.'

'It is all well, Kit,' I said. 'You need not say any more. And you have already stayed too long. What if they followed you?' I rose from the table, Thomas and Kit following.

'Let me pay for the dinner,' Kit said. 'Will you drink another glass with me?'

'It is not safe to do so,' I said, and though I did not mean to be cruel I saw how it hit him. I reached out, and touched his face. 'I am not angry with you,' I said. 'Goodbye, dearest Kit.' He looked into the depths of his empty glass. Then he kissed my cheek, shook Thomas's hand, and went, the briskness of his step only barely decent.

Thomas and I were silent, exhausted by despair as we settled the bill. I knew I could hardly ask him to continue with me in such a slough; and it seemed the baby was further from me than ever. I ached to hold him, one more time. I wondered if we would ever see each other this side of heaven.

As we were paying, the door of the inn opened and I, ever watchful, glanced over to see Emma Elton's housemaid looking around. At the sight of me, her looking stopped and she advanced towards me.

'What do you want?' I said. 'And how did you find me?'

'Stephen followed you this afternoon,' she said. '*Devon*. He was sent by my mistress, on account of him being the swiftest on his feet. He told me where you were. Hasn't stopped moaning about the cold, either.'

'Would you like a drop of ale?' I said, and saw Thomas glance at me. She assented; took her seat with us. She was not as cynical as she seemed; even as she drank, she took in my face, and expression, with a kind of curiosity that showed me I had inspired gossip in the servants.

'So what is your business with us?' I said. 'You were sent for some reason?' I kept my eyes on the door, opening and closing, expecting at any moment to see a constable.

She took a letter from her pocket, and handed it to me. The seal was broken.

'You've read it?'

She shrugged. 'Of course. Why? Are you going to tell on me? I thought on account of you being a servant yourself you might understand. That's the case, isn't it? You served at White Windows?'

'It's not right that you read the letter,' said Thomas, who had ordered himself another ale.

'She probably knows most of the contents of it anyway – don't you?' I said, reading it. 'Perhaps even why it has been sent.'

The servant sat motionless, her dark eyes without expression. She picked up her tankard and gulped down the ale.

'Not telling?' I said, then to Thomas, 'Mrs Elton wants to see us. She says she has more information for us, and would be grateful if we would call upon her tomorrow.'

Thomas looked doubtful.

'Cat got your tongue?' I said to the servant.

'Thanks for the ale,' she said, rising. 'I don't know what she wants to speak to you about. I've never known someone keep things so close to her. She has been a fair mistress to me – good wages, good allowances, and even a kind word now and then – but she doesn't think of me as a person, I know that. And the others say she is capable of great cruelty. So what can I tell you? Nothing I've seen with my own eyes. Will you tell me something, though? How is he? Mr Elton?'

I saw it in her eyes. As I had seen it in the others'. 'Are you in love with him too?' I said. She shook her head. 'Not that. He was kind to me, once. I was sorry when he went away.'

Thomas rose, took her tankard, his and mine, clearing the table and ending the conversation. 'We do not know how he is, and nor do we wish to. Good night.'

We went to our room miserable, but alert. As we reached the top step, I stopped, and grasped Thomas's hand. 'The door is open,' I whispered.

He moved to pass me and go in first. But I shook my head, and went forwards at a run, shoving the door open as hard as I could.

The figure came out from behind the door with the swiftness of a cat's shadow; I swung, my hand was caught, hard, my arm turned and I was dragged to the floor with a shriek. I heard it first: 'whoa, whoa, whoa,' as Thomas ran at the figure, then stopped, and then, from the light of a candle, I saw the familiar shape of the face.

'Bloody hell, lass, I knew you had some fire in you, but would you really batter an old man so?'

As I looked up at him, rubbing my arm, I saw with deep relief that the shadow was Edward Digby.

# CHAPTER THIRTY-FIVE

After both men had sworn copiously, Mr Digby embraced his son, and then looked appraisingly at me.

'You both look like death,' he said. Then he downed the half of porter he had left on the table in the corner. 'No,' he said, 'worse than that.'

'Thanks,' I said.

Thomas was lighting more tapers. 'Aiming to set the house on fire, boy?' said his father, appreciatively.

'You said you'd never come to London again,' said Thomas.

'I did. So you did listen to me? I'm an old man now. Those I associated with here are mostly in the church-yard, no doubt. What harm can they do to me?' I saw the unease in his eyes. 'Besides, there seemed no other way of speaking to you. God knows I don't trust the post from the Cross Keys now. But you leave mighty large footprints for people who are trying to be lost. All I had to do was walk into the tavern next door and describe you. Don't you know what hats and hoods are for?'

'You see?' I said to Thomas, who looked both amused and ashamed. 'He always told me to take my hood down.'

'You told me to lodge here, so you knew where we were. And if we are so obvious why haven't the watch found us?' said Thomas.

Mr Digby laughed. 'Some landlords don't like the watch, and some do. And some watchmen are thicker than others. You've always been lucky, Tom. But they'd have caught up with you soon enough. Anyhow, I am here with important business. You won't have found the child.'

'No,' I said.

'Because the child never left Yorkshire,' he said, and looked concerned as I sat down on the bed. 'Whoever told you he had, was spinning you a pretty tale.'

'Who said it to you?' asked Thomas.

'Jeanne,' I said. 'Jeanne told me.'

'I never liked her,' said Mr Digby confidently. 'Only met her once, but I always say: never trust a woman who plays dumb. We'd best get you out of this city, madam.'

'Where is the baby? Have you seen him? Is he well?'

'Whoa, there. The answers are: I don't know; no; and I don't know. But word is Miss Hester took him to Shawsdrop. One of our friends from the meeting house had sight of him. Trust in God's networks, my girl.'

Shawsdrop. Within sight of the route I had followed

across the moors. I shook my head, numb with exhaustion and disbelief.

Mr Digby sat down beside me. 'If you don't want to go back, you can disappear. I can help you do that – and if you wish to take Thomas with you, well, then. We will grieve, but it will be God's will. God's will be done, is what I say.'

'I cannot disappear. I must claim the child.'

'There's a surprise. And what will you do when you find him? Do you think they will just let you walk out of the house with him? If you take the child from his father they will clap you in irons for stealing, just as if you had taken their blessed silver candlestick. Have you thought of that?'

'Will you all stop asking me such things!' I cried. 'I will gain him. I will see his face again. And then I will find some way of living.' I got to my feet. Walked away, the few steps I could.

'It has been a hard few days, Father,' said Thomas. 'We have much to tell you.'

Mr Digby nodded. I saw the tiredness and the sorrow in his face. 'Let us go, then. See if we can catch the mail coach. I'll settle the bill.'

I turned to Thomas again. 'I must see Mrs Elton, one last time. Let us go there now. We do not need to wait until tomorrow morning. I have had enough of waiting.'

Thomas shook his head. 'No. It is too dangerous.'

'I will go alone if I have to. We have barely scratched the surface of what she knows.'

'I do not doubt it. But there is nothing she can say which will change things. You may be walking into a trap.'

I shook off his touch on my shoulders and walked out. As I ran down the staircase, I heard his footsteps behind me.

# CHAPTER THIRTY-SIX

The door was opened by a butler carrying a wax light. I saw the recognition in his eyes, and wondered if we had passed him earlier when we were led through the downstairs corridors by the footman. He did not question us, but ushered us into the hallway and went out of another door.

A pianoforte was being played in some distant part of the house, the sweet frivolity of its tinkling notes echoing in the stone and tiled room, seeming to create the ghost of a gathering. But there were no voices. Then it stopped.

After a moment the door opened and a man came out, dressed in solemn elegance as though for a ball, his face set in a grave, proud expression. Thomas and I turned, thinking that he was bracing himself to speak to us, but he passed us in the vast hallway without a glance, or a bow, as though we were ghosts. He was coldly, almost unbearably handsome, with a kind of sharpness to his looks; a glittering complexity of beauty. It struck me that I could never have loved such a man. I had been drawn to Marcus by his frailties, and to Thomas by his goodness. I knew instinctively that if this man had any such qualities, they were behind walls so high that none could find them.

The butler returned, and showed us back into the same drawing room we had been in earlier, this time lit with many branches of candles. Even their combined light could not give the room a glow of warmth; there were dark corners and shadows, so that I instinctively walked around it, checking that no one was there. Mrs Elton wished us good evening. Like the man who had passed us she was in evening dress: her white gown cut low over her shoulders and breasts, with puffed white sleeves and skirts gathered with threaded blue ribbon, diamonds at her neck and in her ears. She drank deep from a glass of champagne; I could smell its sweetness on her breath when she spoke.

'Did you pass Mr Colton?'

'We did.'

'He looks like an angel, does he not? He has conceived a passion for me. He is sweet to me, but I have heard that he has jilted other ladies, and not been kind to them. I wonder if, in time, he might not be kind to me.' She gave me a rueful smile. 'It is strange how I can tell you these things, things I would never speak of to anyone else.' She took a mouthful of champagne, and swallowed, as though it was an effort.

'It is because we do not matter,' I said. 'Because you think we will be made to disappear, if we do not do it ourselves.'

She did not agree or disagree. She looked at me carefully.

'As you have a suitor, you will forgive me for asking the question,' I said. 'Do you wish for a new life, Mrs Elton?'

She circled the table with the empty glass on it. I could tell she wanted more. 'What do you mean?' she said, as though I was speaking some inexplicable language that was not known to her. Looking at her incomprehension reminded me that I was a strange creature who had passed through many worlds. Innocent child, servant, wife, defiled woman, now, if the watch had anything to do with it, criminal.

Lost momentarily in my thoughts, I jumped when I felt her hand on mine and looked down on it: cool, smooth-skinned, a soft hand that had never known work. I remembered the laundress, remembered her cracked, bleeding hands, the kind you would bear as a burden in this world.

'I want to know what you mean,' she said. 'Truly, I do.'

I looked at her: her eyes wide, and unquestionably beautiful. That blue, flecked with grey, which had an ache in it, which must have made Marcus wonder at their beauty. He must have seen a kindred soul in their sadness; or perhaps only I could see how alike they were.

'Did you marry him for love?' I said.

'I cannot say,' she said. 'It was my duty, it was the right thing to do, but it was romantic also. Yes, I loved him. I cannot say I feel that any more. It is hard to tell. Bring him into the room, and I will tell you.'

'Our lives would be easier if he was gone,' I said.

'Annaleigh.' Thomas's voice brought a touch of sanity to our conversation.

'You said you wished to see us,' I said. 'And we shall be gone tomorrow, so speak.' I heard Thomas mutter a curse under his breath at my openness.

Her eyes had lit up, and she at last stepped away from the table where the glass sat, thinking no more of it. 'Are you going to White Windows?'

I brought my fist onto the table. There was no other way I could convey my pain, my anger. The glass rattled, trembled and almost fell. 'Speak,' I said. She had taken a few steps back, away from me, and the fire. Did she think I would throw her into it? There must have been violence in my face.

'The baby is ill,' she said. 'He is in Yorkshire. And if you wish to go there, then I must go with you.'

'Ill?' I cried. 'It is it the disease?'

'I do not know,' she said, and rang the bell.

'What are you doing?' said Thomas, coming towards her with a few quick steps. 'Who are you calling?'

'My servant only,' she said, and when the butler came in, she spoke loudly and clearly, as though to show us there was nothing to be frightened of. 'Bring the letter on my bureau,' she said to him, 'and more champagne.'

There was nothing in the man's face to show suspicion, and yet we waited, rattled, and I saw Thomas preparing himself for something, a fight perhaps. But when the man returned, he brought a letter on a silver salver, and a full glass of champagne. She ushered him out, then handed me the letter, taking the glass and drinking deep.

Marcus's handwriting made me catch my breath, half-gag with it, the fear rising in me like water filling a wrecked vessel. It was short.

*My dear,* he had written, *come with all haste. Our boy sickens, and a mother's love is what he needs. M.*

'I am sorry,' said Emma. She said it even before I had finished reading. I dropped the letter. Thomas caught it as it rode the currents of warm air from the fire to the floor.

'He needs me,' I said, groping my way towards the ottoman, trying to see through the tears.

'What does he mean?' said Thomas hoarsely. 'Why would this be sent to you? You are not that child's mother. And if you wish to be, why are you not there now?'

'You must understand that what has happened to you was Marcus's doing, not mine,' she said. 'Marcus has driven it all. I am still his wife, but I have kept my distance from him. He wished for me to go there when the baby was born, but I could not bear to see another child live, and die. They are so fragile when they are small.'

'And yet he writes and asks for you now,' he said. 'He must be confident that you will go there.'

'He is my husband. I could not deny him completely,' she said. 'I agreed that, if the child lived, and seemed to be healthy, I would go there eventually. That we would travel, and begin again, perhaps. I would like to be a mother again.'

She finished the last of her glass of champagne with a quick, nervous action. Then she sat down beside me, taking one of my hands in hers.

'You see why I must go with you now?' she said. 'The baby was intended to replace my lost child.' I turned, and looked at her, and I saw that her eyes were as full of tears as mine. Distressed, angry, full of hate as I was, I recognized her suffering.

'Annaleigh,' said Thomas. 'Get up, we are going now.'

'Why would I tell you this?' she said. 'If I did not mean to help you? I see now that it was wrong.'

'You see *now*?' shouted Thomas, and now it was my turn to ask him to be calm, but he shook off my words as I began to speak. 'We are going now, for I am sure the watch will be on its way soon, if it is not already,' he said.

'Do not be so harsh,' I said. 'She has helped us. Perhaps we can go together back to Yorkshire.'

Thomas pulled me around with more violence than he had ever shown before. 'Are you trying to get us hanged or transported? You have been reported as a thief, and she knows that. She may even have supported the claim herself. Are you out of your wits?'

'If I am, it is because of the man in that miniature, and she knows that,' I said. 'Don't you? He is the cause of everything – my pain, and yours.'

'Yes,' said Emma. 'Yes.'

'Is it you who have notified the watch in London?' said Thomas. 'Saying that Annaleigh has stolen from you?'

'No,' she said. 'It was Marcus.'

'But they gave this address?'

She looked down. 'Yes.'

Thomas seized my hand. 'We are going now. *Now!*' He pulled me across the room. 'Don't ring the bell!' he shouted, for she had walked towards the velvet bell pull. She stopped, turned and looked at us. Met my eyes with hers. I saw then how Marcus had ruined us both. Saw then her pain, how her life had been shaped by him. Both of us mothers, both of us with the best parts of our character destroyed.

'God speed,' she said.

Thomas walked so quickly, I could hardly keep up with him. Some moments, I thought he was trying to lose me, until his hand reached back in the darkness for mine. A touch was enough to make him walk on with renewed vigour, and we stumbled forwards, in the darkness, making our way back to the lodgings. I said sorry to him a hundred times.

'How could you have so much hope of her?' said Thomas, as we reached Piccadilly. 'Do you not see her loyalty to him, still?' He pulled me past a couple staggering, roaring with laughter.

'No, I do not,' I said breathlessly. 'If there is some residue of affection – I can make her see how dangerous it is, how useless and poisonous to her happiness.'

He shook his head. 'You are naive, Annaleigh. That woman's character has been moulded by her marriage, even if Twentyman has not deserved her faith. There is something stubborn in those eyes – no other loyalty can challenge it. Her love has been poured into one vessel, and whatever she may say, there is no changing it or altering the course she has taken. She is still his wife.'

'Only because she does not wish to risk the scandal of a crim con case. If she was free she would marry her Mr Colton in a moment.' I said it with more than a touch of bitterness. A married woman who formed a connection with another man opened that man to a 'criminal conversation' suit from the husband for his trespass on the husband's property. Such suits could be read about in the newspapers, and even in illustrated journals. Whatever the men had done, it was always the woman who bore the stain of shame and disgrace.

Thomas glared at me. 'She is right not to risk it. There is not a court in the land who would not excuse him the occasional dalliance. He has never injured her physically. Other than – the illness, which she would never mention, for the public shame it would cause her. And believe me – those eyes. I have seen that same look in the eyes of horses that have never been any good.'

I laughed then. 'You say such a fine lady is like a horse? Can we leave horses out of this, just for once?'

He looked pained. 'Despite our finer instincts we are still all animals. She has known but one master, and he is her master still.'

353

I could not help the tightness in my voice, though I cursed the tremor in it. 'And do you think he is still my master?'

I could not see his face in the darkness. 'I do not know,' he said, sounding tired, his pace slowing a little as we turned down Swallow Street. 'I would like to say no. But that day I saw you let him lay his head in your lap, I realized I did not know you at all. I cannot get that sight out of my mind, even after everything. You say that you hate him – that you wish to return only because you want your child, and to gain revenge on Marcus, and yet. I saw you. I saw you give in to him.'

'And there are many things you did not see,' I said. Stung at his lack of faith, I felt the splinter of doubt that had been placed in me long ago by Hester. 'Perhaps we are both strangers to each other.'

'What does that mean?'

'It means that I know you as little as you know me – or as well, depending on how you wish to see it. You say you love me. Tell me this: have you ever loved before?'

I saw the bewilderment on his face. 'I have felt affection before. But I have never declared myself to another woman as I have you.'

'I must take that on trust,' I said. 'And you must take it on trust that what I say to you of Marcus is true. The night you brandish before me, that was another place and another time. It feels as though it were years ago. He is an object of hatred to me and I would have destroyed him already if he did not hold the key to finding my poor child.'

I saw his face. 'But I see that troubles you too,' I said. 'What would you have me do?'

'Truthfully?' He was the same Thomas again, his face that of the young man who had ridden across the moor, and first put me on his horse and taken me to White Windows. 'I would have you at peace, Annaleigh, whatever that means. We will go to Yorkshire tomorrow.'

# CHAPTER THIRTY-SEVEN

The watch came looking for me in the night. They came knocking at our lodgings, but our landlady swore she had never seen us. She let them search the ground-floor rooms, begged them not to disturb her sleeping lodgers, and they left satisfied. I still do not know why she did it; I suspect Mr Digby had spoken to her, paid her, sweet-talked her. Perhaps he even knew her from the past; he seemed to know about most things. Whatever he did, she saved me, and Thomas only told me the news when I had woken from what, for once, was a deep and dreamless sleep. He and his father had sat awake all night, he said, armed only with their stick and two knives. Tending the fire, absorbing each other's stillness, protecting me. I woke; they told me of the night's events; and I dressed, ready to leave our room for the last time.

Then came a knock on the door.

Thomas ran to it. 'Who's there?' he said.

'Just me.' It was our landlady.

He opened it, and I saw him step back.

'Who is it?' I said, determined to face whatever had come to me. He let the door open more. Standing beside our landlady, with her hood up, was Emma Elton.

'Oh, Mrs Dunning,' said Mr Digby to the landlady. 'You are a disappointment to me, after our long acquaintance. How much did she pay you?' The landlady cast him a darkling look, and left us alone.

Emma came in slowly, looking around her with astonished eyes, taking in the cramped, dark room, with its two truckle beds, smoking fire and scarred table. I guessed she had not thought we lived in such mean circumstances, and I felt my pride come awake at the sight of her. 'Well?' I said.

'I have called off the watch,' she said, taking her hood down. 'I have reported that there was an error, and that the candlestick has been found. I will not have you chased. You have been through too much already.'

'Whatever you say,' said Thomas, picking up his pack. His father rose, and threw some water on the fire.

Emma saw they would not hear her, so she turned to me. 'Will you let me come with you?' she said. 'It is all as I said. I promise you that. And your words. Last night I kept awake, thinking of everything you said to me. It seems I have been in a kind of madness for a long time, and only you have woken me from it. Let me come with you and I will persuade Marcus to give the baby up to you.'

I looked at Thomas and his father. Saw their doubt, and their dislike of her.

'It may help,' I said.

'We'd best hurry if we are to take our places on the coach,' said Mr Digby.

'If you will wait a little then we need not travel by public coach,' she said. 'Wait but half a day, then we could take my post-chaise.'

'No, we couldn't,' said Thomas. I had never seen him be so harsh to anyone. 'It is conspicuous. Would you have the driver in livery too, just to be sure that we are caught before we get there?'

She blinked at his vehemence, but was unchecked. 'I must accompany you,' she said. She looked at me, and I could not help but admire her resilience.

'You may come with us,' I said.

'We are going on the Waterloo,' said Digby. 'It leaves from the Saracen's Head at Snow Hill at two o'clock. I will see if we can secure you a place. Let me pay Mrs Dunning off. Come now, no dallying.'

As we went down the stairs, Emma following Mr Digby, I stopped Thomas. 'Why are you so hard on her?' I said.

'Because I do not trust her,' he said. 'Do you not see she is the picture of your feelings, rather than her own? I have studied her these last two days. She is the perfect mirror, so full of the desire for affection that she will reflect anything back. She will change at White Windows. I promise you.'

'What did your father say?' I asked him, for I had seen Mr Digby murmur to him as he passed.

Thomas's mouth twitched into a smile. 'He said, "Don't bring the milksop with you". And I agree.'

When we arrived at four in the afternoon of the next day at the Golden Lion, Leeds, there was a letter waiting for us. The harassed landlady of the tavern called Emma's name relentlessly, walking through the press of people, until she went forwards and took it. I saw it as she did: Marcus's hand, and seal.

'Did you write, and tell him we were coming?' I said.

'No,' she said. 'When I received the letter from him saying the baby was ill, I wrote immediately and said I would come as soon as I could. I said nothing of you.'

She opened it, read it, and began to tremble, then gave it to Thomas, running from the room, followed by Mr Digby, who followed her as though she was something that might escape. Thomas read it, then came to me and put his arms around me.

'What is it?' I said, as he held me.

'The baby is dead,' he said. And the cry that came from me seemed not to come from me but from some other place and other world. He caught me, supported me to a bench. The atmosphere in the tavern had softened, the other passengers from our coach watching. This was no London place, where I could have grieved, protected from onlookers by their constant indifference. Here, people watched, and waited, and I buried my head in Thomas's shoulder and felt his arms around me.

'We are too late,' I said, when the sobs had been shaken from me. 'He might have lived if I could have reached him.'

He said nothing, only held me, and when I finally looked up I saw that Mr Digby had returned, with Emma at his side, her face streaked with tears.

'What do you wish to do?' said Thomas, his face near mine. I breathed the sour air of the inn, saw the driver of the Hebden Bridge coach, conversing with the landlady and taking a hot buttered roll and coffee. Our coach would be prepared soon. I had unfinished business to transact.

'*En avant*,' I said, softly, knowing that he would remember our conversation, that first day, on the moors.

He kissed me on the forehead. 'Forwards,' he said. He looked at his father. 'If the weather continues so like this, we will need one of our better carriages. May we borrow one?'

'You need not ask,' said Mr Digby.

We left the Enterprize at Hebden Bridge, and were taken directly from there to the Poole farmhouse, where I had worshipped with the Digbys so many Sundays before. From that place I could look out, over the moors, straining my eyes in the direction of Shawsdrop, where my baby had lived his short life. I wept sometimes, but less than I thought I would. The wound was too raw, too open to be dwelt upon. I knew somehow that if I truly held it as a reality in my mind, in that moment, I would crumble. In time, when I was far from here, I would think of the baby again, and mourn him as I should. For now, just for now, I thought of White Windows. I thought of Marcus.

'Why are we going back there?' Thomas said to me on the second day. 'Is it just to speak to him, Annaleigh? If it is I cannot see why.'

'It is not to speak to him,' I said. 'Or, if it is, it is so that he might make peace with God before he dies.'

He came to me then, sat beside me, and took my hands. 'You cannot mean it,' he said. 'To do some violence to him?'

'She does.' It was Emma. It had been her custom, in the last day, to pace the hall of the farmhouse. Awake in the nights, sharing a room, we had spoken, fitfully, of the baby. We had also spoken of Marcus. Emma had told me to forgive him, and had pressed me to return to London, but I had presented my argument forcefully, and I now felt sure I had convinced her.

'Annaleigh, look at me,' Thomas said. 'My love, I cannot see you in there. Annaleigh! You are not looking at me properly.'

'It is because her eyes are fixed on the next world,' said Emma. 'I have argued with her until my throat is sore. I have told her to turn back. There is no convincing her.'

'Will you be quiet?' he said, angrily. I saw his frustration, his despair. I knew he had come thus far for me, and I was sorry that I had dragged him into it all, but I could not feel it. Sadly, I kissed him on the cheek. 'You do not have to come with me,' I said. 'If I have to walk across the moors, I will do so. But I will be revenged on him. I will hurt him, in some way. I will make my presence felt.'

I looked at Emma. Quiet, composed, she stood there, in her black and white travelling dress, watching me.

*Let me be full*, I thought. *Let me be empty.*

# CHAPTER THIRTY-EIGHT

I listened to the violence of the storm that night, sitting in the Cross Keys. All our preparations were in place, and there was nothing to do but wait. The men of the inn greeted Thomas, then turned to their own affairs. They looked at me and at Emma with kindly eyes, and it was clear in the way they turned away and attended to their conversations that they would not be running to Marcus Twentyman any time soon. They were as solid as the stone walls of this county, I thought. Marcus was as evanescent as the storm outside.

We were shown into a private parlour. 'Just in case he comes in,' said Thomas. Knowing that Marcus was so close to me made me feel not right within myself; my skin prickled with it, cold as the time he had taken me by my wrists, on the day the laundrywomen had ridden away. As though someone had walked over my grave.

'We should go,' said Thomas, downing his ale. Solid Thomas, now with sadness in his eyes that I had put there. Who would do anything to protect me.

I excused myself. As I returned, I stopped briefly, looking at Thomas and Emma, sitting at the trestle table, conversing with each other. His hands rested on the table before him, those large, capable hands, and I remembered how he had always saved me. There had been moments, in London, lying beside him, when I could have reached for him, and I knew he would never have denied me, never seen it as a sin. I had even woken once, knowing what it would have been to be with him, my skin as warm as melted butter, only my slowly healing body, damaged by the birth, keeping me from him. And now this illness lay between us, the possibility of the illness that Marcus had given to me, on that wretched afternoon after the pretence of a wedding ceremony. Through my own passivity I had damned myself never to feel Thomas's touch, when, beneath everything, it was what I had wanted since the first day I arrived at Becket Bridge.

In that moment, I saw Emma reach out, and touch his face. Her beautiful hand rested there, for a moment, before he saw me, and drew away with a sharpness akin to revulsion.

I felt only the briefest of shocks that she had done such a thing. After all, I did not know her at all, not really. Perhaps, even after everything, I did not know him. *A libertine*, Hester had said. What of this world? I thought. What certainties are there? And I wondered what I would have done with my son, had he survived. How I, a penniless, discarded servant, would have kept him. Could I have asked Thomas to have been his father? Thomas, who had just been touched by that soft, white hand, who was being fixed by those haunting eyes? Would I have ended as a destitute woman, as my mother had been, with no Jared to save the child, even after I had gone?

Thomas rose to his feet then, and I went to them. The wind beat against the windowpanes.

'Maybe he will not see the lights on the carriage,' I said.

We pulled up near the tethering stone on the Shawsdrop road, safe by some kind of miracle, and climbed down. The storm was clearing, dissolving, the moonlight bright and ghostly, the quality of the light changing moment by moment as the clouds moved overhead. I alone went forwards, Thomas calling after me as he secured the horses, Emma, perhaps, somewhere behind. Down that path, slipping and sliding in the rain, the moors still running with water, nearly pitching over during the last descent, across that last bank, and through the toothless gateposts into the sodden courtyard. At the porch I took out an unlit torch from the pile Sorsby prepared to put on the gatepost in case it was needed.

I tried the front door and it opened with its normal grating call. No candles were lit, but there was a fire in the fireplace burning brightly; and the clock ticked as though I had never left. I walked swiftly to the fire and lit my torch. Turned, and saw a maid, neatly dressed, standing in the kitchen doorway. As young as me.

'Who are you?' she said.

I saw movement behind her, heard the suggestion of a familiar voice. Sorsby came out from the kitchen and when he saw me he ran at me, growling like a dog, only stopping as I came to meet him and swiped my torch at his head, the fierce light and fire sending him reeling back, an arm before his face. The smell of singed hair filled the room.

I heard the door behind me then, heard Thomas cursing as he ran forwards, Emma's little ineffectual cry as Thomas threw a punch hard at Sorsby's face and laid him out on the floor. The new servant stood, rooted to the spot in the doorway, her face full of terror.

'Are you alone?' I said. 'Is Jeanne here?'

She shook her head. 'She left a few days ago.'

'Get in the kitchen,' I said to her, pointing Thomas towards the door as, protesting, he dragged Sorsby into the kitchen. 'I can smell the liquor on him,' he said. 'He was never like this before, was he?'

The girl went in there with Sorsby, and Thomas tied him to the chair. Then we locked the door.

'What now?' said Thomas. 'They can't be here. They would have come out at the noise.'

'He's here,' I said. I looked at Emma. She had taken down the fur-lined hood of her cloak. She was looking at me steadily, with that same piercing stare she had given me as a child, all those years ago. I thought of her portrait upstairs on the wall. A portrait is presence, Jared had said. She had been here all the time.

'You are mistress here,' I said. 'Open the door.' I gestured to the library.

She did not protest. She walked across the hall, and, with her gloved hand, turned the doorknob.

The scene that greeted us was one I had seen many times before. The fire and candles lit, the light dancing across the glass and the lines of books on the shelves. Marcus and Hester sitting alongside each other, Hester's face turned to the fire. But Marcus was not reading. His hands were clasped in his lap. I wondered if he had been praying. When he looked up at me, and then at Emma, that steady mournful gaze hit me as strongly as a scent from childhood.

'Annaleigh,' he said. 'Have you come to slit my throat?' Then he held out one hand in the direction of Emma. 'My love,' he said. 'I wasn't sure you would come, now that he is dead.'

Trembling, I plunged my torch into the fire, and sat down on the chesterfield opposite them.

'Sister,' I said to Hester, sarcastically. But as she turned to me all of my venom drained away. She looked terrible: her face drawn, and a dozen years older, it seemed, her once fine gown, so carefully washed by me on the Yorkshire hillside, hanging from her frame. She said nothing to me. Her eyes were as dead as mine.

'She grieves,' said Marcus. 'See how she grieves. You think yourself hard done by, Annaleigh, but Hester did not know it would be so hard. She even tried to end her life – did you not, my dear? – she,' his shoulders began to shake, as though he could not control his mirth, 'tried to eat the colours in her paint box. Can you imagine? Such a hideous death, and when she had a full bottle of laudanum at her right hand.'

She murmured something: poor Hester. 'What was that?' he said. 'Speak up, dear.'

'I should be punished,' she said.

I ran at him then. He did not even put up his hands as I beat him on his chest with my fists, and I found his hands resting on my waist. He watched me with those eyes, that same constant mourning. At length I felt a wrench, and Thomas lifted me away, pulling me clear of him. I yanked myself out of his arms, and seized the poker from beside the fire.

'Do you want her to kill you?' said Thomas.

Marcus said nothing.

Thomas pulled at my arm. 'Annaleigh, do not do this. It is what he wants.'

'Where is the baby?' I said. 'Let me see him, let me hold him and grieve over him.'

Marcus shook his head.

'Let me see him!' I was howling now, every piece of energy going into the vision of my dead child. 'Why will you not say it? Why do you sit there, looking at me so, with no thought? Has the word "sorry" ever passed from your lips?'

'Annaleigh.' It was Emma, her calm voice breaking through my sobs. 'Stop this. Stop it. If you go any further

I will testify. I will say that you broke in here, and tried to rob this place. I will say it, I will have you and Thomas hanged for it. Stay your hand.' Her gaze moved to Marcus's face. 'Do not hurt him.'

Thomas looked at me, his gaze stripped of all emotion. I could sense him calculating how we would run from this.

'He told us it was a mistake to bring the milksop along,' I said, echoing his father's words.

'Is that what you think me?' she said. 'I do not think that at all. All these months, years it is now, separated from Marcus. I remember the day he fled London. He lay with me, that last night. I rose to breakfast the next morning and only one place was set. The footman said he had commanded it so. You see, Annaleigh, I waited. It is true that, sometimes, I hate him. But I told you I could only know my heart once I was in the room with him. And I know. Because I have what you do not – faith.'

I swear to God I wanted to batter her then. 'Of course you would have faith, when you have been given everything you ever wanted in life. You have never been cold or hungry. You have never had your child taken from you.'

We looked at each other.

'Have I not?' she said.

'You have faith in nothing,' I said. 'He is nothing.'

'Am I?' said Marcus, and I saw the light of humour in his eyes. 'I should leave you two to argue, about what you think you know. Has Emma told you, Annaleigh, about the sickness?'

I glared at him. 'Yes.'

His eyes were bright with it. 'Its source, I mean? I hazard she spun you a pretty tale, did she not?'

I looked at Emma. She had lowered her head.

'Said I was a libertine, did she? Hint that I spent the early months of our marriage whoring around? When in truth,' he rose, and took a step towards her, 'it was she who infected me.'

'I did not know I was unwell,' she said, softly.

'Which of course excuses you,' he said. 'Don't let that cool beauty fool you, Annaleigh. Inflamed, she is a different person. She was not a virgin when we married. She had dallied with another man. Only briefly, if you believe what she says, but that hardly matters. She pretended she was a maid when we married. Did it well enough to convince me, green, lovesick fool that I was.'

Emma had turned away. He went to her, put his hand on her shoulder. 'Never mind,' he said, lowering his head, and lightly kissing the back of her neck. 'Never mind.' When he turned back, he had recovered his composure.

'You think us men have great loves, don't you? The truth is we do, but they are not normally women. Why would we love such a thing, when it is so easy for us to gain it? My love is not you, Annaleigh, nor Emma, nor any other of those women. It is Gracegrave, my estate. The estate my father inherited, and his father before him. How you look at me, when I say that. But you have never seen it. My brother will inherit it, but he, like me, is sick. He has no children, and his only parlour is the long gallery of the house where he walks, raving, I am told, day and night. So to have a child, and to have one from a virgin, who might even wash me clean before I become what he is – you can understand. I know you can. You are a sensible woman. You have scrubbed laundry, you have scrubbed flagstones, you know what the world is. What dirt is and what clean is. There may be others who do not share my good opinion of you and your like – others might talk of bloodlines, but for me the mother is just the pale oil to hold the colour, as you would say. My son had my blood. That was enough.'

I looked at him: mercifully silent at last, only the crackle of the fire as it consumed the torch, and my laboured breathing. And I remembered Jared's words, when I had asked, long ago, why he kept faith in Richard, even when they argued: some bonds can only be severed by death.

I looked down at the poker, its cold force in my hand, an extension of my muscle and bone, but much, much, harder.

'Anna,' said Tom.

We looked at each other, then I looked at Marcus, at his sad eyes, slightly mocking, the same eyes I had seen that first evening in White Windows, so long ago, yards from here as he reached out and pulled at my dress.

I glanced back at Thomas, hoping that he saw my love for him in my eyes.

'I'm sorry,' I said.

Then I swung.

# CHAPTER THIRTY-NINE

I remember the sound of breaking glass.

The first blow glanced off his chin; my aim was failing, my weakness and distress finally showing through. That, though, was enough to break some of his teeth, and to send him hurtling to the ground, where he stayed for a moment on all fours, spitting blood and fragments of tooth out of his mouth.

I stared at him. Waited for the relief to flood me. The sense of justification, of some kind of fulfilment. But there was nothing. I was the same boiling mess of pain and frustration. Having struck him, there was no way back.

I raised the poker again.

'No, no!'

It was Hester.

'He is alive, he is alive, the baby is alive,' she cried.

Emma stayed where she was. She looked terrified, vehement, and yet unwilling to defend Marcus. Still, her eyes were fixed on him. He was what mattered to her.

I wiped some of the tears from my face. 'You are lying,' I said to Hester.

'I am not,' she said. 'He lives. Emma sent word that she would persuade you to come here with her. Marcus wrote to say the baby was dead because he hoped you would turn back.'

I looked at Emma. 'You said you had told him you travelled alone,' I said.

'I did not wish to debate with you,' she said. 'And I did not think you would really try to hurt him. I told him I would bring you because I knew what effect it would have. I wished to frighten him, and to shake his sense of certainty. It is strange, is it not? The games we play with those we profess to love most in the world.' There was not a trace of shame on her face. I wondered if her tears had been real, in the inn at Leeds. If she had ever cared for my baby, or if Marcus had always been her main concern.

'Please, Annaleigh,' said Hester. 'Do not make your son the child of a murderer. I will let you see him. But if you do this, you may kill me, and Marcus, and you will never know where he is. You will never see him. The arrangements are in place to take him.'

I turned away then, my whole body trembling with the rage that swept through me. And I smashed every piece of glass and crystal in that room, clearing the shelf with a broad sweep of the poker. Smashed it and struck it until the room was ringing with it. No one moved to stop me.

When I had finished, breathless, I pointed the poker at Marcus. 'Give me the child, and I will be done with you.'

'You do not even know his name,' he said. 'You never saw his face. You never nursed him. Why do you presume to own him, in this way, when the only parent he has ever known in his short life is me? And Hester – if you count her. Why, the village wet nurse we hired knows more of him than you.'

'My child,' I said. 'My child.'

'He belongs to me by law,' he said. 'He is to be raised at Gracegrave. And he will live a better life there. You can tear this house down stone by stone, but he will still live a better life there.'

It was the wretched truth, that I had turned away from in London. I saw the years opening up before us. I did not know if Thomas would keep faith with me. I did not know if I would die in the gutter of some London street, the child in my arms, with nothing to keep us.

'You know it,' said Marcus, his voice slightly blunted by the injury. He was pale, the blood smeared across his chin. 'I can see it in your eyes. You always had good sense.' He spat another gobbet of blood onto the carpet.

I looked at Thomas, and could see no guidance there.

'And what if I say no?' I said to Marcus. He was raising himself, touching his mouth repeatedly, and looking at the blood on his hands, but at my words he brought his eyes to my face. Those eyes, full of venom now, full of that frightening heave of emotion that had once intrigued me.

'I will never let you rest,' he said. Thomas stepped forwards and Marcus glanced at him. 'Leave it,' he said. 'She knows I speak the truth. And if it is not me, it will be Emma. And if it is not Emma, it will be my father. There will never be a place you can go that I will not follow you. If I must wait, I will. You can never leave him unattended in his crib. There will be no servant, no friend of yours that I will not pay. And I will pay any price to gain him again. If I have to watch you rot in destitution, if I have to pay someone to take your life, I will. He is mine, as much as he is yours. More so.'

I turned, and gave the poker to Thomas.

'I will see him,' I said. 'Before I decide.'

So we waited, in the long dark hours of the night, all together. And at length Thomas unlocked the kitchen, and gave the maid and Sorsby the chance to go. Sorsby stayed, angry but pacified by beer, tied like a dog to the table. But the maid went, without her locking box, out onto the moors.

# CHAPTER FORTY

They insisted on blindfolds, or nothing, for Thomas and I.
I thought they might cut our throats, not that I cared then.
Despite their subterfuge, I knew where they took us. After
all, I had learned to listen to every noise, to sense every
change of direction. We went to a cottage near Shawsdrop.
A small place, with one parlour, its stone walls heated to
stuffy warmth by the fire.

The wet nurse rose, and curtseyed low to Marcus, the
horror written across her face at the sight of him. He gave
a nervous laugh. 'I took a fall from my horse,' he said.

She was almost as young as me, her skin clear, her eyes
bright. She looked questioningly at me and Thomas, but
Marcus's expression must have reassured her. 'He's asleep,
sir,' she said. 'I took him out in the fresh air today.'

'Is that wise, in the cold?' I said, but Marcus passed

me, touching my arm, and went to the far corner of the room, to a screen, decorated with delicately patterned paper. Hester's work, I thought, and as I walked towards it I wondered if she had sat in this room, with her scissors and her glue, making a scrapbook of a screen for my baby. As I came closer to it I saw it was decorated with handbills from London, song sheets and images, fragments of maps, and I wondered if she had thought of me as she made it. They were things she must have gathered when she lived in London, fragments of a life she had left behind.

But already my eyes were blurring with tears, as Marcus moved back the screen. I went to the cradle – such a beautiful cradle, of carved dark oak, which must have seen generations of babies. And I saw the child there, fast asleep, wrapped tight in his blankets, so that only his face could be seen. 'He has had a little cold,' Marcus said. 'We feared for him. But he is better now.'

My baby was perfect. That was the wonder of him, having come from such imperfection. His skin was pure – no dark mark or telltale scab – and I saw in that small face something of myself, but also of Marcus. A hated face, mixed with mine, and translated into something which could only be loved.

Thomas had come to Marcus's side. 'Move back,' he said roughly. 'Let her be alone with him.'

'She might harm him,' said Marcus, and I sensed there was no spite, only fear, in his words.

'And I might harm you,' said Thomas.

'Enough,' I said.

The wet nurse's eyes were wide, watching us. I heard her take a step towards me when I leaned down and gathered the baby up in my arms.

'What have you called him?' I said, the tears falling from my eyes now, one onto his bonnet.

'William,' said Marcus, 'after my father.'

I held the baby close, smelled his hair and his skin, mineral pure. He half-opened his eyes then, his mouth puckering, and gave a little cry.

'There, there,' I said. And he stopped crying and opened his eyes, drawn up short by it, the sound of a voice which he had heard before. He and I had spent many hours imprisoned in the upper room of White Windows, him swimming against my hand; he and I kicked to the floor by Sorsby. Then something took him – a pain, perhaps – and he began to cry in earnest.

'Let me,' said Marcus, and I gave William to him. Watched how he held him, put him over his shoulder, waving away the wet nurse.

He saw me watching him, as he rocked backwards and forwards.

'Hester loves him so much,' he said. 'I love him so much. I did not expect to love him, Annaleigh.'

'Please, sir,' said the wet nurse. 'It is time for his feed.'

I felt the sharp ache of my breasts. My milk had dried up, but the instinct to feed him had not. I watched Marcus hand the baby over to her, watched William feed, and then fall asleep, without a flicker of knowing in him.

'You can come and see him again tomorrow,' said Marcus.

I leaned over the cot. Smelled his skin, so that I could store the scent in my memory. Laid the briefest touch of a kiss on his forehead. When one tear fell onto his head, the baby stirred just a little. Then he slept again.

At White Windows, the house was being packed up. Sorsby swept up the fragments of crystal, put the books in boxes. He was to stay there, he said, to keep the house as Jack had wished it. The portrait of Emma was wrapped in cloth, propped against the wall in the hallway. I went up to my room, found my locking box, pushed into a corner of the new maid's room. Opened it. She had taken my money and clothes, but left the coral beads and signet ring behind. They were wrapped in the piece of paper with the name of the painter from Leeds on it, written in Jared's hand.

Marcus and I went out, onto the little ridge of moor outside the house.

'If I let you keep my child,' I said. And he looked at me. 'There is a condition. I will have a portrait painted and sent to you, and you will swear to me that it will hang in his rooms, always. My face will look down on him, even if I cannot.'

'I agree. Of course I agree,' he said, as Thomas approached us.

Thomas asked to speak to me. We went further up onto the moor, a little way from Marcus. 'We can keep the baby,' he said. 'My offer of marriage stands.'

'You are the most honourable man I have ever known, I

swear it,' I said. 'But I cannot ask you to do that. If we take William now, we will always be running, Thomas. You heard Marcus, did you not? You know what he said was true, and the law is on his side. The baby is cared for, he is loved, and, though I cannot feel it now, at least he will not have lived the life I have lived. He will belong somewhere.'

'Are you sure?'

'No,' I said. 'I will never be sure.'

'What will you do?'

'Find another situation. Pray, a lot, which was what your father once advised me to do. At the moment I feel I will never smile again, and that I will never be at peace. But I will try and be who I once was. The person you loved.'

I knew that I would struggle to be the Annaleigh I had once been, with the tenderness to seek beauty. There were moments when I believed *that* Annaleigh had gone completely, slipping silently from a shadowy autumn room in a house on the moors; that the ghost of what I had been still haunted that place, the shade of my innocence flitting from room to room, just out of sight. But I could still feel, despite the armour of my anger, and when I knew that, I knew I would eventually be grateful for it. I left Thomas on the moor, went down the bank to Marcus.

'There is one other condition,' I said.

There were times when my hatred of Marcus would infiltrate my dreams, and wake me in the night. But I remember him now with the same dispassion as I remember the moors. The way the land reflected the sky. The sun on the heather; the sudden darknesses and shadows.

Thomas and I drove to Becket Bridge, left the carriage and horses with the Digbys, then went on, with money given by Mr Digby. Thomas was still afraid that the Twentymans might come for me and send for the magistrate with a concocted story, with Hester and Emma as witnesses. I neither cared nor worried. I had not wept, yet. We bought places on the mail coach to Edinburgh. We had not talked of the future.

It was a beautiful day when we left Yorkshire. From the window of the coach I looked out at the shape of the land, beneath a golden light that transformed it: the heather, the grim stone, even the faces of my fellow travellers.

The light was soft yet piercing. It made everything magical and beautiful. The kind of light which medieval people saw saints by, that wakes the superstition of the soul, and makes the sinner whole.

# CHAPTER FORTY-ONE

*Derbyshire, 1820*

In the early morning, before the sun has risen, I wake, and you are with me in the silence. While others sleep, my mind journeys to be with you.

I am with you when you rise to do your lessons, sleepy and cross; when you eat your rolls and cocoa so hungrily; when you wait in the evening to see your grandfather and receive his praise or admonishment in those long, echoing rooms, hung with paintings and glittering with gilding, their windows shrouded in velvet. Do you ask who the woman is, in the portrait that hangs on your wall? If not, never mind. I am with you in your games and, when you laugh, I am in your smile. Blood cannot be separated, you see, and your smile is my secret. Your father lives abroad

382

now, if he is not already dead from the pox, and he is the only one, apart from Hester, who would have recognized it.

In your grandfather's acres, you walk and play, watched over by a governess. I see the sheen of your hair in the light of the low autumn sun. In the distance, your small figure is never still. I imagine the content of your games, and the words you say. And again, your smile, of course. Always that.

You are everything of me, and nothing: like a dream, something I have imagined that has dissolved with the daylight. Yet the knowledge of you clings to me, and will always do so. My husband and I go once a year, when the gathering-in of the harvest at Gracegrave is celebrated. From this one day a year, I build a picture of your life in my mind. Each year I will make the pilgrimage to Gracegrave, until I judge it is enough. On that day I am in your presence, the closest I have been since that last day, when I leaned to kiss your sleeping face. And each time I stand there, beneath the oak tree, as the estate staff drink and dance and roast an ox, I wait for you to turn, and see me, and know it.

A new child swims within my belly now. But know, my firstborn, that there is nothing that can unwrite a mother's love, whether that mother is made by blood or by choice. Ask the woman who walks alongside you on the feast day: the one you know as Mama, with her blue eyes and her golden hair, which lightens a little each year. Ask her why her eyes scan the crowds on that day and, why, sometimes, she catches sight of something which makes her stop, and hold your hand a little tighter. I see how she sickens, her walk a little stiffer than before. That illness comes to her now. Soon she will travel too, to be with your pa, and you will see them no more. Your aunt Hester will be the one who sees you to adulthood.

Instead of polishing silver, you eat with it. Be kind to the maid who brings you your porridge.

It is my prayer you will never know a day without a fire, that the cold will never bed itself into your skin or wake you in the night. There is no abyss of terror or destitution into which you might slip, its shadow always far below your feet, your only foothold the ability to serve those you loathe with a smile. If you live your whole life without that feeling, then I have done enough. Your free soul is my gift to you, formed not just from God's grace but the kernel of my wishes for you.

I feel Thomas's hand on my forehead, the softest touch, not a caress – only to bring me to wakefulness.

'Come back, Anna,' he says. 'Do not stay there too long.'

And I open my eyes, and smile at him, for it is the business of a wife to comfort her husband. I am still well, and I give thanks for it. I pray daily, always the same: *let me be full, let me be empty. Let me have all things, let me have nothing.*

I never tell Thomas that there is a part of me which will always be there, at Gracegrave, watching for you. Because I know the truth now, time has brought it to me, and I have lived it. I may be a servant, but I am the last servant in my line. My children will not live invisible lives. But they will know about the vanishing of the generations before them, about the hopes of their forebears scattered to the wind like dust; they will know it in a place beyond knowing. In you, and in my other child, my anger and love will be carried and passed, and the echo of it will remain down the years, unceasing.

You feel it, don't you? I know you do.

You are part of me, and I am part of you.

And so it follows that you can never be taken from me.

# AUTHOR'S NOTE

I am indebted to Deborah Hayden's book *Pox* (2003) and Linda E. Merian's *The Secret Malady* (1996) for their information on syphilis. The disease is highly infectious for the first two years, then progressively less so up to approximately seven years, thus accounting for Annaleigh's escape from infection.

I am also indebted to Thomas De Quincey's *Confessions of an English Opium-Eater* (1821) for its insights into nineteenth-century drug addiction.

The town of Becket Bridge is fictional, but the Cross Keys tavern is based on the Waggon and Horses, Oxenhope, and the landscape described in the book on the moorland beyond Haworth.

The words of prayer so beloved to Annaleigh and quoted by the Methodist minister and Edward Digby are taken from the traditional Wesleyan Covenant Prayer. I should also add that, although Methodism came to be associated with total abstinence from alcohol later in the nineteenth century, at the time this book is set some drinking would have been tolerated.

The lines of poetry Marcus reads to Annaleigh are from *The Sorrows of Love* by David Malcolm, published in 1814.

# ACKNOWLEDGEMENTS

I am grateful to my editor, Clare Hey, for her great skill and sensitivity as an editor, and for showing such enthusiasm for *The Vanishing*. Many thanks to copyeditor Susan Opie and proofreader Linda Joyce, and to a sterling team at Simon & Schuster, including: Dawn Burnett, Toby Jones, Claire Bennett, Laura Hough, Sally Wilks, Dominic Brendon, Joe Roche, Carla Josephson, Jess Barratt, Sian Wilson and Richard Vlietstra.

My agent, Jane Finigan at Lutyens & Rubinstein, has supported my writing career from the very beginning and I am thankful for her patient and intelligent support. I am also grateful to the staff at Lutyens & Rubinstein, particularly Juliet Mahony, Gillian Fitzgerald-Kelly and Fran Davies.

The shadowy stacks of the London Library have

provided a refuge for writing, my thanks to the helpful staff there.

My colleagues at the Goldsmiths' Company have been very supportive and I am grateful to all of them.

Huge thanks to the friends, near and far, who have cheered me on during the writing process.

Aelred Tobin, Sophie Hardach and Sian Robinson discussed *The Vanishing* with me as I was writing it: I am grateful to all of them for their insightful comments.

Love and thanks, as always, to my mum and dad, for always being there. Love also to my sister Angela and her family.

Huge thanks to my beloved husband, who makes my writing possible with his kindness and practical support.

At the front of this book you will find the names of my sister Lisa and her sons Samuel and Harrison. I am grateful every day for their presence in my life, and this book is dedicated to them with love.

Loved *The Vanishing*?

Turn the page to discover more stunning novels by
Sophia Tobin ...

# The Silversmith's Wife

## Sophia Tobin

'A self-assured, page-turning debut which leaves you guessing until the last – a great read' *Daily Mail*

The year is 1792 and it's winter in Berkeley Square. As the city sleeps, the night-watchman keeps a cautious eye over the streets and another eye in the back doors of the great and the good. Then one fateful night he comes across the body of Pierre Renard, the local silversmith, lying dead, his throat cut and his valuables missing. It could be common theft, committed by one of the many villains who stalk the square, but as news of the murder spreads, it soon becomes clear that Renard had more than a few enemies, all with their own secrets to hide.

At the centre of this web is Mary, the silversmith's wife. Ostensibly theirs was an excellent pairing, but behind closed doors their relationship was a dark and at times sadistic one and when we meet her, Mary is withdrawn and weak, haunted by her past and near-mad with guilt. Will she attain the redemption she seeks and what, exactly, does she need redemption for . . .?

Rich, intricate and beautifully told, this is a story of murder, love and buried secrets.

**Available in print and eBook**

SIMON &
SCHUSTER

# The Widow's Confession

## Sophia Tobin

Broadstairs, Kent, 1851. Once a sleepy fishing village, now a
select sea-bathing resort, this is a place where people come
to take the air, and where they come to hide.

Delphine and her cousin Julia have come to the seaside
with a secret, one they have been running from for years.
The clean air and quiet outlook of Broadstairs appeal to
them and they think this is a place they can hide from the
darkness for just a little longer. Even so, they find themselves
increasingly involved in the intrigues and relationships of
other visitors to the town.

But this is a place with its own secrets, and a dark past. And
when the body of a young girl is found washed up on the
beach, a mysterious message scrawled on the sand beside
her, the past returns to haunt Broadstairs and its inhabitants.
As the incomers are drawn into the mystery and each
others' lives, they realise they cannot escape what happened
here years before ...

A compelling story of secrets, lies and lost innocence ...

**Available in print and eBook**

SIMON &
SCHUSTER